Nina Milne has always dreamed of writing for Mills & Boon—ever since as a child she played library with her mother's stacks of Mills & Boon romances. On her way to this dream Nina acquired an English degree, a hero of her own, three gorgeous children and (somehow) an accountancy qualification. She lives in Brighton and has filled her house with stacks of books—her very own real library.

A former au pair, bookseller, marketing manager and seafront trader, Jessica Gilmore now works for an environmental charity in York. Married with one daughter, one fluffy dog and two dog-loathing cats, she spends her time avoiding house-work and can usually be found with her nose in a book. Jessica writes emotional romance with a hint of humour, a splash of sunshine and a great deal of delicious food—and equally delicious heroes.

Award-winning author Jennifer Faye pens fun, heart-warming romances. Jennifer has won the RT Reviewers' Choice Best Book Award, is a Top Pick author and has been nominated for numerous awards. Now living her dream, she resides with her patient husband, one amazing daughter—the other remarkable daughter is off chasing her own dreams—and two spoiled cats. She'd love to hear from you via her website: jenniferfaye.com.

Snowkissed

NINA MILNE
JESSICA GILMORE
JENNIFER FAYE

MILLS & BOON

First Published in Great Britain 2018
by Mills & Boon, an imprint of HarperCollins*Publishers*
1 London Bridge Street, London, SE1 9GF

SNOWKISSED © 2018 Harlequin Books S. A.

Christmas Kisses With Her Boss © 2015 Nina Milne
Proposal At The Winter Ball © 2015 Jessica Gilmore
The Prince's Christmas Vow © 2015 Jennifer F. Stroka

ISBN: 978-0-263-27464-6

1118

MIX
Paper from
responsible sources
FSC™ C007454
www.fsc.org

This book is produced from independently certified FSC™ paper to ensure responsible forest management.

For more information visit: www.harpercollins.co.uk/green

Printed and bound in Spain
by CPI, Barcelona

CHRISTMAS KISSES
WITH HER BOSS

NINA MILNE

This one is for my dad, because I always remember him at Christmas and always lift a glass to his memory.

CHAPTER ONE

LOITER. SKULK. PANIC. Who knew it was possible to do all three at once? Ruby Hampton shoved her hands into the pockets of the overlong padded coat, worn for the purpose of disguise as well as to keep the bite of the December wind out.

This was nuts. All she had to do was cross the bustling London street and enter the impressive skyscraper that housed Caversham Holiday Adventures HQ. Easy, right? Clearly not, because her feet remained adhered to the pavement.

On the plus side, at least there didn't seem to be any reporters around. Unless they were camouflaged as one of the Christmas vendors touting anything from chestnuts to reindeer-daubed jumpers. Not that she'd studied them too closely as she'd walked through Knightsbridge, head down, in desperate hope that her furry hood and sunglasses would save her from recognition and the mortification of a public lynching.

But so far so good, and maybe the fact there were no paps in hot pursuit meant they had finally got the message and realised that not a single comment would fall from her zipped lips, effectively sewn shut by Hugh's threats.

His American drawl still echoed in her ears.

'One wrong word and my publicity machine will chew you up, spit you out and leave your remains for my lawyers to kick.'

So the paps were better off camping on Hugh's doorstep, where comments flowed in a stream of lies from his glamorous Hollywood lips. No change there. Mind you, she couldn't even blame his legions of fans for their implicit belief in him. After all, she had fallen hook, line and sinker for every honeyed word he'd conned her with. And now...

Now the headlines screamed across her brain.

Ruby Hampton—exposed as two-timing gold-digger!
Hugh Farlane: Hollywood megastar. Heartbroken!
Christmas Engagement Extravaganza off!
Ruby Hampton vilified by Farlane's adoring public!

'Vilified' was an understatement—Hugh's besotted fans were baying for her blood. No one believed in her innocence—instead they believed she had broken Hugh's heart whilst in hot pursuit of filthy lucre. The idea made her toes curl in abhorrence—she'd vowed in childhood never to exist on someone else's handouts and it was a promise she'd faithfully kept. Her parents had produced child after child to reap state benefits to fuel their addictions—had cadged and lied and cheated. No way could she do that.

For a moment shades of the past threatened. Tom... Edie... Philippa... Siblings she'd never see again.

Whoa, Ruby.

The past was over. Done with.

Right now she needed to haul ass and get herself to this job interview—it was time to do what she did best: pick up the pieces and move on. Put Hugh Ratbag Farlane and the past firmly behind her.

Ah...

Therein lay a cracker of a problem—an explanation for

her skulk, loiter and panic manoeuvre in blustery December on a London kerbside.

A piece of her past awaited her inside Caversham HQ—a veritable blast from the past was about to interview her.

Ethan Caversham.

The syllables unleashed another onslaught of nerves. The last man she'd ever expected to lay eyes on ever again. The last man she'd *wanted* to lay eyes on ever again.

Get a grip, Ruby—Ethan was so far in her past he was history. She was no longer that wide-eyed teenager with a ginormous crush. Ginormous and short-lived. She still cringed at the memory of that crush exploding into smithereens, bombed by Ethan's words.

'Stop following me around. I don't want your gratitude. I don't want your help. I don't want you. So please just leave me alone.'

Clearly times had changed, because fast-forward ten years and Ethan had contacted her to offer her an interview. His email, via a business media site, had been short and to the point—no hint of whether he remembered her, not much clue as to what the job even entailed. But that didn't matter. Right now she needed a job—*any* job.

She had been a fool to quit her previous job, but she had believed Hugh.

Frustration at her own idiocy clogged her throat—she'd free fallen for Hugh's persuasive words—had let him mess with her head, believed he needed her by his side. As a result she had given up an incredible job. *Idiot.*

Work was her lifeline—her salvation, her security—and right now no one else would give her so much as an opportunity to ask the time of day. They didn't want to be tainted by all the negative publicity, and she didn't want to sit around and wait until the public furore died down. Not her style.

So… Time to walk the walk, talk the talk and nail this role.

Ethan Caversham meant nothing to her any more—he had walked out on their friendship and as far as Ruby was concerned he was simply a prospective employer with the potential to offer her a job that would enhance her CV.

It would do more than that—crystal-clear determination solidified in her gut. This job would provide her with money and security…the wherewithal to start the adoption process—to have a family. By herself.

Pulling her hands out of her pockets, she urged her feet into walk mode, crossed the street and entered the glass revolving door of the sleek glass-plated building. An elevator ride to the third floor allowed her just enough time to take off her coat and check that the severe professional chignon was still in place, the subtle make-up intact.

The doors slid open, and with a deep in-haul of breath Ruby entered the lobby of Caversham Holiday Adventures.

She braced herself as the receptionist looked up, and on cue there was the expected glare of condemnation. Clearly the svelte blonde woman was yet another of Hugh's legion of fans.

No way would she cower—instead she smiled, and took courage from her carefully chosen outfit: a grey woollen jacket that nipped in at her waist over a tailored black jersey dress. Severe, smooth, *professional*.

'I have an interview with Ethan Caversham.'

The receptionist nodded, tight-lipped. 'I'll let him know you're here.'

'Thank you.'

Adrenalin started to spike and Ruby focused on her surroundings. It was an old childhood trick that had always grounded her in tricky times—helped her concentrate on reality and the importance of the tasks ahead—how to convince social workers that all was well, how to angle a bottle of milk so that the baby didn't cough it up, how to keep her siblings safe…

This backdrop was way different from the squalid environment of her youth—here there was marble flooring, lush green exotic plants, and a lustrous glass reception desk. Imposing photographs graced the walls. Glorious rugged mountains. The turquoise-blue of the sea. A surfer cresting the swell of a wave. The pictures exuded energy and exhilaration.

After a brief telephone conversation the receptionist rose to her considerable height. 'I'll take you to him,' she said.

'Thank you.'

Ruby followed her down a corridor and curiosity, panic and anticipation mingled in her tummy. *Ethan Caversham. Ethan Caversham. Ethan Caversham.* The syllables beat a tattoo in her brain that matched the click-clack of her heels on the parquet floor. Even as she tried to remind herself that he meant zilch to her now.

The receptionist pushed the door open. 'Ethan. Your ten o'clock appointment is here.'

'Thank you, Linda.'

One more censorious look and Linda withdrew, the door snapping shut behind her.

Heart pounding so hard it was a miracle her ribcage remained intact, Ruby stepped forward as a man rose from behind the curved cherrywood desk.

Oh.

Sure, she'd researched him. Sure, the internet had revealed that present-day Ethan Caversham was hot, rugged and handsome. Come to that, teenage Ethan had been no slouch in the looks department.

But now… Now she was adhered to the plush carpet, mouth agape, as she took in his chiselled features, thick brown hair, cool blue-grey eyes. Six foot plus, with a body that had been honed over the years into muscular perfection. The angry vibe of a decade ago had been muted into an edgy aura of toughness; this wasn't a man you'd mess with.

Nerves that had already been writhing serpent-like in her tummy renewed their snaking.

Come on, Ruby. Don't blow this.

Uprooting her feet, she moved towards the cherrywood desk and held her hand out. 'Ruby Hampton.'

The feel of his fingers round hers brought back a blast of memory and an undefinable, ridiculous sense of safety, and for an insane second she wanted to hold on to his broad, capable hand. For a lingering second his eyes met hers and something glinted in their blue-grey depths.

'Good to see you again,' he said.

'You too.'

His eyebrows rose. 'You don't sound convinced.'

'I…I…'

Oh, for heaven's sake. This was ridiculous. She'd known the past would come up and she'd planned to deal with it with brightness and breeze. Unfortunately the plan hadn't allowed for the poleaxed effect on her of this version of Ethan. What was the matter with her? Instant attraction wasn't something she believed in. Any more than she believed in instant coffee.

'I wasn't sure you knew who I was, given we didn't exactly part on the best of terms.' The words escaped her lips with a lot more tartness than she'd intended—more ice-cold than bright and breezy.

'No.'

There was a pause, but it soon became clear that Ethan wasn't planning to vouchsafe any more. For a moment the urge to berate him—to force an apology for a decade-old insult, a hurt she hadn't deserved—tempted her vocal cords.

Bad idea, Ruby.

The past needed to remain firmly anchored in the past.

Plus, no way did she want Ethan to know he could still incite such a seething of emotional turmoil. Truth be told, she wasn't that happy about it herself.

Forcing a cool smile to her lips, she nodded. 'I guess the important thing is that we've both come a long way this past decade.'

He gestured to the chair opposite his desk. 'That we have. Please—have a seat and let's get started.'

Easier said than done.

Annoyance flicked in Ethan at his inexplicable reaction to Ruby Hampton.

Inexplicable? Get real.

Ruby was dynamite. Somewhere in the past decade she had morphed from street urchin to professional beauty— dark hair swept up in a chignon, flawless skin glowing translucent and cheekbones you could climb. The problem was his response was more than physical.

Physical attraction he could deal with—attractive women were ten a penny. But Ruby had awoken something else. Because he'd glimpsed a flash of quickly masked vulnerability in her sapphire eyes. The very same vulnerability that had been there all those years ago. An indefinable yet familiar emotion had banded his chest, and for an instant he could taste those youthful emotions—anger, confusion, panic.

Back then her eyes had held incipient hero-worship too. A look he'd loathed. He had known then, as he knew now, that he was no hero, and the idea of adoration had flayed his soul. Sudden guilt thumped his chest. Pointless guilt. Ten years ago he'd done what had been right for Ruby— ripped her fledgling crush out at the roots before it developed into more. Because then, as now, he had known he couldn't offer more.

Enough, already.

That had been then—this was now. And right now all Ruby's eyes held was a cool wariness as she waited for him to start the interview.

So... 'How did you end up in the catering industry?'

'After you and I...' a small hesitation '...went our separate ways I started a waitressing job and enrolled on an adult education course. I worked every shift I could and studied the rest of the time.' Sheer determination etched her features. 'I wanted out of the hostel and out of the care system. I wanted to make my own way in the world and I wanted to do it as fast as possible.'

'I get that.'

He totally understood the need to spend every second busy, busy, busy, until you fell into bed so exhausted that the past didn't dig its talons into your dreams. He fully grasped the necessity of achieving success for your own salvation.

'Once I got some qualifications the owner of the café I worked in offered me promotion to manager and I took it. From there I moved into hotel work, and...'

As she continued to outline her impressive career trail admiration touched him.

'And your last job was front-of-house manager at Forsythe's?'

Forsythe's being one of London's most prestigious restaurants. Graced by the rich and famous, it adjoined Forsythe's Theatre, run by the Forsythe family for centuries.

'Tell me about your experience there.'

'I worked closely with the manager to give the restaurant a new touch. I introduced a Regency theme—spent hours trawling the internet, art shops and markets, finding some incredible items.'

All wariness clearly forgotten, she leant forward; her hands flying the air as she made a point, her classical features illuminated by enthusiasm as she described finding a genuine two-hundred-year-old sketch of the theatre.

'I researched new menus…liaised with customers—' She broke off and a shadow crossed her face as she sat back in her chair.

'Like Hugh Farlane,' Ethan stated.

'Yes. And many others.' Her tone was noncommittal, her dark blue eyes once again guarded. 'I hope that my experience at Forsythe's ties in with whatever role you have in mind for me?'

'Yes, it does. Let me tell you more about the position.'

And then, if she was interested, he would return to the subject of Hugh Farlane.

'So, how much do you know about Caversham Holiday Adventures?'

'A holiday company with a twist, Caversham offers very high-end packages that incorporate extreme sports and hotels with a difference around the world. Your clients include billionaires, jetsetters and celebrities. Your latest project is a castle in Cornwall.'

'Correct.'

For a second Ethan lingered on his vision for the castle and adrenalin buzzed through him. The brooding Cornish castle had captured his imagination, fired him with a desire to do something different—to mix his business life with his charity work.

'Renovation there is nearly complete, and I'm ready to get the restaurant up and flying. I need a restaurant manager to work with me on the design, the menus and the staff, and to plan a grand New Year's Eve opening. The hotel opens for normal business January fifteenth. I know that's a tight deadline. Especially with Christmas. Can you do it?'

'Yes.' There was not a sliver of doubt in her tone. 'But I'm not sure I understand why you don't already have someone in place.'

'I did. We didn't see eye to eye and he quit.' It had turned out that the guy hadn't bought into Ethan's vision for the castle. 'I've been interviewing for a week or so and no dice. This is an important project and I need the right person. You could be it.'

Her eyes lit up and for the first time since she'd entered the room a small, genuine smile tugged her lips up and sucker-punched him straight in the chest.

'That's great.' Then a small frown creased her brow. 'I can do the job,' she said with utter certainty, 'but as I am sure you are aware I am currently not the public's most favourite person. Social media and the tabloids are awash with vitriol aimed at me—if you hire me there may be a backlash.'

Although her voice was even there was a quickly veiled shadow in her eyes that jolted him. Her words were an understatement—the comments being aimed at Ruby were vicious, awash with menace, and in some cases downright obscene.

Ethan's lips tightened in distaste even as his brain clouded with a black shadow. The knowledge of the tragic consequences that could ensue after such unconscionable bullying twisted his very soul.

Pushing the dark memories away, he focused on Ruby. 'I realise that. It's not a problem. I stand by my employees because I trust them. Which brings me to my next question.'

Her credentials were excellent. Now all he had to do was confirm his gut instinct and make sure he could believe in her.

'Go ahead.' Her body tensed in palpable anticipation.

'Obviously I read the papers, and I've seen the accusations that you are a gold-digger who used your position at Forsythe's to attract Hugh Farlane. At Caversham you would be on the front line, liaising with my clients, so I need to trust that you will be delivering customer service without an eye on their wallets. You haven't denied any of the allegations in the press. Could you clarify the situation for me?'

He leant back and waited for her to do just that.

Instead the smile plummeted from her lips with maximum velocity. Her hands twisted together so tightly that her knuckles clicked in protest, the sound breaking the depth of silence.

Then, 'No comment.'

CHAPTER TWO

RUBY BRACED HERSELF as his brown eyebrows rose. 'You're sure you don't want to expand on that?'

What was she supposed to do? Frustration danced in her tummy even as her brain scrambled for a way to salvage the situation. She knew she was innocent, but logic indicated that she could hardly expect Ethan to give her the benefit of the doubt without some semblance of an explanation.

But there was no way she could risk discussing Hugh Farlane—she *knew* the power he wielded. All it would take was for Ethan to go to the papers with her 'story' and *whoomph*—her life would go further down the toilet.

But, she wanted this job. The thought of a return to her solitary apartment for another ice-cream-eating stint was not an option. However much she liked double-double choc-chip.

Ugh. How had this happened? Ah—she knew the answer. The reason she was in this mess was because she had been a fool—had allowed herself to do the unthinkable and dream. *Again*. Dream that she could have it all—love and a family. *Stupid*. Dreams were fantasies, fiction. In real life she had to concentrate on real goals. Such as this job.

The drumming of Ethan's fingers on the cherrywood desk recalled her to the fact that he was awaiting a response. The slight slash of a frown that creased his brow looked more perplexed then judgemental.

Come on. Answer the man.

'I would like to expand further but I can't risk it. Anything I say could be twisted, so it seems best to me that I say nothing. If you decide to quote me, or post something on social media, it will spark off another barrage of hatred.' And consequences from Hugh that she didn't want to contemplate. 'And I... I don't want that.' She hated that quiver in her voice; she didn't want Ethan to think her scared. 'But I give you my word that if you give me a chance I'll do a fabulous job for you and won't let you down.'

His frown deepened. 'And I give you *my* word that I won't betray your confidence. There is no way that I would aggravate the situation.'

A shadow crossed his eyes and for a second Ruby saw a depth of pain in his eyes that made her want to stretch her hand across the desk. Then it was gone, and yet the deep sincerity of his words echoed in her brain.

For an insane second she felt the urge to tell him the whole truth. 'I...'

Stop, Ruby.

Had she learnt nothing from the debacle of Hugh Farlane? She'd trusted him and look where it had landed her—up to her neck in metaphorical manure.

Yet it was impossible to believe that Ethan Caversham was cut from Farlane cloth. The man had saved her life ten years ago.

Yes, and then he'd vanished from her life without trace. Cut and run.

But he'd also bothered to call her for an interview.

Head awhirl, she hauled in breath. It wasn't as if she'd be a contender for any Best Judge of Character awards right now. There were times when she still felt enmeshed in the illusions and lies Hugh had woven. So the best rule of all was *Trust no one.*

'Okay.' Ethan raised his hands. 'Think about what I've said. If we're going to work together there has to be an element of trust. On both sides. Now let's consider another of my concerns. I need to know that you would be fully committed to this job.'

That was easy. 'I would be. All yours. One hundred per cent.'

For an instant his gaze locked on hers and the *double entendre* of her words shimmered over his desk. She gulped.

'Yet you left Forsythe's after just two months.'

A flush heated her cheeks. 'That was what I believe is known as "a career mistake".' Of monumental proportions. 'I'd got engaged, and at the time it seemed like the right course of action. The Forsythe sisters were very understanding.'

'I get that. Most women would get carried away by the lifestyle of fiancée to a Hollywood movie star compared to working in an all-hours pressured job. I saw the press coverage of those swish parties—you're clearly a natural partygoer.'

'No!'

The world might believe that of her, but she felt affront scrape her chest at the idea that Ethan should join that bandwagon of opinion.

'I loathed those parties. I'm so used to fronting events or serving tables that being a guest was hard. All that glitter and glam and there was nothing for me to do except—' She broke off.

Except play the part of Hugh Farlane's besotted girlfriend.

How could she have fallen for it? For *him*? At first she hadn't been interested in a man with his playboy heartbreaker reputation. Certainly she had wanted zilch to do with his fame, the limelight, his money. But slowly he'd chipped away at her resistance, and then he'd confessed that he needed her, that she was the one woman who could heal him, and his honeyed voice had called to something in her very soul.

After all, she'd failed to heal her family on so very many levels—with heart-rending consequences.

So when he had gone down on bended knee, when he had poured out his desire to turn his life around, her heart had melted and she'd known she would do whatever it took to help Hugh. And if that meant she'd have to embrace a lifestyle she disliked, play the part of the glamorous girlfriend and smile at the paps, then she would do that. After all, playing a part was second nature to her—and Hugh had needed her.

Yuck! Talk about deluded…

'Except what?' A hint of unexpected compassion softened his eyes as he picked up a pencil and rolled it between his fingers. 'Except be Hugh Farlane's girlfriend? Guess it must have been hard to lose your identity…'

For a second her brain scrambled, mesmerised by the movement and the broad capability of his hand, and shocked by his understanding. For a second the impulse to confide in him returned. To tell him just how hard it had been, and how much worse it had made Hugh's subsequent betrayal.

Swallowing it down, she met his gaze. 'If possible I'd like to keep Hugh out of this. I get that I'm asking a lot, but I promise you can trust me. I will do a brilliant job and I will not leave you in the lurch. Give me a chance to convince you.'

This job was perfect for her—exactly up her street—and her fierce desire to achieve this role had nothing to do with the man offering it. *At all*. All she wanted was to put the last few weeks behind her, to consign the whole Hugh debacle to oblivion and move on.

The pencil thunked down on the table with finality and she felt panic glimmer. She'd blown it.

Silence stretched and yawned as his blue-grey eyes bored into her. Then he blinked, and a slight hint of rue-fulness tipped up his lips. 'Okay. I'll give you the job. Trial period until the grand opening. Then we'll take it from there.'

Triumph-tinged relief doused her and tipped her own lips up into a smile. 'You won't regret it. Thank you.'

'Don't thank me yet, Ruby. I'm a hard task master and I'll be with you every step of the way.'

'You will?' Just peachy—the idea sent a flotilla of but-terflies aswirl in her tummy.

'Yes. This project is important to me, so you and I will be spending the next few weeks in close conference.'

Close conference. The businesslike words misfired in her brain to take on a stupid intimacy.

'Starting now. I'm headed down to the castle this af-ternoon. I'll meet you there, or if you prefer I can give you a lift.'

Common sense overrode her instinct to refuse the offer of transport. The only other alternative was a train journey, where the chances of recognition would be high.

'A lift would be great.' The words were not exactly true—the whole idea of time in an enclosed space with Ethan sent a strange trickle of anticipation through her veins. 'Thank you...'

Ethan gave his companion a quick sideways glance and then returned his gaze to the stretch of road ahead. Dressed now in a pair of dark trousers, a white shirt and a soft brown jacket cinched at the waist with a wide belt, she still looked the epitome of professional. Yet his fingers *still* itched to pull the pins out of her severe bun and then run through the resultant tumble of glossy black hair. Even as her cinnamon scent tantalised...

This awareness sucked.

An awareness he suspected was mutual—he'd caught the way her eyes rested on him, the quickly lowered lashes. So why had he hired her? This level of awareness was an issue—he didn't understand it, and the niggle of suspicion that it was more than just physical was already causing his temples to pound.

Employing someone from his past was nuts—he should have known that. The woman next to him triggered memories of times he would rather forget—of the Ethan Caversham of a decade ago, driven to the streets to try and escape the harsh reality of his life, the bitter knowledge that his mother had wanted shot of him made worse by the knowledge that he could hardly blame her.

Shoving the darkness aside, he unclenched his jaw and reminded himself that Ruby was the right person for the job.

But it was more than that.

The quiver in her voice had flicked him on the raw with the knowledge that she was scared—he'd looked across his desk at Ruby and images had surged of Tanya…of the beautiful, gentle sister he'd been unable to protect.

Of Ruby herself ten years before.

A far scrawnier version of Ruby stood in a less than salubrious park trying to face down three vicious-looking youths. He'd seen the scene but the true interpretation of the tableau had taken a moment to sink in. Then one of the youths had lunged and sudden fear had coated his teeth as adrenalin spiked. Not fear of the gang but fear he wouldn't make it in time.

Once he got there he'd take them on—bad odds but he'd weathered worse. Flipside of growing up on a gang-ridden estate meant he knew how to fight. Worst case scenario they'd take him down but the girl would escape. That was what mattered. He couldn't…wouldn't be party to further tragedy.

The element of surprise helped. The youths too intent on their prey to pay him any attention. The jagged sound of the girl's shirt rip galvanised him and he launched knocking the youth aside.

'Run,' he yelled at the girl.

But she hadn't. For a second she had frozen and then she'd entered the melee.

Ten vicious minutes later it was over—the three youths ran off and he turned to see a tall, dark haired girl, her midnight hair hacked as if she'd done it herself. Her face was grubby and a small trickle of blood daubed her forehead. Silhouetted against the barren scrubland of the park, she returned his gaze; wide sapphire blue eyes fringed by incredibly long lashes mesmerised him. Their ragged breaths mingled and for an insane second he didn't see her there—instead he saw his sister. The girl he hadn't managed to save.

He held his hand out. 'Let's go. Before they come back with reinforcements. Or knives.'

'Go where?' Her voice shaky now as reality sunk in.

'Hostel. You can bunk in with me for the night. You'll be safe with me. I promise.'

She'd stared at his hand, and without hesitation she'd placed her hand in his, that damned hero worship dawning in her brilliant eyes.

Present day, and the end result was he'd offered her a job. Because every instinct told him that Hugh Farlane had done her over somehow. Because he would not leave her prey to the online bullies. Because—somehow, somewhere that protective urge had been rebooted.

The dual carriageway had reduced to a single lane. Dusky scenery flashed past the windows—a mixture of wind turbines and farmland that morphed into a small Cornish hamlet, up a windy hill, and then…

'Here we are,' he said, and heard the burr of pride as he

drove down the grand tree-spanned driveway and parked in the car park.

He turned to see Ruby's reaction—hoped she would see in it what he saw.

She shifted and gazed out of the window, her blue eyes fixed to where the castle jutted magnificently on the horizon. 'It's...*awesome*. By which I mean it fills me with awe,' she said.

He knew what she meant. Sometimes it seemed impossible to him that he owned these mighty stone walls, these turrets and towers weighted with the history of centuries, the air peopled by the memory of generations gone past.

Ruby sighed. 'If I close my eyes I can see the Parliamentarians and the Royalists battling it out...the blood that would have seeped into the stone...the cries, the bravery, the pain. I can imagine medieval knights galloping towards the portcullis—' An almost embarrassed smile accompanied her words. 'Sorry. That sounded a bit daft. How on earth did you get permission to convert it into a hotel? Isn't it protected?'

'Permission had already been given, decades ago—I have no idea how—but the company that undertook the project went bust and the castle was left to fall into disrepair. I undertook negotiations with the council and various heritage trusts and bought the place, and now...'

'Now you've transformed it...' Her voice was low and melodious.

Lost in contemplation of her surroundings, she shifted closer to him—and all of a sudden it seemed imperative to get out of the confines of the car, away from the tantalising hint of cinnamon she exuded, away from the warmth in her eyes and voice as she surveyed the castle and then him.

'So, let me show you what I've done and hopefully that will trigger some ideas for you to think about.'

'Perfect.'

The gravel of the vast path crunched under their feet as they walked to the refurbished ancient portcullis. Ethan inhaled the cold, crisp Cornish air, with its sea tang, and saw Ruby do the same, her cheeks already pink from the gust of the winter breeze.

They reached the door and entered the warmth of the reception area. A familiar sense of pride warmed his chest as he glanced round at the mix of modern and ancient. Tapestries adorned the stone walls, plush red armchairs and mahogany tables were strategically placed around the area, with Wi-Fi available throughout.

'This is incredible,' Ruby said.

'Let me show you the rest.'

Ethan led the way along the stone-walled corridors and into the room destined to be the restaurant.

'We believe this was once the banqueting hall,' he said, gesturing round the vast cavernous room also with stone walls and floor.

'Wow...' Ruby stepped forward, her eyes wide and dreamy. She walked into the middle of the room and stood for a moment with her eyes closed.

Ethan caught his breath—Ruby *got* it. She felt the thrill of this place and that meant she'd do her best.

Opening her eyes, she exhaled. 'I can see how this hall would have been in medieval times. Jugglers, singers, raconteurs—a great table laden with food...'

'Let me show you the other rooms.'

Ruby paused outside a large room adjoining the hall. 'What about this one?'

'You don't need to worry about that one.'

Ethan knew his voice was guarded, but he had no wish to share his full vision for the castle with Ruby. There would be time enough to explain, as and when it was necessary. Right now she was on trial.

'But it looks perfect for a café. Your guests won't always want to dine in splendour—they might just want a sandwich or a bowl of soup. I could—'

'I said you don't need to worry about it.'

Seeing the flash of hurt cross her face, he raised his hand in a placatory gesture and smiled.

'Right now I want you to see the parts of the castle that I have renovated—not worry about the ones I haven't. Let's keep moving.'

Another length of corridor and they reached a bar. 'I want the castle to be representative of all periods of history. This room shows the Victorian era,' he explained.

'It is absolutely incredible!' Ruby enthused as she stood and gazed around the room before walking to the actual bar, where she ran a hand along the smooth polished English oak.

Ethan gulped, mesmerised as her slender fingers slid its length. He turned the sound into what even *he* could hear was a less than plausible cough. 'Would you like a drink? The bar's not fully stocked yet, but I do have a selection of drinks.'

'That would be really helpful.'

'Helpful…?'

'Yup. Lots of your guests will sit in here before coming into the restaurant. I want their movement to segue. So if I can just soak up the atmosphere in here a bit that would be helpful.'

'Fine by me. What would you like to drink?'

'Tomato juice with tabasco sauce.'

Ethan went behind the bar, ridiculously aware of her gaze on him as he squatted down to grab a bottle, deftly opened the tomato juice, shifted ice and peppered the mix with the fiery sauce.

A blink and she stepped away from the bar. 'You're a natural.' Her voice edged with added husk.

'I make sure I can stand in for any of my staff,' he said,

placing her drink on the bar, unable to risk so much as the brush of her hand. He gestured towards an area near the Victorian fireplace, with two overstuffed armchairs.

Ruby sat down and looked round the room, blue eyes widening. 'You have done such a *fabulous* job here—I can't really find words to describe it. I know I've never been to any of the other Caversham sites, but I did do a lot of online research and...' Slim shoulders lifted. 'This seems different. I can't quite put my finger on it but this feels more...*personal*. Does that sound daft?'

No, it didn't. It spoke volumes for her intuitive powers. His vision for the castle *was* personal. And it was going to stay that way. An explanation too likely to open him up to accolades—the idea set his teeth on the brink of discomfort. Even worse, it might pave the way to a discussion as to his motivations and a visit down memory lane. That was enough to make his soul run cold and he felt his mouth form a grim line.

Ruby twirled a strand of hair that had escaped its confines. 'I'm not trying to pry, but if you do have a different idea for the castle restaurant then I need to know, so I can come up with the right design.'

Time to say something. 'I feel proud of what I've already done here, and I'm sure we can work together to come up with a concept that works for the castle.'

Another glance around and then she smiled at him, a smile that warmed him despite his best attempts to erect a wall of coldness.

'You're right to be proud, Ethan—you have come so far. You said ten years ago you would make it big—but this... it's gigantically humungous.'

There it was again—the tug back to the past. Yes, he'd vowed to succeed—how else could he show his mother, show the whole world, that he was worth something? That he was not his father.

'I'm truly honoured to be part of it. So if there is anything I need to know, please share.'

Share. The word was alien. Ethan Caversham knew the best way to walk was alone. Ten years ago Ruby Hampton had slipped under his guard enough that he'd *shared* his dream of success. And instantly regretted the confidence when it had seemed to make her want more—now here she was again with a request that he share, and once again the promise of warmth in those eyes held allure, a tempt to disclosure.

Not this time—this time he'd break the spell at the outset.

'I do have an attachment to the castle—I think it's because it does feel steeped in history. That's why I've gone into such detail. You may want to take note of the stone floors. Also the reason the room is predominantly ruby-red and dark green is that there were limited colours actually available then. And did you know that it was only in the eighteen-forties that wallpaper was first mass-produced?'

Excellent—he'd turned into a walking encyclopaedia on Victorian restoration.

Ruby nodded. 'You've got it exactly right with the birds and animals motif, and the faux marble paint effects are spot-on too. As for the fireplace...it's magnificent—especially with all the dried flowers.'

Clearly Ruby had decided to humour the boss and join in with the fact-bombardment.

'I love the brass light fittings as well. And all the ornaments. The Victorians *loved* ornaments.' She rose from the sofa and crouched down in front of one of a pair of porcelain dogs on either side of the fireplace. 'These are a real find. A proper matching pair.'

'They are,' Ethan agreed. 'How come you're so knowledgeable?'

'We looked into the idea of going Victorian in For-sythe's.'

That seemed to cover Victoriana, and suddenly the at-mosphere thickened.

Rising to her feet, Ruby reached out for her glass, drained it and glanced at her watch. 'Would it be okay if I clocked off for today? I need to sort out somewhere to stay—I've got a list of places to ring.'

For a fraction of a second a shadow crossed her sapphire eyes. Then the hint of vulnerability was blinked away as she straightened her shoulders and smiled at him.

'I'll call them, find somewhere, and then grab a taxi.'

Realisation crashed down. She was scared—and who could blame her? Right now the idea of an encounter with the public was enough to daunt the staunchest of celeb-rities.

That instinctive need to protect her surged up and trig-gered his vocal cords. 'Or you could stay here.'

CHAPTER THREE

'HERE?' RELIEF TOUCHED RUBY, but before she could succumb she forced her brain to think mode. 'Why?'

Ethan shrugged. 'It makes sense. It's a hotel. There's plenty of room. You'll have to make your own bed, and there's no housekeeping service, but you can have a suite and work more effectively here. I'll be staying here too, so you won't be on your own.'

Thoughts scrambled round her brain. Truth be told, she would feel safer here. *Because of Ethan.* The thought sneaked in and she dismissed it instantly. This was zip to do with Ethan—sheer logic dictated she should stay in the castle. Nothing to do with his aura, or the slow burn of the atmosphere.

'Thank you, Ethan. If you're sure.'

'I'm sure. Let's find you a bedroom.'

'Um… Okay.' *Freaking great*—here came a tidal wave blush adolescent-style at the word. How ridiculous. As preposterous as the thud of her heart as she followed him up the sweep of the magnificent staircase to the second floor, where he pushed open a door marked 'Elizabethan Suite' and stood back to let her enter.

'Whoa!' The room was stunning, a panorama of resplendence, and yet despite its space, despite the splendour of the brocade curtains and the gorgeous wall-hangings that depicted scenes of verdure, her eyes were drawn with mesmerising force to the bed. Four-poster, awash with luxurious draperies—but right now all she could concentrate on was the fact that it was a bed.

For a crazy moment her mind raced to create an age-old formula; her body brazenly—*foolishly*—wanted to act on an instinct older than time. And for one ephemeral heart-beat his pupils darkened to slate-grey and she believed that insanity must be contagious…believed that he would close the gap between them.

Then Ethan stepped back and the instant dissolved, leaving a sizzle in the air. A swivel of the heel and he'd turned to the door.

'I'll meet you in the morning to finish showing you around. If you're hungry there's some basic food stuff in the kitchen.'

'Okay.' Though her appetite had deserted her—pushed aside by the spin of emotions Ethan had unleashed.

'If you need anything you've got my mobile number. My suite is on the next floor. No one knows you're here, so you can sleep easy.'

For the first time in the two horrendous weeks since she'd walked in on Hugh and a woman who had turned out to be a hooker she felt…safe…

'Thank you. And, Ethan…?'

'Yes?'

'Thank you for today. For…well, for coming to my rescue again.'

A long moment and then he nodded, his expression unreadable. 'No problem.'

'Ethan?'

'Yes.'

'Can I ask you something?'

Wariness crossed his face and left behind a guarded expression. 'You can ask…'

'Why did you call me to an interview?'

Silence yawned and Ruby's breath caught. Foolish hope that he had wanted to make amends for the past unfurled.

'Everyone is entitled to a chance,' he said finally. 'And everyone deserves a second one.'

The words were a deep rumble, and fraught with a connotation she couldn't grasp.

'Sleep well, Ruby. We've got a lot of work ahead.'

The door clicked shut behind him and Ruby sank down onto the bed.

Enough. Don't analyse. Don't think. Don't be attracted to him. In other words, don't repeat the mistakes of the past.

Ethan Caversham had offered her a chance and she wouldn't let the jerk of attraction mess that up. Wouldn't kid herself that it was more than that—more like a bond between them. Ruby shook her head—this was an aftermath...an echo of her ancient crush on the man. Because he'd rescued her again.

Only this time it had to play out differently. Instead of allowing the development of pointless feelings and imaginary emotional connections she would concentrate on the job at hand. Get through the trial period, secure the job as a permanent post and then she would be back on track. Heading towards her goal of a family.

One week later

Ethan gave a perfunctory knock and pushed the door open. Ruby looked up from her paper-strewn makeshift desk in the box room where she'd set up office. His conscience panged at her pale face and the dark smudges under her eyes. She'd worked her guts out these past days and he'd let her. More than that—he'd encouraged it.

Get a grip, Ethan.

That was what he paid her to do—to work and work hard. He had high expectations of all his employees and made no bones about it. Ruby was no different.

Sure. Keep telling yourself that, Ethan. Say it enough times and maybe it will become true.

'Earth to Ethan. I was about to call you with an update. I've got delivery dates for the furniture for the banqueting hall and I've found a mural painter. I've mocked up some possible uniforms—black and red as a theme—and...'

'That's all sounds great, but that's not why I'm here. There's something else I need you to do.'

'Okay. No problem. Shoot.'

'Rafael Martinez is coming for dinner and I need you to rustle us up a meal.'

Her dark eyebrows rose. 'Rafael Martinez—billionaire wine guru, owner of the vineyard of all vineyards—is coming for dinner? Why on earth didn't you mention it before?'

'Because I didn't know. I'd scheduled to meet him later this month, but he called to say he's in the UK and that tonight would suit him. I realise it's not ideal. But Rafael and I are...'

Old friends? Nope. Acquaintances? More than that. Old schoolmates? The idea was almost laughable—he and Rafael had bunked off more school than they had attended.

'We go back a while.'

'Maybe you should take him out somewhere?'

'I'd rather discuss business in private. But if it's too much for you...?'

He made no attempt to disguise the challenge in his tone, and she made no attempt to pretend she didn't hear it, angling her chin somewhere between determination and defiance.

'Leave it with me.'

'You're sure?'

'I'm sure.'

'Look on this as a test of your ability to handle a restaurant crisis.'

'Yippee. An opportunity!'

A snort of laughter escaped his lips. 'That's the attitude. I'll leave you to it.'

Whilst he figured out the best way to approach Rafael with his proposition... Rafael Martinez was known more for his playboy tendencies and utterly ruthless business tactics than his philanthropic traits. But Ethan had been upfront in his preliminary approach—had intimated that his agenda was a business deal with a charitable bent— and Rafael had agreed to meet. Somehow it seemed unlikely that he'd done so to reminisce over the bad old days of their more than misguided youth.

He'd reached the doorway when he heard Ruby's voice. 'Actually...I've had an idea...'

Ethan turned. 'Go ahead.'

'Okay. So it's best if you eat in the bar—it's a pretty impressive room, and I think we should make it a little bit Christmassy.'

'Christmassy?' Somehow the idea of Christmas and Rafael didn't exactly gel. 'I don't think so, Ruby. My guess is that Rafael is even less enamoured with the schmaltz of Christmas than me.'

A shake of her dark head and an exaggerated sigh. 'I'm not suggesting schmaltz. If we were open we would be playing the Christmas card—of course we would.' For a second a hint of wistfulness touched her face. 'Can't you picture it? An enormous tree. Garlands. Twinkling lights—' She broke off and frowned. 'I assume all your other business ventures offer Christmas deals and a proper Christmas ambience?'

'Yes, but I don't do it myself.'

He wouldn't have the first clue how—he hadn't celebrated Christmas Day in the traditional sense since... since Tanya was alive.

For a second he was transported back to childhood. His sister had loved Christmas...had made it magical—she had made him help her make paper chains and decorate the tree, and although he'd protested they'd both known the protest to be half-hearted. She'd chivvied their mum into the festive spirit and the day had always been happy. But after Tanya... Well, best not to go there.

'To be honest, I'm not much of a Christmas type of guy. And I'm pretty sure Rafael isn't either.'

'Well, luckily for you I'm a Christmas type of gal. I'm thinking a tasteful acknowledgement of the time of year so that Rafael Martinez gets an idea of how Caversham Castle would showcase his wine. The Martinez Vineyards offer plenty of Christmas wines. Plus, if we do it right the whole Christmas edge might soften him up.'

Difficult to imagine, but given he hoped to appeal to Rafael's charitable side maybe it was worth a shot. And he believed in encouraging staff initiative and drive.

'Knock yourself out,' he said.

'Fabulous. I'll hit the shops.'

Ruby crouched down and carefully moved the small potted tree a couple of centimetres to the left of the hearth. She inhaled the scent of fir and soil and felt a small glow of satisfaction at a job well done. Or at least *she* thought so—Ethan clearly had reservations about the whole Christmas idea, and her research into Rafael Martinez had shown her why.

Like Ethan Caversham, he had a reputation for ruthlessness, and an internet trawl had revealed images of a man with a dark aura. Midnight hair, tall, with a dominant nose and deep black eyes. Unlike Ethan, he'd left a score of girlfriends in his wake—all glamorous, gorgeous and very, very temporary. For a second Ruby dwelled on Ethan, and curiosity about his love-life bubbled. But it was none of her business.

He's your boss, nothing more.

'Hey.'

Ruby leapt up and swivelled round. *Chill, Ruby.* Ethan was many things, but he was not a mind-reader.

'Hey. Sorry. You startled me.' She gestured around. 'What do you think? I was just making sure the trees don't overshadow Dash and Dot.'

'Dash and Dot?'

Ruby chewed her bottom lip. *Idiot.*

Ethan's lips turned up in a sudden small smile and her toes curled. For a second he'd looked way younger, and she could remember her flash of gratification at winning a rare smile all those years ago.

'You named the china dogs?'

'Yes. In my head. I have to admit I didn't intend to share that fact with anyone. But, yes, I did. Queen Victoria had a spaniel called Dash, you see.' Ruby puffed out a sigh. 'And then I thought of Dot because of Morse code. Anyway, what do you think?'

'Excellent names,' he said, his features schooled to gravity, though amusement glinted in his eyes.

Ruby couldn't help but chuckle, despite the clawing worry that he'd loathe what she'd done. 'I meant the decorations.'

Hope that he'd approve mixed with annoyance at her need for approval. A hangover from childhood, when approval had been at high premium and in short supply.

Surely he had to like it? Her gaze swept over the small potted trees on either side of the fireplace and the wreath hanging above. Took in the lightly scented candles on the mantelpiece and the backdrop of tasteful branch lights casting a festive hint.

'It's incredible.'

'No need to sound surprised.' Sheer relief curved her lips into a no doubt goofy grin. 'Admit it. You thought I would produce something ghastly and flashy.'

'I should have had more faith.'

'Absolutely. Don't get me wrong, I can do tacky schmaltz—in fact I have done. A few years back I worked in a café called Yvette's. Yvette herself was lovely, but she was incredibly sentimental. On Valentine's Day you could barely move for helium-filled heart balloons, and as for Christmas… I provided gaudy tinsel, baubles, mistletoe—and this absolutely incredibly tacky light-up Father Christmas that had to be seen to be believed.'

Ethan glanced at her. 'You're a woman of many talents. But what about you? What kind of Christmas is *your* kind?'

The question caught her off guard and without permission her brain conjured up her game plan Christmas. 'Me? Um… Well… I've spent every Christmas working for the past decade, so I go with my employers' flow.'

'So it's just another day for you? You said you were a Christmas kind of gal.'

'I am.' His words pushed all her buttons and she twisted to face him. 'It's a time of celebration. I'm not overly religious, but I do believe it is way more than just another day. It's a time for giving—a magical day.'

His lips were a straight line as he contemplated her words. 'Giving, yes. Magic, no. That's idealistic. Christmas Day doesn't magically put an end to poverty or disease or crime.'

'No, it doesn't. But it is an opportunity to strive for a ceasefire—to try and alleviate sadness and spread some happiness and cheer. Don't you believe that?'

He hesitated, opened his mouth and then closed it again. Waited a beat and then, 'Yes, Ruby. I do believe that.'

'Good. It's also about being with the people you care about and…'

The familiar tug of loss thudded behind her ribcage… the wondering as to the whereabouts of her siblings, the hope that their Christmas would be a joyful one. It would.

Of course it would. They had a loving adoptive family, and the thought encased her in a genuine blanket of happiness.

Seeing Ethan's blue-grey eyes resting on her expression, she went on. 'And if you can't do that then I think it's still wonderful to be part of someone else's happiness. That's why I've always worked Christmas Day; watching other families celebrate is enough for now.'

'For now?'

'Sure.' *Keep it light.* 'One day I'll have a family, and then…'

'Then all will be well in the world?' His scathing tone shocked her.

'Yes.' The affirmation fell from her lips with way too much emphasis. 'And when I have a family I can tell you the exact Christmas I'll have. An enormous tree, the scent of pine, crackers, decorated walls, holly, ivy, stockings with a candy cane peering over the top. The table laid with cutlery that gleams in the twinkle of Christmas lights. In the centre a golden turkey and all the extras. Pigs in blankets, roast potatoes, roast parsnips, stuffing and lashings of gravy. But most important of all there'll be children. My family. Because *that* is what Christmas is about. And that is magical.'

Ruby hauled in breath as realisation dawned that she might have got a tad carried away.

'Anyway, obviously that is in the far distant future and not something I need to worry about right now.'

It would take time to save enough money to support a family—time to go through the lengthy adoption process.

'No, it isn't.' Ethan's voice was neutral now, his eyes hooded. 'And now isn't the time to dream of future Christmases.'

'It's not a dream. It's a goal. That's different.'

Dreams were insubstantial clouds—stupid aspirations that might never be attained. Goals—goals were differ-

ent. Goals were definitive. And Ruby was definite that she
would have a family. By hook or by crook.

'But you're right. I need to be in the kitchen—or you
and Rafael will be eating candle wax for dinner.'

'Hang on.' His forehead was slashed with a deep frown.
'I meant now is the time to think about present-day Christmas. What are your plans for this year?'

His voice had a rough edge of concern to it and Ruby
frowned. The last thing she wanted was for Ethan Caversham to feel sorry for her—the idea was insupportable.

'I'll be fine. I have plans.'

Sure. Her plan was to shut herself away in her apartment and watch weepy movies with a vat of ice cream. But
that counted as a plan, right? It wasn't even that she was
mourning Hugh—she was bereft at the loss of a dream.
Because for all her lofty words she had been stupid enough
to take her eye off the goal and allow herself to dream.
And Hugh had crushed that dream and trampled it into the
dust. Further proof—as if she'd needed it—that dreams
were for idiots. Lesson learnt. *Again*. But this time reinforced in steel.

'But thank you for asking.'

Ethan's eyes bored into her and the conviction that he
would ask her to expand on the exact nature of her plans
opened her lips in pre-emptive strike.

'What about your plans?'

His expression retreated to neutral. 'They aren't firmed
up as yet.'

Obscure irrational hurt touched her that he didn't feel
able to share his plans with her. Daft! After all, it wasn't
as if she was sharing hers with him.

'Well, I hope they sort themselves out. Right now I must
go and cook. Prepare to be amazed!'

CHAPTER FOUR

ETHAN HANDED RAFAEL a crystal tumbler of malt whisky, checked the fire and sat down in the opposite armchair.

Rafael cradled the glass. 'So, my old friend, tell me what it is you want of me?'

'To negotiate a wine deal. You provide my restaurants worldwide at a cost we negotiate. All except here at Caversham Castle—here I'd like you to donate the wine.'

'And why would I do that?' Rafael scanned the room and the slight upturn of his lips glinted with amusement. 'In the spirit of Christmas?'

'Yes,' Ethan said. 'If by that you mean the spirit of giving and caring. Because I plan to run Caversham Castle differently from my other businesses. As a charitable concern. The castle will be open to holidaymakers for nine months of the year and for the remaining three it will be used as a place to help disadvantaged youngsters.'

For a second, the image of him and Rafael, side by side as they faced down one of the gangs that had roved their estate, flashed in his mind. They had both been loners, but when Rafael had seen him in trouble he'd come to his aid.

'I plan to provide sporting holidays and job-training opportunities. Run fundraisers where they can help out and help organise them. Get involved. Make a difference.' He met Rafael's gaze. 'Give them a chance to do what we've both done.'

After all, they had both been experts in petty crime, headed towards worse, but they had both turned their lives around.

'We did it on our own.'

'Doesn't mean we shouldn't help others.'

Before Rafael could reply the door swung open and Ruby entered.

Whoa. She looked stunning, and Ethan nearly inhaled his mouthful of whisky. Her dark luxuriant hair was swept up in an elegant chignon, clipped with a red barrette. A black dress that reached mid-thigh was cinched at the waist with a wide red sash, and—heaven help him—she wore black peeptoe shoes with jaunty red bows at the heels. Clearly she was giving the new uniform an airing.

A small smile curved her lips as she glided towards them and placed a tray on the table. 'Appetisers to go with your pre-dinner drinks,' she said. 'Parma ham and mozzarella bites, and smoked salmon on crushed potato'.

'Thank you, Ruby.' Attempting to gather his scattered brain cells, Ethan rose to his feet and Rafael followed suit, his dark eyes alight with interest.

'Rafael, this is Ruby Hampton—my restaurant manager.'

'Enchanted to meet you.' Rafael smiled. 'The lady who knocked me off the celebrity gossip pages.'

Colour leached from her face and Ethan stepped towards her.

'I...I hope you enjoyed the respite,' she said, her smile not wavering, and admiration touched his chest. 'I'm not planning on a repeat run.'

Rafael gave a small laugh. 'Well said.' He reached down and picked up one of the canapés and popped it into his mouth. 'Exquisite.'

'Thank you. I'll leave you to it, and then I'll be back with the starters in about fifteen minutes.'

'So...' Rafael said as the door swung shut. 'You've hired Ruby Hampton?'

'Yes.'

'Why? Because you want to give her a second chance?' Rafael gestured round the bar. 'That's what this is about, right? You want people to be given a chance?'

'Yes. I do. I want youngsters who've had a tough time in life to see there is a choice apart from a life of truancy and mindless crime.'

Images of the bleak landscape of the council estate they'd grown up on streamed in his mind.

'And I want society to recognise that they deserve a chance even if they've messed up.'

Rafael leant back. 'You see, *I* think people should make their own choices and prove they deserve a chance. So let's talk business, my friend, and let me think about the charitable angle.'

'Done.'

Ethan placed his whisky glass down. Time to show Rafael Martinez that he might have a philanthropic side, but it didn't mean he wasn't hard-nosed at the negotiating table—helped by the fact that said table was soon occupied by melt-in-the-mouth food, discreetly delivered and served.

In fact if it wasn't for the ultra-sensitive 'detecting Ruby' antennae he seemed to have developed he doubted he would have noticed her presence.

Once the dessert plates were cleared away Ethan scribbled some final figures down and handed them across to Rafael. 'So we're agreed?'

'We're agreed. I'll get it drawn up legally and the contracts across to you tomorrow.'

'And the wine for Caversham Castle?'

Rafael crossed one long leg across his knee and steepled his fingers together as Ruby entered with a tray of coffee.

'Ruby, I'd like to thank you. Dinner was superb. Why don't you join us for coffee?' His smile widened and Ruby hesitated, but then Rafael rose and pulled out a chair for her. 'I insist. I'm sure you and I will have some contact in the future.'

Half an hour later Ethan resisted the urge to applaud. Conversation had flowed and Ethan could only admire the fact that somehow Ruby had found the time to research Rafael sufficiently to engage him on topics that interested him.

Eventually Ruby rose to her feet and held a hand out to Rafael. 'It's been a pleasure—and now I'll leave you two to get back to business.'

Ruby stood in the gleaming chrome confines of the state-of-the-art kitchens and allowed one puff of weariness to escape her lips as she wiped down the final surface.

Tired didn't cover it—she was teetering on the cliff of exhaustion. But she welcomed it. The past week had been incredible. Sure, Ethan was a hard taskmaster, but the man was a human dynamo—and it had energised her. There were times when she could almost believe the whole debacle with Hugh Farlane had been a bad dream. The only whisper of worry was that it wasn't the work that provided balm—it was working with Ethan.

As if her thoughts had the art of conjure, the kitchen door swung open and there he stood. Still suited in the charcoal-grey wool that fitted him to perfection, he'd shed his tie and undone the top button of the crisp white shirt. Her gaze snagged on the triangle of golden bare skin and her breath caught in her throat as he strode towards her.

Cool it, Ruby.

Will power forced the tumult of her pulse to slow. 'All signed on the dotted line?'

'Yes.' His eyes were alight with satisfaction and she could feel energy vibrate off him. 'Rafael just left and I've come to thank you.'

'No problem. Just doing my job.'

'No. You went the extra mile and then some. The meal, the décor…and then you—you charmed the pants off him.'

His words caused a flinch that she tried to turn into another swipe of the counter; panic lashed her as she reviewed their coffee conversation.

'What's wrong?'

She shrugged and straightened up. 'I guess I'm hoping Rafael didn't think that was my aim in the literal sense.'

Comprehension dawned in his eyes. 'He didn't. You did your job. You liaised.'

His matter-of-fact assurance warmed her very soul. 'Thank you for seeing that. Problem is, I'm not sure everyone will. The world believes I trapped Hugh whilst *liaising* on the job.'

He stepped towards her, frustration evident in the power of his stride, in the tension that tautened his body. 'Then deny the allegations.'

'I can't.'

'Why not? Unless you do feel guilty?' Blue-grey eyes bored into her. 'If he dazzled you with his wealth and charm that doesn't make you a gold-digger. When you start out with nothing it's easy to be swept off your feet—to welcome the idea of lifelong security and easy wealth. There is no need for guilt.'

'I wasn't dazzled by his wealth. I always vowed that I would earn my keep every step of the way.' Wouldn't set foot on her parents' path. 'I wasn't after Hugh's cash.'

And yet…

A small hard lump of honesty formed in her tummy. 'But I suppose with hindsight I am worried that I was dazzled by the idea of a family. He said he wanted kids, and…'

Yes, there had been that idea of it being within her grasp—the idea that she'd finally found a man who wanted a family. Not a man like Steve or Gary but a man who could provide, who needed her and wanted her help to heal him… What a sucker she'd been. Never again—that was for sure.

'I assume he lied? Like he's lying now? That is his bad. Not yours. So fight him. I had you down as a fighter.'

'I can't win this fight. Hugh Farlane is too big to take on. It's unbelievable how much clout he has. He has enough money to sink a ship…enough publicity people to spin the Bayeux Tapestry.'

'What about right and wrong?'

'That's subjective.'

It was a lesson she had learnt the hard way. She'd fought the good fight before and lost her siblings. Lord knew she was so very happy for them—joyful that Tom and Edie and Philippa had found an adoptive family to love them all. But it had been hard to accept that they would never be the happy family unit she had always dreamed they would be.

So many dreams…woven, threaded, embroidered with intricate care. Of parents who cleaned up their alcohol and drug-fuelled life and transformed themselves into people who cared and nurtured and loved… And when that dream had dissolved she had rethreaded the loom with rose threads and produced a new picture. An adoptive family who would take them all in and provide a normal life—a place where love abounded along with food, drink, clothes and happiness…

She'd fought for both those dreams and been beaten both times. Still had the bruises. So she might have learnt the hard way, but she'd sucked the lesson right up.

'Yes, it is.' His voice was hard. 'But you should still fight injustice. You owe it yourself.'

'No! What I owe myself is to not let my life be wiped out.' *Again.* 'I've worked hard to get where I am now, and I will not throw it away.'

'I don't see how denying these allegations equates to chucking your life away. Unless…'

A deep slash creased his brow and she could almost hear the cogs of his brain click into gear. For a crazy moment she considered breaking into a dance to distract him. But then…

'Has he forced you to silence? Threatened you?'

Ethan started to pace, his strides covering the resin floor from the grill station with its burnished charbroiler to the sauté station where she stood.

'Is that why you aren't fighting this? Why you haven't refuted the rubbish in the papers? Why Farlane knows he can slate you with impunity and guarantee he'll come up drenched in the scent of roses.'

Just freaking fabulous—he'd worked it out. 'Leave it, Ethan. It doesn't matter. This is my choice. To not add more logs to already fiery flames.'

His expulsion of breath tinged the air with impatience. 'That's a pretty crummy choice.'

'Easy for you to say. You're the multimillionaire head of a global business and best mates with the Rafael Martinezes of the world.'

'That is irrelevant. I would take Hugh Farlane down, whatever my bank balance and connections, because he is a bully. The kind of man who uses his power to hurt and terrorise others.'

Ruby blinked; the ice in his voice had caused the hairs on her arms to stand to attention.

'If you don't stand up to him he will do this to someone else. Bully them, harass them, scare them.'

'No, he won't.'

'You don't know that.'

'Yes, I do…'

Ruby hesitated, tried to tell herself that common sense dictated she end this exchange here and now. But, she couldn't. Her tummy churned in repudiation of the disappointment in his gaze, the flick of disdain in his tone.

'The whole engagement was a set-up.'

The taste of mortification was bitter on her tongue as the words were blurted out.

Ethan frowned. You two were faking a relationship?'

'No. *We* weren't faking. Hugh was. It was a publicity stunt—he needed an urgent image-change. His public were disenchanted with his womanising and his sex addiction. Hugh was keen to get into the more serious side of acting as well, and he wanted to impress the Forsythe sisters, who are notorious for their high moral standards. So he figured he'd get engaged to someone "normal". I fell for it. Hook line and sinker.'

His jaw clenched. 'So it was a scam?'

'Yup. I thought he loved me—in reality he was using me.'

Story of her life.

'I resigned because he asked me to—so that I could be by his side. He told me it was to help him. To keep him from the temptation to stray. But really it was all about the publicity. I can't believe I didn't see it. Hugh Farlane…rich, famous…a man who could have any woman he wanted… decided to sweep *me* off my feet, to change his whole lifestyle, marry me. He said we would live happily ever after with lots of sproglets.' She shook her head. 'I of all people should have known the stupidity of believing *that.*'

Her own parents hadn't loved her enough to change their lifestyles—despite their endless promises to quit, their addictions had held sway over their world. Rendered them immoral and uncaring of anything except the whereabouts of their next fix.

'How did you find out?'

Ethan's voice pulled her back to the present.

'He "confessed" when I found him in bed with another woman. A hooker, no less. Turned out he'd been sleeping around the whole time. He'd told me that he wanted to wait to sleep with me until we got married, to prove I was "different".'

Little wonder her cheeks were burning—she'd accepted Hugh's declaration as further evidence of his feelings for her, of his willingness to change his lifestyle for her, and her soul had sung.

'In reality it was so that he could be free at night for some extracurricular action between the sheets.'

For a second a flicker of relief crossed his face, before sheer contempt hardened his features to granite. Both emotions she fully grasped. If she'd actually slept with Hugh she would feel even more besmirched than she already did. As for contempt—she'd been through every shade, though each one had been tinted with a healthy dose of self-castigation at her own stupidity.

'Anyway, once I got over the shock I chucked the ring at him, advised him to pay the woman with it and left. Then his publicity machine swung into action. Hugh's first gambit was to apologise. It was cringeworthy. Next up, ironically enough, he offered to pay me to play the role of his fiancée. When I refused, it all got a bit ugly.'

Ethan halted, his jaw and hands clenched. 'You want me to go and find him? Drag him here and make him grovel?'

'No!'

But his words had loosed a thrill into her veins—there was no doubt in her mind that he would do exactly that. For a second she lingered on the satisfying image of a kowtowing Hugh Farlane and she gave a sudden gurgle of laughter.

'I appreciate it, but no—thank you. The point is he said he'd never bother to pull a publicity stunt like this again. So I don't need to make a stand for the greater good. To be honest, I just want it to blow over; I want the threats and the hatred to stop.'

Ethan drummed his fingers on the counter and her flesh

goosebumped at his proximity, at the level of anger that buzzed off him. It was an anger with a depth that filled her with the urge to try to soothe him. Instinct told her this went deeper than outrage on her behalf, and her hand rose to reach out and touch him. Rested on his forearm.

His muscles tensed and his blue-grey gaze contemplated her touch for a stretch. Then he covered her hand with his own and the sheer warmth made her sway.

'I'm sorry you went through that, Ruby. I'd like to make the bastard pay.'

'It's okay.' Ruby shook her head. 'I'm good. Thanks to you. You gave me a chance, believed in me, and that means the world.'

Lighten the mood. Before you do something nuts like lean over and kiss him on the cheek. Or just inhale his woodsy aroma.

'If it weren't for you I'd still be under my duvet, ice cream in hand. Instead I'm here. Helping renovate a castle. So I'm really good, and I want to move forward with my life.'

'Then let's do exactly that.' Ethan nodded. 'Let's go to dinner.'

'Huh?' Confusion flicked her, along with a thread of apprehension at the glint in his eye. 'Now? You've had dinner, remember?'

'Tomorrow. Pugliano's. In the next town along.'

'Pugliano's? You're kidding? We'd never get in at such short notice.'

'Don't worry about that. We'll get a table.'

'But why do you want us to go out for dinner?' For a scant nanosecond her heart speeded up, made giddy by the idea that it was a date.

'To celebrate making your appointment official. You're off trial.'

'I am?' A momentary emotion she refused to acknowledge as disappointment that it was not a date twanged. To be succeeded by suspicion. 'Why?'

Shut up, shut up, shut up.

This was good news, right? The type that should have her cartwheeling around the room. But...

'I don't want this job out of pity.'

'Look at me.' He met her gaze. 'Do I look like a man who would appoint someone to an important business role out of pity?'

'Fair point. No, you don't. But I think your timing is suspect.'

'Nope. You've proved yourself this past week. You've matched my work drive without complaint and with enthusiasm. Tonight you went beyond the call of duty with Rafael and now you've told me the truth. No pity involved. So... Dinner?'

'Dinner.'

Try as she might the idea sizzled—right alongside his touch. His hand still covered hers and she wanted more.

As if realisation hit him at the same instant he released his grip and stepped backwards. 'It will be good for you as well. To see how Pugliano's works.'

'Good...how?' Hurt flickered across her chest. 'I've researched all your places. I've talked to your restaurant managers in Spain and France and New York. Plus I know how a top-notch restaurant works already.'

'Sure—but as a manager, not as a guest.' He raised a hand. 'I know your engagement to Hugh was filled with social occasions in glitzy places, but you said it yourself you didn't enjoy them and now I get why. I want you to see it from the point of view of a guest. Experience it from *that* side of the table.'

Despite all her endeavour, the bit of her that persisted in believing the date scenario pointed out that she would positively *revel* in the experience alongside Ethan.

The thought unleashed a flutter of apprehension.

Chill, Ruby. And think this through.

This was *not* a date, and actually... 'I'm not sure it's a good idea. What if it reactivates the media hype? What if people think that I'm moving in on *you*, shovel in hand, kitted out in my gold-prospecting ensemble?'

His broad shoulders shrugged with an indifference she could only envy. 'Does it matter what people think?'

'It does if it starts up a media storm.'

'We can weather the storm. This is a business dinner, not a date, and I don't have a problem going public with that.'

'Well, *I* do. I can picture it—sitting there being stared at, whispered about...the salacious glances...'

'But once they see two people clearly in the process of having a business dinner they will lose interest and stop gawping.'

'What about the negative publicity viewpoint?'

'You are my *restaurant manager*. You do your job and I will deal with any negative publicity. I stand by my employees. Look, I get that it will be hard, but if you want to move on you need to face it. I'll be right there by your side.'

'I get that it will be hard... You need to face it...I'll be right there by your side.'

The phrases echoed along the passage of a decade— the self-same words that the younger Ethan Caversham had uttered.

Those grey-blue eyes had held her mesmerised and his voice, his sheer presence, had held her panic attacks at bay. It had been Ethan who had made her leave the hostel, who had built her confidence so she could walk the streets again, only this time with more assurance, with a poise engendered by the self-defence classes he'd enrolled her in.

Yes—for weeks he'd been by her side. Then he'd gone. One overstep on her part, one outburst on his, and he'd gone. Left her. Moved out and away, leaving no forwarding address.

Ruby met his gaze, hooded now, and wondered if he had travelled the same memory route. She reminded herself that now it was different—*she* was different. No way would she open herself to that hurt again—that particular door was permanently closed and armour-plated.

So Ethan was right—to move forward she needed to put herself out there.

'Let's do this.'

CHAPTER FIVE

ETHAN RESISTED THE urge to loosen his collar as he waited in front of the limo outside the castle's grand entrance. This strange fizz of anticipation in his gut was not acceptable—not something he'd experienced before, and not something he wanted to experience again.

Fact One: this was *not* a date. A whoosh of irritation escaped his lips that he needed a reminder of the obvious. The word date was not in Ethan Caversham's dictionary.

Fact Two: Ruby was an *employee* and this was a business dinner, to give her a guest's viewpoint and to show her—an *employee*—his appreciation of a job well done. Perhaps if he stressed the word *employee* enough his body and mind would grasp the concept...

Fact Three: yes, they had a shared past—but that past consisted of a brief snapshot in time, and that tiny percentage of time was not relevant to the present.

So... Those were the facts and now he was sorted. Defizzed. Ethan Caversham was back in control.

A minute later the front door opened and every bit of his control was blown sky-high, splattering him with the smithereens of perspective. Moisture sheened his neck as he slammed his hands into his pockets and forced himself not to rock back on his heels.

Ruby looked sensational, and all his senses reeled in response. Her glorious dark hair tumbled loose in glossy ripples over the creamy bare skin of her shoulders. The black lacy bodice of her dress tantalised his vision. A wide black band emphasised the slender curve of her waist and the dress was ruched into a fun, flirty skirt that showcased the length of her legs.

But what robbed his lungs of breath was the expression on her face and the very slight question in her sapphire eyes. That hint of masked vulnerability smote him with a direct jab to the chest.

'You look stunning.'

'Thank you.' Her chin angled in defiance. 'I decided that if people are going to stare I'd better scrub up.'

'You scrub up well.'

With a gargantuan effort he kept his tone light, pushed away the urge to pull her into his arms and show her how well, to try to soothe the apprehension that pulsed from her.

'Your limo awaits.'

'You didn't need to hire a limo.'

'I wanted to. We're celebrating, and I want to do this in style—tonight I want you to enjoy the experience of being a guest.'

To make up in some small way for what Hugh had put her through. All those high society occasions where he'd groomed her to act a part she'd disliked. Sheer anger at the actor's behaviour still fuelled Ethan—to have messed with Ruby's head like that was unforgivable. So tonight it was all about Ruby. As his *employee*. His temple pounded a warning—perspective needed to be retained.

'So that you can use the experience to help you at Caversham Castle. Speaking of which...I've issued a press statement.'

'Good idea.' The words were alight with false brightness as she slid into the limousine. Waited for him to join her in sleek leather luxury. 'What did it say?'

'"Ethan Caversham is pleased to announce the appointment of a restaurant manager for his new project, Caversham Castle in Cornwall. Ruby Hampton has taken on the role, and both Ethan and Ruby are excited at the prospect of creating a restaurant that sparkles with all the usual Caversham glitter and offers a dining experience to savour."'

'Sounds good.'

After that, silence fell, and Ethan forced his gaze away from her beauty and instead gazed out at the scenery. A quick glance at Ruby saw her doing the same. There was tension in the taut stance of her body and in the twisting of her hands in her lap.

'You okay?' he asked.

'Sure.' The word was too swift, the smile too bright.

'It's all right to be nervous. You've been in hiding for weeks.'

'I'll be fine.' Slim bare shoulders lifted. 'I just loathe being gawped at. You know…? Plus, you *do* realise there is every chance people will chuck bread rolls at me, or worse?'

'Not on my watch,' he said as the limo glided to a stop. 'But if they do we'll face it together.' The words were all wrong. 'As employer and employee—colleagues…professionals.' Okay… Now he was overcompensating. 'You can do this, Ruby.'

A small determined nod was her response as the car door was opened by the driver. Ethan slid along the leather seat and stepped out, waited as Ruby followed suit. Before she could so much as step from the car a bevy of reporters flocked around them. Quelling the urge to actually move closer to her, Ethan turned to face them, angled his body to shield Ruby.

'So, Ruby, have you decided to break your silence about Hugh Farlane?'

'Ethan, is it true that you've *hired* Ruby, or is this something more personal?'

Ethan raised his hands. 'Easy, guys. Give Ruby some space, please. We get that you're pleased to see her, but she needs to breathe. I need my new restaurant manager to be fully functional.'

Next to him, he sensed the shudder of tension ripple through her body, heard her inhalation of breath—and then she stepped forward.

'Hey, guys. I'm happy to chat about my new role— which I am *very* excited about as the next step in my career—but I have nothing to say about Hugh.'

His chest warmed with admiration at the cool confidence of her tone and the poise she generated.

'That's old news,' he interpolated. 'Our concern is with the future and with Caversham's new venture. Ruby is already doing an amazing job, and I'm looking forward to continuing to work with her.'

'Best keep an eye on your wallet, then, Ethan!'

'What about you, Ruby? Is this a new game plan? To get your mitts on Ethan and the Caversham bank balance?'

She flinched, and Ethan swivelled with lethal speed, the urge to lash out contained and leashed, his tone smooth as ice.

'My wallet is perfectly safe, but many thanks for your concern. I have no doubt that Ruby has the same game plan as me. Right now I'm concentrating on the grand opening of Caversham Castle—the guest list is shaping up nicely. My plan is to grant exclusive coverage to a magazine— though I haven't decided who yet. Perhaps we'll discuss it over dinner.'

The implication was clear. *Drop the gold-digger angle and you might be in with a chance.*

The reporters dispersed, oiled away with ingratiating smiles, and satisfaction touched him. They would stop ripping Ruby to shreds, Hugh Farlane would in turn back off, public interest would die down and the bullies and the nutcases would retreat.

His aim was achieved—his anger channelled to achieve the desired result. Control was key—emotions needed to be ruled and used. When you let your emotions rule you then you lost control. And Ethan was never walking that road again.

Without thought he placed his hand on the small of her back to guide her forward and then wished he hadn't. *Too close, too much*—a reminder that the physical awareness hadn't diminished.

It was with relief that he entered the warmth of the restaurant and Ruby stepped away from him. Her face flushed as her gaze skittered away from his and she looked around.

'Wow!'

'Tony Pugliano is a fan of Christmas,' Ethan said.

The whole restaurant was a dazzling testament to that. The winter grotto theme was delicate, yet pervasive. Lights like icicles glittered from the ceiling and a suspended ice sculpture captured the eye. Windows and mirrors were frosted, and each table displayed scented star-shaped candles that filled the room with the elusive scent of Christmas.

'It's beautiful…' Ruby breathed.

'You like it?' boomed a voice.

Ethan dragged his gaze from Ruby's rapt features to see Tony Pugliano crossing the floor towards them.

'Ethan.' Tony pulled him into a bear hug and slapped his back. 'This is fabulous, no? Welcome to my winter palace. Ruby—it's good to see you.'

'You too—and it's glorious, Tony.'

The grizzled Italian beamed. 'And now, for you, I have reserved the best table—you will be private, and yet you will appreciate every bit of the restaurant's atmosphere. Anything you want you must ask and it is yours, my friends.'

'Thank you, Tony. We appreciate it.'

'We really do,' Ruby said as they followed in Tony's expansive wake to a table that outdid all the other tables in the vicinity.

Crystal glasses seized the light and glittered from each

angled facet, a plethora of star candles dotted the table, and the gleam of moisture sheened the champagne already in an ice bucket.

'Sit, sit…' Tony said. 'I have, for you, chosen the best—the very best of our menu. You need not even have to think—you can simply enjoy.'

Ruby watched his departing back and opened her mouth, closed it again as a waiter glided towards them, poured the champagne and reverently placed a plate of canapés in front of them.

'Made by Signor Pugliano himself. There is *arancini di riso* filled with smoked mozzarella cheese, radicchio ravioli, bresaola and pecorino crostini drizzled with truffle oil, and Jerusalem artichokes with chestnut velouté, perfumed with white truffle oil.'

'That sounds marvellous,' Ruby managed.

Once the waiter had gone she met Ethan's gaze, clocked his smile and forced her toes to remain uncurled. It was a smile—nothing more.

'This is almost as miraculous as what I just witnessed. I am considering how to lift my jaw from my knees.' She shook her head. 'Tony Pugliano is renowned as one of the toughest, most brusque, most temperamental chefs in the country and round you he's turned into some sort of pussycat. How? Why? What gives?'

His smile morphed into a grin. 'It's my famous charm.'

'Rubbish.' However charming Ethan was—and that was a point she had no wish to dwell on—it wouldn't affect Tony Pugliano. 'Plus, I know Hugh eats here, so I'm amazed he seemed so happy to see me.'

'You are underrating my charm capacity,' Ethan said.

Picking up a canapé, she narrowed her eyes. Nope—she wasn't buying it. This was zip to do with charm, but clearly Ethan had no intention of sharing. No surprise there, then.

'Especially given his less than accommodating attitude when I applied for a job here after my break-up with Hugh. Whereas now, if you asked him to, he'd probably give me any job I asked for.' Seeing his eyebrows rise she shook her head. 'Not that I *want* you to do that!'

'You sure?' There was an edge to his voice under the light banter.

Disbelief and hurt mingled. Surely Ethan couldn't possibly think she would go after another job. 'I am one hundred per cent sure. You gave me a chance when no one else would give me the opportunity to wash so much as a dish. So you get one hundred per cent loyalty.'

'I appreciate that.'

Yet the flatness of his tone was in direct variance to the fizz of champagne on her tongue. 'Ethan. I mean it.'

His broad shoulders lifted and for a second the resultant ripple of muscle distracted her. But only for a heartbeat.

'There isn't such a thing as one hundred per cent loyalty. Everyone has a price or a boundary that dissolves loyalty.'

The edge of bitterness caught at her. Had someone let him down? All of a sudden it became imperative that he believed in her.

'Well, *I* don't. You're stuck with me for the duration.'

His large hand cradled his glass, set the light amber liquid swirling. 'If you had an opportunity to have a family then your loyalty might lose some percentage points. Likewise if I stopped paying your salary your allegiance would be forfeit.' He pierced a raviolo. 'That's life, Ruby. No big deal.'

'It is a *huge* deal—and I think I need to make something clear. I do want children, but that does not take precedence above this job. Right now my top priority is to see Caversham Castle firmly ensconced as the lodestar of Caversham Holiday Adventures. I have no intention of starting a family until I am financially secure, with a house, savings in the bank and the ability to support one. But even if I won the Lottery I would not let you down. As for you not paying me—I know you would only do that in a crisis. I would always believe that you'd turn that crisis around, so you'd still have my loyalty.'

Ethan didn't look even remotely moved—it was as if her words had slid off his smooth armour of cynicism.

Dipping a succulent morsel of artichoke into the chestnut velouté, she savoured the taste, wondered how else she could persuade him. She looked up and encountered an ironic glint in his eyes.

'Forget the Lottery. What if Mr Perfect turns up and says he wants a family right now? I wouldn't see you for dust.'

The words stung—what would it take to show him that he could trust her? 'That won't happen because I'm not planning on a meeting with Mr Perfect. I don't *need* Mr Perfect—or Mr Anyone. My plan is to be a single parent.'

His grey-blue eyes hardened, all emotion vanishing to leave only ice.

The advent of their waiter was a relief and a prevention of further conversation. As if sensing the tension, he worked deftly to remove their used plates and replace them.

'Here is langoustine cooked three different ways. Roasted with a hint of chilli and served with puy lentils, grilled with seared avocado and manuka honey, and a langoustine mousseline with manzanilla,' he said swiftly, before making a dignified retreat with a discreet, *'Buon appetito.'*

Ethan didn't so much as peek down at his plate, and Ruby forced herself to hold his gaze even as regret pounded her temples. Of all the idiotic conversational paths to take, telling Ethan about her single parenthood aspirations rated right up there as the Idiot Trail. Her intent had been to prove her loyalty was genuine, to *reassure* him. Which was nuts.

Ethan was a billionaire…head of a global business—he did not need reassurance from one restaurant manager minion.

'This looks delicious,' she ventured.

'Enjoy it whilst you can. Single parenthood doesn't offer much opportunity to eat like this.'

Was he for real? A trickle of anger seeped into her veins. 'That's a bit of a sweeping statement, don't you think?'

His snort of derision caused her toes to tingle with the urge to kick him.

'No. Do you have any idea of the reality of single parenthood? How hard it is?'

Swallowing down the threat of a mirthless laugh, she slapped some of the langoustine mousse onto some bread and took a bite. Tried to concentrate on the incredible hit to her tastebuds instead of the memories that hovered before her—memories of those childhood years when she had effectively looked after her siblings. Dark-haired Tom, blue-eyed Philippa and baby Edie…

Yes! she wanted to shout. Yes, she did know how hard it was—but she also knew with all her being that it was worth it.

'I fully understand how enormous a responsibility parenting is and I know it will be hard. But I also know it will be incredibly rewarding.'

Ever since she'd lost her siblings, understood she would never be with them again. Ruby had known with every cell of her body and soul that she wanted a family.

Desperately she tried to neutralise her expression but it was too late—his blue-grey eyes considered her and his face lost some of its scowl.

'Those are words, Ruby. Easy to say. But the reality of caring for a family and supporting them at the same time on your own is way more daunting.' His voice sounded less harsh, yet the words were leaden with knowledge.

'I know it won't be easy.'

'No, it won't. Plus it's not all about babies and how cute and sweet they are.'

'I get that.' Her teeth were now clenched so tightly her jaw ached. 'I am not a fool, basing a decision like this on a baby's cute factor.'

Given her plan to adopt, it was more than possible that she'd opt for older children. Children such as she and her siblings had been.

'Babies grow up—into toddlers, into schoolchildren and into teenagers. Sometimes when you're on your own, trying to do it all, it can go wrong.' A shadow darkened his features and he scoured his palm over his face as if in an effort to erase it.

For a heartbeat doubt shook her—Tom had been five, the girls even younger when social services had finally hauled the whole family into care. If that hadn't happened would it all have gone wrong for them? Maybe it would—but that was because back then she'd been a child herself. This time she had it all *planned*.

'I told you. I won't embark on having a family until I have sufficient resources to make it possible. I will make sure I can work part-time, I will have the best childcare known to mankind, and—' Breaking off, she picked up her fork and pulled her plate towards her. Shook her head. 'I have no idea why I am justifying myself to you. Who made you the authority on single parenthood?'

'No one. But I am concerned that you are jumping the gun. Just because Hugh Farlane turned out to be a number one schmuck it doesn't mean you have to dive into single parenthood. Maybe this desire for kids on your own is a reaction to how badly it worked out with Hugh. I don't think you should make any hasty decisions, that's all. It's a mighty big step to take.'

His deep tone had gentled, the concern in it undoubtedly genuine, and that was worse than his scorn. That she could have dismissed, or countered with anger. But care triggered in her an alarming yearn to confide in him, to explain that her desire for a family was way more than a whim activated by Hugh's perfidy.

Bad idea. Yet she had to say something.

'I know that.' She did. 'But this is not a rebound decision from Hugh. Truly it isn't. It feels right.'

'Why?'

Ruby hesitated, picked up her glass and sipped a swirl of champagne, relieved to see their waiter approaching. Her brain raced as he placed the next course in front of them, rapidly explained that it consisted of crispy skinned chicken breast with black truffles, spinach and a white port sauce, and then discreetly melted into the background.

This would be the perfect opportunity to turn the conversation. Yet surely there was no harm in answering the question—maybe it was time to remind herself of her goals and her motivations...set it all out.

A warning chime pealed from the alcoves of her mind. This was meant to be a professional dinner. It was hard to see that this conversation was anything *but* personal. But for some indefinable reason it seemed natural. The ding-dong of alarm pealed harder. This was how it had felt a decade before. Curled up in a chair in the beige metallic confines of a hostel room, the temptation to talk and confide had ended up in disaster.

But it was different now, and...and, *truth be told*—she wanted him to know that she was all grown up...not some daft girl who hadn't thought through the idea of going it alone into parenthood. So one last explanation and then she would move the conversation into professional waters.

CHAPTER SIX

ETHAN KNEW THAT the whole discussion had derailed spectacularly and that it behoved him to push it onto a blander path.

But, he couldn't. Intrigue and frustration intermeshed at the idea of Ruby launching herself into the murk of single parenthood through choice.

Chill, Ethan.

There were many, many excellent single parents—he knew that. But it was a tough road; he knew from bitter personal experience exactly how difficult it was—had seen how it had played out for his mother.

'So why single parenthood?' he repeated.

Ruby carefully cut up a piece of chicken and for a moment he thought she would change the subject, then she put her cutlery down and shrugged.

'Because I'm not exactly clued up at choosing good father material.'

'Just because Hugh didn't work out…'

Ruby snorted. '"Didn't work out" is a bit of an understatement. But the point is that it's not just Hugh. You see, Hugh wasn't the first person to tug the wool over my eyes. Being taken in is my speciality—I could write a thesis. When I was nineteen there was Gary. I believed Gary to be a misunderstood individual who had been wrongfully dismissed. Turned out he was a drunken layabout who'd been quite rightly fired. Then a few years later there was Steve—a self-confessed gambler who swore himself hoarse that he was trying to quit. In reality he was keen on extracting as much money from me as possible to fund the local betting shop.'

A wave of her fork in his direction.

'Hugh you know about. So surely you can see the theme here. I am not a good judge of character. So it makes sense to do this alone.'

'But why do it at all? Or at least why do it now? You're twenty-six.'

'You are thirty. Most thirty-year-olds aren't billionaire CEOs of their own global business. Ten years ago I knew I wanted a family and you knew you wanted to make it big. You've done that through grit and hard work and drive. Well, now I am doing the same to get a family.'

A frown slashed his brow. 'Children aren't an acquisition.'

'I am not suggesting they are.' She gave an expressive roll of her eyes as she huffed out a breath that left her exasperation to hover in the air. '*Sheesh*. What is wrong with wanting to have children?'

'Nothing.'

For Pete's sake—he'd muttered the word, and now his lips had pressed together as a barrier to the further words that wanted to spill from his lips with unprecedented freedom. To stem the explanation that having children could lead to devastation not joy.

His mother had been deprived of her daughter—her pride and joy. For an instant the image of Tanya's lifeless body assaulted his brain. His sister—driven to take her own life. And he hadn't known—hadn't been able to protect her.

His mother had been left with him, her son, a mirror image of her violent criminal husband. The son she had never been able to love but had done her duty by. Until he'd driven her to snap point and she'd washed her hands of him.

For a split second the memory of the packed case and the hand-over to social services jarred his brain. No fault of hers—in her eyes he'd been on the road to following his father's footsteps. His impassioned pleas for forgiveness and promises to reform would have simply been further shades of the man she despised.

Ethan shut down the thought process and concentrated on Ruby's face. Those sapphire eyes, delicate features and that determined chin. Her expression of challenge had morphed into one of concern and he forced his vocal cords into action and his face into neutral.

'There is nothing wrong with wanting children. I just think you need to give single parenthood a lot of thought and not enter the whole venture with rose-coloured spectacles. That's all.'

End of subject, and Ethan picked up his knife and fork and started to eat.

Ruby twirled a tendril of hair around her finger. 'What about you? Where do you stand on the venture into parenthood? Don't you hope for a family one day?'

'No.'

The idea of a family was enough to bring him out in hives. Family had brought him nothing except a one-way channel to loss, heartbreak and rejection. So what was the point?

'Never?' Surprise laced her tone.

'No.' Perhaps monosyllables would indicate to Ruby that this wasn't a topic he wished to pursue.

'Why not?'

Clearly the indirect approach hadn't worked—so it was time to make it clear.

'That's my personal choice.'

Hurt mingled with anger flashed across her features. *Fair enough, Ethan.* He'd been mighty fine with a personal conversation when it was *her* personal life under discussion.

'In brief, it's not what I want. Like you. I've worked hard to get to where I am and I don't want to rock the boat. I'm exactly where I want to be. And I know exactly where I'm going.'

'Isn't that a bit boring? I mean, will that be your life for ever? Buy another property…set up another venture? What happens when you run out of countries?'

Ethan blinked at the barrage of questions. 'Boring? I run a global business, travel the world on a daily basis, have more than enough money and a pretty nifty lifestyle. So, nope. Not humdrum.'

'But…' A shake of her head and she turned her attention back to her plate.

Following suit, he took another mouthful, tried to appreciate the delicacy of the truffles, the infusion of port, the tenderness of the meat. To his own irritation he couldn't let it go.

'But what?'

Her shoulders lifted and for a second his gaze lingered on the creamy skin, the enticing hint of cleavage.

'That world of yours—that non-rocking boat of yours—only contains you, and that sounds lonely. Unless you're in a relationship that you haven't mentioned?'

'Nope. It's a one-man vessel and I'm good with that.'

'So you don't want a long-term relationship or kids? Ever?'

'I don't want any type of relationship. Full stop. I make sure my…my liaisons are brief.' Like a night—a weekend, tops.

Ruby's eyed widened and his exasperation escalated as he identified compassion in her.

'But you've worked so hard to build up Caversham. What's the point if you don't have someone to hand it over to?'

'That's hardly a reason to have a child.'

'Not a reason, but surely part of being a parent is the desire to pass on your values or beliefs. A part of yourself.'

The very idea made him go cold. 'I think that's a bit egocentric. You can't have children just to inculcate them with your beliefs.'

'No!' She shook her head, impatience in the movement. 'You're making it sound as if I want to instil them with questionable propaganda. I don't. But I *do* believe we are programmed with a need to nurture. To love and be loved.'

'Well, I'm the exception to the rule.'

Her chin angled in defiance. 'Or your programming has gone haywire.'

Ethan picked his glass up and sipped the fizz. No way would he rise to that bait.

'The point is, even if you're right, it is wrong to put that burden on someone. That responsibility. You shouldn't have a child just because you want someone to love and love you back. There are enough people out there already. The world doesn't need more.'

'Actually...' Ruby hesitated.

'Actually, what?'

'Nothing.'

Before he could respond the boom of Tony Pugliano's voice rang out. 'So, my friends. It was all to your liking?'

Ruby's thoughts whirled as she strove to concentrate on Tony's question, primed her lips to smile. Maybe this was an intervention from providence itself—a reinforcement of her decision to cease with the confidences.

'It was incredible, Tony!' she stated.

'How could it be anything else?' the chef declared. 'And now we have the perfect end to the perfect meal—I have for you a sample of the very best desserts in the world.'

He waved an expansive hand and the waiter appeared with an enormous platter, which he placed in the middle of the table.

'I, Tony Pugliano, prepared these with my own hands

for your delectation. There is praline mousseline with cherry confit, clementine cheesecake, almond and black sesame pannacotta and a dark chilli chocolate lime *torta*.' He beamed as he clapped Ethan on the shoulder. 'And of course all this is on the house.'

There went her jaw again—headed kneewards. *On the house.* She doubted such words had ever crossed Tony's lips before.

'You look surprised. No need. Because never, *never* can I thank this man enough. You saved my Carlo—my one and only child. You are a good man, Ethan, and I thank you with all my heart.'

Tony seemed sublimely unaware of Ethan's look of intense discomfort. Yet the shadow in Ethan's eye, the flash of darkness, made her chest band in instinctive sympathy.

'I think this meal goes a long way towards thanks,' she said. 'It was divine. I don't suppose you would share the secret of the truffle sauce in…?'

The tactic worked. As if recalled to his chef persona, Tony gave a mock roar and shook his head.

'*Never.* Not even for you would I reveal the Pugliano family secret. It has passed from one generation to the next for centuries and shall remain sacrosanct for ever. Now—I shall leave you to enjoy the fruit of my unsurpassable skills.'

Once he had made a majestic exit, Ethan nodded. 'Thanks for the change of subject.'

'No problem.' Ruby reached out and selected a minidessert. 'I knew it took more than charm to get Tony Pugliano grazing from your hand. Whatever you did for his son must have been a big deal.'

Ethan shrugged his shoulders, the casual gesture at variance with the wariness in his clenched jaw. 'I was in a position to help his son and I did so. Simple as that.'

'It didn't sound simple to me. More like fundamental.'

'How about another change of subject?'

Picking up a morsel of cheesecake, he popped it in his mouth. His expression was not so much closed as locked, barred *and* padlocked—with a 'Trespassers Will Be Prosecuted' sign up to boot.

'I think our dinner conversation has gone a bit off the business track.'

He wasn't wrong. In fact she should be doused in relief that he didn't want to rewind their conversational spool. Because she had been on the cusp of intimacy—tempted to confide to Ethan that her plan was to adopt, about to spill even more of her guts. And a girl needed her intestines to survive. Something she would do well to remember.

Her family plans were zilch to do with Ethan Caversham. And similarly there was no need for her to wonder why he had decided to eschew love of any sort from a partner or a child. Over the past week she'd gained his trust, they had built up an easy working relationship, and she would not risk that. She mustn't let this man tug her into an emotional vortex again. Ten years ago it had been understandable. Now it would be classed as sheer stupidity.

'So,' he said. 'How about we start with what you think of this restaurant? With your guest's hat on?'

'Modern. Sweeping. The glass effect works to make it sleek, and his table placement is extraordinary. I love the balcony—it's contemporary and it's got buzz. Those enormous flower arrangements are perfect. As for the Christmas effect—it is superb.'

Maybe she could blame the glitter of the pseudo icicles or the scent of cinnamon and gingerbread that lingered in the air for flavouring their conversation with intimacy...

'Definitely five-star. But is this what you want for Caversham?'

'Five stars? Absolutely.'

'I get that, but I have an idea that you're holding some

information back. About your plans for the castle.' Something she couldn't quantify made her know that what Tony Pugliano had achieved wasn't exactly what Ethan was after. His body stilled and she scooped up a spoonful of the cheesecake, allowed the cold tang of clementine to melt on her tongue. 'Am I right?'

Ethan drummed a rhythm on the table. 'Yes,' he said finally. 'But it's on a need-to-know basis.'

'Don't you think that as your restaurant manager I "need to know"?'

'Yes—and when it's the right time I will tell you. For now, I'd like to discuss the grand opening.'

Determination not to show hurt allowed her to nod, relieved that the movement shook her hair forward to shield her expression from those all-seeing eyes.

'Fair enough.'

An inhalation of breath and she summoned enthusiasm—she *was* excited about her ideas for the event and she would not let Ethan's caginess shadow that.

'I thought we could have a medieval theme—maybe even a ball. And what do you think about the idea of making it a fundraiser? I know we've already confirmed the guest list, but I think people will happily buy tickets for a good cause. Especially if they also get publicity from it. We could offer exclusive coverage to one of the celebrity gossip mags and—'

Ruby broke off. Ethan sat immobile, his silence uninterpretable.

Then… 'It's a great idea,' Ethan said. A sudden rueful smile tipped his lips and curled her toes. 'In fact it ties in perfectly with my ideas for the castle. So I guess you now "need to know".' His smile vanished and left his lips in a hard straight line. 'In brief, I want to run Caversham Castle as a charitable venture. So kick-starting it with a fundraiser would work well.'

It was as if each word had been wrung from him and confusion creased her brow. 'I love the idea, but can you tell me more? Is it a particular charity you want to raise money for? The more information I have the more successful I can make the event.'

'The money raised will go to a charity that helps troubled teens. Gets them off the streets, helps them back on their feet if they've been in juvie.'

It took a few moments for the true meaning of his words to make an impact, and then it took all her will-power not to launch herself across the table and wrap her arms around him. Only the knowledge that they were in a public place and the suspicion that Ethan would loathe the display kept her in her seat. But the idea that Ethan Caversham, renowned tough guy and entrepreneur, had a different side to him made her tummy go gooey. He'd experienced life on the streets, been a troubled teen himself and now he wanted to help others.

'I think that is an amazing idea. Brilliant. We will make this the best fundraiser ever.' Her mind was already fizzing with ideas. 'How about we go back to my suite for coffee and a brainstorm?'

Ethan bit back a groan and tried to get a grip. Better late than never, after all. Somehow he'd utterly lost his grasp of events—the conversation had spiralled out of control and now he could see more than a flicker of approval in Ruby's eyes. An approval he didn't want.

Time to try and relocate even a shard of perspective.

Ruby was his employee—one who could help make this fundraiser work. Therefore he should be pleased at her enthusiasm and accept her approval on a professional level, not a personal one.

So... 'Coffee and a brainstorm sound good.'

'Perfect.' A blink of hesitation and then she reached out

and covered his hand with her own. 'I will make this *rock*. I remember how it felt to be a teenager on the streets. It was like being shrouded in invisibility. Even the people who dropped a ten pence piece in front of me did it without even a glance.'

A small shiver ran through her body, and her eyes were wide in a face that had been leached of colour.

'The idea of subsisting on people's charity made me feel small and helpless and angry and very alone.'

The image of Ruby huddled on the streets smote his chest.

'It is an endemic problem. I know there are hostels and soup kitchens and the like, and that is incredible, but I want to do something more hands-on, more direct—' He broke off.

The image of a homeless Ruby had set him galloping on his hobby horse.

'Like what?' She leant forward, her entire being absorbed in their conversation. 'Come on, Ethan—spill. I want to help.'

Her sincerity was vibrant and how could he quench that? It would be wrong.

'My idea for the castle is to open it as a luxury hotel for nine months of the year and then use the proceeds to utilise it differently for the remaining three months. As a place for troubled teens. Surfing holidays but also training courses, so they can learn job skills—maybe in the hotel industry.'

He'd explained his idea to Rafael, but somehow the words were much harder to utter now—maybe because Rafael understood his need for redemption, retribution, second chances. Ruby didn't. And there it was—the dawning of approbation, the foretaste of hero worship simmering in her beautiful eyes.

'That is an awesome idea,' she said quietly. 'Truly. Tony was right. You are a good man.'

The words were not what he wanted to hear—there was too much in his past for him to have earned that epithet.

'I'm not quite ready for a halo—all I plan to do is use the profits from a business venture to try and do some good. That's all. Don't big it up into more than it is.'

A push of the nearly empty dessert plate across the table.

'Now, eat up and then let's go brainstorm.'

There went her chin again. 'You're not just raising money—you have a hands-on plan that will help some of those homeless kids out there. That's pretty big in my book, and nothing you say will change my opinion. Now, we'd better find Tony and say goodbye.'

One effusive farewell later and they were outside. Next to him, Ruby inhaled the cold crisp air and looked up into the darkness of the sky. 'Do you think it will snow?'

'Unlikely.'

'So no white Christmas?' Ruby said with a hint of wistfulness. 'It's a shame, really—can you imagine how beautiful Cornwall would be covered in snow?' She shook her head. 'On the subject of Christmas…how do you feel about a Christmas party at Caversham? Not on Christmas Day, obviously, but maybe Christmas Eve drinks? Or eve of Christmas Eve drinks? For suppliers and locals. A lot of the staff we've taken on are local, so I think it would be a nice idea. Bank some goodwill…show the Caversham community ethos.'

Ethan considered—it was a good idea. But not in the run-up to Christmas.

'It doesn't fit with my plans.' More plans he didn't wish to share. 'Maybe we could think about it later? After New Year? Anyway, I know you said you had Christmas plans as well. So take some time off. From the twenty-first—that's not a problem.'

'Okay. Thanks.'

Enthusiasm was not prominent in her voice and Ethan

swallowed the urge to ask her exactly what her plans were. Not his business—and not fair, as he didn't want to share his own.

The limo pulled up and he held the door open for Ruby to slide in, averted his eyes from the smooth length of her leg, hoped the tantalising cinnamon smell wouldn't whirl his head further. *Employee, employee, employee.*

As soon as the car started she leant forward; now her enthusiasm shone through the dim interior of the car.

'So—for the medieval banquet…I've already done loads of research and I've got some fab dishes we could use. What do you think about eels in a thick spicy purée, loach in a cold green sauce and a meat tile—which is chicken cooked in a spiced sauce of pounded crayfish tails, almonds and toasted bread, garnished with whole crayfish tails. Or capon pasties—or even eel and bream pasties. I've spoken to a medieval re-enactor and I reckon he'll know someone who will come along and cook us some samples. We could even put together a recipe book and sell it—raise some extra funds.'

'Excellent ideas. Though…what is loach?'

'It's a freshwater fish. Mind you, I'm not sure you can get it here.' A quick rummage in her evening bag netted a small notebook and pen. 'I'll check. What about an auction?' A sudden grin illuminated her face. 'Hey! You could talk to Tony. Auction off a cooking lesson with Antonio Pugliano. What do you think?'

His breath caught as his lungs suspended their function. One thought only was in his mind—Ruby was so beautiful, so animated, so unutterably gorgeous, and all he wanted was to tug her across the seat and kiss her.

CHAPTER SEVEN

RUBY BROKE OFF as all her ideas took flight from her brain in one perfect V-shaped swoop, evicted by an across-the-board sweep of desire. Ethan's pupils had darkened and the atmosphere in the limousine morphed. Words withered on her tongue she shifted towards him, propelled by instinct, pulled by his mesmerising eyes.

His features seemed ever so slightly softened by the shadows in the dim interior. Or maybe it was because now she had gained some insight. This man cared about so much more than profit and business domination. He hadn't let ambition consume him to the point where he forgot people in need. Forgot the Ethan and Ruby of a decade ago.

'Ethan…' she whispered.

Somehow they were right alongside each other, her leg pressed against the solid strength of his thigh, and she let out a small sigh. The closeness felt right, and she twisted her torso so she faced him, placed a hand over his heart, felt the steady beat increase tempo. Then his broad, capable hand cupped her jaw oh so gently, his thumb brushed her lip and she shivered in response.

His grey-blue eyes locked onto hers with a blaze of desire that melted all barriers, called to something deep inside her. She parted her lips, sheer anticipation hollowed her tummy—and then with precipitous speed his expression changed.

'What am I doing?'

The words were muttered with a low ferocity as his hand dropped from her face, left her skin bereft.

He hauled in an audible breath. 'This is not a good idea. I wish it were, but it isn't.'

It took a few seconds for the words to register, to make sense, and then reality hit. Forget Ethan. What was *she* doing? This was her boss…this was Ethan Caversham… this was a disastrous idea.

The idea that a reporter with some sort of lens able to penetrate tinted windows might have caught them on camera made her cringe. But even worse than that was the sheer stupidity of getting involved in any way with Ethan. There was an edge of danger—a foreshadow she recognised all too well and that urged her to scramble back to her side of the seat.

'You're right. I…I guess we got carried away. Food, champagne, limo… It's easily done. We'll forget it ever happened, yes? But would you mind if we took up the brainstorming tomorrow?'

She needed time to detonate that near-kiss from her psyche, scrub it from her memory banks. Right now the idea of Ethan in her suite was impossible to contemplate. A few hours by herself and she would rebuild the façade, resume the role of Ruby Hampton, Restaurant Manager. Then all would be well—because this time the mask would be uncrackable, fireproof, indestructible…

Unable to stop herself, she glanced nervously out of the window, checking for reporters.

Ethan noticed, and his lips pulled into a tight, grim line. 'Worried about the paps? You're safe in here, you know.'

'I know.'

And she did—deep down. Thanks to Ethan, who had neutralised the reporters with smooth, cold ease and rendered them powerless. The memory triggered a small thrill that she hastened to suppress. Yes, Ethan had protected her—but he had done so on principle. To him, the Hugh Farlanes and the paps out for a story at any price were scum and he would shield anyone from them. It wasn't personal. He would champion anyone broken or wounded or hurt.

But that near-kiss was pretty personal, pointed out a small inner voice. Which was exactly why he'd shut it down. And she should be grateful for that—would be once she'd escaped this limousine, where the air swirled with might-have-beens and what-ifs.

When they arrived back at the castle Ruby practically shot from the car through the grand entrance. 'I'll see you in the morning,' she called over her shoulder.

An expletive dropped from Ethan's lips, making her pause and turn on the stairs. He scrubbed a hand down his jaw, looking weary.

'Listen, Ruby, we need to get rid of the awkwardness. We have a lot to do in a minimal amount of time to upgrade the opening dinner to a ball. So we must manage it—nothing happened and nothing will happen. It was one fool moment and I will not let that ruin the professional relationship we have established.'

'You're right. It wasn't even a kiss. No big deal, right?'

An infinitesimal hesitation and then he nodded. 'No big deal.'

Ethan's head pounded as he looked across at Ruby. Seated at her desk she was back in professional mode—glossy black hair pinned back into a svelte chignon, dressed in dark grey trousers and a pinstripe jacket over a crisp white shirt. Her posture spoke of wariness and her eyes held a matching guard. The spontaneous trust, the spark doused and if Ethan could have worked out a way to kick himself round Cornwall he would have.

She straightened some papers on her desk, the action unnecessary. 'If it's OK with you rather than brainstorm I'll put together a presentation.'

Which meant he'd miss out on seeing her features light

with enthusiasm as she came up with ideas. Mind you it was that illumination that had led to his disastrous impulse the night before. Impulses never ended well—he knew that to bitter cost.

Ruby was a woman with a plan to have a family—she was barely out of a demoralising relationship, and he had no business kissing her. 'Sounds good. Come down to my office when you're ready.' Maybe he'd rustle up some stilts to shore up the conversation. As he clicked the door shut he vowed to himself that by hook or by crook he'd win back their former camaraderie. It was necessary in order to maximise their productivity and their ability to pull of this ball. It was zip to do with a desire to see her lips curve up into a genuine smile.

So first he'd throw himself into work, get himself back on track and then he'd charm Ruby back to the status quo. But one conference call later a perfunctory knock heralded the appearance of Ruby and camaraderie looked to be the last thing on her mind—in fact she could have personified the cliché spitting mad.

'I have a message for you.' Annoyance clipped each syllable.

'Shoot.'

Her chest rose and he could almost see metaphorical steam issuing from her. 'It's from Tony Pugliano.'

Ah... 'Why didn't you put the call through to me?'

'Obviously I tried to, but you were engaged, and then Tony said it didn't matter—he could discuss it with me. Which was when he informed me that he will make a delivery of super-special pizzas on the twenty-second of December. Explained how happy he is to support such a worthy cause and how much he admires your plan to give these teens in care a wonderful time over the Christmas period. So there you go—message delivered.'

With that she swivelled on one black-booted foot and headed for the door.

That wasn't just anger that radiated off her—there was hurt as well.

'Ruby—wait.'

A heartbeat of hesitation and then she turned to face him. 'Yes.'

'I should have told you.'

Her shoulders lifted. 'It's your business—you don't have to tell me everything.'

'No. But I should have told you this.'

'So why didn't you?'

'We have been and will be working full-time until the ball. I figured you'd deserve a break—those days will be pretty full-on. Plus the kids will be here from the twenty-second to the twenty-fourth, and I know you have Christmas plans. I didn't want you to feel obliged to cancel them, or to feel guilty. It's no big deal.'

All the truth—though nowhere near the complete truth. But it was difficult to explain his utter disinclination to let her see the full extent of his charitable activities.

Her expression softened as she studied his face, though a small frown still nipped at her wide brow. 'Your idea of what is a big deal and mine is different. But you're right—you should have told me. Now I know, I would like to help.'

Bad idea… The previous night had amply demonstrated that a break would do them good. 'No need. I have it all covered here. There is nothing for you to do—so go and enjoy yourself.'

'Ethan, I don't want to go and enjoy myself. I know I can help. Why don't you want me to? Is it because…?' Her voice faltered for a second and then she met his gaze full-on. 'Because of what happened last night.'

'No. I don't want you to help because I don't want you to

get burn out. There is a huge amount of work to be done in the next few days. You'll need a break. I've got it covered.'

Ethan could feel the grooves in the floor where his heels were dug in. Instinct told him that if they weren't careful, complications would abound.

'I bet you haven't.' Her chin angled, pugnacious. 'Tell me your plans and if I can work out how to improve them I get to help. Deal?'

Great! Instinct had made another express delivery—this was über-important to Ruby and it went deep, though he wasn't sure why.

Expelling a sigh of pure exasperation, he shrugged. 'Fine. I wanted to do it all actually on Christmas Day, but that didn't work out. So…a busload of teenagers will arrive here on the twenty-second. They are all either in children's homes or in foster care and they've all got a chequered history. We'll have a pizza, DVD and games night. I've ordered a billiards table and a darts board. On the twenty-third I and a few surf instructors will take them out for a day of water sports. We'll come back and I'm having caterers in to serve up a Christmas dinner. Another relaxed games evening, then to bed. Another morning's water sport on Christmas Eve and then they head back.'

There—you couldn't say fairer than that surely? So who knew why Ruby was shaking her head?

'What you have scheduled is brilliant, but I can make it better,' she said flatly.

'How?'

'Can I sit?'

Once he'd nodded she lowered herself onto a chair, rested her elbows on the desk and cupped her chin.

'I think you've missed something.'

'What? Another game? A…?'

'The magic of Christmas. You've mentioned Christmas dinner, but otherwise it could be any weekend. This is about the spirit of Christmas even if it's not actually Christmas Day. So what about a tree?'

'I thought about that and I figured the last thing they'll want is a tree and lots of schmaltz. These kids are tough and they've been through the mill. They'll want to obliterate Christmas—suppress the tainted memories it evokes.'

'Maybe some of them think like that—maybe that's what they need to think in order to get through Christmas. Dissing Christmas is their method of self-defence. But deep down they are still kids, and they deserve to be given a real Christmas—to see that Christmas doesn't always have to suck, that it can be wonderful and magical. It could be that what they're going back to is dismal, or lonely, or grim, so this two days you give them has to be something precious. Maybe to help them dilute those tainted memories.'

Her words strummed him... They spoke of a deep, vibrant sincerity and an underlying genuine comprehension, and Ethan knew that such empathy could only come from one place.

'Were you ever in care?' he asked. 'Is that why this is so important to you?'

She blinked, as if the question had zinged out of nowhere and caught her completely on the hop, skip and jump.

A flush seeped into her cheeks and then she shrugged. 'Yes—and yes. I was in care, and that's why I want to be part of this. I was eleven when it happened, and although I know that foster care can sometimes work out well it didn't for me. Looking back, I can see I was a difficult child to care for—so no surprise that I was moved from place to place. Including a stint in a residential home. I empathise with these kids. Because I remember vividly how awful holiday times were. Especially Christmas. But that doesn't mean I've given up on Christmas. And I don't want these kids to either.'

'I'm sorry the care system didn't work for you.'

'Don't be. I'm not after sympathy. I'm after your agreement to let me loose on this Christmas break. What do you think?'

Ethan drummed his fingers on the table. Of course he could shut this down and tell her no, but what kind of heel would that make him? To turn away someone who fervently wanted to help with a cause he fervently believed in?

'Go for it. You have carte blanche.' His smile twisted a little 'If you can give these kids some of the magic of Christmas then that would be a great thing. But I'm not sure it'll be easy. Some of these kids come from a very notorious estate and they have all been in serious trouble at one time or another.'

Images of the estate dotted his retina like flash photography. Depressing grey high-rise buildings, tower blocks of misery, with the smell of urine up the stairs, lifts that never worked. Vandalised park areas daubed with graffiti where kids roamed in gangs, so many of them caught in a vicious cycle of young offenders' units and truancy, the product of misery and neglect. Guilt stamped him—because he hadn't had that excuse for the road he'd chosen to walk.

Suddenly aware of Ruby's small frown, he shook his head to dislodge the thoughts. 'Just keep it in mind that you may need more than a magic wand and sprinkle of glitter,' he said.

'Sure…'

The speculative gaze she planted on him sent a frisson of unease through him. It was as if she were considering waving that wand and glitter pot at him.

He tugged his keyboard across the desk. 'Now you're here let's start that brainstorm session and get down to business.'

Time to make it clear this was a non-magical, glitter-free zone.

CHAPTER EIGHT

'THROUGH HERE, PLEASE.'

Two days later Ruby directed the three men toting the most enormous Christmas tree she'd ever seen into the library—the room Ethan had designated as Teen Base.

'That's perfect,' she stated, refusing to allow the battalion of doubts that were making a spirited attempt to gain a foothold in her brain.

It was the tyrannosaurus rex of spruces. Once the delivery men had left she contemplated the sheer enormity of actually decorating the tree, and for a second considered enlisting Ethan's help.

No. The tree had been her idea—plus she had vowed not to orchestrate any time with Ethan that could be avoided. Somehow she had to squash the urge to try to entice him into the idea of liking Christmas—had to suppress the urge for closeness that threatened at every turn.

The problem was the more they discussed the medieval ball and ways to raise money and publicity for their cause, the more she learnt about his ideas for Caversham Castle and the worse her gooey tummy syndrome became. The more he spoke about the youths he wished to help, the more sure she was that his empathy came from his own experiences. Which in turn led to her nutty desire to enmesh Ethan in the magic of Christmas.

Only it was clear he had no wish to enter her net. In the past two days his demeanour had been always professional, with the high expectations she'd become accustomed to, alleviated by a polite charm and appreciation for her work. But there was a guardedness, a caginess that kept her at a distance.

A distance she needed to respect—to welcome, even. Because Ethan Caversham was synonymous with danger. It was an equation she had to remember—because linked to her desire for emotional intimacy was the ever-present underlay of attraction. It was a lose-lose situation all round.

So she'd better get on with the decorations herself.

Inhaling the evocative spruce aroma that now tinged the air, Ruby opened the first box of ornaments with a small sigh of pleasure. This tree would exude Christmas and be the Christmassiest tree ever seen. Or at least the bits she could reach would be...

'Ruby.'

The sound of Ethan's deep voice nearly sent her tumbling from the stepladder.

'Here you are. We're meant to be doing the final run-through of the seating plan.'

Ruby twisted round to face him. 'I am so sorry. I lost track of time.'

'No worries.' His glance rested for a second on the tree. 'Looks good.'

'Good? Is that all you can say.' Ruby stepped backwards to assess her handiwork so far. 'It's flipping marvellous, if I say so myself. I know I've only managed to get less than half done, but I think the bold and beautiful theme works.'

Reds, purples and golds abounded, though she had made sure that the lush green of the pine was also on display. The ornaments were tasteful, but with a vibrant appeal that she thought would at least mean the tree would be noticed.

'So come on. Surely you can do better than "good" as an adjective.'

'Eye-catching,' he said, and she frowned at the obvious effort.

The syllables sounded forced. It was almost as if he didn't want to look at the tree or at her. Well, tough! He'd agreed to her plan to try to offer these youths some Christmas spirit, so the least he could do was be polite.

Better yet... 'Do you want to help me finish decorating it? As you can see it's pretty big—and you're taller than me. Plus it might be fun.'

The challenging smile slid from her lips as she clocked his sudden leaching of colour, his small step backwards. As if he'd seen a ghost.

He scraped a hand down his face as if to force his features into a semblance of normality. 'I'll pass, thanks. Trust me—you wouldn't want me bah-humbugging about the place.'

It was a credible attempt to lighten his expression, marred only by the wary ice-blue flecks in his eyes and the slight clenching of his jaw.

Every instinct told her he was hurting, and without thought she moved towards him and placed her hand over his forearm—the texture of his skin, the rough smattering of hair embedded itself into her fingertips.

'Look what happened to Scrooge. The ghosts of Christmases Past do not have to ruin the possibilities of Christmas Present.'

She'd expected him to scoff at the concept of ghosts—instead he simply shook his head. There was something intangible about him that she didn't understand—the way his blue-grey eyes zoned in on her, haunted, glittering with something elusive, as if they could see something she couldn't.

'Leave it, Ruby. The tree is incredible; you're doing a great job. Find me when it's done. No rush.'

His voice was so flat that instinct told her his spectres hovered close. It seemed clear what she ought to do—let him go, remember his disinclination to get close, the danger signs she had already identified, his need for distance. But she couldn't… She didn't know what had triggered his reaction, doubted he would tell her, but maybe she could help.

'Don't go.'

A frown descended on his brow at her words and she clenched her fingers into her palm and forced herself to hold her ground.

'Ethan. Stay. Try it. Let's decorate together.'

Gathering all her courage, she squatted down and hefted a box of purple baubles.

'Here. I get that you don't want to, and I get that sometimes the past taints the present, but these kids will be here the day after tomorrow and there's lots to be done.'

'You're suggesting tree decoration as some form of therapy?' He was back in control now—on the surface at least—and his voice was a drawl. 'Or have you bitten off more than you can chew?'

'A bit of both… This tree needs help. So—are you in?'

Was he in? Ethan stared down at the box of purple ornaments. Why was he even considering this idea?

Because Ruby had a point. From a practical point of view this gargantuan tree did need to be finished, and if he left Ruby to it she probably wouldn't get it done until past midnight.

And that was a problem because…?

Ruby was the one who had ordered the tree in the first place—and since when had he cavilled at the thought of his staff working overtime? Ethan gusted out a sigh. Since now, apparently. Because—tough business guy or not— if he walked out of this room now he would feel like an A-class schmuck.

He'd have to get over the memories and get on with it.

The shock had hit him with unexpected force. For a

vivid second the memory of Tanya had been so stark he
might have believed he'd been transported back in time.
He'd heard his sister's voice persuading him to help decorate the tree, remembered arranging the tinsel and the
scruffy, cheap but cheerful decorations under her instruc-
tion.

The memory had receded now, and as he looked at
Ruby's almost comically hopeful expression he shrugged.

'I'm in.'

That way maybe there'd be a chance of getting some
actual work done that day.

Whoa, Ethan, play fair. He'd agreed to this whole magic
of Christmas idea; he just hadn't reckoned on the extent
of Ruby's enchantment scheme.

'Excellent,' she said. 'So you're in charge of purple.
I'll do the red.'

For a while they worked in a silence that seemed oddly
peaceful. To his own irritation he found himself stepping
down at intervals, to check the effect of his handiwork. A
snort of exasperation escaped his lips and Ruby's subsequent chuckle had him glaring across at her.

'Sorry. I couldn't help it. You look so...*absorbed.*'

'Yes, well. If I do something I make sure I do it properly.'

For no reason whatsoever the words travelled across the
pine-scented air and took on an unintended undertone...
one that brought an image of kissing Ruby with attention
to every detail. It was an effort not to crane his neck in a
search for mistletoe. Instead his eyes snagged on the lush
outline of her lips and desire tautened inside him.

Her fingers rose and touched her lips. He heard her intake of breath and forced his gaze to return to the tree.

'So...' His voice resembled that of a frog. *Try again.*
'So, believe me, my share of this tree will rock and roll.'

A small shake of her head and then her lips tilted into a full-wattage smile. 'See? It is kind of fun, isn't it?'

Ethan blinked—to his own surprise, it was…but it would be a whole lot better if he could tell himself that the reason had zip to do with his fellow decorator. Maybe her palpable belief in the magic of Christmas was contagious. Dear Lord—he'd lost the plot big-time. If he didn't take care he'd find himself with a pillow round his middle in a red suit.

'Could be worse,' he muttered as he stretched up his arm to thread a silver-spangled ball on to a branch.

Hmm… Alarm bells started to toll in his brain. If Ruby had gone this over the top with the tree, what other schemes were afoot?

'So…any other magical plans apart from the tree?'

Ruby expertly unhooked a strand of tinsel and rearranged it. 'I've planned a bake-off.'

'A bake-off?'

'Yup. I think they'll go for it because of all the TV shows. My plan is that everyone has a go at Christmas cookies and gingerbread. It will be friendly—they can judge each other. Or the ones who really don't want to bake can judge. It will make a nice start to the festivities. Then they can eat Tony's pizzas and chill, play some games, maybe catch a Christmas movie. I'll make popcorn.'

'That sounds like a lot of work for you.' Ethan hesitated; he didn't want to hail on her parade or dim her enthusiasm, but… 'You do know that these kids…they may not appreciate your good intentions.'

'Don't worry. I know I'm coming across all Pollyanna, but I have kept a reality check. I've got in extra fire extinguishers, plus I've cleared out all the sharp knives, though I've decided cookie cutters won't be lethal. I know there is a chance none of them will engage. But…' Reaching up, she attached a gold bauble. 'I've got to try. Because if we get through to even one of these kids and create a happy memory of Christmas then it will be worth it. Even if they aren't in a place to show their appreciation.'

'The "dilute the tainted memories" approach?' he said.

'Yup.'

For a second Ethan wondered if that were possible—then knew he was deluded. It wasn't. He wasn't even sure he wanted it to be.

Once he'd believed the best thing to do was obliterate the chain of memories with mindless anger. Beat them into oblivion. Especially the memory of the Christmas after Tanya's death. His mother, him, and the ghost of Tanya. In the end rage had overcome him and he'd hurled the microwaved stodgy food at the wall, watched the gravy trickle and blend in with the grungy paint. Once he'd started he hadn't been able to stop—had pulled the scrawny tree from its pot, flung it down. Stamped on it, kicked it—as if the tree had been the bully who had driven Tanya to her death.

His mother hadn't said a word; then she had left the room with a curt, 'Clean it up.'

Seconds later he'd heard the sound of the television and known that it was the end of Christmas. By the following Christmas she'd consigned him to social services and he'd taken to the streets, consumed by grief, anger and misery. Then finally he'd decided to take control—to leash the demons and channel his emotions in order to succeed.

With an abrupt movement he stood back. 'I'm done.'

Seeing the snap of concern in her blue eyes, he forced his lips into a smile. Ruby's way wasn't his way, but that wasn't to say it wasn't a good way—and she was right. If her way could help even one of these teenagers then it was worth every moment.

'It looks spectacular.'

That pulled an answering smile, though her eyes still surveyed him with a question. 'It's a work of art.'

It was definitely a work of *something*—though Ethan wasn't sure what.

'Hang on,' she said. 'We need to do the star. It's the *pièce de résistance*.' She walked across the room and rummaged around in a box before twirling round. 'What do you think?'

Ethan blinked, all darkness chased away by a star that could only be described as the Star of Bling. 'Wow. That's...'

'Eye-catching?' Ruby handed it up to him. 'I think you should do the honours. Really.' Her voice softened. 'This is your scheme. I know I'm banging on about the magic of Christmas, but without you these teens wouldn't be going anywhere. So I think it's right that you should put the star on top.'

Ethan hesitated, a frisson of discomfort rippling through him at her tone. Too much admiration, too much emotion... best to get this whole interlude over with.

In an abrupt movement he placed the star on top of the tree, nestled it into the branches and jumped down off the stepladder.

'There. Done. Now, how about we get some work done?'

'Sure...'

Ethan frowned at the note of hesitation in her voice, saw her swift glance at her watch and sighed. 'Unless you have more Christmas magic to sort?'

'Not magic...just something I need to do. But I can do it later. It's not a problem.'

Curiosity warred with common sense and won. 'Okay. I'll bite. What needs to be done?'

'Now I'll sound like Pollyanna on a sugar rush. I've bought them all gifts. Out of my own money,' she added quickly.

'The money's not an issue.' Affront touched him that she'd thought it would be.

'I know that! I just wanted to make it personal. I'll sign

the tags from you as well. Though it would be better if you—' She broke off.

'If I signed them myself? I can do that.'

'Fabulous. I'll run up and get all the gifts now. Maybe we could wrap them whilst we discuss the seating plan?'

Ethan opened his mouth and then closed it again. What he'd meant was that Ruby could give him the tags to sign. No need for him to see the presents—presumably she'd bought them all chocolates or key rings. But she looked so pleased...

'Sure,' he heard his voice say.

'I'll be back in a mo...'

'Bring them to my office.' At least that way he could pretend it was work.

Ruby toted the bags out of her bedroom and paused on the landing. Time for a pep talk. It was wonderful that Ethan had bought into her ideas, but she had to grab on to the coat-tails of perspective before it disappeared over the horizon. Sure, he'd helped decorate the tree, but that was because she had given him little choice—he'd done it for those teens and so that she could resume her restaurant manager duties more quickly. Not for *her*.

It was time to get these gifts wrapped and get on with some work.

So why, when she entered his office, did she feel a small ripple of disappointment to see Ethan behind his desk, intent on his computer screen, exuding professionalism?

His glance up as she entered was perfunctory at best.

She hesitated. 'If you want to get on with some work I can wrap these later.'

'No, it's fine.' One broad hand swept the contents of the desktop to one side.

'Right. Here goes. I've got a list that details each person and their gift.'

His body stilled. 'You bought individual gifts?'

'Yes. I called the social workers, got a few numbers for foster carers and residential home workers and chatted to some people. Just to find out a bit about them all, so I could buy something personal.'

His eyes rested on her with an indecipherable expression.

'Hey… Like you would say, it's no big deal.'

'Yes, it is.'

'No—really. To be honest, it's kind of therapeutic. In a weird way I feel like I'm doing it for myself. The me of all those years ago. Because I can remember what it was like in care, being the person with the token present. That was the worst of it—having to be grateful for gifts that were impersonal. Don't get me wrong—some carers really tried. But they didn't know me well enough to know what I wanted. Others couldn't be bothered to get to know me. So I'd get orange-flavoured chocolate when I only liked milk, or a top that I loathed and that didn't fit.'

For heaven's sake!

'That all sounds petty, doesn't it? But I want these kids to get a gift they *want*—not something generic.'

'Like a key ring or a chocolate bar?' he said, and a rueful smile touched his lips.

'Is that what you thought I'd bought?'

'Yes. I guess I should have known better.' Ethan rose to his feet. 'Come on.'

'Where to?'

'Let's do this properly. We'll wrap in the bar and you can show me what you bought everyone and brief me on what you found out about them. I'll light the fire and we'll have a drink.'

'What about work?'

The rueful smile became even more rueful, mixed with charm, and Ruby concentrated on keeping her breathing steady.

'I think we have done all we can do. The seating plan looks fine, the food is sorted, the wine is sorted, the auction is sorted and the band is booked. The banqueting hall furniture arrives after the Christmas period. All in all, I think we may have run out of work.'

He was right—and she knew exactly why that smile was now packed with regret…because without work to focus on what would they do with themselves?

She looked down at the presents she carried. The answer to that problem was to wrap fast, then flee to bed. *Alone.*

CHAPTER NINE

RUBY WATCHED AS Ethan lit the fire, his movements deft, the tug of denim against the muscles of his thighs holding her gaze as he squatted by the flames.

Stop with the ogling.

She forced herself to lay out the silver paper patterned with snowflakes and the list of gifts on the table. A sip of the deep red wine Ethan had poured for them both and then she waited until he sat opposite her.

'Here,' she said, and handed over the first present. 'This one is for Max: he's one of the boys in residential care and he's really into music—specifically rap, which I have to admit I know nothing about. So I did some research, conferred with his key worker at the home, and we came up with this T-shirt. It's the right size, and it's a cool label, so…'

Ethan shook the T-shirt out and nodded approval at the slogan. Folding it up again, he kept his eyes on her. 'It must have taken a fair amount of time to research each and every one of them and then find what you wanted. You should have told me. I'd have lightened your workload.'

'No way. I was happy to do it on my own time. Plus, you've hardly been idle yourself. You've briefed the surf instructors, sourced the caterers, the billiards table, co-ordinated all the paperwork—and you're also running a global business.'

Ruby frowned, wondering why he never seemed to re-alise just how much he did.

He broke off a piece of tape with a deft snap. 'What I've

done is generic—I could have set this up for any group of teenagers in care. You've made it personal.'

'Yes, I have. But I couldn't have done that if you hadn't set it up in the first place. Plus…' She hesitated. 'What you've done is personal too. You're giving them what helped you. The opportunity to surf, to do other water sport, to expend energy and vent frustration in a positive way. So what you've done isn't generic, and I won't let you believe it is. You care about these kids.' With a sudden flash of insight she blurted, 'Did *you* grow up on an estate? Like the one some of these kids are from?' The one he'd described as 'notorious'.

For a second she thought he wouldn't answer; the only sound was the crackle of the logs. Then he dropped the wrapped T-shirt into a bag and lifted his broad shoulders in an I-suppose-there's-no-harm-in-answering shrug.

'Yes, I did. So I relate to where these kids have come from—a tough background, maybe abuse, neglect, parents on drugs and alcohol or in prison. It's easy for them to get into trouble, join a gang, because there's nothing else to do and no one to stop them. And then they do what their parents did—steal, deal…whatever it takes. All these kids are in that cycle, and I'd like to show them there are other choices. Not just by giving them Christmas, but by giving them incentive. If they can go away from here and stay clean for a few months they can come back and take other opportunities if they want to. I want to give them a chance to get off the wheel.'

'Like you did?'

'No.'

His voice was harsh now, and the dark pain that etched his features made her yearn to reach out.

'I didn't have their excuse. My dad was a lowlife—apparently he yo-yoed in and out of prison—but my mum tossed him out when I was tiny. The time he went down for armed robbery she said enough was enough. Mum didn't drink or do drugs, and any neglect was because she was out at work all day so she could put food on the table. God knows, she did her best—but it wasn't enough. I jumped onto the wheel all by myself. Like father, like son.'

The words sounded like a quote, the derision in them painful, and Ruby tried to gather her scrambled thoughts. 'I'm guessing you got into trouble—but it's like you said yourself. In an environment like a troubled estate that's understandable. The point is you got off that wheel and out of trouble. Look at you now—your mum must be proud.'

It was the wrong thing to have said; his face was padlocked and his eyes flecked with ice. Surely his mother hadn't been the one to make the father-son comparison?

Disbelief morphed into anger as she saw his expression. 'You are *not* a lowlife.'

'That's a matter of opinion.' His eyes were dark now, his voice vibrating with mockery, though she wasn't sure if he was mocking her, himself or the world.

'I don't care. Opinion doesn't make you into your father. It doesn't work like that. I know that because *I* am not my parents. Not either of them. And I never will be.'

Her fingers clenched around the edges of the table as she faced him.

'My parents were addicts. Booze, heroin—whatever they could get their hands on, whenever they could get their hands on it. At whatever cost. Food and paying bills and shoes were all irrelevant.'

She gestured down to the reams of Christmas wrapping paper.

'For them the festive period was an excuse to justify extra excess—which led to extra verbal violence or extra apathy. Turkey, decorations and presents didn't feature.'

For a moment she was back there—in the past. Feeling the tingle of childish anticipation that scratched her eyelids as she lay on the verge of sleep. The twist of hope that Santa was real…that she'd open her eyes and see four stuffed stockings for her siblings and herself. More importantly her parents, groomed and sober, would watch them opening them with love. Then reality would touch her with the cold fingers of dawn. The smell of stale cigarettes and worse would invade her nostrils and she'd know it would be another Christmas of playing avoid-the-abuse and hide-from-notice, ensuring her siblings stayed out of the line of fire.

The memory gave steel to her voice. 'I am not like them. I won't ever let addiction become more important than my children. *Ever.*'

His hands clenched on his thighs and his whole body vibrated with tension. His foot jumped on the wooden floor. As if he wanted to somehow change her past for her.

'Ruby. I am so sorry. I don't know what to say—except that it sucks that you had to go through that.'

She gave an impatient shake of her head. 'It did suck, but that's not the point. The point is *I* am not my parents and *you* are not your father.' His jaw was set and she could almost see her statement slide off him unheeded. 'I mean, do you even know where he is now?'

'No. My guess would be in a prison cell.'

'Well, you aren't. You are here, trying to make a difference and do good.'

'In which case I'd better get on with it.' His tone was light, but with an edge that emphasised the end of the subject. 'But first…' and now his gaze was filled with warmth and compassion '… I can't imagine what you went through, but I am full of admiration for the wonderful woman that child has become.'

'Thank you.'

Frustration mixed with a yen to get close to him—to make him see that his achievements deserved kudos just as much as hers. Yet already she could see the shutters had been pulled down to hood his eyes as he picked up the tape again.

'We'd better get a move on,' he said. It's a big day tomorrow.'

'Wait.'

Something—she had to do *something*. Loathing touched her soul at the idea that Ethan had such a deep-rooted, downright skewed vision of himself. Without allowing herself time to think she moved round the table and took his hand, tugged at it to indicate she wanted him to stand. He rose to his feet and she kept her fingers wrapped around his, tried to ignore the frisson that vibrated through her at the feel of his skin against hers.

'Come here.'

The small frown deepened on his forehead as she led him to the ornate gold Victorian mirror—an oval of gilt curls and swirls.

'Look at yourself,' she said firmly, 'and you will see you. Ethan Caversham. You are you. You may look like your dad, but you are not like him. This I know.'

His reluctance palpable, he shrugged. But he complied, and as he glanced at his reflection she hoped against all hope that he would see what she could. It was an optimism that proved foolhardy as his jaw hardened and a haunting mockery speckled his blue-grey eyes.

She stepped forward and turned so that she faced him, stood on tiptoe and cupped his jaw in her palms. The six o'clock shadow was rough against her skin as she angled his face and met his gaze.

'You are a good man,' she whispered, and reached up to kiss him.

Heaven knew she'd had every intention of pressing her lips to his cheek, but instinct overcame common sense and the burning of need to imprint her sincerity onto his consciousness prevailed. Her lips brushed his and she gave a small sigh as desire shimmered and sizzled, and then his broad hands spanned her waist and pulled her against him.

For a second she thought he'd kiss her properly, deepen the connection that fizzed, but as if he'd suddenly caught sight of his reflection he gently moved her away and stepped backwards instead. He lifted a hand and ran a finger against her cheek in a gesture so gentle she felt tears threaten.

'Thank you, Ruby. I appreciate the endorsement.'

A smile redolent with strain touched his lips and then he turned and headed back to the table, sat down and picked up the scissors.

This was a *good* thing, right? Of course it was. Kissing Ethan was a bad, bad idea—that was an already established fact. So she needed to crush the absurd sense of disappointment and follow suit.

Two days later Ethan watched the busload of teenagers depart round the curve of the driveway. A sideways glance showed Ruby still waving, a smile on her face, though he knew she must be exhausted.

'Come on,' he said. 'I'll make you a cheese toastie and a cup of tea.'

'We've just had lunch.'

'No. You just made everybody else lunch. You didn't actually eat. No protests.'

'Okay. I am hungry. Thank you.'

Twenty minutes later he made his way to the lounge, to find her curled up on an overstuffed armchair, dark head bent over her phone as she texted.

'Hey…' she said, looking up as he deposited the tray on a small table next to her. 'I'm texting Tara. To tell her I meant it when I said I'd keep in touch.'

Her expression was serious, her brow creased, as she picked up the sandwich.

He eased onto the sofa opposite and stretched his legs out. 'You bonded with her, didn't you?'

'Hard *not* to bond with someone who scares the beje-sus out of you!'

Ethan shook his head; he could still feel the cold glug of panic that had hit his gut two days earlier.

Everything had been going so well. Nearly all the kids had wanted to have a go at the bake off, and had gath-ered in the kitchen with no more than some minor banter. Ruby had set up each person with a station with all the ingredients set out. There were recipes and she was at the front to demonstrate the technique. There had been a few flour-bomb incidents but after a couple of interventions by the social worker they settled down and soon everyone had been absorbed in the tasks at hand. The scent of cin-namon and ginger pervaded the kitchen and Ethan had relaxed enough to start a conversation about the follow-ing day's surf trip.

It had all happened so fast.

A dark-haired boy had been in discussion with his neighbour a blonde petite teenager. Ethan clocked the vi-olent shake of her head and just as his antennae alerted him that there was trouble, the youth stepped too close. Uttered a profanity so crude Ruby's head whipped round from where she'd been helping someone else. As Ethan headed over, the girl whipped out a flick knife.

Ethan's lips straightened to grim as he strode forward but before he could get there Ruby had put herself directly in the girl's path and Ethan's gut froze. The girl looked feral, her pupils wide and he could only hope that she wasn't doped up on anything.

The knife glinted in her hand. Behind Ruby, the dark-haired boy had tensed and Ethan knew any second now

*the situation would blow. No way would that boy be able
to keep face if he backed down to a girl—the only reason he hadn't launched yet was the fact that Ruby was in
the middle.*

*She held her hand out to the girl. 'Tara, give me the
knife. No one is going to hurt you. Not now and not later.
Not Max, not anyone.' Ruby's voice betrayed not a flicker
of fear. She swept a glance at Ethan and gave a small shake
of head and he slowed his stride. Ruby clearly didn't want
him to spook the girl. Instead Ethan ducked round so that
he could manoeuvre Max out of the equation, saw the boy
open his mouth and moved straight in.*

'Quiet.' Max took one look and kept his mouth shut.

*'Come on, Tara,' Ruby said. 'It's OK. Look round.
You're safe. Look at me. You have my word. Now give me
the knife and it will all be fine.'*

*Tara had shaken her head. 'It'll never be fine,' she
stated with a flat despair that chilled Ethan's blood. Then
the knife fell to the floor, the clatter as it hit the tiles released some of the tension in the room. Ruby put her foot
over the weapon, then stooped to pick it up.*

*'You want to keep going?' she asked Tara. 'It's OK. No
repercussions.' She turned to Max and there was something in her stance that meant business. 'No repercussions,' she repeated.*

*Next to him Ethan saw the social worker open his mouth
as if to intervene and he stepped into action. 'I second that.
No repercussions from anyone. This is not what this all
about. You guys want to make a difference to your lives.
It starts here. And this incident ends here.'*

'Now back to baking,' Ruby said.

Looking back now, it occurred to Ethan how seam-
lessly he and Ruby had acted together, so attuned to the
nuances of the scene, the risks, the threat, the best way to
defuse the tension.

Ruby picked up her mug and cradled it. 'You know what she told me?'

Ethan shook his head. His chest panged at the pain sketched on Ruby's features.

'She told me she wished there *had* been repercussions. That if she'd ended up inside it would have been better for her than her life now.'

Ruby's voice was sad and heavy with knowledge.

'I don't blame her for having that knife. Her home life makes mine look like a picnic in the park. Her dad is a violent loser and she is so damaged no carer can cope. That's why she's in a residential home. That's why she reacted to Max like that—he was in her space and she panicked. Oddly enough after the incident Max tried to befriend her.' She glanced at him. 'Your doing?'

'I did talk to him.' He had tried to tell him there were other ways—told him that there were consequences to actions.

'That's fab, Ethan. Maybe they can help each other. I hope they'll all come back in September. Once they let their guard down they were all so full of potential—I mean, did you see them after surfing? They had a blast.'

So had he. All the teenagers had been stoked to be in the water and he'd watched them—some of them carbon copies of himself and Rafael. Tough...so tough...and always out to prove it. Because if they didn't there was the fear of being taken down. All swagger, all bravado—but up against the waves, up against the spray and the sea salt, they had met an element stronger than themselves that they could challenge with impunity. And they'd loved it. Enough, he hoped, to incentivise them to keep out of trouble until September.

A soft sigh escaped her lips. 'I wish...I wish I could help. Take them all in and house the lot of them.' She placed her empty plate down with a *thunk*. 'Maybe one day I will. No—not maybe. Definitely.'

'How are you going to do that?'

Her chin tilted. 'I'm going to adopt,' she said. 'That's my single parenthood plan.'

Maybe it shouldn't surprise him—after all, Ruby had been in care and he understood why she would want to help children like the child she had been. Hey, *he* wanted to do that. But adoption by herself...

Her eyes narrowed. 'You don't think it's a good plan?'

'I didn't say that.'

'Then what? You think I can't hack it?'

'I didn't say that either.'

'Then say something. What do you think?'

'I think it's a very, very big thing to take on.' He raised a hand. 'I'm not saying you couldn't do it. I think you would be a fantastic person for any kid to have in their lives.' And he meant that—he'd seen the way she'd interacted with all the kids, seen her capacity for care and love. 'But taking on older children... It's a huge commitment—especially on your own.'

'I know that.'

There was no uncertainty in her voice and he couldn't help but wonder at the depth of her need to do this even as he admired her confidence in herself. The idea of any-body—let alone a child...let alone a child who had already been through the system—being dependent on him for their well-being made his veins freeze over. To those kids Ruby would be their salvation, and he knew that saving wasn't part of his make-up.

But concern still niggled. 'You said you'd decided on single parenthood because you can't pick good father ma-terial. Don't you think you should rethink that strategy?'

'What do you mean?'

'I mean why not open yourself up to the idea of a relationship? Find a man who will support you emotionally and be a great father to your family. You're too young to give up on having love and a family.'

'You have,' she pointed out.

'That's because I don't want love *or* a family. You can't give up on something you've never wanted in the first place. You do want love—you'd never have been sucked in by Hugh or those other two losers otherwise.'

'See?' Tucking her legs beneath her, she jabbed her finger at him. 'That's exactly it. Three out of three losers. That's a one hundred per cent miss rate. I can't risk what is most important to me—having a family—by taking a side quest for love. Plus, if I pick wrong it could have a terrible effect on any children. I need to stay focused on my ultimate goal. I thought you of all people would get that. You want Caversham world domination and I want children. I won't be sidelined by anything else.'

Well, what could he say to that?

'I can see the "but" written all over your face, Ethan. I know it will be tough but it will be incredibly worthwhile.' The finality in her tone suggested that any argument would be futile. 'Like these past two days have been.'

'Two days is one thing. A lifetime is another.'

He pressed his lips together. Ruby was right—she had her goal and he had his, and hers was none of his business. What did he know? It was not as if he thought love was a good idea, so why push Ruby towards it? He didn't want the bright light of hope to be extinguished from those eyes by some idiot. But that wasn't his problem or his decision to make—it was Ruby's. So…

'You're right I think the past two days were a success—and a lot of that is thanks to you. The tree, the gifts, the food…and the karaoke carols were superb. You did a great job.'

Relief touched her face at the change of subject and he wondered if she regretted telling him of her plans.

'So did you. Thanks muchly. And thanks for letting me be part of it.' A glance at her watch and she straightened up in the chair. 'Right. I'll start the clear-up procedure and then I'll be on my way. Leave you to your Christmas plans.'

Her voice was a smidge too breezy, and her eyes flicked away from his as she rose to her feet.

'Don't worry about clearing up,' he said as he stood, his eyes fixed on her expression. 'You've already spent so much time and effort on this—I want you to start your break as soon as possible.'

Deliberately casual, he stepped towards her.

'Where did you say you were going, again?'

'Um…' For a heartbeat she twisted her finger into a stray curl, then met his gaze with cool aplomb. 'I didn't.' As she moved towards the door she gave him a small smile. 'Any more than you shared *your* plans.'

Her pace increased to escape speed and instantly he moved to bar her path.

'That's easily remedied. My plan is to stay here.'

Surprise skittered across her face. 'Alone?'

'Yup. My original plan was to host the teens over Christmas—when that changed I didn't bother making different plans for Christmas Day. It's just another day, after all. But I know you don't agree with that. So what are your plans, Ruby?'

Her eyes narrowed slightly as she realised she'd walked straight into that. 'I… Look, why does it matter to you?'

'Because you have worked so hard, and made such a difference to those teenagers—I don't want to think that doing that has ruined your plans.'

'Oh. It hasn't. Truly.' A gust escaped her lips as he raised his eyebrows. 'You aren't going to let up, are you? Look, I haven't got any specific plans. I never did.'

A slight look of surprise tilted her features.

'It's odd, actually. My original plan was to shut myself away with some weepie movies and a vat of ice cream. But now I don't want to do that. In fact if I wanted to I could go out and paint the town red. Since your press release lots of people who had dropped me like the proverbial hot root vegetable are now keen to be my friend again. Or I could probably even rustle up an invite from a real friend. But I don't really want to do any of that either. So I think I'll just head home and use the time to relax. Read a book. Watch some sappy Christmas movies.'

Ever so slowly she started to edge around him for the door.

'Not so fast.' The idea flashed into his mind like a light-ning bolt, zigzagged around and sparked a mad impulse. 'I have a better idea.'

'What?'

'Let's go away for Christmas.'

'Who? You and me?' Incredulity widened her eyes—clearly the idea was risible.

'Yup. We've worked incredibly hard and we deserve a break. You said you wanted snow—how about the Alps?'

The realisation that he was making this up as he went along triggered a ring tone of alarm.

'Are you serious?'

For a second excitement lit her blue eyes and Ethan ignored the warning blare of instinct—the reminder that mad impulses never ended well.

'Of course I'm serious. Why wouldn't I be?'

'Because... Well... We can't just up and leave.'

'Last time I looked I was the boss and I say we can.'

The idea gave him a sudden surge of exhilaration—the kind he usually felt on a surfboard. It morphed into a mad desire to take her hands and twirl her round the room.

Which was every kind of nutty—from peanuts to Brazil. *Rein it in, Ethan.* What exactly was he suggesting, here?

Welcome rationalisation kicked in. 'I'd like to check out the Alps anyway—as a possible Caversham location.'

'But you haven't even opened the castle yet.'

Ethan shrugged. 'Gotta keep on moving, Ruby. I told you I want to make it big, and momentum is key.'

Plus, it made sense—it would make this a business trip and not a mad impulse at all. With any luck he'd get there, feel the buzz of a new venture—and the odd, unwanted emotions that Ruby stirred within him would dissipate. Come to that, once the ball was over—which was a few scant days away—he wouldn't need to spend as much time here. He'd see Ruby less, and his life would regain its status quo.

'So what do you think? Shall we go and get a feel for the place?'

Ruby wasn't sure she *could* think. Or at least think straight. His idea had conjured up cosy warm scenes. Snow, mountain peaks, magical Christmas card scenery... Ethan and Ruby walking hand in hand...

As if.

Ruby hauled in a breath and instructed her brain to think, to oust the temptation that had slunk to the table— a late and uninvited guest at negotiations. Ethan had probably never held hands with anyone in his life, and the very fact that the picture had formed in her mind meant she needed to be on her guard.

In fact... 'It's a crazy idea.'

'Why? We both deserve a break. I have a good gut feeling about the Alps as a Caversham location, you've done a lot of research into the Caversham ethos, and I'd value a second opinion from you.'

It all sounded so reasonable. His words slipped into her consciousness like honey. From a professional viewpoint her boss had asked her to go on a business trip. It was a no-brainer.

Plus, if she said no would he take someone else? A sudden vision of gorgeous blondes and curvy brunettes paraded in her brain and her nails scored into her palm in instinctive recoil.

'I think it sounds fabulous. Let's do it.'

Temptation gave a smug smile of victory and panic assailed her nerves. Because all of a sudden thrills of anticipation shot through her veins. *Chill, Ruby.* Who wouldn't look forward to Christmas in the Alps? Obviously those little pulse-buzzes had zilch to do with the prospect of one-on-one time with Ethan. Because that would be personal. To say nothing of certifiably stupid.

Ethan nodded, his expression inscrutable. 'Okay. I'll check flights and we'll take the first available one.'

'Fantastic.'

Though it occurred to Ruby that this whole idea could be better filed under 'Terminally Stupid'.

CHAPTER TEN

RUBY GLANCED ACROSS at Ethan and tried to stop her tummy from a launch into cartwheels. Tried to tell herself that her stomach's antics were a Braxton-Hicks-type reaction to non-existent air turbulence. Why on earth had she consented to this? Why in this universe had *he* suggested it?

Because it was work. That was why. Ethan wanted to scout out the French Alps and had decided that this was an ideal time. Plus he was a generous man, and this was his way of showing appreciation for all her hard work.

Work, Ruby. That was what this was and she had best remember that. After all it was Christmas Day, and apart from a perfunctory 'Merry Christmas' Ethan hadn't so much as referred to the fact.

Though she could hardly blame him. Organising their departure had been his priority, and she could only admire the efficiency that had achieved a super-early trip to her London apartment to pick up her passport, followed by a trip to the airport that had given her sufficient time to pick up the extra cold-weather clothes she needed as well as time for a spirited argument over who would pay for said clothing.

Now here they were, on board a flight to Geneva, where they would pick up a car. So who could blame Ethan for not making a hue and cry about it being Christmas—he was taking her to a magical Christmas place after all.

On a business trip.

What else did she want it to be?

Yet as she studied the strength of his profile, the potent

force of his jaw, an obscure yearning banded her chest—as if she were a girl with her nose pressed against the glass pane of a sweet shop. Gazing, *coveting*, but unable to touch.

As if he sensed her gaze he turned to look at her and the breath hitched in her throat. The man was so gorgeous—but it was more than that. The way he had been with those teenagers had filled her with admiration. He'd shown them respect and invited respect in return—the fact that he'd cared about them had shone through, and it had triggered this ridiculous gooeyness inside her.

Enough. Say something. Before you embarrass yourself.

To her relief panic mobilised her vocal cords and she burst into speech. 'I was wondering—where are we staying?'

'The travel agent managed to find us a chalet; there weren't many options but she assured me that it would be perfect. And I've organised an itinerary.'

For a second his voice sounded almost gruff...even vulnerable...and she thought there was a hint of colour on the strong angles of his face.

'What sort of an itinerary?'

'The kind that will give us an idea of what other resorts offer.' Now his tone had segued to brusque—she was an idiot. What had she thought? That he'd picked things out for her?

'Great.'

The chalet was presumably part of a resort—which would be good. There would be hustle and bustle and other people, and they would be kept so busy with work that the two days would pass by in a flash.

'Sure is.' Ethan nodded a touch too enthusiastically. 'I've got the address, so once we land we'll pick up the hire car, put the location into the satnav and be on our way.'

This had to be a joke right? Ethan stared through the windscreen of the four-by-four that had negotiated the curving mountain roads and treacherous hairpin bends to bring them to the chalet that the satnav had announced was their destination. He'd swear the robotic voice had a gloat to it.

He was going to track down that travel agent and have serious words. She had described the chalet as 'just the place' and left Ethan with the impression that it was part of a busy resort, awash with people and activities. Though maybe he'd been so distracted by Ruby, so caught up in the mad impulse of the moment, that he'd heard what he'd wanted to hear.

Because it turned out that the chalet was a higgledy-piggledy structure nestled in the fold of a valley and it looked like it had come straight out of a fairy tale. Set in a circular grove of snow-heaped birches, the property was made completely of wood. It practically *glowed*. Quaint wooden shutters boxed in the windows and there wasn't another person in sight.

It looked as if it had descended from the clouds especially for Christmas. It was a surprise that it wasn't wrapped up in festive paper with a bow on top.

Ethan resisted the urge to thunk his forehead on the chunky steering wheel. Instead he glanced across at Ruby, who had fallen asleep on the motorway and slept like the proverbial infant for the entire drive. Perhaps if he started the car he could drive them to the nearest hotel and blag them two rooms. Or he could phone the travel agent and...

Too late.

Next to him Ruby stretched sleepily and opened her eyes; her sleep-creased face looked adorably kissable.

'Can't believe I fell asleep.' Her blue eyes widened as she took in the scene. 'Oh, my goodness me! We get to stay here?'

'Looks like it.'

'It's as if we've been beamed into a fairy tale. Or a Christmas card.'

Or a nightmare.

'It's magical. I reckon it may even be made of ginger-bread.'

'Which wouldn't exactly be very useful, would it?'

Chill, Ethan. Snapping wouldn't change the setting.

'Plus, I don't much want to be trapped in a cage by a wicked witch and fattened up. In fact maybe we should go and find somewhere else to stay.'

Her gurgle of laughter indicated that she'd missed the fact he'd meant it as a genuine suggestion. 'I didn't have you down as a fairy tale expert.'

'I'm not.'

For a second he remembered Tanya reading to him, his laughter at the funny voices she'd used for the different characters.

'You should go on stage,' he'd told her, and she'd shaken her head.

'I'd be too shy, Thanny,' she'd said in her soft voice. 'But I love reading to you.'

He pushed the memory away and glared at the chalet. 'I'm serious. Wouldn't you rather stay somewhere busier? Less isolated? Less over-the-top?'

'I…' She gave her head a small shake. 'Sorry, Ethan, I must still be half asleep. It just looks perfect for Christmas, but I guess it's not a good idea to stay somewhere so…' She trailed off.

So romantic, so small, so intimate.

Conversely the words challenged him—was he really saying that he was incapable of being in a romantic fairy tale chalet with Ruby? Talk about an overreaction. In truth the cutesy atmosphere should serve as a reminder that romance was anathema to him. Plus he could see from her expression that she had fallen for the place.

After the amount of work she'd put in these past weeks she deserved the chance to stay where she wanted to. With all she had been through in life she deserved a Christmas with some magic in it just as much as those teenagers had. Ethan might not believe in the magic of Christmas but Ruby Hampton did, and he would be a real-life Grinch if he denied her this.

'Why don't we go in and have a look round? Then decide what to do. The agent said the key would be outside, under a pot.'

Minutes later they crossed the threshold and irritation touched his brow as he realised he was holding his breath. What did he expect? A wolf dressed up as a grandma to jump out at them?

Instead he saw an open-plan area that brought the words *cosy, intimate* and *snug* to mind. Timber walls were decked with bright, vivid textiles and prints, there was a purple two-seater sofa, a fireplace piled with freshly chopped logs, a circular rustic pine table. Bright light flooded through the floor-to-ceiling window that looked out onto the crisp snow-covered garden. One corner of the room showcased an abundant Christmas tree decorated with beautifully crafted wooden decorations interspersed with red baubles.

'This is…dreamy…' Ruby said as she headed over to the table. 'Hey! Look! It's a hamper. Christmas coffee… Gingerbread… Nougat… Champagne…' Picking up a card, she twirled to face him. 'The larder and fridge are stocked with supplies as well.'

Okay, Ruby loved it, and for one disorientating second the look of wonder on her face made Ethan want to give her whatever she wanted.

A sudden sense that he was losing control sent an unfamiliar swirl of panic through his gut, caused him to strive for practicality. One swift glance took in the kitchen area, tiled and warm with pine and pottery, and another door through which he glimpsed a washing machine and a shower room. Which left…

'Oh!' Ruby gasped. 'Look! The ladder must lead up to the next storey. It's like a scene from *Heidi*.'

If there was a hayloft up there he would definitely sue the travel agent.

Ruby headed towards the ladder and started to climb, her long dark ponytail swinging a jaunty rhythm, her pert denim-clad bottom snagging his gaze.

Jeez. Get a grip, Ethan. They were in enough trouble.

Ruby stepped forward from the ladder-top and gazed around the cosy confines of the bedroom. The view from the window pulled her across the floor. Mountains sculpted the horizon, almost impossible in their precipitous snow-crested magnificence. A miracle of nature, of strata and formations that had resulted in a strength and enormity that dazzled— added to the swirl of emotions that pulsed through her. It was as if the chalet had indeed exerted some kind of Christmas spell over her.

Made her forget that this was a business trip, that any glimmer of attraction between them was impossible. Instead all that mattered to her was the fact that this place reeked of romance, oozed intimacy from every wooden beam and panel.

So much so that she couldn't think straight: images waltzed and corkscrewed through her mind. Cast her as the princess and Ethan as the knight in spotless armour. Setting the scene as the place where they would…

Her gaze plunged to the snug double bed, with its patterned quilt and simple wooden headboard. More vivid pictures tangled in her imagination: herself snuggled up to Ethan, falling asleep in dappled moonlight, warm and safe from the bitter cold outside, seduced into wakefulness by the trail of his fingers on her skin…

'On my way up.'

The sound of Ethan's voice was like an ice bucket of

reality. What was the matter with her? Panic knotted her tummy as she leapt across the room to an interconnecting door and wrenched it open.

She swung round as Ethan mounted the ladder, willed her heart-rate to slow down, ordered her brain to leave the mushy fantasy world it had stupidly decided to inhabit. She should never have fallen asleep in the car. Falling asleep on a motorway and waking up in fairyland had obviously decimated her brain cells.

'The bedrooms…' she said.

Talk about a statement of the obvious.

He crossed the mezzanine floor and poked his head into the second room, so close that she had to close her eyes to combat the urge to touch him, to inhale his clean sandalwood scent. Whatever influence this place exerted had to be shaken off.

Holding her tummy in, she sidled past him towards the ladder-top.

'It's tiny,' Ethan said. 'It's for children. It's only got a minuscule bunk bed in it. That decides it. We can't stay here.'

A glitter of relief flecked his eyes and she clocked the almost imperceptible sag of those broad shoulders.

Ruby knew it was wrong, but the knowledge that Ethan Caversham was worried about staying here with her triggered a feminine satisfaction.

The fact that she had managed to breach the professional wall he'd built up since that near-kiss prompted her to step forward.

'I wouldn't mind sleeping in there. There's no way you could manoeuvre your way into the room, let alone the bed. But I'll be fine. I'm flexible.'

Unable to help herself, she gave a little shimmy to demonstrate the point and his jaw clenched again. *Whoa.* Probably best not to bite off more than she could nibble. But this chalet called to something deep inside her. It was a magical place, made for dreams, and even though she knew dreams were a fallacy surely there could be no harm in two days of magic? It was Christmas, for crying out loud.

'I think we should stay here. I mean, it's quirky—it's different. Maybe you could build a resort with places like this. Plus, it's a good place to work. No distractions.'

Bwa-ha-ha-ha! went her hormones as they rolled on the floor with mirth. As a small voice shrieked in the dark recesses of her brain, pointed out that all those diversions she'd dissed would have equalled an effective chaperon service.

'I'd like to stay here, but if you think it's too difficult...'

Too late it occurred to her that Ethan had never been able to resist a challenge. His eyebrows rose and suddenly the room seemed even smaller.

'So you want to stay here?'

'Yup.'

Determination solidified inside her—her ill-advised hormones would *not* govern her actions. This place was magical, and magical was what she wanted. Not just for herself, but for Ethan as well. Surely even his cynicism, his determination to treat Christmas as just another day, wouldn't be proof against this chalet?

He gave so much—wanted to make a difference in the lives of Max and Tara and others teens like them. Maybe it was time someone tried to make a difference for Ethan. That darkness she'd sensed inside him a decade ago—the darkness that still remained despite the aura of success— she wanted to change that, to lighten him up with some magic. How could that be wrong?

That small, insistent voice at the back of her mind clamoured to be heard—warned her that he hadn't wanted her help ten years before and he didn't want it now. It was advice she knew she should heed—she didn't know how to change people...never had, never would. So she should back off. Instead she met his gaze.

'Yes,' she repeated. 'I do want to stay here.'

Two days. It couldn't harm.

His broad shoulders lifted. 'Then so be it.'

The enormity of her own stupidity nearly overcame her. 'Fabulous,' she squeaked. 'So let's go and sample some of that Christmas coffee and gingerbread.'

And get out of the bedroom.

Repeating the mantra 'We are professional' under her breath, Ruby busied herself in the small kitchen area. Focused on the beautifully crafted pottery and the blue and white ceramic tiles as she made coffee. Inhaled its nutty roasted aroma and hoped it would defuse her disastrous awareness of Ethan.

Tray loaded, she headed to the lounge area. Flames crackled in the hearth and the sweet spicy scent of the logs infused the air.

Pouring out the coffee, handing out the gingerbread and lowering herself warily onto the sofa to avoid any form of thigh-to-thigh contact consumed all of five minutes.

The search for conversation turned out to be problematic. Ridiculous. Over the past days she and Ethan had spent hours in comfortable silence. Unfortunately right now comfort had legged it over the horizon into the alpine peaks.

Next to her Ethan shifted; she sipped her coffee as the silence stretched on.

This was madness—what had she been thinking? The ideal solution would have been to have let Ethan move them out of here. *Here* was the sort of place where couples came on honeymoon, cuddled in front of the flickering logs and cooed sweet nothings. Or the sort of place for a family holiday—a place where kids could build snowmen in the garden and sleep in that storybook bunk bed.

This must be anathema to Ethan, and yet he'd agreed to remain here. So the least she could do was come up with some conversation. A sideways glance noted that he looked brooding, one hand drumming on his knee almost as if he were waiting for something. Conversation, presumably.

'So, if you go ahead here would you set up your own ski school, complete with equipment hire and guides? Or use an existing school and arrange for some sort of commission?'

'They are both options I'll consider. It depends.'

That seemed to cover that. She reached out for another piece of the spicy gingerbread—oh, so aware of the jiggling of Ethan's leg, the tap-tap of his foot on the wooden floor. Silence reigned until Ethan put his coffee cup down with a clunk just as a jingling noise came from outside.

Turning, he cleared his throat. 'Right on time,' he declared, with a glance at his watch.

'What is?'

'Look out of the window.' Rising, he gave a sudden smile, an odd mix of relief and trepidation in the tipping of his lips.

Despite the temptation to absorb the impact of that smile, she unsnagged her gaze from his mouth, rose to her feet and headed for the expanse of glass.

The breath cascaded from her lungs—outside on the snow-laden road was a horse-drawn carriage. Not any old carriage, either—this one was in the style of a sleigh, complete with large red and black wheels and a fur-hooded roof. The sturdy brown horse was adorned with a festive bridle, resplendent with images of Father Christmas, and a blanket in deep red and green. The driver was bundled in coats and a high fur hat and lifted a hand in greeting.

'It's amazing...' Ruby breathed as she turned to Ethan.

'I thought you might like it,' he said, almost abruptly.

'I don't just like it. I love it! Thank you.'

For a second that seemed infinite he met her gaze and something flickered in his eyes—only to be doused as he scrubbed a hand over his jaw.

'I thought it would have mass appeal if I were to offer high-end romantic Christmas breaks in the Alps.'

Wow—he couldn't have made it clearer that this wasn't personal. Hurt flashed across her ribcage…until she registered the slight croakiness to his tone, as if he were forcing the words out. She didn't believe him. Ethan had done this for *her*—had chosen this particular activity with her in mind—she knew it.

For heaven's sake.

She had to get a grip. Of course she didn't know it—it was another case of believing what she wanted to believe. Just as she'd believed her parents would change—had taken any stray kind word and built it up into a pointless dream. Just as she'd trusted that Gary and Steve and Hugh would change for her. Each and every time she had been blind and foolish.

Not any more.

'Let's get our coats.'

Curse words streamed through Ethan's brain—talk about acting like a class-A schmuck. What was he trying to prove? So what if he had chosen the itinerary with Ruby in mind? The whole point had been to give her a magical Christmas. To palliate the hurt of her Christmases Past—to do for her what she had done for Tara and Max and all those teenagers. There was nothing wrong with that—and yet panic continued to churn in his gut.

Deal with it, Ethan.

Sure, the last time Christmas had been magical for him had been when Tanya was alive. That magic hadn't stopped his sister from leaving this life scant months later. But that had zip to do with Ruby, and he wouldn't let his own past ruin this day for her.

'Wait!'

Ruby swivelled round on one booted foot, her poise

back in place, her initial happiness and subsequent hurt both erased.

'Yes?'

'I apologise. I'm not good at this whole Christmas scenario, but I don't want this to be awkward. I want you to enjoy the ride and the itinerary and...'

And he wanted to kiss her so badly his lips tingled and his hands ached with the need to reach out for her. Somehow a kiss would show her what he meant when words seemed to have deserted his tongue...

Somehow he needed to get with it and recall Ethan Caversham, man-in-control, to the building.

'So how about we get this carriage on the road?'

Her gorgeous lips turned up in a smile so sweet that he knew she had intuitively understood what he meant even if he didn't.

'It's a plan. But first maybe this is the right time for me to give you your Christmas gifts.'

Surprise slammed into him. 'You bought me gifts?'

'No need to sound so shocked. Yes, I did. Hang on.' Anticipation etched her features as she walked over to her case. 'This one I bought ages ago. I was going to leave it at the castle for you to find. And this one was an impulse buy at the airport.'

'Thank you.'

In truth he had no idea what to say—he couldn't remember the last time he had been on the receiving end of a personal gift. His lips twisted in a rueful smile—in a sense he was still on a par with Max and Tara, *et al*.

Slipping a hand into his pocket, he retrieved his present for Ruby and sudden trepidation shot through his nerves. 'Here's yours. Ladies first.'

'Oh... You didn't have to. I know you don't really believe in Christmas.'

Ethan shrugged. 'I...I thought that...seeing how much

effort you put into the teens' gifts…the least I could do was—' He broke off. He was doing it again. 'I wanted to.'

He had wanted Ruby to have a present that someone had thought about. Okay. Make that agonised over. How long had he spent in that stupid jewellery shop? Irritation caused his fingers to drum on his thigh as he felt his heart thud faster—he wanted her to like it way too much.

A yearning to see her eyes light up banded his chest as she carefully unwrapped the green embossed paper, held the dark blue jewellery box and then snapped it open and gasped, her lips forming a perfect O of wonder.

The pendant glittered, diamonds on white gold, shaped into an exquisite simple star. When he'd seen it an image of Ruby as she'd handed him the star to adorn the Christmas tree had popped into his mind.

'Ethan. I…I…can't accept this. It's not right. It's…'

'It's yours.'

Though by 'not right' maybe she meant she didn't like it…

An image of his mother that terrible first Christmas after Tanya's death flashed across his mind. Her wooden expression as she opened his gifts. The sear of knowledge that he'd got it wrong. That without Tanya he meant nothing to her, couldn't get it right. All those hours spent agonising for naught.

Maybe he should have learnt—stuck to something generic for Ruby. Better yet, he should have given her a Christmas bonus—a cheque, a banker's draft. Going personal had been a mistake. Ethan Caversham didn't do personal.

'You can exchange it if need be.'

'Exchange it?' she echoed. 'Why would I do that? It's beautiful. I meant it's too much.'

'It's a gift, Ruby.' It occurred to him that she was no more used to gifts than he was. 'I want you to have it.'

'Then thank you.'

As she took it from the box he thought for an instant that she would ask his help to put it on. Relief warred with disappointment when she lifted it herself—the thought of his fingers brushing the sensitive skin of her neck had strummed a jolt of pure desire through him.

'Now open yours.'

An absurd sense of excitement threaded his gut as he unwrapped the first gift, the bright paper covered in images of Father Christmas bringing a smile to his lips. It was a smile that grew as warmth touched his chest.

In his hands was a painting of Caversham Castle. The artist had captured the sheer brooding history of the craggy mound of medieval stone, imposing and grand, made to defend and dominate the landscape.

'It's perfect. Thank you.'

'Open the next one.' A small frown creased her forehead. 'Like I said, this was an impulse buy and if you don't like it I won't be offended...'

As he pulled the jumper out of its silver wrapping paper a chuckle fell from his lips. 'A Christmas jumper.' A cable knit in dark blue, it was patterned with reindeer. 'It's inspired—and what better time to wear it?'

'You mean it?'

Surprise and a smile illuminated her face, and for one heartbeat full of exhilaration he nearly succumbed to the temptation to sweep her into his arms and kiss her.

No! There was personal and there was *personal*.

Instead he tugged the jumper over his head 'Of course. Now, let's go!'

A few minutes later and they were all layered up. Once outside, Ethan sucked in the cold air; welcomed the hit to his lungs and brain. Perhaps the cold would freeze some sense into him.

CHAPTER ELEVEN

RUBY STOLE A sideways glance at Ethan and tried to confine the tornado of her thoughts. *Yeah, right.* Containment continued to elude her, effectively held at bay by the sheer nearness of Ethan as they settled under the heap of blankets on the carriage seat. Ruby clenched her jaw—she would not even contemplate the word snuggle.

Somehow she had to keep perspective, had to chillax and not read more into Ethan's actions than there was. After all, she had earned a diploma in that. Yes, he had bought her a beautiful Christmas gift—instinctively her hand rose to touch the diamond pendant—but that was because Ethan was a good man who tried to give people second chances.

No doubt he had simply wanted to do for her what he had wanted to do for all those troubled teenagers. In fact he had practically said so…so there was no point to this continued analysis.

Time instead to concentrate on the beauty of her surroundings, which was enough to catch the breath in her throat. The ground was covered in snow, as if someone had taken the time to weave a thick white duvet to cover the landscape and then sprinkled the bare branches of the trees with a dazzling glitter. It was beautiful—glorious—magical. The silence was broken only by the chime of the horse's bells, the huff of his breath and the crunch of his hooves in the snow.

'This is beyond incredible,' she murmured with a sideways glance.

Ethan's expression was unreadable, but the vibe she

got from him was edgy—as if he too battled complicated thoughts.

Her words caused him to blink and give a small shake of his head. 'I'm glad you're enjoying it,' he said. 'Not too cold?'

'Nope. The last time I saw snow was in London, and it had turned to slush before I could truly appreciate its beauty. This is spectacular.'

Now a genuine smile touched his lips as his gaze rested on her expression. 'I hope you'll like the next item on our agenda.'

'Which is…?'

'Sledging.'

'For real?'

Excitement fizzed inside her and collided with a pang of emotion as a memory jolted her brain. Years and years ago she'd taken her siblings out into the snow. She'd carried Edie, who hadn't been able to walk yet, Philippa had toddled beside her and Tom, aged just four, had raced ahead with a joyous whoop. They hadn't gone far, just to a local park to watch the children sledge.

How she had yearned to have a go. But there had been no sledge, and she hadn't wanted to draw attention to themselves. But it had still been a good day—they had made a snowman, thrown some snowballs, before Ruby had realised that there were some adults clearly wondering why they were unaccompanied and she'd quickly herded her siblings together and left.

'Is that okay?' A small frown touched Ethan's face as he studied her expression and she did her best to erase the hint of wistfulness, the shadow of memory from her face.

'It's better than okay. I've never sledged before and I would absolutely love to.'

Ruby let the memory go with the silent hope that her siblings had had plenty of opportunity to sledge with their new family. Allowed the fizz of excitement to take ascendancy.

Minutes later the carriage drew to a halt and Ethan helped her alight. 'Here we are. It's a resort, but we have passes.'

They lingered for a moment to thank the driver and pat the horse, and then she turned and once again the scenery caused the breath to whoosh from her lungs. Snow glistened in the distant trees of the forest and crunched underfoot, thick and soft all at the same time—the way she had imagined stepping on clouds would be as a child.

They entered the resort and headed to the sledge hire desk.

The woman behind the counter smiled. 'Would you like a paret, a disc or a toboggan?'

Ruby stared at the options. 'I'll go for a toboggan.' On the basis that it looked the safest. The paret looked to be a mixture of a tricycle without wheels and a stool, and the disc looked as if it might well career round and round out of control. As that was her current mental state, there was no point adding a physical element.

The woman smiled. 'I promise they are all safe, *mademoiselle*. They are designed to be safe for children as well as adults.'

'I'll try the paret,' Ethan said.

Ruby narrowed her eyes. 'Show-off.'

That garnered a smile. 'Think of it as research. It's occurred to me that I could offer moonlit paret sledging as a part of a holiday package.'

They exited the building and she inhaled the tang of snow and pine, absorbed the bustle of people and the sound of laughter. Took courage from the happy vibe.

Until they reached the top of the slope.

'Um…' Ruby peered over the edge.

Suddenly the snow was reminiscent of clouds only in

the way that if you tried to walk on a cloud you would plummet downwards. The ground was a turreted mass of white, under which surely there would lurk hidden dangers.

'You worried?'

Daft. She was being daft. This was an official slope, suitable for tiny kids. All she needed to do was look around again and observe them.

Her heart gave a sudden thump. Just a few feet away a mother with a baby in a sling helped two children get onto a sledge. A dark-haired boy and a younger little girl with blonde curls. The world seemed to fall into slow motion and for an absurd second she nearly ran towards them— until common sense drummed its beat.

That wasn't Tom and Philippa. Tom would be twenty now, and Philippa nineteen. Even if they were here she wouldn't recognise them. They were adults.

For a second, loss shredded her insides.

'Ruby?' Ethan's rich voice held a question and a heap of concern.

For a mad minute she wanted to tell him the truth, in the hope that he could soothe the pain.

With muscle-aching effort she pulled herself together. Confiding in Ethan would only add to the intimacy she was trying to fight. In any case Ethan didn't welcome emotional intensity; he hadn't ten years before and he wouldn't now.

'I'm fine. Just chicken, I guess. Why don't you show me how it's done?'

'No. You look like you've seen a ghost. We're going to the café.'

'I…'

'No arguments. First rule of snow sport. You don't do it unless you're focused.'

Maybe he was right. Either way he wasn't taking no for an answer and willy-nilly Ruby followed him towards the café.

* * *

Ethan held the café door open. The smell of coffee jumbled up with the aromas of vanilla and almond and Christmas spices. Carols filled the air with a choral hum—a festive backdrop to the chatter of families and the clink-clank of cutlery. Usually the scents would have triggered a smile, but Ruby seemed enmeshed in thought.

Even an almond croissant and hot chocolate didn't bring more than a perfunctory smile to her face.

'You want to talk about it?' Even as he spoke the words he knew it was a foolhardy query. The invitation to confide, to *share*, was not one he would ever make as a rule. Panic threatened—an echo of a decade ago. He was letting her get too close. But how could he help it? When she looked to be in such pain, with her usual vividness drained? He wanted to help, to make it better for her.

If he had any sense he would never have let things get to this point—maybe he should have let history repeat itself and cut and run.

Chill, Ethan.

Time to remember that he was ten years older now, ten years wiser, and this time he would be able to control the situation. There could be no danger in an offer of support and it would be an impossibility to withhold that support.

'If you want to talk I'm here.'

Her eyes met his with a hint of surprise, palpable hesitation, and a small determined shake of her head. 'It's Christmas. You've gone to all this trouble. I'm sorry to be a Debbie Downer.'

'You aren't. I promise. Ruby, we both know that Christmas can be an emotive time for people with difficult pasts. Talk to me. I know your childhood Christmases were grim. Maybe I can dilute some of your tainted memories.'

One more heartbeat of a pause and then she exhaled. Picked up the steaming mug of hot chocolate and cradled it, her eyes wide. 'I guess for a moment out there the past arrived from nowhere and knocked me for a half-dozen. Those children on the sledge next to us… For an instant they reminded me of my younger brother and sisters.'

The words registered in his brain—generated a host of questions. If Ruby had siblings where were they now? Why did the memory of them haunt her?

Her gloved hand pushed a tendril of hair from her face and she sighed. The noise escaped into the chatter-tinged air with the sound of age-old sorrow and weariness.

'Tom, Edie and Philippa,' she continued. 'I told you my parents were addicts. One of the ways they funded their addictions was via benefits. The more children they had, the more money they got. I was the oldest, then Tom, Philippa and Edie. I was six when Tom was born, and I can still remember the awe I felt when I first saw him—such a tiny scrap of humanity. I felt welded to him. Same with the girls. All I wanted was for us to stay together as a family, and I vowed I would do whatever it took. Mum and Dad told me that it was up to me—that they couldn't do it so I had to be strong. I had to be responsible. I had to lie to social workers and school teachers. Had to make sure everyone believed we were a happy family.'

Ethan's chest constricted at the sight of her face, whiter than the snow that glittered and glinted outside. He could picture a much younger Ruby, her expression oh, so serious, tucking an unruly curl of dark hair behind her ear as she concentrated on changing a nappy or manoeuvred a heavy pan of water onto the hob.

'That must have been tough,' he said softly.

'It was and it wasn't. I loved them all so much, you see—and I told myself that Mum and Dad loved us really. But the cold hard truth is that they used us. More fool me for ever thinking otherwise. Even after it all went wrong, when I screwed it up, for ages I still kidded myself that they loved me.'

'What happened?'

'I couldn't hold up the façade and it crumbled down. We were whisked away into care. They couldn't find a carer to take all four of us so we were split up. We went from being a family unit to having visits in a social worker's office once a week if we were lucky.'

'That must have been beyond terrible.'

'It was.'

Her words were flat and in that moment he knew that it had been unfathomably horrific.

'I fought for us to be placed together, or at least near each other. But nothing I said made any difference. The social workers said that we were better off like that than with our parents. But it didn't seem that way to me. Sometimes I even pictured my parents missing us so much that they would turn over a new leaf and we'd all go back to them.'

She laughed—the noise devoid of mirth.

'I take it that didn't happen?'

'Nope. They turned up to see me once—stoned and drunk—hurled abuse at me and the social worker ended the meeting. I've never seen them again. No idea if they are alive or dead.'

He placed his hand over hers, wished he could find words to convey his feelings.

'Time went—and one day a social worker came and told me she had good news. An adoptive family had been found, but they would only take three children—Tom, Edie and Philippa. I was too old and too difficult. I'd been acting out, and they figured it would be bad for the others if I was placed with them.'

She paused, her blue eyes wide and unfocused, as if she had teleported through time to relive the moment.

'The social worker explained that if they waited, kept

trying to find someone to take all of us, it might end up that none of us got adopted—or that Tom, Edie and Philippa would end up separated. She promised me there would still be contact. I'd still see them. But it didn't go down like that. Tom Edie and Philippa moved in with their new family and I was told there would be no contact whilst they settled in. I fought it—I went on and on to the carers, to the social workers. They told me I had to wait. That I was being selfish. Then one day I decided to take matters in my own hands. I bunked off and went to their school. I was so desperate to see if they were okay. That's all I'd ever done, you see.'

Her hands gripped the mug of hot chocolate so hard he leant over and prised her fingers free, retained her hand in his grasp. He could envisage her so clearly; frantic and determined, fuelled by a love that gave her the strength to do anything for the sake of her siblings.

'It was the end of school—I saw them run out to a woman who I knew must be their new mum. She looked so pretty, and like she adored them, and they looked so happy. It just needed Mary Poppins to make it complete. Not me.'

'Oh, jeez, Ruby...'

What could he say? What could he do to fix this? To mend the void that echoed from her voice? Helplessness gnawed at his insides and he did the only thing he could. Moved his chair round the table in the hope that his body, his presence, would offer some comfort.

'After I saw that I knew what I needed to do. I told the social worker that I didn't want to see my siblings for a while. That I understood it was better for them to integrate into their new family. Eventually, with a social worker's approval, I wrote them a letter to tell them I loved them but a clean break was better for all of us. I knew it was right—my presence in their lives would only make everyone feel bad. Their new family would feel bad for not being able to take me, and Tom and Edie and Philippa's loyalty would be divided. That wouldn't have been good for them. So I decided there and then that I would try and be happy for them.'

Her slim shoulders lifted.

'And I *am* happy for them. But occasionally I still miss them so much it hurts.'

A solitary tear seeped from her eye and he reached out and caught it on his thumb. The moisture glistened on the pad of his glove and he pulled her into his arms.

'It's okay, Ruby. Cry it out.'

Her body tensed and he rubbed her back in a gentle circular motion. Felt her relax as she snuggled into his chest and wept. From somewhere he found soothing words as he rested his cheek on the silkiness of her hair. He realised he couldn't remember a time when he had done this. Offered comfort. Oh he'd tried with his mother, after Tanya, but she'd pushed him away, her whole body stiff with grief. Her eyes had told him what she had later confirmed in words—the wish that it had been him who had died rather than his sister.

He pushed the thoughts away—right now it was all about Ruby. His past couldn't be changed or fixed—his mother had no wish to mend fences in any way. Tracey Caversham wouldn't even take his money, let alone any affection. But he was grateful that Ruby seemed to derive some comfort from his actions.

After a while she placed her palms on his chest and gently pushed herself upright. 'Phew,' she said as she looked up at him, tear-swept eyes glistening. 'I'm sorry. What you said was so beautiful, and suddenly I could see them so vividly. Memories deluged me and turned me into a watering pot.'

'There's no need to apologise. At all. I'm glad you told me. Tell me more about them. About Tom, Edie and Philippa.'

So she did, and as she spoke he could visualise the energetic, dark-haired Tom, with his cheeky grin, see the chatterbox Philippa with her blonde ringlets and quiet, straight-haired Edie who sucked her thumb.

When she'd stopped speaking Ruby squeezed his hands. 'Thank you. Mostly I try to leave the past in the past. But sharing the good memories has made the bad memories easier to bear. I feel lighter. Thank you, Ethan—and I mean that. If you ever want to talk I'm here for you.'

Her words triggered a strange reaction—for a second he allowed himself to ponder that scenario. Tried to picture the concept of sharing. Sharing with Ruby the way his mother's face had always twisted at the sight of him, the continued rain of comments as to how he reminded her of his dad. How Tanya had shielded him with her love, but how that shield had been tragically removed by her suicide. His terrible grief and its aftermath. How spectacularly he had let his mother down and the devastating consequences.

Discomfort rippled in his gut, along with a healthy dose of denial, and he felt his lips curl with distaste. *Not happening.* If there was one thing his past had taught him it was the need to control emotion—all the release of it could achieve was pain. If he had only retained control after Tanya's death then he wouldn't have walked the road that had led to his mother handing him over to social services. To confide in Ruby would open up an emotional vortex and that was not going to happen.

So... 'I'll bear it in mind,' he said as he pushed her plate towards her. 'So what now?'

Ruby picked up the almond croissant. 'I'd like to eat this, and then—if it's okay with you—I'd still like to sledge.'

'Then that's the plan.'

It truly felt as if a bulk had been hefted from her very soul. The sadness was still there, but more manageable. As they exited the café the snow seemed even brighter, and now the sight of children filled her with a sense of hope and determination. Because one day she would adopt, and she vowed that she would take her children sledging.

A sideways glance at Ethan filled her with relief—his blue-grey eyes rested on her with warmth, but not a hint of pity, and she honoured him for that. For his innate realisation that pity would be anathema to her.

There was a bond between them now—she could see it shimmer in the air between them. They had both pulled themselves from the gutter and survived events that had had the potential to destroy. That was worthy of admiration—not pity. But she knew she felt more than admiration, and she needed to be careful. Because right now that gooey warmth had multiplied, and instead of being mortified at having wept all over him she felt energised... awash with dangerous feelings of intimacy. An intimacy he would abhor.

Sure, he had just proved himself capable of emotional understanding, but his withdrawal at the thought of sharing his own past had been crystal-clear.

She had to rein it in. Her goals and Ethan's goals were as far apart as it was possible to be. Ethan wanted to sit in his un-rocked boat on his own—he wanted a life alone—and she wanted as many children as she could manage. So her best hope was that she and Ethan could become friends.

Yet right now she wanted more...couldn't help herself. The tug of attraction, the tug of emotion, the tug towards him in general asserted a magnetism she somehow had to control. Because there couldn't be anything else, and she couldn't let herself fall headlong for yet another unsuitable man. Another man who would not or could not change his lifestyle for her.

Instead it would be better to focus on what she could share with Ethan—like this wonderful Christmas Day he had given her. Maybe she needed to focus on a headlong ride on a sledge... A peek down the slope and she felt a surge of anticipation.

'Take it away, maestro,' she said.

His smile was the genuine article—it lit his grey-blue eyes and her tummy clenched in response.

'As you wish,' he said, and he turned, dropped down onto the disc sledge and launched himself down the slope. Tore down the slope, swerved and manoeuvred, flew over the snow.

Once at the bottom he looked up and gave her the thumbs-up sign before beginning his ascent. She watched him climb back up, legs strong and body lithe. What was it about him that made him stand out? Maybe his aura— one that meant she would be able to spot him anywhere in the world.

'There—see. Easy.'

Ruby looked down at the toboggan doubtfully. 'I'm still not convinced I won't fall off.'

'It's all about balance.'

'Very Zen...'

His chuckle caught on the crisp breeze, and unlocked something inside her. The sight of his smile and the tang of snow made her breath catch, made her heart hop, skip and jump. and she felt her lips tilt into a grin.

'Zen or not, you are going down that slope, Ruby. We'll go together. This is one childish dream that you *will* fulfil. Come on. Sit. I'll fit in behind you.'

Huh?

She squatted, placed the plastic toboggan on the snow and wriggled on, intensely aware of him as he lowered himself behind her. This was daft—they were both in Eskimo-level layers of clothing on a populated slope— not sunbathing on an isolated beach in bikini and trunks.

Ethan placed one arm round her waist and she swallowed her small gasp. His touch defied physics, felt electric through all the layers.

'So all you have to do to steer is use this stick on the side, or your hands or feet.'

Was it her imagination or was his voice deeper than normal—the sort of deep that made her think of dark chocolate with a hint of ginger and spicy mulled wine? Panic mixed with a tummy-tingle of need.

Do something, Ruby.

'Let's go!'

They took off, skimmed over the snow. Exhilaration heated her veins as she let go, with no time to think or analyse or worry. She existed in the second, fuelled by adrenalin and sheer excitement as the world flew by until they reached the base and glided to a stop.

Pure elation frothed inside her as she shifted to look up at Ethan. 'That was incredible. Like an out-of-body experience.'

Ruby stared at him. He looked…utterly gorgeous. And in this mood of sheer instinct she knew with a blind, horrible clarity that she wanted him to kiss her. That the tingles that coursed through her body were no longer due to her sledging experience. This attraction existed. No—it did more than that. Right now it burned…just like his gaze that was focused on her parted lips.

His pupils darkened; desire flared.

'Ethan…?'

The question whispered across the snow-tinged air. Her heart pounded in her ribcage as her lips parted and she twisted round, propelled by an instinct older than time, her body no longer at home to the voice of reason.

CHAPTER TWELVE

ETHAN COULDN'T TEAR his gaze from her—she was so incredibly beautiful. Her cheeks flushed from the cold, her entire face animated by desire. And, heaven help him, he couldn't help himself—couldn't stop himself.

Leaning forward, he covered her lush lips with his own as precipitous need overcame all capacity for thought. It felt so right. He could taste Ruby—the tang of almond with a hint of chocolate. Her lips, cold at first, heated up and she gave a small mewl. The sound triggered a further yearning for more and he pushed his fingers under the hood of her parka, tangled his fingers in the silk of her hair. Her lips parted and her tongue touched his in a tentative flick. And he was lost in a desire to block out the world and kiss her until...

Until what?

The knowledge that the universe could not be ignored was one he carried with him every second of the day; there were always consequences. Problem was at this instant he couldn't care less—which was dangerous beyond belief. He mustn't let her close. For both their sakes. Ruby wanted a family and she deserved to have that—she might believe now that she wanted single parenthood, but he hoped that one day she would find love with a man who could give her everything she deserved. Ethan was not that man— and he would not mess with her head.

With a supreme effort of will he pulled back and for a long second they gazed at each other, puffs of breath mingling in the cold.

'I...' Her voice trailed off as she lifted her fingers to her lips again. As if they stung in sheer frustration.

Well he could empathise with that. All of him was tingling with spikes of unfulfilled need.

'I...um...what now?'

'I don't know.'

What could he say? There was no point trying to dismiss what had happened. That kiss had been off the Richter scale and it had changed everything. Which was a problem.

'But I apologise.' From somewhere he pulled a smile—this Christmas Day would *not* be ruined by his stupidity. 'We need to forget that happened. And whilst we try to do that let's keep sledging.'

Truth be told, he couldn't think what else to do. The alternative was to hotfoot it back to the chalet and haul her into the bedroom.

A silence, and then she essayed a small, determined nod. 'Okay,' she agreed. 'This is such an amazing place to be, and I am having a wonderful Christmas Day, so don't apologise. We can chalk it up to an inevitable moment of foolishness.'

To his surprise there was no awkwardness in the next few hours—Ruby took to the snow like the proverbial duck to water, and swerved and dipped and dived over the slopes. They raced each other and laughed over the results, argued with mock ferocity over a handicap system, and sledged until dusk hit.

'Time for the next stop,' Ethan said. 'Gaston should be back with the carriage and then it's time for Christmas drinks and dinner in town.'

The knowledge was a relief, because despite all his efforts the air still hummed with the undercurrent of attraction and they needed time before they returned to the problematic fairy tale chalet, with its solitude and adjoining bedrooms.

'Great.' Ruby clapped her hands together to get rid of the last vestige of snow and leant with natural grace to pick up her toboggan.

The carriage journey into town was silent—but not a silence of an awkward or grim calibre. Ethan would have classed it as one infused with an undercurrent he wasn't sure he grasped. Every so often Ruby would glance at him with a sideways sweep, her eyes wide in thought as one finger curled a tendril of dark hair that escaped from her red bobble hat.

And then the horse came to a halt and they disembarked into the Christmas card scene of the Alpen town. The atmosphere was lively, and the artful array of high-end shops was combined with an olde-worlde charm.

'It's gorgeous…' Ruby breathed.

As was she.

They walked down the snow-dusted street, illuminated by the glow of lights from the multitude of bars and restaurants and the twinkle of lights that decked the air. Next to him Ruby had subsided back into silence. She broke it with a quick look up at him.

'Where are we having dinner?'

'A Michelin-starred restaurant owned by the resort. We're a bit early, but we can have a drink before.'

'How about in here?' she suggested, stopping outside a bar that resembled an old coaching inn.

'Sure.'

They stepped over the threshold into the warmth of the bar. Chatter in a variety of languages mingled with universal laughter and the chink and rattle of glasses and cutlery. The aroma of fondue and beer was mixed with the tang of snow.

'What would you like?'

'A small glass of white wine, please.' Ruby eyed him with something very near speculation as she tugged her bobble hat off.

'Coming right up.' He shrugged out of his jacket and dropped it on the back of a chair whilst she seated herself at the round wooden table. As he headed through the throng to the bar he was aware of her eyes as they followed his progress.

Minutes later he returned and placed her wine and his tankard of beer on the table. He sat down and surveyed her thoughtful expression. Something had shifted and he wasn't sure what it was. The idea that they were on the brink of new territory sent a conflict of anticipation and panic to his synapses.

Ruby lifted her glass. 'To us. And how far we've come.'

Her words seemed imbued with meaning. The crowd and the hum of conversation seemed to fade, to leave only Ruby and himself. Perhaps he should make a stalwart attempt to pull the conversation round to work, but the idea refused to be translated into words.

The moment they had avoided so dextrously refused to be ignored any longer. That kiss—the mammoth in the room—was sitting right next to them, drink in hand. All he could think about was how her lips had felt, the wonder and the beauty and the sheer pleasure of that kiss. A kiss he'd waited a decade for...the desire he'd run from all those years ago. And now...

Ruby leant forward, her sapphire eyes sparkling as she tucked a stray tendril of hair behind her ear. 'I've been thinking, and I want...' Her cheeks flushed with a tinge of pink. 'I want...I want—' She broke off. 'Maybe it's better to start with what I don't want. I don't want a relationship with you. I don't want to climb into your boat or to rock it in any way whatsoever. My goal is adoption, and I will not let anything stand in my way.'

A pause whilst she sipped her drink.

'But I would like to explore this further. You and me. Just whilst we're here. Like a bubble of time between our pasts and our futures. I'd like to enjoy the now. With you. A two-night holiday fling. That's what you normally do, isn't it?'

No! It was an enormous effort to haul the syllable back. But instinct revolted, because Ethan knew that whatever happened between him and Ruby it didn't class with his usual liaisons.

'No.' The word was gentle. 'No, Ruby. You are different. If we do this I need you to know that.'

If they did this.

Ethan tried to think—when all he wanted to do was punch the air in triumph, sling Ruby over his shoulder caveman-style and get back to the chalet pronto. But he couldn't do that. Ruby had thought this through and he needed to do that as well.

Hours before he had ended their kiss because he had believed it was a bad idea—succumbing to emotion and impulse would land him in trouble. Worse, it could land *Ruby* in trouble, and he wouldn't let that happen. She'd been messed around enough by the men in her life—he wouldn't add to that.

'Ethan, I won't get hurt.'

Great. Clearly she could read him like a picture book.

'This is *my* idea. As soon as we get on the plane back home we revert to normal. Boss and employee. And we throw ourselves into making the ball a success. This will work.'

Her words held conviction and sense. Ruby did not want a relationship with him—she wanted a fling. There would be no further expectation, so he would not be messing with her head. Ruby wanted a family—he didn't. There could be no future. Her words.

For a scant second a warning bell clanged at the back of his brain—he didn't want to let Ruby close, remember? But Ethan wasn't in danger—how could he be? This was a fling—purely physical, no emotions on the table.

'Let's do it,' he said.

Ruby held her breath, giddy with sheer disbelief—had she really propositioned Ethan Caversham? *Yup*—she believed she had. For a scant second she wondered if she'd lost her mind. Yet if her sanity had gone walkabout she was in no hurry to get it back. Not when Ethan's eyes raked over her, glinting with a promise of fulfilment that sent shivers dancing up her spine.

'Let's go,' she said. 'Would you mind skipping dinner? I don't think I could eat a thing. But if you're hungry...'

Be quiet, Ruby. Before he changes his mind.

'I don't want dinner.'

His voice sent the tingle into acrobatic overdrive and sheer anticipation wobbled her legs as she slipped off the bar stool. As he encased her hand in his she knew her smile rivalled that of a plethora of Cheshire cats. This was all about the moment, and this moment felt fabulous, unrestricted by the past or the future.

Even the wait at the taxi stand, the journey back, felt alight with possibility—and then the magical glow of the chalet welcomed them.

Without releasing her hand Ethan manoeuvred the door open and tugged her straight across the lounge area.

Ruby disengaged her grasp to scramble up the ladder and into the bedroom. Now the reassurance of his touch had gone a sudden shyness threatened, caused her to circumnavigate the bed and approach the window.

The hairs on the back of her neck stood to attention as she sensed his presence behind her, and then his warmth enveloped her. His hands rested on her shoulders and began to knead gently. Tension ebbed away as she gazed out at the garden, where moonbeams danced on the birches and skittered in gleams on the duvet of snow.

Ethan swept her hair from her nape and she gasped as his lips grazed the sensitive flesh. An urge to see him overcame her, and as if he instinctively knew he stepped back and gently turned her to face him.

'So beautiful...' he murmured, one thick finger stroking her cheek.

His grey-blue eyes shone in the moon's illumination, the light played on the planes of his face and emphasised their strength. Her heart melted and ached and she reached up for him, greedy for the devastation of his kiss.

It was a kiss that seemed to take up from where they'd left off—only this time with the knowledge that there was more to come. There was no need to think or analyse or worry, and that added a sharp edge to a desire that dizzied her. Propelled by instinct, she gripped his shoulders and Ethan lifted her effortlessly, so her legs wrapped his waist and his hands cupped her bottom.

He carried her to the bed, their lips still locked, and Ruby moaned as he slid her down the hard length of his body before tumbling her onto the mattress.

Hours later Ruby opened her eyes, aware of an immense contentment that swathed her limbs in languorous satisfaction. For a long moment she lay and gazed up at the ceiling, cocooned under the weight of Ethan's arm, his dark brown head next to hers. A gentle shift and she could study his face, bathed in the streaks of dawn that slid through the slats of the shutters. Softer in sleep, yet still his features held a tautness—as if even in slumber he were loath to relinquish complete control.

A qualm tugged at her heart as it hopped, skipped and jumped. But there was nothing to worry about—she had decided that she wanted to grasp this opportunity, to live in the moment and just be herself. Because with Ethan that was who she could be—she'd shared her past and she'd shared her future. Now she wanted this time with him to explore their attraction.

Though somehow the theory no longer seemed so simple. Certain flaws had popped into her mind. These past hours had shown her an attraction that flamed with a heat she hadn't envisaged. But the fire would burn itself out. Though when fires burnt themselves out didn't they often leave a whole lot of collateral damage...?

His eyes opened and instantly focused—barely a fraction of a second between oblivion and awareness.

And she doused every qualm as his smile warmed her. She was being daft. They only had a day and a night left. Then it would be over. So what was the point of worry? It was not as if she had any intention of calling a halt to proceedings. Of not experiencing the wonder of the previous hours again...not falling asleep in the safe cocoon of his arms—the idea was unthinkable.

'Ruby? You okay?'

'Of course I am.'

Of course she was. *Jeez.* She really needed to work on her live-in-the-moment technique. The whole point was to enjoy each and every moment of the next twenty-four hours.

Twenty-four hours. Tick-tock went a metaphorical clock.

Concern lit his eyes and she summoned a smile. 'Just hungry. Guess it's time to eat. Not that I have a single regret for missing that Michelin-starred Christmas dinner.'

'Me neither. Our evening was spent in far more enjoyable ways. But now you mention it I am pretty hungry. I think we need to build up our strength,' he added with a wiggle of his eyebrows that made a giggle bubble up to the surface.

'And why would that be, Mr Caversham?'

Leaning over, he nuzzled her ear. 'In fact, perhaps I could muster up my last reserves of energy right now...'

'Hmm...' Desire sizzled through her with intoxicating speed—perhaps enjoying each and every moment would be a cinch after all.

An hour later he grinned lazily at her. 'Now would be a good time for breakfast.'

'How about I whip us up a brunch fondue?'

'Sounds perfect. I'll check our Boxing Day itinerary.'

'Okay. And thank you for a magical Christmas Day— the planned bits and the...the...' Her cheeks heated up.

'Impromptu night-time activities?' he supplied, with a wicked smile that curled her toes.

The morning hours swept by and she could almost see the magical motes of happiness fleck the air. Magic infused them both—brought laughter and warmth, enabled Ethan to dance round the kitchen disco-style whilst she sang along into a wooden spoon in lieu of a microphone.

Even the fondue worked—the mixture of Emmental, Gruyère and Comté provided a tang that burst onto their tastebuds, and the consistency of the bubbling cheese and wine was neither too thick nor too thin. Perfect for dunking cubes of baguette.

'Ruby, that was awesome. I am truly replete. Why don't you relax by the fire and I'll wash up?'

'You wash. I'll dry. You did help cook.'

'That's a generous interpretation of grating cheese.'

'You did an excellent job of stirring as well.'

Ruby looked over her shoulder as she carried their plates towards the kitchen area and glanced at the clock. A sudden sense of panic touched her. *Tick-tock.*

Stop it, Ruby.

This was an interlude—it couldn't go on for ever and

she wouldn't want it to. Work was way too important, along with her goals and her future life. A future in which Ethan would only feature in a professional sense.

'Anyway, we'd best get this cleared up quick—the carriage will be back to take us into town for the Boxing Day market, followed by a mountain ascent.'

'Sounds brilliant.'

Maybe Ethan was right—the key was to keep moving, garner the maximum number of precious memories from this time capsule.

The hustle and bustle of the town square soothed her. It was littered with stalls, and the air was alight with chatter, wafting with a cluster of glorious scents. As she stood and inhaled the tang of gingerbread, the scent of the pine so evocative of the Christmas Day just gone, her qualms faded away along with the concern they had created.

This was all about a magical interlude and for once she was in control. There was no question of delusions or false dreams or hopes. This fling had been her idea, entered into with the knowledge that Ethan wouldn't change, and she was good with that.

She opened her eyes to find Ethan's grey-blue eyes fixed on her and she smiled at him, drank in the craggy features, the breadth of his shoulders, his aura of strength. Desire lodged deep in the hollow of her tummy—this freaking gorgeous man was hers. For now… And that was enough. For now she would live in the moment.

'This is such a wonderful place,' she said. 'I'd come on holiday for the market alone.'

The fresh produce was enough to make her tastebuds explode in anticipation. Cheeses abounded, bowls heaped with olives glistened, dried meats and *saucissons* hung in tempting displays.

'Shall I buy ingredients for dinner tonight?' she asked, the words so deliciously intimate. The idea of the evening ahead enticed her: cosy in the chalet, preparing dinner, a glass of wine, music in the background, smooth conversation, the exchange of a kiss here and there...

Purchases made, she espied the Christmas stalls, still piled high with festive adornments. Wooden gifts, bright wrapping paper, carved toys and gaudy sweets. Simple carved Christmas decorations, each one chunky and unique. One of the reindeer looked back at her, its antlers glistening in the afternoon sun.

Surprise laced her as Ethan picked it up and studied it. Then he nodded at the stallholder. 'I'll take one of each.'

'What are you doing? We did Christmas already. Anyway, I thought you weren't into decorations.'

'They're for you. To keep for your perfect Christmas. I know it'll happen for you.'

Tears prickled the back of her eyes. 'Thank you.'

A vision strobed in her mind. But it was wrong... Because there was Ethan, standing by a Christmas tree as he helped a small brown-haired boy hang the decorations. Around the other side of a tree a slightly older dark-haired girl was being helped by a teenager to thread a garland of tinsel.

Squeezing her nails into the palms of her hands, she erased the imaginary scene and shoved it firmly into her brain's 'Deleted' file. Time to concentrate on the moment, on the here and now. On the imposing grandeur of Mont Blanc as it towered over the town...on the fact that she was about to ascend a high mountain peak with this gorgeous man.

The stallholder handed her the bag and she smiled. 'They are perfect. Now, we had better get going—before we miss the ascent.'

CHAPTER THIRTEEN

ETHAN STRODE DOWN the street, an unfamiliar warmth heating his chest. It was as if this bubble of time theory had freed him to…to what? To *feel*? A soupçon of worry trickled through the fuzzy feel-good haze. Feelings netted nothing but pain and loss.

Chill.

Once they got on that plane in less than twenty-four hours everything would snap back to normal. Work would become paramount and all these strange feelings would dissipate.

'You okay?' she asked.

'I'm good.'

Without thought he took her hand in his and they made their way towards the ticket office. Picked up their tickets and joined the press of people in the gondola. When was the last time he had held someone's hand? Not since childhood, when he'd teetered along holding Tanya's hand.

The concept was strange, and for a moment he stared down at their clasped hands before releasing Ruby's hand under the pretence of losing his balance. The motion was abrupt, and it left him with a strange sense of bereavement as he fixed his eyes on the view as they ascended the steep elevation.

Ruby too was silent, until they disembarked at very top, when she halted, her lips parted in a gasp that denoted sheer wonder. Ethan stared too. The incredible vista was one that emptied the lungs and constricted the throat. Panoramic didn't cover it.

They walked slowly across the terrace and Ruby hesitated as she approached the rail.

'You okay?' he asked. 'The altitude could be making you dizzy.'

'I do feel a little light-headed, but I think that's because I am awestruck.'

'Ditto.'

The snow-covered expanse stretched and stretched; the sky surrounded them in a cerulean blue cloak.

Ruby gestured towards the now far-distant town that looked as if it might be made from building bricks. 'Wow! Being up here, encompassed by Nature's might—it puts things into perspective. We are here for such a minuscule slice of time compared to this universality. It makes me feel insignificant.'

'You could never be insignificant.'

Not this woman, with her determination, courage and her capacity to give.

She tugged her hat further down her head and he stepped closer to her to share his body warmth; the icy temperature permeated their thick padded layers.

'That's kind, Ethan, but it's not true. One day I hope I *will* be significant—help turn someone's life around. But until then...'

'No.' The idea that she believed herself insignificant did not sit well with him. 'You have already touched so many people's lives. Look at what you did for your brother and sisters.'

She shook her head. 'I did my best, but you know the saying—the road to hell is paved with good intentions. If I'd been stronger I wouldn't have shielded my parents for so long. I believed what they said—believed they would turn their lives around for us. So I lied, I pretended, but I was a fool. There were times when there wasn't enough food, when we slept in squalor—parties when things could have gone so horribly wrong. If I'd spoken up Tom, Edie and Philippa would have had a better start in life. I let them down.'

'No!' The syllable was torn from him. 'You didn't let anyone down. You gave Tom and Edie and Philippa the right start in life, you kept them safe and you gave them love. I promise you, hand on heart, that you gave each one of them something incredibly precious. Something every baby and every child deserves. Your parents let you all down. The system let you down. *You* didn't let anyone down. This I know.'

'Thank you.' The words were polite, but she turned away as she spoke them to survey the vast expanse and he knew she had dismissed his words as so much bunkum.

'Why don't you ask them?'

That caught her attention and she twisted to face him, her breath white in the crisp cold air.

'I'm sure you would be able to trace them.'

'I won't do that.' Her chin tilted in a stubborn determination that spoke of a decision made.

'Why not? I understand the decision you made back then. But now... Now surely it would be good for you all to reconnect?'

She shook her head. 'I don't want to rock *their* boat. You should understand that. They are young adults now, and they have their own lives to lead. The last thing I want to do is complicate those lives. That's partly why I changed my name years ago—a clean break, a fresh start.'

'It sounds like there was a deep bond between you. I think they would want to hear from you.'

A sigh puffed from her lips and stricken eyes met his. 'They have each other and their adoptive parents. They don't need me.'

Ethan frowned, hearing the stubborn lilt to her voice.

'It's not about need, Ruby. Maybe they'd like to hear from you. Maybe they want to know what happened to you.'

He knew that if he could turn back time and somehow spend even five more minutes with Tanya he would move heaven and earth to do so.

His body tensed as Ruby turned again, rested her arms on the railing and stared out into the cold vastness of unforgiving beauty.

'It's a bit more complicated than that.'

'How?'

'What if I try and contact them and they say thanks, but no thanks? I've already lost them once and…' She gestured over the terrace rail. 'It was like plummeting into that chasm. I'm out of the pit now and I've got my life together. I can't face the prospect of falling back in.'

Her voice was small and lost and compassion touched him. 'It's okay to be scared. But that doesn't mean you shouldn't take the risk.'

'That's easy for you to say. You're never scared, and risk is your middle name. Given half a chance you'd leap off here and ski down the mountain.'

'That's different. That's about physical fear—it helps create a buzz; it's a good feeling. The fear of contact with your brother and sisters not working out is an emotional one, and it takes far more courage to overcome that then it does to climb a mountain.'

'But you don't have any emotional fears either.'

That was because he didn't let himself feel any emotion that he couldn't control. 'This isn't about me. This is about you. And I believe you should do this. Otherwise you're letting your fear conquer something that could make an enormous difference to your life and theirs.'

Her eyes shot anger at him—a dark blue laser. 'It's not your decision to make. All due respect, Ethan, but you don't know how this feels.'

'No, I don't. But…'

His turn now to look away, to absorb the vast chill of white that would remain there long after he and Ruby had returned to normality.

'But what?'

The exasperation had left her tone and she shifted closer to him, placed a hand on his forearm. Her touch brought a soothing heat and somehow gave him the incentive to step into the chasm. To help Ruby make the decision he felt to be right.

'But I do know what it feels like to lose a sibling. I had a sister.' His voice cracked—the word was rusty with disuse. 'An older sister. Tanya. She died, and I would do pretty much anything to have the chance to see her again. So I am telling you, Ruby. Contact them. You have the chance of a future that has them in it. Take that chance.'

Her body stilled next to him and then she let out an exhalation of shock as her grip tightened on his arm. 'I am so sorry. I don't know what to say or do, but I am so very sorry.'

She closed the gap between them completely, so that her body pressed against his, and he took comfort from her closeness. For a long moment they stared out at the view, and then he heard her intake of breath.

'Do you want to talk about it?' she asked.

Did he? Disbelief rippled in his gut at the fact he was even considering the hitherto impossible. But he was. Because he knew that once they left the Alps there would be no more of this. It was too emotional; too many layers were being unravelled and he couldn't risk his emotions escalating out of control.

But here and now the temptation to share his memories of Tanya nigh overwhelmed him, and images of his beautiful gentle sister streamed in his mind. He realised that he wanted Ruby to 'know' Tanya—to 'see' the sis-

ter he missed so much. Ruby had told him that talking
about Tom, Edie and Philippa had reminded her of the
good memories. Maybe Tanya deserved that—to be remembered.

His voice caught as he nodded his head. 'I think I do.
But not here. Let's go back to the chalet.'

As they entered the chalet Ruby fought down the urge to
throw herself onto his chest, wrap her arms around him
and just hold him. Though…why not? For the next few
hours at least she could be herself, could show feelings
and emotions, and right now the desire to offer comfort
overrode all else. But she knew that this was unmapped
territory for both of them.

He shrugged his jacket off and hung it on a peg, watched
her almost warily as she approached. Standing on tiptoe,
she kissed his cheek, inhaled his woodsy scent, felt the
solid bulk of his body against hers. She stepped back and
took his hands in hers. The smile he gave was a little
twisted, but his grasp tightened around hers as she tugged
him towards the sofa.

'I'll light the fire,' he said.

Sensing that it would be easier for him to talk whilst
in action, she nodded. 'That would be great. You want
coffee?'

'No, thanks.'

He busied herself with the fire, loaded the logs, and
Ruby curled up on the purple cushions, her whole being
attuned to him.

'Tanya was three years older than me. Mum was always
out—she worked so many jobs to make ends meet—and
that made Tanya and I extra close. Tanya was…'

His deep tone faltered and he paused, scraped a match
against the side of the box and lit the wood. Sat back on
his haunches and gazed at the flicker of red and orange.

'She was so very gentle, so kind.' Wonder touched his voice. 'It was as if she was something rare and beautiful and fragile on that estate. She had chestnut hair, long and thick, and brown eyes, and the warmest smile in the world—the kind that made you feel like you could do anything.'

The fire whoomphed and caught, illuminated the planes of his features, touched with sadness now. Ruby slipped off the sofa, and as if aware of her movements he shifted, so that they both ended up on the floor with the sofa at their backs. Without speaking she placed a hand on his thigh, tucked her body next to his.

'She wanted to make something of her life. Her dream was to write, to travel, to see the wonders of the world. Mum encouraged her, and Tanya flourished—she loved books, absorbed information like a sponge. She'd tell me about all the countries out there and we'd hatch dreams of travel.'

'She sounds wonderful—and it sounds like you loved each other very much.'

No wonder Ethan had rejected love—he'd had the most important person in his world snatched by death. Yet the darkness of his expression told her that it was even worse than that.

'We did. It was Tanya who kept me on the straight and narrow for a long time. But as I got older it became harder for her.'

'What about your mum?'

'Mum was… Mum and I… It was difficult. I am the spitting image of my father. She hadn't actually wanted a second child with him and she never really engaged with me.'

Ruby felt her nails score her palm—it sounded as though Ethan felt he'd deserved the indifference she read from his words. 'That wasn't your fault.'

A shrug greeted this and she held her peace.

'No, but my behaviour was my own choice. The estate was my reality and I began to believe that Tanya's aspirations could never happen. I started to bunk off school, began to go off the rails. But Tanya held me in check; I would have done anything for her. If she'd let me.'

Foreboding touched Ruby, drizzled her skin with dread. 'What happened?'

'She was bullied. I didn't know—she didn't tell me, and we were at different schools by then. Tanya was doing A levels, and that meant a bunch of kids had it in for her. It started out as small-time stuff, teasing with a nasty edge, and then it became sabotage of homework, and then it became worse and worse. They stalked her, threatened her with rape, and eventually she couldn't take it any more. She killed herself.'

The words buzzed in the air like dark, malignant insects, and for a moment Ruby couldn't take in the enormity of his words. Once they hit her she raised her hand to her mouth to stifle the cry of protest. 'Ethan…' The anguish on his face was enough to make her weep.

'I found her. She'd overdosed—she'd found a stash of Mum's sleeping pills and swallowed the lot.' His voice jerked the words out, raspy and abuzz with a raw, jagged pain. 'At first I thought she was asleep, and then…'

Ruby swallowed the lump of horror that clogged her throat, pressed her lips together to stop herself from crying out. The image was so clear in her brain—she could only imagine how etched it was on his. A younger Ethan—lanky, tall, unsuspecting—calling his sister, entering the room… And then the awful paralysed second when he would have realised the grim truth and his life had changed for ever.

'Ethan…' Her voice was a whisper as compassion

robbed her breath. 'I am so very sorry. I cannot imagine what you and your mother went through.'

The words were inadequate against such calamity, and she could only hope that the tragedy had brought mother and son closer.

'Mum was devastated. It was a dark time.'

For a long moment he stared into the flames and then he shifted slightly. Scored his palm down his face as if in an attempt to erase the memories.

'Do you think we could change topic? I'm kind of talked out.'

'Of course we can.'

Ruby tried to pull her thoughts together, her heart aching for what he had been through. For what he had told her and for the troubled relationship that he had with his mother. But now she wanted to lighten the mood, hoping that their conversation had been cathartic.

'How about a picnic and some board games?'

Surprise touched his face, and then his lips tipped into a small smile. 'That sounds perfect.' As she rose he followed suit and placed a hand on her arm. 'Thanks for listening.'

He cupped her jaw in his palms and dropped the lightest and sweetest of kisses on her lips. And her heart ached all the more.

As dawn slipped through the shutter's slats Ethan slipped quietly from the bed, pulled on his jeans and gazed down at Ruby, her cheek pillowed on her hand, her dark hair in sheer contrast to the white of the pillowcase and the cream of her skin. Her beauty touched him on a strata that he didn't want to identify and, turning away, he reached down for his shirt, thrust his arms into the sleeves and headed for the ladder.

Panic strummed inside him, made him edgy. Somehow Ruby had got right under his skin, and the idea caused angst to tighten his gut as he prowled the lounge and kitchen.

Memories of the past evening itched and prickled—they'd drunk cocoa in front of the lambent flames of the fire, talked of anything and nothing, laughed and philosophised. Then they'd gone to bed and… And there weren't words, truth be told, and he wasn't sure he even wanted to find any.

The panic grew—as if his actions had opened the floodgates. Letting her in had been a mistake, and nothing good could come of it. He wasn't capable of closeness.

'Ethan?'

He swivelled round, saw her at the top of the ladder. How long had she been there, watching him pace?

With an effort he forced his lips up into a relaxed smile. 'Morning!' he said, and his heart thumped against his ribcage as he took in her tousled hair, the penguin pyjamas.

Silence stretched into a net of awkwardness as she climbed down the ladder, paused at the bottom to survey him. Impulse urged him to walk over and carry her right back upstairs, and he slammed his hands into his jeans pockets and rocked back on his heels. No more impulses—because his emotions were already ricocheting off the Richter scale.

'Coffee?' he offered.

'Yes, please.'

Trying to keep his body rhythm natural, he headed to the kitchen. The endeavour was a fail and he passed her, breath held, unsure what to do, ultra-careful not to touch her. Yesterday he'd have teased her mercilessly about the penguins, dropped a kiss on her lips, taken her hand… Now he sidled past.

Ruby stood stock-still, one finger tugging a strand of hair. 'I'll…I'll go change,' she said, the words stilted, and relief rippled with regret touched his chest.

Because he knew she'd gone upstairs to armour herself in clothes. For this bubble of time she had been herself—no façade needed. Same for him. But now… Now it was time to go back to normal. Because being himself was too raw, too hard, too emotional. And emotion was not the way he wanted to go—he wanted the status quo of his un-rocked boat.

So he filled the kettle and assembled the ingredients for breakfast. The bread they had bought yesterday, the succulent strawberry jam, the pastries Ruby loved so much.

The sound of her shoes tapping on the wooden floor forced him to look up.

'Looks great,' she said, the words too bright, underscored with brittleness.

Her glorious hair was tamed into a sleek ponytail, not even a tendril loose. The knowledge sucker-punched him—never again would he run his fingers through those smooth silky curls, never again would he touch her soft skin, hear the small responsive gasp she made…

Enough.

A sudden urge to sweep the breakfast off the table, to get rid of the false image of intimacy, nearly overwhelmed him. The intimacy was over, and the sooner they exited this cloying atmosphere the better.

Too many emotions brewed inside him now, but at all costs he had to remember this was not Ruby's fault. If he had miscalculated it would not rebound on her. Instead he would haul back on all this feeling and return to professional normality. Though right now, in the line of her direct gaze, work seemed almost surreal. Which was nuts. Work was his life.

Jeez, Ethan.

Now he'd gone all drama king. Maybe he'd actually shed some brain cells these past days. In which case it was time to use the ones he had left. Fast.

No point in rueing the fact that he'd agreed to this fling in the first place. His eyes had been open to the fact that it would be different from his usual liaisons—he simply hadn't realised how that difference would play out. But there was no time for regrets. None at all. Regret was an indulgence—the important thing now was momentum.

With determination he lifted a croissant, went through the motions of spreading butter and jam. Then he glanced at his watch. 'We'll need to hit the road soon. I thought we could do a drive-round and get a visual of any areas or properties suitable for Caversham. I'll do a computer trawl whilst you pack up. Then maybe you can take over whilst I pack.'

'No problem.'

The cool near formality of her tone smote him even as he forced himself to pick up his coffee cup.

A gulp of coffee and she pushed her plate away. 'I'm on it.'

CHAPTER FOURTEEN

RUBY LOOKED AROUND the banqueting hall of Caversham Castle and tried to summon more than a token sense of pride and achievement. It looked fabulous, and she knew the sight would usually have prompted a victory dance or three around the room.

Actually it looked better than fabulous—she had worked flat-out the past two days, and all the work she had put in prior to Christmas had paid off. Medieval-style trestle tables fashioned from oak were arranged round the restaurant floor. The ceiling boasted an intricate mural depicting knights, princesses and acts of valour. The whole room seeped history, with maps of Cornwall through the ages and Cornish scenes from centuries ago adorning the walls.

Soon enough the room would be filled with the bustle of one hundred celebrity guests, the sound of troubadours and the scent of a genuine historic feast and Ruby knew the evening would be a success.

If only she cared.

She resisted the urge to put her head in her hands—of course she cared. This would be a career-tilting event—it would show the world that Ruby Hampton was the business. The restaurant at Caversham Castle would be launched in style, and she had little doubt that by the time they opened for normal custom in two weeks they would be booked up months in advance. Which was even better, because then she would be rushed off her feet.

Which would hopefully be the catalyst for the cessation of the stupid, mad feelings that swamped her every time she saw Ethan. The strange ache in her tummy when she wasn't with him...the stranger ache in her heart when she was. It would almost be preferable to discover that it was an ulcer rather than what she suspected—she missed him. Missed the Ethan she had glimpsed for forty-eight precious hours.

Unfortunately that Ethan had vanished—had donned the cloak of professionalism and left the building. How did he do that? Maybe the same way she did. After all, hadn't she been the epitome of a perfect restaurant manager? Could there be a possibility that he was hurting as she was?

But even if he was...what difference did it make? There could be no future. Her plan was to adopt and Ethan didn't want a family. Ethan didn't want *anything*.

In two days the ball would be over—it would be a new year and a new start. Ethan would waltz off to his usual business concerns and she would be able to get her head back together.

The back of her neck prickled and her whole body went to code red—a sure indicator that Ethan was in the vicinity.

'It's looking good,' he said. 'I need the final auction list, please. Rafael's on his way and he wants to look at it en route.'

'Sure. It's good of him to be auctioneer.'

'Yes.'

The terse edge of near indifference that veiled his tone made her foot itch with the urge to kick him even as she matched it. 'I'll email him the list straight away.'

'Ruby?'

The sound of Cora Brookes's even, well-modulated voice had her swivelling on her heel in relief. Cora, the new hotel administrator, had arrived two days before, and already Ruby was impressed by her smooth competence— though Cora had equally smoothly avoided all attempts at anything other than professional conversation.

'I thought you should see this.'

'What's up? Don't tell me the caterers have cancelled? Rafael Martinez has pulled out?'

For a second a faint look Ruby couldn't interpret crossed Cora's face. Then the redhead shook her head. 'Nothing like that. Why would he? It's great publicity for him... Plus it's not often a playboy like him gets to feature in a celebrity magazine in a charitable light.' She shook her head. 'Anyway, here you are.'

Ruby accepted the netbook and looked down at a celebrity magazine's website.

Breaking News!
Hugh Farlane engaged.
'This time it's the real thing,' Hollywood star proclaims.

What?

Disbelief churned in her tummy. She'd barely given Hugh a thought in the past days. Apart from feeling a vague relief that he had obviously decided to stop offering her up as sacrificial goods to the press.

Mere weeks after his break-up with Ruby Hampton, now working within the Caversham Holiday Adventures empire, Hugh has announced his engagement to his long-term PA, Portia Brockman.

Portia? Beautiful, devoted to Hugh's interests, she'd worked for him for years—the woman had to know him better than anyone else, so why on earth would she marry him? Surely it was another stunt. Or... She looked down at the image of Portia, who was gazing up adoringly at Hugh. Maybe a better question would be did Portia *know* it was a stunt?

Next query—what was Ruby going to do about it?

Which led on to another question: if she thrust a spoke in Hugh's wheel what would he do? A flicker of fear ignited at the memory of his expression, taut with threat, as he'd ensured her silence.

It was a flicker she knew she had no choice but to ignore.

With a start she realised Ethan had removed the tablet from her grasp and was reading the article. A formidable frown slashed his brow as he handed it back to Cora.

'I'll have to go and sort this out,' Ruby said briskly. 'I'll get a train up to London—I should be back late this evening. Cora, thanks for bringing this to my attention. Can I leave a few things for you to do while I'm gone?'

'Of course.'

'Great. I'll catch you before I leave.'

Ruby nodded and turned, headed for the door.

'Hold on.' Ethan's stepped into her path, his tone peremptory.

'Yes?' Slamming to a halt, she tried to sound cool, as if her proximity to his chest, delectably covered in a white T-shirt, wasn't playing havoc with her respiratory system. Who wore T-shirts at the end of December, anyway?

'I'll come with you.'

'That is not necessary.'

Cora glanced from one to the other. 'Let me know what you need, Ruby. I'll be in my office or you can call me.'

Once the redhead had glided away, with admirable discretion, and the door had clicked shut, Ruby glared at Ethan.

'*So* not necessary,' she amended.

'I disagree—I told you I stand by my employees.'

All of a sudden a wave of pure white-hot anger flooded her—as if every molecule of built-up frustration from the past four days had all exploded into rage simultaneously.

'So you're going to hop on your charger and come and protect me because I am your *employee*?'

'What is wrong with that?'

'Everything. Everything is wrong with that.' Had he forgotten Christmas? Had some sort of brain transplant? 'Forget it. You have made it perfectly clear that you want our relationship to be professional.'

'We agreed that once we got back here we would revert to being professional.'

There was no arguing with that—if he took it a step further he might even point out that it had been *her* fool idea in the first place.

'You're right. So since my business with Hugh is *personal* I will deal with it myself.'

There was no indication that he'd even heard her. 'I don't want you to face him alone.'

'Why not? I'm sure I'll have to face plenty on my own when I adopt. There will be social workers and carers and teachers and who knows what else? Will you be there when it gets tough then?'

'That is hardly a valid argument.'

'It is extremely valid from my side.'

The air was tinged with exasperation as he folded his arms. 'That scenario is set in the future. This situation with Hugh is now. He's threatened you in the past, the man is a liar and a bully, and I don't see the problem with you accepting some support.'

Oh, crap!

As she stared at him, absorbed the frown that slashed his brow and the determined set of his mouth, drank in his sheer strength, the icy cold fingers of realisation dawned. Seeped into her soul. She knew exactly why this was a problem—she *wanted* Ethan to come with her. But she wanted his presence because he cared about her as person, not as an employee.

Panic squeezed her chest. She'd fallen for Ethan Caversham. Again. Or maybe she'd never got over him. This stubborn, generous, flawed man had called to something deep within her and her heart had responded without her permission.

She wanted him in her present *and* in her future.

Shock doused her veins, made her skin clammy. How had this happened? Ethan would never want a family. Would never change from being the workaholic, driven man he was. So why was her heart—the self-same heart that wasn't supposed to be involved—aching with a deep, bitter sting?

His frown deepened as he studied her expression and she desperately tried to think—tried to work out what to do with this awful, awesome knowledge.

Nothing. That was what she should do.

Ethan had made it more than clear that he had negative desire for a relationship, let alone a family. It wasn't his fault she'd been stupid enough to fall for him. If she told him how she felt he would recoil, and she wasn't sure she could bear that. Let alone the fact that it would make any work relationship impossible.

Maybe that would be impossible anyway. Maybe her best course of action would be to leave. Otherwise she would have to spend her life erecting a façade of lies, playing a part, watching him from afar, living in hope that one day he'd return her love. The idea made her tummy churn in revolt. It would be a replay of her childhood.

'Ruby?' There was concern in his voice now, as well as an assessing look in his blue-grey eyes that indicated the whirring of his formidable brain.

With an effort she recalled their conversation. 'Ethan, I need to do this by myself. Plus, tomorrow night is too important to blow—too important for kids like Tara and Max. You need to be here to supervise any last-minute glitches.'

He shook his head. 'Cora can cover that. So can Rafael.'

Somehow she had to dissuade him—all she wanted to do now was run. Achieve some space. Get her head together. Enough that she could hold the façade together for a while longer until she could find him a replacement restaurant manager.

'No. Cora and Rafael are great, but you need to be here. This is your show.' For a heartbeat she felt the sudden scratch of tears—this would be one of the last times they were together, and emotion bubbled inside her. 'You're doing such good here.'

Instinct carried her forward, so close to him that she could smell the oh-so-familiar, oh-so-dizzying woodsy scent of him. One hand reached out and lay on his forearm as she gazed up at him, allowed herself one last touch.

'Don't.' His voice low and guttural.

'Don't what? Tell the truth?'

He shook his head, stepped back so that her hand dropped to her side. 'Don't look at me like that. Don't make me a hero. Because I'm not.'

'I didn't say you were a hero. But you are a good man, and you do so much good. Why won't you acknowledge that and accept something good in your life.'

What was she doing? The sane course of action would be to get out of there at speed, but some small unfurling of hope kept her feet adhered to the floor.

'Whatever you did in the past can't change that.'

'You don't know about my past, Ruby.'

'Then tell me.'

For a long moment he looked deep into her eyes, and for a second she feared that he could read her thoughts, her emotions, could see the love that she was so desperately trying to veil.

His gaze didn't falter, though the clench of his jaw and the taut stance of his body betrayed his tension.

'I told you that even before Tanya died I was beginning to go off the rails—I'd bunk off school every so often... I'd taken up smoking, graffitied the odd wall. But after she died I was so angry; I wanted vengeance on those bullies who'd made her last months on this earth a torment. But what could I do? I couldn't take them all on myself—they were a group, part of one of the most intimidating gangs on the estate. Mum was falling apart, and I was full of frustration and rage.'

Her lungs constricted as she imagined how the teen-aged Ethan must have felt. So helpless, so alone. With a mother prostrate with grief and the sister he'd looked up to driven to take her own life.

'So it all went downhill. School became ancient history. I took up petty crime—shoplifting. I got into fights. I did dope...I drank. I swaggered around the estate like an idiot. I became everything Tanya would have abhorred.'

'Tanya would have understood. You were a child full of anger, pain and grief. Didn't your mum do anything?'

'She was too immersed in grief to notice.'

There was no rancour to be heard, but it seemed to Ruby that everything he had done must have been in an effort to make his mum notice—step in, *do* something. She couldn't bear the fact that he'd judged himself so harshly—that he couldn't see the plethora of mitigation around his actions.

'God knows what might have happened, but finally I got caught stealing from one of the high-street clothes stores. I went nuts—went up against the security officer. I lost it completely and they called in the cops. I was arrested, taken down to the police station, and they contacted my mother.'

'What happened?'

'As far as she was concerned it proved I'd morphed into my father. Reinforced her fear that history would repeat.'

'But...but she must have seen that this was different?'

His silence was ample testament to the fact that she hadn't, and the dark shadow in his eyes was further proof that neither had he. Foreboding rippled through her. 'What did she do?'

'Packed my stuff and handed me over to social services.'

Words failed her as anger and compassion intertwined—no wonder Ethan had judged himself as guilty when his own mother had disowned him.

'Hey. Don't look like that. For Mum the loss of Tanya was more than a tragedy—it was innately wrong. It should have been me.'

'Did she say that?'

'Yes.'

The syllable was spoken as if it was to be expected and Ruby's heart tore.

'I get that. She had a point.'

'No, she did not!' The words were a shout, but she couldn't help it.

'I let her down, Ruby. It is as simple as that. No one made me act that way.'

'You were her *son*, Ethan—her child. You were acting out of your own grief and anger.'

Ruby clenched her fists. Why was he being so obdurate? But, of course, she knew the answer. Hope. Why had she persisted in believing in her own parents, long after they had proved they would never change? Same answer. Hope.

'Have you seen your mum since?'

'No. She is still on the estate, and every year I send her a cheque and a letter. Every year she doesn't bank the cheque and she doesn't answer the letter.'

The unfairness, the tragedy of it, banded her chest. 'I understand that your mother had her own issues, but they were *her* issues. Would you ever do to a child what she did to you?'

Something flashed across his eyes and then he rubbed

his hand down his face, made a derisive sound in his throat. 'Jeez. Let's end this conversation. Okay? I've come to terms with it all and it's no—'

'If you say it's no big deal I'll scream. It's a *huge* deal. You told me to fight for justice, that right and wrong matter. This matters, and this is injustice. Ethan, you told me you thought I would be a good parent.'

'You will be.'

'Well, a social worker told me once that damaged children like me repeat their parents' mistakes. I don't believe that has to be true and neither do you. That's why you want to help kids like Max and Tara—because you believe they deserve a chance. So do you.' Ruby hauled in breath. 'You have judged yourself and you've judged wrong. Whether your mum can see it or not, you're a good man, Ethan Caversham.'

For a second she thought she'd made some sort of impact, but then his broad shoulders lifted.

'Sure, Ruby. Whatever you want. I'm a good man.'

The self-mockery evident.

'You are. And you deserve love. Real, *proper* love.'

It all seemed so clear to her now—exactly why Ethan had his heart under such a guard, his emotions in lockdown. The only person who had loved him was the sister he felt he had let down—a sister he had lost so tragically. The mother who should have loved him had condemned him from birth.

'You do not have to be alone in that boat, Ethan. All family relationships do not have to end in tragedy. Love doesn't always have to go wrong.'

Discomfort etched his face, was clear in his stance as he rocked back on his heels, hands in his pockets. 'Leave it, Ruby.'

'I can't. You deserve love.' How could she make him see that? 'For what it's worth, I love you.'

His face was leached of colour; blue-grey eyes burned with a light she couldn't interpret. Eventually he stepped back.

'It's not love. It's what you felt for Hugh, for Steve, for Gary. You said it yourself—you're not a good judge of character.'

'Ouch. That is below the belt.'

'No, it isn't. You don't love me—you want to heal me because you see me as broken. And I don't need to be healed. As for deserving love—that is irrelevant. I don't want love; I don't need love. I have come to terms with my past and I am moving forward. I'm not going to change. Any more than Gary, Steve or Hugh. So please don't waste your time thinking you love me. Find someone who will be good for you and to you. Someone who will father your children, whichever way you choose to have them. That man isn't me.'

The words were so final, so heavy, that she could feel her heart crack.

'Then I'd best get to London.'

What else was there to say?

CHAPTER FIFTEEN

THE CLICK OF the door unglued Ethan's feet from the floor, sent him striding forward, her name on his lips. Only to stop. What was he doing? He'd rejected her love so why was he following her? To do what?

His gut churned. He didn't want to hurt Ruby—hadn't wanted to a decade ago and didn't want to now. Somehow he had to make her see that he was right—she did not love him, whatever she believed. All he needed to do was convince her of that.

Maybe she'd work it out herself. See that every word he'd said was the truth. The past was over and he had come to terms with it. Had worked out that the best way forward was to move on, to channel his anger into becoming a success and using that success to help others. That worked for him—he didn't need love or a family. Didn't want love.

So why did he sound as if he was trying to convince himself?

The door swung open and Ethan swivelled round, his heart hammering in irrational hope that she had come back. Instead he saw Rafael Martinez, his expression creased in a small puzzled frown. 'A red-haired woman brought me here. Who is she?'

Pull it together, Ethan.

'Cora Brookes. My new hotel administrator.'

'I see.' Rafael frowned and rubbed his jaw. 'I had the distinct impression that Cora Brookes doesn't like me. She walked me here at the rate of knots and avoided all eye contact. Yet she looks familiar. Anyway it doesn't matter.

I'm here, and ready to auction like a pro tomorrow. I also have a business proposition I want to discuss with you. But you look as though business is the last thing on your mind.'

He needed to get it together. This was Rafael Martinez and this was business.

'I'm fine. Happy to talk business. Why don't we go to my office?'

Get away from this banqueting hall with all its memories of Ruby.

Rafael's dark eyes surveyed him with what looked like amusement. 'And how is the lovely Ruby Hampton?'

'Fine.' If Rafael was about to show even the most tepid interest in Ruby, Ethan had every intention of ramming his teeth down his throat. Business or no business. 'Why do you ask?'

'Whoa!' Rafael lifted his hands in the air. 'I was just curious. I get that she is off-limits.'

'Yes, she is.'

Rafael's eyebrows rose. 'Well, if you have an interest there you should know she has left the castle at speed—with a suitcase.'

Ethan paused as his brain attempted to compute the situation. Why would Ruby have taken a suitcase when she planned to return the same day? Unless she'd figured the journey there and back was too far? Needed some space? That must be it. Yet panic whispered in his gut.

There was a knock at the door and Cora entered, glanced at Rafael and then away again. 'Ethan. I'm not sure if I should mention this or not, but Ruby seemed upset and I'm not sure she's coming back.'

'What do you mean? It's the ball tomorrow.'

'I know.' Cora hesitated. 'It's just… She gave me the whole breakdown of the event in intricate detail—as if it was possible that she wouldn't be here. I mean…to be honest I can cover the admin side, because you and Ruby have planned it all down to the last detail. But I can't meet and greet or mingle with the guests. We agreed that.'

Her even voice held the hint of a quaver as her turquoise eyes met his and Ethan nodded. She was right. They had.

As if aware of Rafael's gaze as he studied her expression, Cora shifted so her back was to him. 'And, more importantly, as Ruby put all the work in I think she should be here to see the success I am sure it will be. I thought you should know.'

Ethan hauled in breath, tried to think.

Of course Ruby wouldn't leave.

You sure, Ethan?

The truth was the ball could go ahead without her and she knew it. It could be she was running—exactly as he had a decade ago. The irony was more than apparent.

Images of Ruby filtered through his brain. Her elfin features illuminated by enthusiasm, haunted by sadness, etched with compassion, lit up by desire. The gurgle of her laugh, the beauty of her smile… The idea of losing her, the idea that she might not return, sent a searing pain to his very soul.

Alongside that was fear…the terror of what it would feel like to let go, to allow his emotions full rein. Fear that he would somehow let Ruby down. If he allowed love to take hold he would screw it up, not be the man she deserved. That added up to a whole lot of scared.

The question now was what was he going to do about it?

Ruby approached the swish London hotel—the very same one where she had discovered Hugh's infidelity and perfidy in a double whammy. For a scant second she wondered why the idea of facing Hugh now didn't have the power to intimidate her. Possibly because she felt numb—had felt a cold, clammy sense of 'ugh' since she'd filled her suitcase and fled Caversham Castle.

Right now all she wanted was to get this over with, because she didn't want Portia to go through the same pain and disillusionment. In addition, it was about time she stood up to Hugh Farlane.

As she entered the imposing lobby—all fancy uniformed staff, marble and fluted pillars—one of Hugh's assistants rushed over to her.

'Come with me,' he said, his eyes roving the area. 'We don't want any bad publicity.'

'Hi, Greg. Good to see you again. Thanks for arranging this.'

The young man flushed. 'Sorry. It's good to see you too. But Hugh is very emphatic that I get you up there fast.'

'So he hasn't decided how to spin it yet?'

Greg declined to answer, shifting from foot to foot in an agony of discomfort, and then hustled her to the lift.

Once inside the sleek metal box, she felt a sliver of worry permeate the anaesthetic of hurt. Hugh Farlane had the power to crush her like an insignificant bug, and she didn't have Ethan's protection to fall back on now. In her own mind at least she was no longer a Caversham employee.

The irony was that she'd come full circle.

No! Not true. Weeks before she hadn't had the courage to stand up to Hugh. Now she did. In the past weeks she'd learned so much—on a professional *and* a personal level.

Before, the thought of any contact with her siblings had been an impossibility—now the idea seemed feasible. Because Ethan had shown her a new perspective. Somehow he had shown her her own inner strength. Which was a further irony. Because now she would have need of that strength to get over Ethan.

Not now. Put the pain aside and channel that inner power.

Her vertebrae clicked as she straightened up. The lift

doors swooshed open and she stepped forward and followed Greg along the plushly carpeted floor to the ornate door of the penthouse suite.

'Good luck,' Greg murmured as he knocked and then faded discreetly away.

The click as the door swung open set her heart pounding but she managed a smile.

'Ruby...' Hugh stepped forward, the familiar smile full of charm on his lips. 'Great to see you. Come right on in.'

Could the man have had some sort of amnesia attack?

'Drop the charm, Hugh,' she said. 'I've come here to give you fair warning.'

'Of what?'

'If this is another scam I won't stand by and let it happen. I will not let you do it to Portia.'

A roll of his deep brown eyes. 'And what exactly do you think you can do to stop me? Wait.' He raised his hand. 'I can answer that for you. There is nothing you can do. Portia believes in me, and as far as she is concerned you are a gold-digging vixen. And that's the way it's going to stay. In fact...' A casual shrug accompanied his words. 'It may get a bit heated for you in the press again. We'll be giving interviews, and Portia does feel very strongly about you.'

'That's a joke, right?' Her imagination went into boggled mode. 'You want me to take the flak *again*?'

'Yes.' Hugh smiled—a smile that would reduce half the population to its knees but left her utterly unmoved. 'That's not a problem, is it?'

'What if I say it is?'

Goodbye to the smile and any pretence of charm. 'Then you'll leave me no choice. I'll take you for everything you have. You'll lose your job like a shot. You may think Ethan Caversham will protect you, but how long do you think he will do that if I really go to war? Threaten to get one of my friends to sue him?'

'Sue him for what?' Disbelief and a smidge of fear touched her.

'For improper safety procedures—I could rig an accident, no sweat.' Tipping his hands in the air, he switched the smile back on. 'I don't *want* to do it, Rube. I don't… But I need this marriage to happen. Those Forsythe sisters have got a bit suspicious…my agent is on my back again. Yada-yada.'

'In other words you've reverted to type,' Ruby interjected.

'Whatever. Point is, Portia is my salvation.'

Ruby stared at him, and suddenly so much seemed clear to her. 'Ethan will never cower before your so-called might. And neither will I. Not any more. So I suggest you tell Portia the truth. Because if you don't, I will. And if you lie about me one more time in the papers then I will call you on it. I will give an interview of my own and then if you want to retaliate you go for it. Bring it on.'

A burst of adrenalin shot through her system. Ethan was right—the only way to deal with a bully was to stand up to him.

Hugh's eyes narrowed. 'I could drag you through the mud.'

'Go right ahead. But I will not let you do this to Portia. Or to me. I want you to tell her the truth and I want you to issue a statement saying that we have sorted our differences and you were mistaken about my gold-digging tendencies.'

He deflated before her eyes, sank onto a chair. 'You don't understand. I'm scared I'll lose my career…'

'Then fight for it. Clean up your act. Change. But do it for real and fight clean.'

Even as she spoke the words it occurred to her that she had hardly put her own money where her lips were. With Ethan she'd accepted rejection as if it were only to be expected. She hadn't put up so much as a vestige of fight—had let him write off her love as false.

Was that the person she'd become? Sure, years ago she'd lost the fight to keep her family together, but that did not mean she had to lose every fight. The truth was, it was easier, less painful, to expect and accept defeat. After all, the harder you fought the more you risked losing.

A hard rock of determination formed inside her. 'Your choice, Hugh. I've got to go.'

'Okay. I'll do it.'

Ruby nodded, already en route to the door. Her thoughts swirled as she figured out how long it would take her to get back to Cornwall. Should she call first? Text? Email?

The elevator felt claustrophobic, stupidly slow, and she jogged from foot to foot as impatience seized her.

Finally the doors opened and she stepped outside—and there was Ethan.

Thank goodness. Ethan's heart thumped against his ribcage as Ruby erupted from the elevator—he'd already paced a layer off the marble floor of the lobby.

Ruby skidded to a stop and stared at him as if he could be some sort of hologram. 'Ethan?'

'In the flesh.'

'But…what are you doing here?'

'We need to talk. How did it go with Hugh?'

'Good. All sorted. He'll tell Portia the truth and issue an apology to me.'

'That's fabulous, Ruby.'

'Is that why you came here? To check I could cope with Hugh?' Wariness tinged her expression now as she tugged at an errant strand of hair.

'Nope. Were you planning on coming back to Caversham Castle?'

'No. But…'

Ethan held a hand up, not sure he could bear to hear any more. Fear strummed him. She had believed the sheer baloney he had spouted earlier. Somehow he had to convince her to give him another chance.

'Not here. We need to talk properly.'

She nodded. 'There are loads of cafés round here. Or...'

'It's okay. I have it covered. Come on.'

Within seconds of leaving the lobby Rafael's loaned car glided to a halt in front of them. The chauffeur climbed out and opened the car door for Ruby, who slid inside with a puzzled look.

'Why didn't you drive your own car?' she asked.

'Actually, Rafael lent me his helicopter, as well as Robert and this car, to meet me on arrival.'

'You *flew* here from Cornwall?' Her eyes widened and a half-laugh dropped from her lips. 'Why?'

Ethan shrugged. 'Impulse. I needed to see you. To apologise and...'

Her eyes narrowed. 'Apologise for what?'

Here goes.

Time to put himself on the line. Along with some emotional honesty. 'For my reactions. I panicked. Just like I did ten years ago. I've been alone a long time; the only person who has ever got close has been you. Ten years ago I ran. I told myself I did it for you, because I could see that you had developed a misguided crush on me, but in reality I panicked.'

'And this time?' The question was soft, almost tentative.

Clenching his hands round his knees, he hauled in breath. 'This time I don't want to run, and I don't want you to run. For ten years I have avoided emotion, locked it down because I associated emotion with bad choices, rejection and tragedy. I decided to channel my anger and use it to create momentum—to build Caversham into some-

thing bigger and bigger, to allow me to do good via charitable efforts.'

'And you succeeded—you turned your life around.'

A twist of her body and she faced him now, her face
illuminated in the dusky light of the limo's interior, her
cinnamon scent whirling in his head.

'You should be proud of that.'

'I am. But the whole time I have been scared of emotion,
scared of rocking the boat, because I thought my whole
new life would tumble down. These past few weeks you
have shown me that doesn't have to happen. With you I
have run the gamut of emotions—each day I have felt more
and more. Caring, desire, happiness, sympathy, a need to
give and take comfort. You've unlocked something inside
me. You've helped me remember Tanya as she deserves
to be remembered—not just with bitterness and guilt, but
with the memory of all the good she did in my life. You've
let me look down the dark tunnels of the past and realise
that along with the darkness there was also light. And
there's something else you did too...'

'What?'

Her voice caught and fear and anticipation rollicked
through him.

'You taught me how to love. I love you, Ruby.'

For a heartbeat her expression registered no more than
shock, and the fear escalated. What if she had changed her
mind—realised that loving him was foolhardy? Then he
would change her mind if it took him his whole life to do
it. Then her expression morphed into a smile that touched
and warmed him as she launched herself across the limo
seat and into his arms.

'I love you too. So very, *very* much. And I swear to you
it is nothing to do with a need to heal you. Because I don't
need to do that—I love you exactly as you are. You're kind
and generous and caring and stubborn and demanding and

deep and complicated, and I love you for all those traits. You don't need to change for me.'

She nestled onto his lap, her hands cupping his jaw, and he felt a thrill of happiness. This woman loved him, and he knew he was the luckiest man in the universe.

'That realisation has been an epiphany for me. You see, all my life I have associated love with need. I wanted to be needed. My parents didn't love me enough to change their lifestyles for me, so I equated someone loving me with them being willing to change for me. Because that would give me self-worth. You've taught me how to have self-worth all by myself. You've shown me how to be brave, to stand up for what is right, and you've taught me to risk again—to risk rejection, to risk pain, because sometimes that is the right thing to do. So you don't have to change to prove your love or mine. I love *you*.'

'And I love you.'

He could quite cheerfully have continued in this conversational vein all day. His heart gave a happy jump and his whole body fizzed with a joy he could barely believe.

The limo glided to a stop and he dropped a kiss on her lips. 'Now that is sorted you need to come with me.'

'Where to?'

'Wait and see.'

The door opened and Ruby scrambled off Ethan's lap, sneaking a quick glance at the impassive face of the chauffeur and figuring he'd probably seen worse as Rafael Martinez's driver.

She looked around in an attempt to work out where they were. Not that it mattered—all that mattered was Ethan's proximity and the sheer sense of wonder that doused her. Ethan *loved* her. The urge to cartwheel, to grab passersby and tell them of her sheer happy feelings nigh overwhelmed her.

Instead she looked round and took in a tree-lined canal, with moored narrowboats of all colours bobbing up and down on the water. Cream Georgian architecture abounded, and the whole area felt like a quirky peaceful oasis in the midst of London's sprawl.

A quick tour of her mental knowledge told her they were in Little Venice.

'Come on,' Ethan said.

His grin was so boyish, so relaxed, that her heart threatened to burst.

'Close your eyes.'

Ruby scrunched her eyes shut and wrapped her fingers round Ethan's capable hand, anticipation unfurling as he guided her along the pathway.

'Okay. You can look.'

A small gasp escaped her lips as she surveyed the boat—gaudy, cheerful, bright red. It looked as though it had a personality all its own.

'Ta-dah!' Ethan beamed at her. 'Welcome to the *Oasis*. Fifty-eight feet long, six foot ten inches wide, she'll be able to take us all over England's canals.'

The grin dropped from his face, to be replaced by a serious expression, his blue-grey eyes full of passion and determination. 'It's symbolic. I want you on board my boat, Ruby, and I don't care how much it rocks or rolls or even if it capsizes, as long as we are on it together.'

The words caused a prickle of tears and he looked at her, consternation written all over his face.

'Hey, don't cry!'

'I can't help it. That is so beautiful and...' She gulped. 'I can't believe you bought a boat!'

'Come and see.'

Ruby followed him inside and felt an instant sense of home. The interior had a clean, homey, compact feel, with the space used to incredible effect. The kitchen area gleamed with pine, and as she explored she gave a small gurgle of delight at the dexterity of the storage space. Already she could picture rustling up meals as they chugged along England's canalways.

Walking further in, she saw the tiny but functional bathroom and shower room. 'There's even a dining area!'

'Well, meals are an important consideration. And look—when we don't need the table it can be folded away and we convert it into a lounge. Plus there are two cabins— a double room and a twin. Tight fit, but...'

Ruby stilled. 'Why the twin bedroom?' she asked.

'Because one day I hope that we will have children. Adopted or birth or a mixture of both.'

His words caused her to freeze, unsure whether to believe him or not, and needing him to understand that she truly loved him for himself. Only him. That he was way more than enough.

'You don't have to say that. I meant what I said. You are who I want. I want my future to be with you—to wake up every day wrapped in your arms.'

'I get that, Ruby, but you have changed me. You've opened my heart. And I have enough love in there for you and for children. Of course I'm scared—scared I'll mess it up, terrified I'll let them down—but I also know I will strive every day to be the best parent I can. Because you were right earlier. I don't blame my mum for what she did, but I could never do that to my child. I would never give up and I would never stop loving them. I'll be there for them, Ruby. I swear I will.'

'There is no doubt in my mind, or in my heart.'

Of course he was scared—after his childhood how could he not be? But she knew that Ethan would be a wonderful dad, and she wanted to whoop with joy that he too wanted a family.

'I know you will be a wonderful dad, and I so want us

to be a family. I've decided to try to trace Tom, Edie and Philippa as well. Make some new memories.'

The idea still scary, but with Ethan by her side, there to catch her if she fell, as she would be there for him, it seemed less daunting.

'I'll support you one hundred per cent. In this and everything, Ruby. Now and for ever.'

His smile was so full of love her breath hitched in her throat.

He gestured towards a corner of the lounge area. 'And right now why don't you have a look in your stocking?'

'Huh?' Following the trail of his hand, her eyes alighted on a small Christmas tree, still in its pot, decorated with silver strands of tinsel and red, purple and gold decorations. Pinned next to it was a bulging striped stocking, with a candy cane poking out of the top.

'I know it's not Christmas anymore. But I figured there was still some Christmas magic left in the air,' he said.

There were those tears of joy. *Again*. 'How on earth did you manage to do all this?'

A grin and the wicked wiggle of his eyebrows banished her tears in favour of a chuckle.

'Consider me all-powerful. Actually, it wasn't too hard. The helicopter only took an hour or so... Rafael's driver picked me up at Battersea... A few stops on the way and then straight here to Little Venice, where the ex-owner of *Oasis* waited. I cleaned the place, set up the tree, and then I went back to the hotel to wait for you.' Eagerness lit his expression as he shifted from foot to foot. 'Come on—open it.'

Unhooking the stocking, Ruby sank onto the cushioned sofa and dived her hand inside. Pulled out a heart-shaped box of chocolates, a gorgeous bath bomb that exuded lavender and chamomile, a pair of fluffy woolly socks... And then, nestled in the toe, her questing fingers found a box.

Heart pounding, mouth parched, she tugged it out and opened it. Inside was a ring—a glorious cluster of sapphires and diamonds.

'Sapphires to match the sparkle of your eyes,' Ethan said. 'Diamonds because diamonds are for ever. Will you marry me, Ruby?'

'Yes.' The assent dropped from her lips and happiness blanketed her as he slid the ring onto her finger. 'It's *so* beautiful.'

'Not as beautiful as you. Now, look up.'

There above them was a sprig of mistletoe, and as Ethan's lips covered hers she knew that her happiness was complete. They would sail their boat together over the horizon, into a life that would hold ups and downs, rain and sunshine. But she knew with all her heart that their love would ride every swell, weather every storm and bask in each ray of happiness.

EPILOGUE

The Caversham Castle Ball

RUBY FELT AS if she were walking, floating, *dancing* on air as she greeted each and every guest at the ball. Time seemed spun with the shining threads of pure happiness as she rested her gaze on Ethan, listened to his speech—his words powerful, emotive and drenched with compassionate belief in his cause.

'He's a good man.'

Ruby turned to see Cora Brookes by her side.

'He is.'

Instinctively she looked down at her left hand, even though she and Ethan had decided to keep their engagement under wraps until the end of the ball. Ruby had insisted that the ball was about fundraising—she didn't want to dilute the impact in any way.

They watched as Ethan introduced Rafael and the tall, dark-haired man took the podium; his aristocratic lips upturned in a captivating smile—within minutes he had them riveted by his words as the bids climbed to outrageous heights.

Cora gazed at him. 'He has the charm of the devil,' she murmured under her breath.

'He's putting it to a good cause.'

'Men like Rafael Martinez only have one cause—their own.' A strand of bitterness tinged Cora's tone. 'I'm surprised he and Ethan are so close.'

Ruby frowned. 'Ethan sees the good in everyone, and he

is a great believer in second chances. Plus, you shouldn't believe everything you read in the papers. Trust me on that. Unless, of course, you know Rafael?'

Cora hesitated. 'No,' she said finally. 'I don't.' A perfunctory smile and then she gestured towards the door. 'I'll go and check the champagne is ready for midnight.'

Ruby turned as Ethan headed towards her.

'All okay, sweetheart?' he asked. 'Why the frown?'

'I was just wondering why Cora doesn't like Rafael...'

'Lots of people don't like Rafael. But he has his good points. Or at least I hope he does. He and I have decided to invest in a business venture together. Spanish vineyard holidays.'

'Maybe we could honeymoon in Spain?'

Ethan shook his head, his expression serious. 'We are *not* going on a working honeymoon, my love. I have way better plans than that, I promise you.'

'I can hardly wait.'

He grinned down at her—a smile that lit his face— and his blue-grey eyes were flecked with a love that stole her breath.

'I think Rafael has everyone's attention,' he murmured. 'So let me snag us a glass of champagne...I want to toast our future under the stars.'

And as he twined his strong hand in hers Ruby basked in the healing lessons learnt from the past, the wondrous glow of joy of the present, and the glorious promise of the future.

* * * * *

PROPOSAL AT THE WINTER BALL

JESSICA GILMORE

For Charlotte and Flo

Charlotte for so selflessly allowing me to pillage her
commuting woes and for being such a brilliant
sounding board, co-plotter, and very patient
(and talented) editor.

Flo for making 'The Call' that changed everything, for
guiding me so patiently through the whole publishing
process, and for being a fab co-presenter extraordinaire
and late-night wine-drinking companion.

Thank you both x

CHAPTER ONE

'A GLASS OF white wine and make it a large one.' Flora sank onto the low leather seat and slumped forward, banging her forehead against the distressed oak table a couple of times. She sat back up and slouched back in her chair. 'Please,' she added, catching a quizzical gleam in Alex's eyes.

'Bad day?' He held up a hand and just like that the waiter glided effortlessly through the crowds of office-Christmas-party escapees and Friday-night drinkers towards their table, tucked away in the corner as far from the excited pre-Christmas hubbub as they could manage. Flora could have waved in the waiter's general direction for an hour and he would have ignored her the whole time but Alex had the knack of procuring service with just a lift of a brow; taxis, waiters, upgrades on flights. It was most unfair.

What was it about Alex that made people—especially women—look twice? His messy curls were more russet than brown, his eyes undecided between green and grey and freckles liberally splattered his slightly crooked nose. And yet the parts added up to a whole that went a long way beyond plain attractive.

But then Alex *was* charmed—while Flora's fairy

godmother must have been down with the flu on the day her gifts were handed out. Flora waited not too patiently, ready to finish her tale of woe, while Alex ordered their drinks. A humiliation shared was a humiliation halved, right?

Finally the waiter turned away and she could launch back in. 'Bad day I could cope with but it's been a bad *week*. I think I'm actually cursed. Monday was the office manager's birthday and she brought in doughnuts. I bit into mine and splat. Raspberry jam right down the front of my blouse. Of course it was my nicest white silk,' she added bitterly.

'Poor Flora.' His mouth tilted with amusement and she glared at him. He was still in his work suit and yet looked completely fresh. Yep, unfairly charmed in ways that were completely wasted on a male. Flora's seasonally green wool dress was stain free today but she still had that slightly sticky, crumpled, straight-from-work feel and was pretty sure it showed…

'And then yesterday I left work with my skirt tucked into my knickers. No, don't laugh.' She reached across the table and prodded him, his chest firm under her fingers. 'I didn't realise for at least five minutes and…' this was the worst part; her voice sank in shame '… I wasn't even wearing nice knickers. Thank goodness for fifteen-denier tights.'

Alex visibly struggled to keep a straight face. 'Maybe nobody noticed. It's winter, surely you had a coat on?'

'I was wearing a jacket. A *short* jacket. And judging by the sniggering the whole of Holborn noticed. But even that was better…' Flora stopped short and buried her face in her hands, shame washing over her as she mentally relived the horror of just an hour ago.

'Better than?' Alex leaned back as the waiter returned carrying a silver circular tray, smiling his thanks as the man put a pint in front of him and a large glass of wine in front of Flora. She picked up the glass, gratefully taking a much-needed gulp, the cold tartness a welcome relief.

'Better than tonight. I didn't mean to...' The old phrase tripped off her tongue. Flora's mother always said that they would be her last words, carved onto her grave.

Here lies Flora Prosperine Buckingham.
She didn't mean to.

'I was just so relieved to see a seat I all out ran for it only I threw myself in a little too vigorously, misjudged and I ended up... I ended up sitting on a strange man's knee.'

She glared at Alex as he choked on his pint. 'It's not funny! The whole carriage just stared at me and the man said...' She stumbled over the words, her cheeks heating at the memory. 'He said, "Make yourself comfortable, pet. I like a girl with plenty to grab hold of."'

She took another gulp, ignoring the guffaws of laughter opposite. The words had stung more than she cared to admit. So she was tall with hips and a bosom that her mother called generous and her kinder friends described as curvy? In the nineteen fifties she would have been bang on trend but right now in the twenty-first century she just felt that bit too tall, that bit too wide, that bit too conspicuous.

Of course, sitting on a strange man's lap in a crowded Tube carriage hadn't helped her blend in. There had probably been people from her office in that very carriage on that very train, witnesses to her humiliation. Thank goodness her contract ended next week, although the thought of even one week of whispers and sniggers was bad enough; if only she could get a convenient dose of flu and call in sick. A week of rest, recuperation and isolation was exactly what she needed.

Though sick days meant no pay. Flora sighed. It was no fun temping.

Alex finally stopped laughing. 'That was very friendly of you. So you've made a new friend?'

'No!' She shuddered, still feeling an itch in the exact spots where the large hands had clasped her. 'The worst thing was I just had to sit there and pretend nothing had happened. No, not on his lap, idiot! On the seat next to him. I'm surprised I didn't spontaneously combust with mortification.'

How she would ever get back onto that Tube, onto that line, even onto the entire underground network again she had no idea. Maybe she could walk to work? It would only take a couple of hours—each way.

'Will you go back there after Christmas?' It was as if he had read her mind. Alex was far too good at that.

Flora shook her head. 'No, I was covering unexpected sick leave and she should be back after the holidays. Luckily January is always a good time for temps. All those people who decide to *carpe diem* on New Year's Eve or do something outrageous at the Christmas party.'

'Come on, Flora, is that your grand plan? Another

year temping? Isn't it time you *carpe diem* yourself? Look, it's been two years since you were made redundant. I know it stung but shouldn't you be back in the saddle by now?'

Flora put her glass firmly on the table, blinking back the sudden and very unwanted tears. 'It's not that easy to find design work and at least this way I'm paying the bills. And no...' she put up her hand as he opened his mouth '... I am not moving in with you and I am not moving back home. I don't need charity. I can do this on my own.'

Besides, it wasn't as if she wasn't trying. Since she had been made redundant from her job at a large but struggling pub chain she had sent out her portfolio to dozens of designers, retail head offices and agencies. She had also looked for freelance work, all too aware how hard it was to land an in-house position.

Most hadn't even bothered to reply.

Alex regarded her levelly. 'I'm not planning on offering you charity. I'm actually planning to offer you a job.'

Again. Flora swallowed, a lump roughly the size of the *Titanic* lodging itself in her throat. Just great. It wasn't that she envied Alex his incredible success; she didn't spend *too* much time comparing the in-demand, hotshot team of architects he headed up with her own continuing search for work. She tried not to dwell on the contrast between his gorgeous Primrose Hill Georgian terrace, bought and renovated to his exact design, and her rented room a little further out in the far ends of North London.

But she wished he wouldn't try and help her. She didn't need his pity. She needed him to believe in her.

'Look,' she said, trying to stop her voice from wobbling. 'I do appreciate you offering me work, just like I appreciate Mum needing a runner or Dad an assistant every time I'm between contracts. But if I learned anything from the three years I was with Village Inns it's that mingling the personal and the professional only leads to disaster.'

It *could* have been a coincidence that she was made redundant shortly after breaking up with the owner's son and heir apparent but she doubted it.

And yes, right now life was a struggle. And it was more than tempting to give in and accept the helping hands her family and best friend kept holding out to her. But if she did then she would just confirm their belief that she couldn't manage on her own.

At least a series of humiliating, weird or dull temp jobs kept her focused on getting out and getting on.

'I'm not offering you a role out of pity. I actually really need you. I need your help.' His mouth quirked into a half-smile.

Flora gaped at him. Had she heard right? The cheesy blend of Christmas tunes was already pretty loud and amplified even more by the group at the bar who were singing along a little too enthusiastically. 'You *need* me?'

That potentially changed everything.

'You know the hotel I designed in Austria?'

Did she know about the high-profile, high-concept boutique hotel Alex had designed for the über-successful, über-exclusive Lusso Group? 'You might have mentioned it once or twice.'

'I've been offered an exclusive contract to design their next three. They pick stunning natural loca-

tions, like everything to be as eco-friendly and locally sourced as possible and each resort has an entirely
unique look and vibe. It's a fantastic project to work
on. Only the designer I used for Austria has just accepted a job with a rival hotel brand and can't continue
working with me.'

This was a lot bigger than the small jobs he had been
pushing her way for the last two years. It was too big
to be a pity offering; his own reputation was at stake
as well. Hope mingled with pride and for the first time
in a long, long time Flora felt a smidgen of optimism
for her future.

Only to be instantly deflated by Alex's next words.
'I'm flying out tomorrow for the launch of the Austrian
hotel and while I'm there I plan to present my initial
concepts for the Bali hotel complete with the interiors
and overall look. I thought Lola had at least made a
start on it but when I called her today to ask her to fax
her scheme over she told me cool as anything that, not
only hadn't she started, but thanks to her new job she
wasn't intending to.' He blew out a long breath, frustration clear on his face. 'This job better work out for
her because there's no way I'll be recommending her
again, no matter how insanely gifted she is.'

Ouch, ouch and ouch again. Flora's fingers tightened on her glass stem. So it wasn't her talent he was
after, it was her availability?

But maybe it was time to swallow her pride. A job
like this would propel her into the next league. She
leaned forward, fixing an interested smile onto her
face. 'So what do you want me to do? Study your plans
and email my ideas over?' Her tiny box room of a bedroom, already crammed with material, her sewing ma-

chine and easel, wasn't the most inspiring surroundings but she could manage. Or she could travel back to her parents a week early and work from there—at least she would be warm and fed if not guaranteed any peace and quiet or, indeed, any privacy.

'Email? Oh, no, I need you to come to Austria with me. That way you'll get a real feel for their taste.' He fixed her with a firm gaze. 'You need to follow the brief, Flora. There's no room for your whimsy.'

Her whimsy? Just because her private designs were a little fantastical didn't mean she carried her taste into her professional work. She knew the difference between indulging her creativity in her personal work and meeting a client's brand expectations, no matter how dull they might seem. She narrowed her eyes at him. 'Of course, I *am* a professional.'

Alex held her gaze for a long second before nodding. 'Good. I'll talk you through my plans on the flight to Innsbruck'

The reality of his words hit her. A trip abroad. She hadn't been on a plane since her redundancy. 'Tomorrow? But I have another week of my temp job to go.'

'Can't you get out of it?'

'Well, yes. Although my agency won't be best pleased.'

'It's a temping agency. I'm sure they will be able to replace you.'

'Yes. Of course.' A fizz of excitement began to bubble through her. No more Tube trains and oppressive offices. No, she would be spending the next week in a gorgeous hotel. No more spreadsheets or audio typing or trying to put salespeople off, she would be flexing her creative muscles instead.

'It's a shame it isn't Bali. I could do with some winter sun.' Flora shivered despite the almost oppressive heat in the overcrowded wine bar. Her last holiday had been a tent in the Cornish countryside. It had all sounded idyllic on the website, which had deliriously described the golden beaches and beautiful scenery. The reality had been freak storms and torrential rain. She didn't think she'd been truly warm since.

Alex set down his pint. 'This isn't a holiday, Flora.'

'I know.' She leaned forward and grabbed his hand. 'I was teasing you. I'd go to the Antarctic for a chance like this. What do I need to do?'

His fingers curled around hers, warm and strong, and Flora's heart gave the all too familiar and all too painful thump at his touch. 'Be ready tomorrow morning, early. Pack for snow and some glamorous events, you know the kind of thing.'

No, she didn't. Not recently but there was no way she was going to tell him that. 'Warm yet dressy. Got it.' A thought struck her as the group by the bar began to roar the chorus of yet another overplayed Christmas classic. 'When are we due back? Mum and Dad are expecting both of us home on Christmas Eve. They'd be gutted if you don't turn up. Horatio is on duty at the hospital so it'll just be Minerva, her perfect spouse and her perfect twins.'

She could hear the bitter note in her voice, feel it coat her tongue and took another sip to wash it down. What she meant was she couldn't cope with Minerva and her Stepford family without Alex.

'No Horry?' Alex raised his eyebrow. 'That's a shame. I do like watching your mum trying to fix him up with the local eligibles. He's so beautifully oblivious.'

'I think it's a defence mechanism.' Flora eyed Alex speculatively. 'Anyway, you should be glad he never takes the bait. If Mum wasn't worrying about her permanent bachelor son she might turn her matchmaking skills onto you.'

'You're her youngest child,' he countered sweetly. 'I wouldn't worry about me, Flora. It'll be you she'll be launching forth next.'

'Don't be ridiculous.' But she wasn't as sure as she sounded. Now thirty was just a year away there had been ominous rumbles about settling down along with the usual thinly veiled hints about getting a proper job, buying her own house and why couldn't she be more like her elder siblings? 'You're one of the family. Better. The Golden Boy. You know they think you can do no wrong.'

Alex had spent every single Christmas with the Buckinghams after the year his father and new stepmother had chosen to spend the festive season in St Bart's leaving eleven-year-old Alex at home in the housekeeper's charge. The next Christmas Flora and her family had taken it for granted he would join them, a stocking with his name on the chimney breast, a place set at the table.

Five years later he had packed his bags and left his father's house for good, taking up permanent residence in the attic bedroom next to Flora's own. He'd never told her just what had led up to his bitter estrangement from his father and Flora had never pried.

Turned out there were places even best friends didn't dare go.

'Don't worry, we'll be back for Christmas. There's no way I'm missing out on your father's Christmas dinner. He's promising goose this year. I watched him prepare it on a video on the Internet. Nothing is keeping me away.'

'That's all right, then.' She took a deep breath of relief. One day surely even Alex would manage more than six months with one of his identikit, well-bred girlfriends and would have to spend the holiday season with *her* family, not the Buckinghams. Each year they managed to hold onto him was a bonus.

She stared at her empty glass regretfully. 'If I need to pack, find my passport and be ready before the crack of dawn I'd better get going. What time shall I meet you?'

'Oh, no.' Alex pushed his chair back and stood up, extending a hand to Flora to help her out of her seat. 'I'm not risking your timekeeping, Flora Buckingham. I'll send a car for you. Five a.m. sharp. Be ready.'

Alex looked down at his tablet and sighed. So much for briefing Flora on the flight—although to be fair he should have known better. It was a gift he envied in her. No matter where they were, what the time was, she would fall asleep at the first sign of motion. She'd slumbered as the taxi took them through the dark, wintry pre-dawn streets of London to the airport, waking long enough to consume an enthusiastic breakfast once they had passed through passport control, only to fall back asleep the second the plane began to taxi down the runway.

And now she was snoozing once again. She would definitely give Sleeping Beauty a run for her money.

He elbowed her. 'Flora, wake up. I want you to take a look at this.'

'Mmm?' She stretched. 'I wasn't asleep, just dozing. Oh! Look at that.' She gazed, awestruck, out of the car windows at the snow-covered mountains, surrounding them in every direction. 'It's just like a Christmas card.'

'What do you think—is it as pretty as you imagined?'

She turned to him, mouth open in indignation, and he stifled a smile. She was far too easy to wind up. 'Pretty? It's so much more than mere prettiness. And look, there are actual chalets. Everywhere!'

'Well observed, Sherlock.'

She didn't react to his sardonic tone. 'I didn't realise Austrian people actually lived in them. I thought it was like thatched cottages. You know, people assume England is all half-timber and cottage gardens but in reality you're far more likely to live in some identikit house on a suburban estate. Oh, I wish I lived in a chalet. They are utterly beautiful.'

'I hope you feel the same way about the hotel.' It was the moment of truth. She had a keen eye, could always see straight through to the heart of his ideas. Would she appreciate the stark simplicity of the hotel, or think it too modern, anachronistic in this natural paradise?

'I always love your designs but this one sounds even more exciting than usual; I have to admit I am really looking forward to seeing it in all its finished glory.'

The car had been steadily taking them along the busy roads that led towards the Tyrolean capital, Innsbruck, but now it veered away to follow a smaller road that wound ahead, climbing into the footholds of the

Alps. The snow lay inches upon inches deep on the sides of the roads.

'Just look at it, look at the light.' Flora's fingers flexed. 'Oh, why didn't I pack my sketchbook? Not that I could really capture it, not the way the sun plays on the snow. Not that light—it's like a kaleidoscope.'

A knot unravelled in the pit of Alex's stomach. She saw what he saw. The interchange between light and the snow. She would get the hotel.

'I have never seen so much snow in my life, not if I took every winter and added them together.' Yep, she was fully awake now, her dark eyes huge as she stared out at the mountains. 'How come England grinds to a halt at just the hint of snow and yet everything here is running normally despite tonnes of the stuff?'

'Because this stuff is what keeps the local economy ticking over. You can't market yourself as a winter wonderland without the cold white stuff.'

'It's like Narnia.' Flora leaned back and stared with enraptured eyes as the car took them higher and higher. On one side the mountains soared high above them, on the other the town was spread out like a child's toy village, the river cutting through the middle like an icily silver scarf. 'How much further? I thought the hotel was in Innsbruck itself.'

'No, it's above the town, close to the ski lifts. The guests are transported in and out at will so they get the best of both worlds. That's the idea anyway, nothing too much effort for them.'

'They are paying enough for it,' Flora pointed out. 'I cannot believe I get to stay somewhere this luxurious. Even the staff quarters are probably one up on a tent in the rain.'

'You're not in the staff quarters. Could you really see Lola in anywhere but a suite? You're doing her job, you get her room. Tomorrow is the soft opening so nobody who stays at the hotel this week is an actual paying guest. We'll be helping to wow travel journalists, bloggers and some influential winter sports enthusiasts.'

He paused, searching for the right words. He knew how awkward she felt in crowds and amongst strangers. 'Flora, it's crucial that they all leave at the end of the week completely bowled over. And it's equally crucial that I leave with fully approved designs. You can manage, can't you? I can't emphasise enough what a big deal this week is. For me, for my firm as well as for Lusso Hotels.'

'Really? How good of you to warn me. I might have put my foot in it otherwise.'

Warning bells tolled through Alex's mind. She sounded frostier than the branches on the trees outside. It was the same tone she'd used the day he'd told her that one day she would grow out of boy bands, the tone she'd used the day he had told her that her first boyfriend wasn't good enough. The same tone she'd used the never to be forgotten day she'd chopped her hair into a pixie cut and he had agreed that, yes, she did look more like a marine than like Audrey Hepburn.

'I only meant...'

'I know what you mean: be professional, don't mess this up. Well, I won't. I need this too, Alex. I might not have founded a "Top Ten Up and Coming Business" while in my twenties, I might not be the bright young thing in my profession. Not yet. I have a lot to prove and this is my big chance. So don't worry about me. I've got this covered.'

Alex opened his mouth to point out that she hid in the kitchen at every single party she attended and would rather face a den full of lions than make small talk but he shut it again. He needed to warn her just how much networking lay ahead of her but not now. He'd wait until she was a little mellower.

Luckily the car turned down a single-track road, cut into the side of the mountain, a dramatic drop on one side showcasing the valley spread out below. 'We're here,' he said instead with some relief. The car slid to a stop and Alex unbuckled his seat belt. 'This *is* Der Steinadler—The Golden Eagle. What do you think?'

She had been looking at him intently, forcing her point home, but at his words she turned and looked out of the window. Her mouth fell open. 'Holy cow. You did this? This is it?'

'Yep, what do you think?'

'I...' She didn't answer, clambering out of the car instead, muttering as her trainer-clad foot sank into the snow and pulling her quilted jacket more closely around her as the sharp chill of the wintry mountain air hit. She turned to him as he joined her. 'All that time spent playing with building blocks as a kid wasn't wasted, huh?'

The hotel was built on the narrow Alpine shelf and looked as if it were suspended above Innsbruck spread out in the valley below, the mountains opposite a living, breathing picture framed through the dramatic windows. Alex had eschewed the traditional chalet design; instead he had used the locally sourced golden wood as a frame for great sheets of glass. The hotel should have looked out of place, too industrial for the tranquil setting, and yet somehow it blended in, the trees and mountains reflecting back from the many panes of glass.

Every time he saw it, it was like being punched in the chest. He couldn't believe he had made his ambitious vision a reality. 'You like?'

Her cheeks were glowing and her large, full mouth curved into a smile. 'I love it. Alex, it's wonderful.'

Relief flooded through him. He wasn't sure why her opinion mattered so much. It wasn't just that she was his oldest friend. No, he trusted her taste. If she didn't get it then he wouldn't have communicated his vision properly. 'Come on, then. Let's go inside. I think you might combust when you see the swimming pool.'

CHAPTER TWO

'SHOW ME AROUND, ALEX! It's not every day a girl gets the architect providing the grand tour.'

'Don't you want to see your room and freshen up first?'

She shook her head. 'No, I'm quite fresh, thank you, and you can conclude the tour at my room.' Flora watched the bellboy pile her bags and coat onto his trolley and sighed happily. 'This is a lot better than lugging a tent over three fields—and then having to go back for the beds. Besides, you want me to get an idea of what the client wants? The best way is for me to take a detailed look around.'

Her first impression was of luxurious comfort rather than cold, chic elegance. The whole interior of the hotel was the same mix of glass and wood as the outside but softened with warm colours and plenty of plants, abstract prints and comfy-looking cushions and sofas to mellow the potentially stark effect.

Alex shrugged off his designer ski jacket, a coat that had probably cost more than Flora's entire suitcase of clothes, and gestured. 'Where do you want to start?'

'Bottom and work our way up?'

'Okay, then, get ready to combust. We're heading down to the pool.'

If Flora didn't actually burst into excitable flames when she saw the swimming pool it was a close-run thing. Housed a floor below the hotel entrance in a space carved out of the alpine shelf, the high-ceilinged pool was enclosed by a dramatic wall of glass. Swimming up to the edge of the pool must feel like swimming to the very edge of the mountain itself, she thought, staring out at the white peaks, as if you might plunge over the side, dive down to the valley below.

The lights were low and intimately flattering, padded sofas were dotted around in discreet corners, and whirlpools, saunas and steam rooms were hidden away behind glazed sliding doors. Tables held jugs of iced water and inviting platters of fruit; thick fluffy towels were piled up on wooden shelves.

'Oh.' She pivoted, taking in every single detail. 'I just want to grab a magazine from that beautifully overstuffed bookshelf, pull on a robe and move into this room for ever. May I? Please?'

But Alex ignored her. 'Come on, next stop the lounge and then I'll take you to your room.'

By the time they reached her room Flora had scribbled down plenty of notes and photographed enough details to give her a good place to start. Obviously the designs she came up with for the Bali hotel would need to be unique, to marry with Alex's vision and the setting, but it was good for her to have an idea of the owner's tastes. She could see why Lola had used the palate she had; it was warming, sumptuous and complemented the natural materials prevalent throughout the building. The soft furnishings and décor were all shades of soft cream, gold, bronze and orange, whether it was the bronze and orange stripes on the cushions or the subtle champagne of the robes and the towels, the same colour in the crisp blouses and shirts worn by the staff.

It was clear that whatever look she designed for the Bali hotel would have to flow through every single detail, no matter how tiny.

'Okay.' Alex stopped at a cream door and gestured. 'This is you.'

Flora held her breath as she slid her keycard into the slot and turned the handle. Yes, she was here to work but there was no reason why she shouldn't enjoy it and after a few long years of penny-pinching and worrying it was rather splendid to be in such indulgent surroundings.

She stepped in and stopped, awestruck. 'Wow. Oh, Alex.'

At one end was the ubiquitous wall of glass and the ubiquitous stunning winter-wonderland view—not that it was getting old. Flora thought she could live here for ever and it would still be as breathtaking as the very first heart-stopping glimpse. The ceiling was high, arched and beamed, the walls a pale gold. The bed, a floating platform, was made up in white linen accented with a bronze silk throw and matching cushions.

Her suitcase had been placed on a low chest at the foot of the huge bed, the cheap, battered case more than a little incongruous in the spacious, luxurious suite. A reminder that this luxury was borrowed, that she had to earn her place here. Now she was here the jeans, jumpers and one good dress she had packed didn't seem enough. Not for the weather or for the hotel itself.

'You like it?' Alex stepped into the room, a smile

playing on his lips as he watched her dart around, peering into every door.

'Like it? Do you realise that this walk-in wardrobe is bigger than my bedroom? In fact this suite is bigger than the house I live in—and I'm including the garden!'

She stopped by the glass screen that separated her bed from the small seating area and stared at the other screen, which stood between her bed and the bath, a huge tub affair perched on a dais right in the centre of the room.

'Thank goodness the toilet's in its proper place and not on show, otherwise this would feel more like an oddly luxurious prison cell than a hotel room!'

'It's looking good.' Alex took a few steps further in and turned slowly. 'I haven't seen most of the suites since they were decorated and the fixtures installed.' He stopped by the bath and ran one finger along the bronze trim. 'At least you'll be clean while you're staying here. It can be so difficult to drag oneself away from the bed to the bathroom, don't you find?'

Flora tested out the sofa, wincing as the rigidity of the cushions rejected her attempt to relax. It looked good but she wasn't sure she would want to actually sit on it for any length of time. 'Was the bath in the centre of the room your idea, Mr Fitzgerald? Have you been watching *Splash* again because I don't think there are many mermaids in the Austrian Alps.'

He grinned. 'Nope, not guilty, the fixtures are all Lola's vision. Apparently this particular suite is the epitome of romantic.'

'That's where I've been going wrong, all that old-fashioned bathing in private nonsense. Although it could be just a *leetle* awkward if I was sharing a room with a friend, not a romantic interest. Is this…erm… motif in all the rooms?'

'Not at all,' he assured her. 'In most of them the baths are tucked away respectably in the room for which they were intended. Okay. If you are ready, they are laying out *Kaffee und Kuchen* for us. I thought we could go and look through my design ideas in the lounge while we have a snack.'

'*Kaffee and Kuchen?* Coffee and cake?' Flora jumped to her feet. 'Never did words so gladden a girl's heart. I'm ready. Lead on, Macduff. Take me to cake.'

The coffee and cakes were laid out in the lounge, the social heart of the hotel, situated on the ground floor at the very front of the building to ensure it took full advantage of the stunning views. Once again Flora stood by the huge floor-to-ceiling windows and her stomach fell away at the terrifying illusion that there was nothing between her and the edge of the mountain.

Clusters of comfy bronze and red velvet sofas and chairs surrounded small tables, bookshelves full of books, games and magazines filled one wall and a huge wood-burning stove was suspended in the middle of the room. Somehow the lounge managed to feel cosy despite its vast size, easily capable of seating the sixty people the boutique hotel was designed to hold.

'Right.' Alex seated himself on one of the sofas and laid out his sketch pad in front of him. It would, she knew, be filled with exquisite pen-and-ink drawings. This was just the first phase, the visionary one. From here he would proceed to blueprints, to computer models, to hundreds of measurements and costings and attention to a million tiny little details that would transfer his vision from the page to reality.

But she knew this, the initial concept, was his favourite part. In many ways neither of them had changed that much from the children they had once been, designing their dream houses, palaces, castles, tree houses, igloos, ships in absorbed companionship.

But in other ways… She ran her eyes hungrily over him, allowing herself one long guilty look at the bent tousled head, at the long, lean body. In other ways they had both changed beyond recognition—not that Alex had noticed that.

No, in his eyes she was still the dirty-faced, scabby-kneed little girl he had met the first time he had run away from home. He'd only made it half a mile along the lane before bumping into Flora and together they'd built him a den to stay in. Planned for Flora to bring him bread and milk and a blanket.

He loved her, she knew that. And there weren't very many people who could claim that. Outside Flora's own family probably none.

He just wasn't *in* love with her. There had been a time, way back when, she had wondered. But her one attempt to move things up a level had ended messily.

Flora curled her fingers into fists, trying to block out the memory. Block out the way he had put his hands on her shoulders, not to pull her in closer but to push her away. Block out the look of utter horror in his eyes.

He had kissed a lot of girls that summer and subsequent springs, summers, autumns and winters. But not Flora; never Flora.

And here she was, all these years later, still hoping.

Pathetic. One day she'd stop being in love with him. She just had to try a little harder, that was all.

Neither of them noticed the light outside fading, replaced by the gradual glow of the low, intimate hotel lighting. It wasn't until the huge Christmas tree dominating the far corner of the lounge sprang into brightly lit colour that Alex sat back, took off his work glasses and rubbed his eyes.

'So, what do you think?'

Flora chewed on her lip. 'I think I really need to take a trip out there to fully get your vision,' she said solemnly. 'At least three weeks, all-expenses-paid.'

'Play your cards right, convince Camilla Lusso that you can do this and you will do,' he pointed out. 'I told you that part of the brand promise is ensuring each hotel is both unique and part of its environment—and to leave as small a carbon footprint as possible. You'll need to source as much from local suppliers as possible.'

'Very worthy.' Flora pulled the pencil out of her hair and allowed the dark brown locks to fall onto her shoulders. 'Will the guests arrive in a canoe, paddled only by their own strokes with the help of a friendly wind?'

He bit back a grin. Trust Flora to see the big glaring hole in the whole eco-resort argument. 'Unlikely. But it's a start, don't knock it.'

'If I get to travel to Bali I promise not to give it as much as a second thought. Do you think they'll go for it? The glass-bottomed hotel?'

'I don't know. They've already decided to set the hotel in the rainforest—which is a pretty interesting decision. After all, most people expect a sea view in a place like Bali, so I really want to still have that water element. And although it would be nice to build out over the sea the local laws won't allow it—and the whole "surrounded by the sea" concept is a little "honeymoon in the Maldives" obviously.'

'Obviously.' Flora sounded wistful and he nudged her.

'Come on, work with me here. If I can't convince you I'm doomed. I actually think this might be even more breathtaking. Not just building over the lagoon but using glass floors to make the lagoon part of the hotel—the water as one of the design materials.'

'And I can bring that detail to bear inside. The lovely local dark woods and the natural blues and greens. Yes.' She nodded. 'I can work with that. Thanks, Alex.'

Alex pushed himself to his feet and walked over to the bar, a long piece of polished oak on the other side of the room. 'Glass of wine or a stein of Austrian beer?'

'I'm not sure what a stein is. A glass of white wine please.'

Alex ordered their drinks from the barmaid who was hovering discreetly at the far end.

He carried their drinks over and handed her the wine, taking a long appreciative gulp of his own cold beer, a heavy weight in the traditional stein glass. 'Cheers, or should I say *prost*?'

She raised her glass to his. 'Cheers. You were right. A job like this is just what I need.'

Alex paused. He knew it wasn't easy for her, younger sister to such high-achieving siblings, daughter of well-known experts in their fields. He knew her mother's well-intentioned comments on everything from Flora's hair to her clothes cut her to the quick. He knew how self-conscious she was, how she hated her conspicuous height, her even more conspicuous figure, her dramatically wide mouth and showy Snow White colouring. She really truly didn't know how stunning she was—when she wasn't hunching herself inside one of the sacklike dresses or tunics she habitually wore.

But she was twenty-nine now. It was time she believed in herself.

'You could have had work before,' he pointed out. 'How many times have I asked you to freelance for me? You were just too proud to accept—or too afraid.'

Her mouth shut again, her lips compressed into a tight, hurt line. 'There's nothing wrong with wanting to stand on my own two feet.'

'No, there isn't.' He fought the urge to backtrack; he'd always hated upsetting her in any way. 'But there's nothing wrong with accepting a helping hand either. Sometimes I think you're so determined to prove yourself you actually hold yourself back.'

Her eyes blazed. 'I can't win, can I? Once you accused me of not knowing my own mind, now you're telling me I'm too stubborn.'

'If you mean I told you not to apply to vet school then I stand by that. Just like I stand by telling you not to take that job at Village Inns. I still don't know why you did.'

Flora set her wine down on the table and glared at him. 'Why were you so set against it? No one lands the perfect job straight from college. It made sense to get some experience.'

'No, but your heart was never in that job, just like it wasn't in veterinary medicine. You applied for that to please your mum.'

Flora jumped to her feet and walked over to the window, staring out at the dark before turning to face him. 'So you were right that I wasn't vet material. Right that I couldn't hack it. So it took me a while to work things out. Excuse me for not being driven, focused on the goal like you, Mr Super Architect of the Year.'

He ignored the dig. So he was driven. Wasn't that the point? It was why they were here after all. 'Art school was far more you—but then you took the first safe job you could find even though designing those trendy pubs and twee restaurants drove you crazy. And when that didn't work out you went into lockdown mode. Took it personally, as if *you* had failed.'

'No, I didn't!' She paused, looked down at the floor. 'Well, maybe a little.'

'Look, Flora. You know the last thing I want to do is hurt you. In any way.' It was truer than she knew. Alex didn't know where he would have ended up, what he would have been without Flora's friendship. It was why he had never been able to confide in her, not fully. He had never wanted to see the warmth in her eyes darken and chill. To be judged by her and found wanting.

God knew he judged himself enough for both of them.

'Thank goodness.' She looked at him directly then, her blue eyes shadowed. 'I'd hate to hear what you would say if you wanted to hurt me.'

'I just want you to follow your dreams. *Yours*, not your mother's or mine or trying to beat your sister at her own game. I want you to go for what you want. Do what makes you happy. Not hang back for fear it doesn't work out or in case you get knocked down again. Take each rejection as a challenge, get back up and try again. Harder each time. Here is your chance. Seize it.'

'I was trying to before my temporary boss and arrogant best friend decided to have a go at me.' But the anger had drained out of her voice. 'I'm not so good at the seizing, Alex. We didn't all get the Masters of the Universe education, you know.'

Alex had hated every single day at his elite boarding school. The only thing in its favour was that every day he had spent there was a day not at home. 'I dropped out of sixth form to slum it at college with you so I missed the Advanced World Domination course. But I tell you what I do know, Flora. We're all mostly faking it. Tell yourself you can do it, tell yourself you deserve it and make yourself go for it. That's the secret. Now, I don't know about you but those cakes seem like hours ago and I know the kitchen is hoping to do a last trial run on us before the guests arrive tomorrow. Let's go eat.'

'That was amazing. Although I don't feel I can ever eat again.' Flora patted her stomach happily and curled up on the velvet sofa.

'Not that cosy though, just the two of us in a room set for sixty.'

'Oh, I don't know.' It had felt a bit incongruous at first, the two of them waited on alone in a vast room, but a couple of glasses of the delicious wine had soon set her at her ease and when Alex suggested they went back into the lounge for one last look at the plans and a *digestif* her original plans for a bath and an early night were forgotten.

She had only drunk schnapps once before and it

hadn't been pretty. But it was the national drink, after all; it would be rude not to sample it.

Alex was leaning back in his chair, his glass held loosely in his hand. Flora was usually so very careful about how she looked at him. If he ever caught her staring. If he ever guessed how she felt...

Alex was her oldest and best friend. His was the shoulder she cried on after break-ups and heartbreaks. He was her go-to person for advice. He knew all her vices and nearly all her secrets. But there were two things that lay between them. Two secrets; a chasm that could never be bridged.

He had never confided in her why he had left home, and why he was so against any kind of reconciliation with his father.

And she had never told him that she loved him.

Not as a friend, as a confidant, but in every way it was possible for a woman to love a man. Sometimes Flora thought she had fallen for him that very first day, that skinny red-headed boy with a look of determination on his face—and desolation in the stormy eyes. The hair had long since darkened to a deep auburn, his body had filled out in all the right places, but he was still determined.

And he hid it well, but at heart he was still as alone as he had been then. Not one of his girlfriends had ever got through to him. Was that why she had never told him how she felt? He was right, she *was* afraid.

Afraid of not being good enough for him. Afraid he would turn away in disgust and horror, just as he had all those years ago. Afraid that this time she would lose him for ever.

Flora downed the schnapps in one satisfying gulp,

choking a little as the pungent, sharp liquor hit the back of her throat. Hmm, not as bad as she'd thought. In fact, that warm feeling at the pit of her stomach was really quite pleasant. She refilled her glass.

She gazed into the amber depths as his words rolled round and round her mind. *'Get back up and try again. Tell yourself you deserve it.'* He was right. She never had. She took every rejection as a final blow whether it was work or her heart. It was easier not to put herself out there. Easier to lock herself away and hope.

Hope that somebody would see her Internet site and say, 'Hey, you amazing talent, come work for me!'

Hope that Alex would turn round, look into her eyes and realise, just like that, she was the only girl for him.

Hope that her parents would tell her that she made them proud.

She just sat back and let life pass her by. Hoping.

Flora raised her glass and downed the schnapps. It wasn't quite as fierce this time. Not as hot. More...mellow. She had definitely underrated schnapps.

She reached out and closed her hand around the bottle, wondering why it took a few goes to clasp it properly, and pulled it towards her.

'Another one?' Alex's eyebrows rose. 'We had quite a lot of wine at dinner. Are you sure?'

'Yes, Dad.' She grinned at him. 'I like your hair like that.'

Alex touched his head, staring at her in confusion. 'My hair?'

Flora put her head to one side. 'It's all glowy with the Christmas lights behind you. Like a halo. Angel Alex.'

She didn't see him move but the next thing she knew

he was by her side, one firm hand on hers, removing the bottle from her grasp.

'If you're talking about angels then you have definitely had enough. Come along.' He slid the bottle out of her reach and pulled at her hand, helping her rise to her feet. Flora swayed and caught his shoulder and he grimaced. 'Bed time for you. I forgot you and schnapps don't mix.'

'We mix just fine.' Flora regained her footing and stopped still, her hand still on his shoulder. She loved that Alex was taller than her. She looked up at him, his dearly familiar face so close to hers. The greeny-grey of his changeable eyes, the long lashes, the faded freckles on his nose, the curve of his cheekbones. The curve of his mouth. So close. Kissing distance. Her stomach clenched, the old exquisite pain. And yet all she had to do was stand on her tiptoes, just a little, and move in.

His words ran through her mind. *Try again. Harder each time.*

Maybe that was all she had to do. Try again. Maybe Alex was waiting for her to step forward, to make the move. Maybe it had always been within her power to change things but she had just never dared.

Maybe...

Before she knew it the words were tumbling out, words she had spent the last thirteen years keeping locked up deep, deep inside, more plaintive than demanding. 'Why didn't you kiss me back?'

'What?' His eyes widened in alarm and he took a step back. She moved with him, still holding on as if he were all that kept her anchored. He was lean, almost rangy, but there was a solidity when she touched him, the feel of a man who was fighting fit. 'What are you talking about?'

'All those years ago. Why did you push me away? Have you never wondered what would have happened if you hadn't?'

'It's never crossed my mind.' But his eyes shifted to her mouth as he spoke.

He's lying. Her throat dried as she realised what that meant.

He *had* thought about it. And that changed everything. Almost unconsciously she licked her lips; his throat tightened as he watched the tip of her tongue dip onto her top lip and, at the gesture, her heart began to beat faster.

Emboldened, Flora carried on, her voice low and persuasive. 'All those nights we stayed up talking till dawn. When we visited each other at uni we slept in the same bed, for goodness' sake. The tents we've shared... Have you never wondered, not even once? What it would be like? What *we'd* be like?'

'I...' His eyes were on hers, intent, a heat she had never seen before beginning to burn bright, melting her. 'Maybe once or twice.' His voice was hoarse. 'But we're not like that, Flora. We're more than that.'

Flora was dimly aware that there was something important in his words, something fundamental that she should understand, but she didn't want to stop, not now as the heat in his eyes intensified, his gaze locking on hers. If she pushed it now, he would follow. She knew it; she knew it as she knew him.

She also knew that whatever happened the consequences would be immense. There would be repercussions. Last time they had pretended it had never happened. It was unlikely that would happen again; their friendship would be altered for ever. Could she live with that?

Could she live without trying? Laugh it off as lack of sleep and too much schnapps? Now she had come so far…

No, not when he was looking at her like that. Heat and questions and desire mingling in his eyes, just as she had always dreamed. *I want you to go for what you want*. That was what he'd told her.

She wanted him.

'Kiss me, Alex,' she said softly. And before he could reply or pull away Flora stepped in, put her other hand on his shoulder and, raising herself on her tiptoes, she pressed her mouth to his.

CHAPTER THREE

HE SHOULD HAVE walked away. No, he *should* walk away, there was still time. Only there wasn't. Time was slowing, stopping, converging right here, right now on this exact spot, somewhere above Innsbruck. All that was left was this moment. The feel of her mouth against his, her hands, tentative on his shoulders. He shouldn't, he couldn't—and yet he was...

Because it was all he had dreamed it might be, those shameful, secret dreams. The crossing of boundaries, the touching the untouchable. Her touch was light, her kiss sweetly questioning and despite everything Alex desperately wanted to give her the answers she was seeking.

He stood stock-still for one long moment, trying to summon up the resolve to walk away, but the blood hummed through his veins, the noise drowning out the voice of caution; her sweet, vanilla scent was enfolding him and he was lost. Lost in her. Lost in the inevitable.

With that knowledge all thought of backing off, backing out disappeared. One hand slipped, as if of its volition, around the curve of her waist, pulling her in tightly against him, the other burying itself in the hair at the nape of her neck; a heavy, sweet smelling cloud.

And Alex took control. He kissed her back, deepening, intensifying the kiss as the blood roared in his ears and all he could feel was the sweetness of her mouth, the softness of her body, pliant against his.

Her touch was no longer tentative, one arm tight around his neck. Holding his head as if she didn't dare let him go. The other was on the small of his back, working at the fabric of his shirt, branding him with the fevered heat of her touch.

If she touched his flesh he would be utterly undone.

Like the animal he was he could take her here and now. Not caring about the consequences, not caring that they weren't in a private space. That the staff could walk in any minute. That once again there would be no going back.

That once again he could take things too far. And once again he could lose everything.

He had learned nothing.

Alex wrenched his mouth away; the taste of her lingered, intoxicatingly tempting on his tongue. But he had to sober up. 'Flora.' His breath was ragged as he stared into her confused dark eyes. 'I...'

'Am I interrupting something?' Both Alex and Flora jumped slightly as the rich, Italian tones, tinged with a hint of mockery, floated across the hotel lounge. Alex didn't need to look around to know who he would see—the owner of this hotel and the woman who had employed him to design three more, Camilla Lusso.

'*Buongiorno*, Camilla.' He took a deep, shuddering breath, willing his overheated body to cool, his spinning brain to slow. 'I wasn't expecting to see you until tomorrow.' He turned, fixing a cool, professional smile on his face as he greeted his biggest and most influential client.

'That's rather clear.' Still that hint of mockery in her voice, her eyes assessing and cool as she looked at Flora, clearly not missing a single detail as she took in the mussed hair, the swollen lips, the wrinkles in the baggy dress.

Camilla Lusso could have been any age between thirty-five and fifty-five although Alex suspected she was at the top end of the age range, but her expensively styled hair, subtle make-up and chic wardrobe made her seem timeless. A glossy, confident and successful woman. A professional woman who demanded top-class professionalism from everyone who worked with and for her.

Flora was supposed to be impressing her, not being found drunkenly making out with the architect.

Why now? Why tonight after all these years? He could blame the schnapps, he could blame the mountains framed through the windows, the warmth of the fire burning in the stove. It was a scene out of *Seduction 101*. But the only person he could really blame was himself. He should have backed off, backed away, laughed off the conversation—not been struck dumb with the thought of an alternate world. A world in which he might have been worthy of the adoration and desire shining out of Flora's dark eyes.

He had to fix this. Camilla's eyes had narrowed as she assessed Flora. If she found her wanting in any way then Alex knew she'd turn her away, no matter how good her work.

'I owe you an apology, Camilla. When I recommended Flora to you I wanted you to appreciate her for her own talent and so…' He paused, searching for the right words, the right way to make this all right. There was only one way. To make the whole embarrassing scene seem perfectly normal.

'I didn't tell you that we're dating. I'm sorry, I should have mentioned it but we agreed to be discreet this week, to put our relationship on the back burner.' He allowed himself a wry smile. 'Starting from tomorrow.' He took Flora's hand in his, pinching her in warning, hoping the shock of the last five minutes had sobered her up. *Play along.*

To his relief she picked up his cue. 'Pleased to meet you. I am very excited to be working with you and to help breathe life and colour into Alex's designs. I didn't realise I would have the honour of meeting you this evening otherwise…' Flora gestured at her wrinkled dress, at her mussed-up hair '…I would have made more of an effort.'

'But no.' Camilla's face had relaxed—as much as her tightened skin would allow—into a smile. 'The apology is all mine. I should have warned you that I had changed my plans. I have interrupted your last evening of privacy.'

'Oh, no.' Flora's cheeks were pink and her hand hot in Alex's. 'Not at all, we have mostly been working…' Her voice trailed off at the knowing look on Camilla's face as she said the last word.

'It all looks absolutely fantastic, just as I envisioned.' Alex took over the conversation, taking pity on Flora. 'And the staff seem to know their roles perfectly—not that I would expect anything else from a Lusso Hotel. What time can we expect the guests tomorrow?'

Camilla accepted a glass of wine from a discreetly

hovering waiter and sat down on one of the chairs by the stove. 'We're expecting the first to arrive after lunch tomorrow. I am so pleased you agreed to spend this opening week with us, Alex. The majority of the guests are influential travel journalists and bloggers and I am sure they are going to have lots of questions about your inspiration for this beautiful building. But please, not all work, eh? You must take full advantage of the facilities while you are here.'

Again she swept a knowing look up and down the pair of them. Alex gritted his teeth. 'It's my absolute pleasure. It's not often I get to spend so much time in a building I designed after completion. It will be really interesting to watch it fulfil its purpose.' Alex stole a glance at Flora. She was no longer flushed, rather she had turned pale, as if all the life had been leached out of her apart from the dark circles shadowing her eyes. 'However, if I'm to ensure the Bali designs are perfect for our meeting at the end of the week and socialise appropriately I think we'd better turn in. We were on the road at five a.m.'

'Of course. I look forward to seeing your designs, Miss Buckingham. Alex has been singing your praises. I can't wait to be impressed.'

Flora had thought she knew all about humiliation. She was the high priestess of it, dedicated to short sharp bursts at regular intervals. There was the awful day her university boyfriend announced he was in love with her sister; the even more awful day her subsequent boy-friend admitted he was in love with Alex; the time she thought her last boyfriend had been proposing when he had, in fact, been breaking up with her.

She had been going to refuse him, of course. But that *so* wasn't the point.

Her redundancy and the nasty smile on Finn's face as he had watched her gather up her pitifully small box of belongings and get escorted from the building like a thief.

Yep. High priestess of humiliation. Case in point: the week of catastrophes she had just experienced.

But, nope. None of them equalled the scene just now. She would rather sit on a hundred strange men's laps on any sort of public transport than relive the scene she had just left.

Flora squeezed her eyes shut as if she could block out the memory by will alone. *Kiss me, Alex.*

Oh, but he had. And it had been...it had been...

Flora flopped onto the bed and searched for the word. It had been wonderful. Right until the moment he had pushed her away with horror in his eyes and disgust on his face. That bit had sucked.

No. That had been the worst moment of her life. Bar none. Much, *much* worse than last time. At least she hadn't asked him, *begged* him to kiss her then. She'd just misjudged a moment. She should have learned her lesson. She wasn't what he wanted. Not in that way. Not then, not now.

She could never face him again. She should pack her bags and escape down the mountain, at night, in thick snow. She couldn't ski, didn't have a car and Innsbruck was several miles below. But that didn't matter, the exit plan itself mere details. The important thing was that she needed to escape and to pretend she had never ever laid eyes on Alex Fitzgerald with his crooked smile and red-brown curls.

But then he would spend Christmas alone. And without her family what did he have? He would never show it, of course, never say anything but she *knew*. She saw the look of relief when he stepped through the front door into her parents' hall. Saw him almost physically set down whatever burdens he carried around along with his overnight bag. Watched him relax, really relax, as he talked sport with Horatio—not that Horry had much of a clue but he tried to keep up. Watched the laughter lurk in his eyes as he half teased, half flirted with Minerva in a way no other mortal, not even her own husband, could get away with.

He helped her dad in the kitchen, talked through work problems with her mum and was on Flora's side. Always.

No, he couldn't be allowed to leave them. She would just have to grin, bear it and blame the schnapps. Not for the first time.

And she would work hard. She would blow the caramel-haired, caramel-clad, tight-skinned Camilla Lusso's designer socks off with her colour schemes, materials and designs. She would make Alex proud and this would be just a teeny footnote in their history. Never to be mentioned again. Never to be…

What now? A knock on the door interrupted her fervent vowing. Flora pushed herself off the bed, smoothed down her hair. *Please don't let it be Camilla Lusso.* There was no way she was ready for round two. 'Come in.'

A bellboy pushed the door open and smiled politely. 'Excuse me, Fraulein. I have Herr Fitzgerald's bags if now is convenient?'

If now was *what*?

'I beg your pardon?'

'Frau Lusso asked me to move Herr Fitzgerald's bags into your room.' He opened the door a little wider, pushing a trolley through heaped with Alex's distinctive brown leather bags.

'But...' Flora shook her head. Was she dreaming? Hallucinating? Had she been drinking absinthe? That would explain a lot. Maybe the whole hideous evening had been some weird absinthe-related dream.

'Mr Fitzgerald has his own room.'

'Not any more,' Alex stepped into the room, just behind the bellboy. His voice was light but there was a grim set to his face, his eyes narrowed as he stared at her. 'Camilla very kindly said there was no need for us to be discreet and we absolutely shouldn't spend the week before Christmas apart. Nice bath. Do you want first dibs or shall I?'

'You can't stay here.' Flora sank back onto the bed and stared at the pile of bags. It was most unfair; how did Alex have proper stuff? They were more or less the same age. How had he managed to turn into an actual functioning grown-up with matching luggage filled with the correct clothes for every occasion?

'What do you suggest?' He seemed unruffled as he opened up the first, neatly packed suitcase and began to lay his top-of-the-line ski kit out onto the other side of the bed.

'Well, we'll just say we're not ready for this step. Say we're waiting.'

'We're waiting?' An unholy glint appeared in his eye. 'How virtuous.'

'People do...' Her cheeks were hot and she couldn't

look at him. All desire to discuss anything relating to love or sex or kissing with Alex Fitzgerald had evaporated the minute she had caught the disgust in his eyes. Again.

'They do,' he agreed, picking up his pile of clothes and disappearing into the walk-in wardrobe with them. 'Why haven't you unpacked?'

Flora blinked, a little stunned by his rapid turn of conversation. 'I have. Those clothes there? They're mine.'

'But where are your ski clothes? You can't hit the slopes in jeans.'

Flora winced. She had a suspicion that hitting would be the right verb if she did venture out on skis—as in her bottom repeatedly and painfully hitting the well-packed snow. 'I don't ski.'

Alex had reappeared and was shaking his tuxedo out of another of the bags; somehow it was miraculously uncreased. Another grown-up trick. 'Flora, we're here to mingle and promote the hotel. In winter it's a ski hotel. I don't think staying away from the slopes is optional. Did you pack anything for the dinners and the ball?'

The what? 'You didn't mention a ball.' Unwanted, hot tears were pricking at her eyes. Any minute he'd inform her that she needed to cook a cordon-bleu meal for sixty and she would win at being completely inadequate.

'You'll have to go shopping tomorrow. You need a ski outfit, another couple of formal dresses for dinner and something for the ball.'

Flora leaned forward and covered her face with her hands, trying to block the whole scene, the whole evening, the whole day out. If she wished hard enough then maybe it would all go away. She'd wake up and be back on the train, squashed onto the knee of a leering stranger, and she'd know that there were worse ways to make a fool of herself.

'I can't afford to go shopping for things I'll only wear once. I cut up my credit cards so I wouldn't be tempted to go into debt and until I get paid next Friday I have exactly two hundred and eight pounds in my account—and I need to live on next week's pay until I go back to London after New Year. We don't all have expense accounts and savings and disposable income.'

It was odd, arguing over clothes and money when so much had happened in the last half-hour. But in a way it was easier, far better to worry about the small stuff than the huge, shattering things.

'You're doing a job for me so you can use my expense account. We'll go into Innsbruck tomorrow morning.'

His tone suggested a complete lack of interest in pursuing the subject. It just ramped up Flora's own annoyance.

'How very convenient.' She was going for icy hauteur but was horribly afraid she just sounded sulky. 'Typical Fitzgerald high-handedness.' She glared at him. 'Will you stop that, stop unpacking as if you are planning to stay here? Just say you need the space to work and there simply isn't the privacy in this room.' She cast a desperate look at the bath. She'd never dare use it now.

'I tried that and Camilla offered me her office. Look, Flora…' Alex put down the pile of jumpers and ran a hand through his hair. 'If we act like this is a problem then she'll get suspicious. I probably shouldn't have lied but I didn't want her to think badly of you. She's very strict on first impressions and professional behaviour from everyone she works with. You and I know that what happened didn't mean anything, it was just a silly moment that got out of hand...'

Whoosh. His words kicked Flora right in the stomach.

'But look at it from her point of view. It'll look even worse if she thinks we lied. What's done is done, it's only a week.' He was so dismissive, as if this was no big deal. But then it wasn't a big deal for him, was it? 'I'll take the couch. Your virtue is safe with me.'

That was only too clear. Unfortunately.

'Come on.' He grabbed a pillow and a quilt from the wardrobe and took them over to the sofa. 'Let's grab some sleep. It was an early start and we've a busy day tomorrow. You can have first go in the bathroom and tomorrow...' He smiled but it didn't reach his eyes. 'Tomorrow we'll figure out a privacy rota for the bath.'

Flora might have got the bed rather than the low, modern, 'easy on the eye but far less easy on the body' sofa but that didn't make sleep any easier. She'd shared rooms with Alex before. Heck, she'd squeezed into a misleadingly named two-man tent with him many times at festivals. But tonight, hearing the slow, easy sounds of his breathing, sleep eluded her.

Flora was more aware of Alex than she had ever been before in her entire life. She had known him as a lanky, red-headed, freckled boy, sleeping on her floor in his striped boarding-school-approved pyjamas, crying out for his long-dead mother in his sleep. She had watched over him as he began to grow into those long limbs, as muscles formed in his shoulders and legs, as other girls began to cast covert—and not so covert—glances at him. And she had watched him learn to glance back.

But she didn't know him at all tonight.

And yet she couldn't stop sensing him. Sensing the strength in his arms, the artistry in the sensitive fingers. She knew without looking just how his jaw curved, how his hair fell over his forehead, how his eyes were shuttered, hiding his thoughts even from her. Especially from her. She felt every movement as if he were lying right next to her, not with what might as well be acres of polished floorboards between them.

She had to stop loving him once and for all or else she risked losing him for ever. And if she lost him then where would he go? Would he lose himself in short-term relationship after fling, trading one gazelle-like blonde for another as carelessly as if they were new shirts? This whole nightmare was a wake-up call. Alex was right. She had to grow up.

And grow out of loving him.

CHAPTER FOUR

IF ALEX EVER needed a new job then he could always audition for work as an actor. As long as the role demanded he was asleep throughout. He'd spent an entire night rehearsing for just such a role.

Lying still but not so still it seems unnatural? Check. Breathing deeply? Check. Resisting the temptation to add in the odd snore? Check. Playing word games, counting sheep and alpine cows and blades of grass? Oh, yes. Very much check.

Doing anything and everything to keep his mind away from the bed just a few feet away—and from the warm body occupying it? Check. Not dwelling in miserable detail on the long limbs, the tousled hair and the wide, sensual mouth just made for kissing? No, no check. He'd failed miserably.

It was all too reminiscent of his last summer in his father's house. Lying in his bed at home during the long school holidays, wishing he were in the little attic room that Flora's family only half jokingly called his or even, on the worst nights, wishing he were back at school in the dorm room filled with the cheesy, musty scent of adolescent boys.

It wasn't as bad when his father was at home. Then

he just had to listen to the noise. The drinking, the laughing, the noisy lovemaking. But his father was so seldom home.

He didn't know what was worse. The way he had dreaded the creak of the door when his stepmother came in to 'check on him'—or the way he had anticipated it. The musky smell of her shampoo. The way the bed dipped where she sat. The cool caress on his cheek. Her whisper. *'Alex, are you awake?'*

And so he had practised his breathing, kept his eyes lightly closed and pretended that he wasn't. He didn't think he ever had her fooled. And in the end she stopped asking if he was awake. Stopped waiting for permission.

In the end he had stopped pretending.

No. He rolled over, the narrow sofa uncomfortable beneath his hip. No. He mustn't think of his stepmother and Flora in the same way, at the same time. They were nothing alike. He couldn't, wouldn't taint Flora with that association. She was better than that. Better than him.

Far too good for him. He had always known that.

And that was why he had to step away. Just as he had all those years ago. He'd broken up his childhood home with his out-of-control desires. He'd been so lucky that Flora's family had stepped in and offered him a second home, an infinitely better home. He couldn't, absolutely couldn't let desire infiltrate that space. No matter what.

He opened one eye, relieved to see the room turning grey with the pre-dawn light. Slowly, stealthily he slid off the sofa, wincing as he straightened his legs; he felt like the princess must have after her night sleeping on a pea—if her bed had also been too narrow to allow her to turn and a good foot too short. He tiptoed to the door and slid it open. He could have sworn he heard a sigh of relief from Flora as the door slipped shut behind him.

He needed a run. He needed a swim. And most of all he needed a very long and very cold shower while he figured out just how he was going to survive the rest of the week.

'I hope you slept well?' Camilla smiled in welcome when Alex walked into the dining hall two hours later. Darn, he had hoped to have more time to gather his thoughts but it was too late. They were on. Time to be convincing.

'Like a baby,' he lied, searching for a subject that didn't involve sleep, Flora or the suite they were now sharing. 'Look at the morning light in here. It's spectacular.'

'It should be. You designed it that way.'

'That's true, I did.' And he had. But it was always an unexpected joy to see his dreams made real.

The hotel was on the western slopes facing Innsbruck and so the huge windows were always most effective in the evening when the sun hung low in the evening sky and began to set. To counter this and to ensure the dining room didn't feel too dark during the day, Alex had designed it as a glassed-in roof terrace with dramatic skylights positioned to capture as much morning sun as possible. Balconies ran around the entire room so summer visitors could enjoy the warm Alpine sun as they ate.

Like the rest of the hotel the floor was a warm, golden oak, the same wood as the tables and chairs and the long counters that ran along one side. Guests could help themselves to juice, fruit and a continental breakfast; discreetly hovering staff were there to take orders for hot breakfasts. There was no menu; the kitchen was prepared for most requests.

Alex strolled over to the counter and poured himself some orange juice before spooning fresh berries into a bowl. 'Coffee, please.' He smiled at the hovering waitress. 'And scrambled eggs, on rye bread. That's all, thanks.'

He took his fruit and drink over to the square table where Camilla sat, basking in the sunlight like a cat. Her plate was bare and she had a single espresso set in front of her. In the two years they had worked together Alex had never seen her eat. He suspected she ran off caffeine, wine and, possibly, the blood of young virgins.

Camilla took a dainty sip of her espresso. 'I think I made the right call on the mattresses. I know they were expensive, but a hotel like this needs the best, hmm?'

Alex nodded, wishing he had had the opportunity to sample the mattress himself. 'Of course. Your guests wouldn't settle for anything less.'

Camilla eyed him shrewdly. 'A hotel tracksuit? Very good of you to live the brand, Alex.'

He speared a blueberry on a fork. 'Early morning workout. I didn't want to wake Flora. Good idea to have them where anyone could borrow them. I wonder how many people will slip one into their suitcase?'

She shrugged dismissively. 'Let them. They pay enough—and it's all good branding.' She looked over at the door. 'Good morning, Miss Buckingham.'

'Good morning.' Flora wandered over to the table,

a glass of juice in her hand. Alex gave her a quick critical look. She had on more make-up than usual, as if she was trying to conceal the dark shadows under her eyes. It might fool anyone who didn't know her. It didn't fool him for a second.

Had she been pretending to sleep as well?

A little belatedly Alex remembered his role as adoring lover and got to his feet to give her a brief peck on the cheek. He closed his eyes for a brief second as her warm, comforting scent enfolded him. 'Morning.'

Her eyes flew to his. He couldn't read her expression at all. He expected anger, discomfort maybe. Instead all he saw was determination.

Interesting—and very unexpected. She looked different too. Her dark hair pulled back into a loose bun, the dark green tunic belted over her jeans not left to hang shapelessly. She'd accessorised the whole with a chunky silver bead necklace and earrings. She looked smarter, more together.

And, yep, she looked determined. For what he wasn't entirely sure.

'I need to go into Innsbruck this morning,' Flora said after giving her breakfast order to the waitress. Alex's coffee arrived as she did so and he gratefully poured a cup of the delicious, dark, caffeinated nectar, offering it to Flora before pouring his own.

It was all very domesticated.

'I only brought work clothes. I didn't realise that I would be participating in the week's activities.' She smiled over at Alex. 'Apparently I won't be able to avoid learning to ski any longer although I'm sure I'd be far more useful concentrating on all the lovely après-ski activities.'

Camilla drained her cup. 'I think learning to ski is an excellent idea. You really should look at the hotel's ski lodges. I'd be interested to hear what you think of the materials and colours. They're accessible by ski lift but the only way back down the mountain is on the slopes.'

Flora grimaced. 'I can't wait to see them but I have to admit I'm a little nervous about the whole "two bits of plastic on snow" part. I can ice skate but other than that my balance is decidedly wonky. But hey, *carpe diem* and all that. It's good to try new things.'

Alex looked up. What was going on with her? Something was definitely different. Her tone, the way she was dressed. Did this have anything to do with yesterday? Their disagreement—or what happened later?

He should step back. This was what he wanted for her, right? For Flora to be more confident, to start living. And he could do with his space too. To make sure he cleared any lingering sentiments from that darned kiss from his system so they could go back to being easy with each other.

He looked out of the window. It was a glorious day, the sun already high in the blue winter's sky, lighting up the snowy peaks in brilliant colour. He should stay in and work—but the contrast to the damp fog he had left behind in London was almost painful. He yearned to get out, to clear his lungs and his mind in the cold, clear air.

Besides, Flora had never skied before; she had no idea what she needed—an easy target for anyone wanting to hit their sales targets. And it *was* his company's expense account on the line. 'I'll come in with you. Unless I'm needed here, Camilla?'

'No, no.' His client shook her head. 'You have a lovely day. Visit the Christmas markets and enjoy Innsbruck. I'll be doing the tour of the hotel when the guests arrive. I don't need you for that. This evening I am planning a mulled-wine reception and sledge rides for my guests. It would be nice if you were here for the reception so that I can introduce you.'

'Absolutely. Sounds great.'

Flora didn't say anything while Camilla sat with them but as soon as she sauntered away Flora pushed her plate away and narrowed her eyes at Alex. 'I don't need a chaperone. I hate shopping enough as it is. The last thing I want is you hanging around looking bored.'

'I love shopping,' he promised her, reaching over and nicking a small Danish pastry from her plate. 'Don't worry about me. I'll be absolutely fine.'

She smacked his hand as he carried the pastry away. 'I wasn't worrying about *you*. I'm going to try out the swimming pool first while I can be sure of having it to myself if you want to go and get changed.' Her cheeks flushed pink and she avoided his eyes. 'I'll be at least an hour so you have plenty of time to, you know… Change.'

He did know. She didn't want to walk in on him. Last summer when they had shared a tent at the festival she'd been content to stand outside the tent flap and yell an imperious demand to know whether he was decent or not. Those more innocent days were gone, maybe irrevocably. He tried for a light humour. 'We should have a code. Like college students—a ribbon on the door handle means don't come in.'

'I'd be tempted to keep one on there all the time.' But she smiled as she said it, a welcome attempt at the old easy camaraderie. 'I'll see you in the foyer at around eleven. You bring the credit cards and arms ready to carry lots of bags. I'll just bring me.'

It was annoying. She was annoying. Annoying and pitiful. Annoying, pitiful and pathetic. Yep, that just about covered it. Flora grimaced at herself in the half-steamed-up changing-room mirror. She shouldn't be glad that he wanted to spend the day with her. She should tell him to stick his pretend relationship and his begrudging job offer and his expense account— and then she should go spend the day sightseeing be-fore jumping back onto a plane and heading home to re-evaluate her life.

All of it.

But instead she was taking extra care drying her hair and reapplying the make-up she had swum off— and not just because this wide room, tiled in bronze and cream, was the most comfortable and well equipped changing room she had ever set foot in. It was going to be very difficult going back to her local council gym with its uncomfortable shared changing facilities and mouldy grout after the thick towels, rainforest show-ers and cushioned benches.

No, she couldn't deny it; she was looking forward to the day ahead. Because when all was said and done he was still Alex Fitzgerald and she was still Flora Buck-ingham. Life-long best mates, blood brothers and con-fidants and surely one embarrassing drunken episode and one insanely hot kiss couldn't change that.

She wouldn't let it change that.

And she wasn't going to sulk and dwell on his words from the previous afternoon either. Flora's hands stilled as shame shot through her, sharp and hot. He knew her too well, knew how to hit a tender spot, how to pierce right through the armour of denial she had been building up. She was too afraid of messing up. So scared of getting it wrong that she had ignored her instincts and selected purely science A levels in a bid to show her parents that she was as clever as her brother, as her Oxford-educated, high-flying sister.

But in the end what had she proved? Nothing. Quitting her vet course might have been the right thing to do but in the end it had just confirmed all their ideas. That she wasn't quite as robust as the rest of her family, not quite as determined.

Flora resumed drying her hair. For once it was going right, the frizz tamed, the curls softened into waves. Maybe this was a good omen for the weeks ahead. The truth was even now she wasn't sure she knew what she *really* wanted, deep down inside. Was she so determined to find more work as an in-house designer simply because that was easiest, hiding behind somebody else's brief, somebody else's brand? Or should she be trying to step away from the corporate world and indulge what he called her *whimsy*?

The little designs she played with might indeed be whimsical, fantastical even, but they had their fans. After all, her little online shop selling scarves and cushion covers in her designs ticked over nicely. Imagine how it would do if she actually gave it all her attention.

She smoothed some gorgeous-smelling oil onto her hair and twisted it back into the loose bun. Three hotels, three design briefs. This could buy her the time and income she needed to find out where her heart lay.

Or was she going to wander from dream to dream for ever, never quite committing? Always afraid of failing. Of falling.

No. This week was a wake-up call in all kinds of ways. And she was going to make the most of it.

She smiled her thanks at the chambermaid who was already collecting her towels and returning the changing room into its pristine state ready to wow the expected guests. Flora knew that along with the journalists and bloggers a few influential winter-sports fanatics had been invited; a couple of ex-Olympians and several trust-fund babies. They would expect only the best even from a free jolly like this one and Camilla and her staff were determined they would get it.

Maybe that could be her career? Travelling from luxury hotel to luxury hotel to be pampered and indulged in the hope that she would say something nice about it. How long would it take to get bored of that? She was more than willing to find out.

She wandered up the stairs to the large, high-ceilinged foyer. It would be the first impression of the hotel for all future guests and so it had to set the standard: light, spacious, with quality in every fitting. Would the people expected here later notice—or did they take such attention to detail for granted? It would be nice to be that jaded...

Yes. Nice was the word. Although she was a long, long way from jaded. Driven into Innsbruck, attentive service in all the shops and, best of all, the hotel driver stayed ready to collect her bags and whisk them back. If only she'd been buying something useful like fabric rather than over-priced, over-stuffed shiny clothes.

'I could get used to this,' Flora confided, watching her bags get loaded into the small hotel city car, ready to be delivered back to her room—their room—and hung up ready for her return. 'I think I was always made to be part of the other half.'

'It's not the other half,' Alex pointed out. 'It's the other one per cent and, I don't know, I think it would do them good to carry their own bags some of the time.'

'Don't spoil my fairy tale. Expense accounts and my every whim taken care of? I feel like a Christmas Cinderella.'

'And who am I? Buttons?'

He hadn't cast himself as Prince Charming. Flora ignored the stab of disappointment and linked arms with him, just as she usually would. *Act normal, remember?* Alex gave a barely susceptible start before falling into step with her.

'No,' she said sweetly. 'You are my fairy godmother. I can just see you in pink tulle.'

He spluttered a surprised bark of laughter and despite herself her heart lifted. They could get back on track even if they did have to share a room. As long as neither of them used that darned bathtub. It had been the first thing she had seen when she opened her eyes that morning, taunting her with its suggestion of decadence.

'I don't remember the fairy godmother having such a hard time convincing Cinders to try on clothes.'

'That's because she wasn't making Cinders wear clothes that made her arse look huge, her bosom matronly and her hips look capable of bearing triplets. Ski clothes and curves do not mix. In fact, winter clothes and curves don't mix.' She had allowed Alex—or rather

Alex's firm—to buy her the thermal turtle neck and leggings, the waterproof padded trousers and jacket, the fleece neck warmer, hat and gloves but had felt the whole time like a tomboy toddler being forced into a frilly bridesmaid dress. At least she had talked him out of the hot pink and gone for a less garish turquoise and white look. But she was pretty sure she'd still look and feel like a child playing dress up.

At least she was fairly happy with the dresses she had bought, even the formal dress for the ball. Actually, if she was honest with herself, she was secretly delighted with it—although whether she'd actually have the courage to wear it in public was a whole other matter. The sales assistants had been enthusiastic but then again that was their job. Just look how gushing the saleswoman had been when she had tried on the Bavarian-barmaid-inspired bridesmaid dress for Minerva's wedding. Even her father hadn't been able to summon up a heartfelt compliment for that particular outfit.

A little part of her wished she hadn't sent Alex away for what he rather insultingly called 'a restorative coffee' when she had started dress shopping, But it had been bad enough having him there assessing her while she tried on padded trousers. The thought of his eyes skimming over her in dress after dress was far too uncomfortable an image.

Innsbruck had no shortage of designer boutiques and stores but Flora had felt even more out of place in them than she had in the bustling board shops. It had been such a relief when she had stumbled on the vintage shop with floors and floors of second-hand and reproduction clothes. Usually she felt too self-conscious to wear anything that drew attention to herself—and with her height vintage always made a statement—but in this town of winter glamour it had been a choice between vintage inspired or designer glitz. No choice at all.

And it *was* a glamorous town. The old, medieval streets surrounded by snow-capped mountains gave Innsbruck a quaint, old-fashioned air but there was a cosmopolitan beat to the old Tyrolean town. People came here to shop at the Christmas markets and to enjoy the myriad winter sports aimed at all levels. There was a palpable sense of money, of entitlement, of health and vigour.

'Look at them all.' Flora stared down the main street at what seemed like a sea of glowing, youthful faces. 'It's like they've been ordered out of a catalogue. I've never seen so many gorgeous people.'

'Even him?' Alex indicated a man sitting in the window of a café, his sunglasses perched high on his unnaturally smooth face, his skin the colour of a ripened orange. Flora bit her lip, trying not to laugh.

'Or her?' He nudged her in the direction of a skeletally thin woman, swathed from neck to ankle in what Flora devoutly hoped were fake furs, incongruously bright yellow hair topping her wrinkled face.

'Maybe not everyone,' she conceded. 'But most people seem so at home, like they *belong*.' No one else bulged out of quilted jackets, or had hair flattened by their hats. The girls looked wholesomely winsome in thick jumpers and gilets, their hair cascading from underneath their knitted hats, their cheeks pink from the cold. The men were like Norse gods: tall, confident as they strode down the snow-filled medieval streets. Alex fitted the scene like the last piece of a jigsaw. Flora? She was the missing piece from a different jigsaw that had somehow got put in the wrong box.

'What did I tell you, Flora? No one really belongs, they just act like they do. You just need to stand tall and look people in the eye.'

'Not easy when everyone is wearing shades.' It was a feeble joke and Alex just looked at her, concern in his eyes. She winced; somehow she had managed to provoke almost every response going in the last forty-eight hours. She made herself smile. *See, joking.*

'We don't have to be back at the hotel for a few hours yet, you're respectably kitted out and I have even managed to clear my emails while you were dress hunting. What do you fancy doing?'

Flora pulled at her coat. 'I should work. What if Camilla wants to see my ideas? All I have are a few online mood boards.'

'That's all she wants at this stage. I can promise you, she'll change her mind a million times and in the end your first concept will be the winner.'

'Then why drag me here for the week?' Oh, no. He hadn't forced her over here as some sort of intervention, had he? He could just imagine him on the phone to her mother, reassuring her that he had it all in hand. That he would put an end to this temping nonsense quick smart.

'Not that I'm not grateful…' she added unconvincingly. Just think, if he'd left her alone she could have been cosying up to the man on the train again tomorrow morning. Maybe she'd misjudged him and his grabby hands. He might just be plain-speaking and tactile. They could have told their kids and grandkids about how they'd met on an overcrowded commuter train a week before Christmas. Just like a film.

'Flora, Camilla can snap her fingers and have the best at the touch of a button. It's the story, the package that she needs to see. She loves that I'm young, terribly English, well educated, have my own firm and I'm tipped for the top.' His laugh was a little self-conscious. 'It's an easy sell, makes a good interview, adds that extra little detail when she's publicising the hotel. You're here so she can see that you can do the same—that's why it's so important that you look right, that you say the right things.'

That she what? Panic churned in her stomach, the snow dazzling as she stared at the ground, her eyes swimming. 'I'm here to schmooze? You didn't tell me that!'

'I didn't hide it. You know who the invited guests are. Look, Camilla knows I wouldn't recommend anyone who wasn't talented and creative. She needs to see that you can mingle with the right people, chat to journalists, help sell her creations. And, Flora, you can.'

'But I can't…' He wanted her to what? *Chat to journalists? Sell?* Flora gulped in air, rooted to the spot, oblivious to the crowds passing her by.

'You've done it before.' He didn't add *Many times* but the words hung in the air. 'At least this time you won't have to baste chickens or pipe icing while you're talking.'

Flora still couldn't joke about her childhood spots in front of the camera. To be honest she wasn't sure she ever would reach that state. 'Can you imagine what it was like going into school after Dad's shows aired? Me this tall and this…' She sketched an arc around her chest. She had been the tallest in her class from nursery onwards—and the most developed from the end of primary school. 'The last thing I want to do is talk about me, you know that. And if I chat to journalists they'll know who I am…'

'And they'll love it. Youngest daughter of food writer and TV chef, Ted Buckingham and TV doctor Jane Buckingham? They won't try and catch you out, Flora. We're talking travel sections, maybe some lifestyle blogs. I promise you. It'll be a lot less stressful than your dad's Internet videos of family get-togethers.'

'Horry says neurosurgery is less stressful than the Internet get-togethers.'

'All you have to do this week is have fun. Try to ski, chat to people, talk colours and materials and be enthusiastic. If Camilla offers you the commission then you can worry about the other side of it later, but if I were you I'd think about how a little publicity in the right places could send your stock sky-high. Come on, Flora. You never know, you might even enjoy it. Now, Christmas markets or ice skating? Your choice.'

Flora took in a deep shuddering breath. Alex was right, if he'd mentioned any of this before she would have hightailed it back to London before he could say *prost*. Minerva positively fed off their parents' fame, using it as a springboard when she opened her PR firm, and Horry was oblivious. Flora, on the other hand, had always found it mortifying, whether appearing on her dad's cookery programme or listening to her mother talk about Flora's first period on national TV. She wasn't sure the scars from that particular episode would ever fade.

Still, silver linings and all that—she hadn't thought

about the kiss or their sleeping arrangements once in the last half-hour. It turned out there were only so many things even she could stress about.

'I haven't been ice skating for years.'

'Indoors or outdoors?'

Flora looked around, at the blue sky, the sun warm despite the chill of the air. 'Oh, outside, please.'

'Come on, then, I challenge you to a backwards-skating race. Loser buys the mulled wine.'

CHAPTER FIVE

THIS WHOLE WEEK was doomed. Alex had known it from the minute he'd got Lola's email. Camilla Lusso liked to work with people she could show off. Extroverted, larger than life, Lola had fitted the bill perfectly. Flora? Not so much. But she did have the training, after all. It wasn't as if he had thrown her in unprepared; she'd been brought up with camera crews, journalists and interviewers traipsing through the house, had been expected to converse intelligently at dinner parties and receptions since she'd hit double figures.

Of course, that didn't mean she *enjoyed* any of it. Alex knew all too well that if he'd been completely honest with her at the start she'd have run a mile.

Maybe that would have been for the best. No Flora, no kiss, no sleepless night.

Because, try as he might, he just couldn't shake the memory of the warmth of her mouth, the sweetness of her lips, the way his hands had held her as if she were made just for him, every curve slotting so perfectly against him.

There had been far too many kisses from far more women than Alex cared to remember. Not one had stayed with him, not for a second. This one he could still taste. He had a feeling he would still feel it imprinted on his lips in fifty years' time.

And it was all he could do not to put his hands on her shoulders, turn her around and kiss her once again. And this time there would be no stepping back. Not ever.

But he couldn't. She deserved better than him. She needed someone who wasn't dead inside, someone who could match her sweetness and generous spirit. Sometimes Alex thought that Flora could be the saving of him—but he'd be the damning of her. His father's last words echoed around his brain yet again.

You taint everything you touch. You were born bad and grew up worse.

And his father was right.

But he wouldn't taint Flora, never Flora.

'I haven't been ice skating in years.' She worried away at her lower lip as they walked through the twisty streets. 'Not since we used to go to the ice discos on a Friday night. Not that you did much skating. You were usually in a corner snogging some random girl.'

He had been. A different girl each week. The worse he'd behaved, the more they'd seemed to find him irresistible. He had hated himself every single Friday night as he'd smiled across at yet another hopeful—but it hadn't stopped him moving in while last week's conquest had watched from a corner.

Had anything changed? He went in for relationships now, not kisses in a booth by an ice rink, but he didn't commit as much as a toothbrush to them—and Flora had a point when she said that each of his girlfriends was interchangeable. A warm body to lose himself in, a talisman against the dark.

Could he change that—did he even want to? Or would it be just as lonely with one woman by his side as it was with dozens?

He shook off the thought. 'It'll be just like riding a bike—the skating, not the snogging.' Why had he said that? He was pretty sure that the red in her cheeks had nothing to do with the cold and she ducked her head so that he couldn't see her expression.

It'll get easier, he told himself. But he hoped it was soon. He couldn't imagine being this awkward in front of her parents. He knew Flora thought they favoured him but there was no contest—she was their little girl and if he hurt her they'd take her side. As they should.

It made him aware just how alone he was in the world. Was there anyone who would be on his side no matter what?

There were lots of ice rinks in and around Innsbruck, the prettiest on naturally frozen lakes, but the one Alex had chosen had a charm all of its own. It was a temporary rink right in the centre of town, just a short walk from the bustling Christmas markets. The early afternoon sun was too bright for the Christmas lights hanging overhead and bedecking every tree to make any impact but Alex knew that once dusk fell the whole town would light up, a dazzling, golden winter wonderland of crystal and light.

The rink was busy and it took a while before they could pay and order their skates. The boots were tight and stiff, unfamiliar on his feet, a reminder as he awkwardly stood up just how long it was since he had last been skating. Judging by Flora's awkward gait, she felt the same way. Gingerly they walked, stiff-legged and heavy-footed, to the wide entrance and peered at the whirling crowd. Even the toddlers seemed to have a professional air as they flew round and round, their mittened hands clasped behind their backs.

Alex grimaced. 'I'm not sure about that backward race; right now just going forwards feels like it might be a struggle.'

Flora slid her foot forward, wobbling like a fawn who had only just found her feet, her arms windmilling madly as she found her balance. 'Come on, we just need to find our feet. It'll be fine. I used to be able to dance on the ice.'

'Synchronised moves to pop. It wasn't exactly figure skating,' he pointed out as he put a tentative toe on the white surface, his eyes following a slight figure who did seem to be practising figure skating as she looped elegant circles round and round. 'I don't think we ever got to Austrian standards.'

Flora slid out another cautious foot and then another, a smile playing around her mouth as she began to pick up speed. 'Speak for yourself! You should have spent more time skating, less time being the local Casanova,' she yelled over her shoulder as she struck out for the centre of the rectangular rink.

Alex took a quick look around. On the far side the tented café was open to the rink and filled with cheerful onlookers clutching hot drinks and waving at family members as they skated close. At both ends spectators paused in their shopping to watch the sport. Christmas music blared from speakers and a giant, lit-up Christmas tree occupied the very centre of the rink.

He could stay here, clinging to the handrail, or he could venture out. Come on, he used to spend every weekend doing this. His body must remember the moves. Grimly he let go and began to move.

That was it, knees bent, body weight forward, letting the blades cut at an angle and propel him forward. The air chilled on his face as he got up some speed, the rest of his body warming with the exertion. Where was Flora? Squinting through a gang of teens, arms locked as they swung round in matching step, he saw her, weaving nimbly in and out of the other skaters. He'd always liked to watch her on the ice. She lost all self-consciousness, graceful as she pirouetted around.

She saw him and skated an elegant figure of eight, the ice swishing under her skates as she pulled up alongside him.

'Hey.' She smiled at him, any trace of reserve gone in the wide beam. 'This is brilliant. Why don't we do this any more?'

'Because we're not sixteen?'

'That's a rubbish reason. Look, there are plenty of people here way older than us.'

'And way younger.' Alex nodded towards one of the toddler prodigies and Flora laughed.

'He must have been born with skates on. Come on, let's go faster...'

She grabbed his hand and struck out and with a shout of alarm mixed with exultation he joined her, their gloved hands entwined, their bodies moving in swift, perfect synchronicity as they whirled faster and faster and faster round and round and round. All he could hear was his blood pumping in his ears, the roar of the wind and the beat of the music; colours swirled together as they moved past, through and round other groups until someone's foot, he wasn't sure whose, slipped and they crashed together, a sliding, flailing, unbalancing. Somehow he managed to grab hold of Flora and steady her before she fell completely onto the ice and they backed carefully to the side, holding onto each other, laughing.

'That was brilliant.' Her eyes shone, her cheeks were pink with exertion and her breath came in pants. She had never looked more magnificent, like some winter naiad glorying in the ice.

'Yes.' He wanted to say more but all the words had gone. All he could see were her long lashes, tipped with snow, her wide laughing mouth, a mouth made for kissing. All he could feel was her softness, nestled in next to him.

He had held her before, stood this close to her before. If he was honest he had wanted her before. But he'd hidden it, even from himself, every single time before. It was as if yesterday's kiss had opened the gates, shown him the forbidden fruit concealed behind them and now that he had tasted he wasn't sure he could ever stop craving.

It was a bad idea. But God help him he'd forgotten why. And when she looked at him like that, tentative, hopeful, naked desire blazing from those dark, dark eyes, he was utterly undone.

It was a bad idea. But Alex pushed that thought away as the air stilled, as the beat of the music faded away replaced with the thrum of need beating its own time through his veins, through his blood. He stood, drinking her in like a dying man at an oasis. All he had to do was bend his head…

He paused, allowing the intoxicating possibility to fill him—and then he stood back. 'Come on.' His voice was rough, rasping like yesterday's beard. 'We need to get back.'

It was a bad idea. If only it didn't feel so wickedly, seductively good. If only doing the right thing didn't rip his heart right out of his chest.

He turned and skated away. And didn't look back once.

He'd nearly kissed her. She knew it completely. She'd seen it as his eyes had darkened to a stormy grey, as his breath had hitched and a muscle had pulsed on his cheek. She'd felt it as his arm had tightened around her shoulders, as her body had swayed into his. She hadn't thrown herself at him; she couldn't blame the schnapps, not this time.

No, Alex Fitzgerald had looked at her as if she were his last hope.

Of course, then he had turned and skated away as if all the Furies were chasing him down, but still. They had had a definite moment.

Which was pretty inconvenient because hadn't she vowed that this was it and she was going to Get Over Him no matter what? And then he had to go and look at her like that and all her good intentions were trampled into the ground like yesterday's snowfall.

Because that look went beyond mere lust. It *did*. It wasn't just wishful thinking. No, she had felt it penetrate right through to the core of her.

Flora sighed and nudged the hot tap with her foot and let another fall of steaming water into the tub. It felt decadently wrong to lie naked in the middle of such a big room, wearing just hot water and scented oils. The view from the bathtub might be incredible but it seemed, a little disconcertingly, as if she were bathing right outside in the middle of a mountain glade.

Still, it was pretty relaxing—as long as Alex stuck to his timetable and didn't walk back in.

What if he did? Would he look like that again or would he back away terrified again?

Something was going on. *I need answers,* she decided, allowing herself to slip deep into the hot, almost to the point of discomfort, luxuriantly smelling water. She couldn't go on like this.

It was one thing thinking he was indifferent; horrid to think he was repulsed. But now? She had no idea. It was as if she were sixteen again. His face had that same remote, shuttered look it had worn all that long, hot summer.

She couldn't let him slip back to that place, wherever it was. She had been too shy, too unsure to ask questions then, to demand answers.

But maybe he needed her to ask them? Maybe by letting whatever had happened lie festering all these years she had done him a disservice. It didn't mean he would end up declaring his undying love for her, she knew that. It might change things for ever. But if she loved him then she needed to be strong, for once in her life. No matter what the personal cost.

And she wouldn't get anywhere lying in this bath, tempting as it was to stay in here all night long.

Although she wanted to try out one of the dresses she had bought that day, the prospect of a potential sledge ride made her think again and in the end Flora opted for her smartest black skinny jeans and a long, soft grey jumper with a snowflake motif. She started to automatically twist her hair into a ponytail but instead she let it flow freely across her shoulders, thankful that the wave had held and it hadn't been too flattened by the hat.

She stood before the mirror and looked down at the last purchase of the day, an impulse buy urged upon her by the shop assistants in the vintage shop. There was no way, they told her, that she could team her formal dress with her usual, insipid shade of lipstick.

She untwisted the top and stared down at the deep, dark red. A colour like that would only draw attention to her mouth and Flora had done her best to disguise its width since the day she had bought her first make-up. It had been the first thing she had been teased about— the kids at school had called her the wide-mouthed frog until she'd started to develop. The names after that had been cruder and even less original.

A sigh escaped her. It was just a colour. And nobody here knew her, would think twice about what colour she chose to paint her mouth. That was it, no more thought. She raised the small stick and quickly dabbed it across her lips, blending in the deep, rich colour. Then before she could backtrack and wipe it off again she turned on her heel and walked away from the mirror. No more hiding.

'This one seems to be ours.' Alex reached out and helped Flora into the old-fashioned, wooden sleigh. She climbed up carefully and settled herself onto the padded bench, drawing the fleecy blankets closely round herself, her feet thankful for the hot bricks placed on the floor. 'Four horses? They must have heard about the six cakes you put away during *Kaffee* and *Kuchen*.'

'At least I stuck to single figures,' she countered as

he swung himself in beside her. Very close bedside her. Flora narrowed her eyes as she tried to make out the other sledges, already sliding away into the dark in a trample of hooves and a ringing of bells. Were they all so intimately small?

The driver shook the reins, causing a cascade of bells to ring out jauntily, and the sledge moved forward. She was all too aware of Alex's knee jammed tight against hers, his shoulders, his arm. The smell of him; like trees in spring and freshly cut grass, the scent incongruous in the dark of winter.

'Have you had a good time at the reception?' He was as formal as a blind date. It was the first time they had spoken this evening, the first interaction since she had taken a long deep breath and walked into the buzzing lounge. To her surprised relief the reception had been a lot less terrifying than she had anticipated. It was informal, although waitresses circled with glasses of mulled wine, spiced hot-chocolate rum and small, spicy canapés, and most people were more than happy to introduce themselves. The vibe was very much anticipatory and relaxed—the whole hotel felt very different, felt alive now that it was filled. It was no longer their private domain.

'You know, I actually have.' She turned and smiled at him. 'I had a lovely chat to Holly, she writes travel blogs and articles. Did you know her parents are journalists too? Her mum writes one of those family confessional weekly columns and Holly spent her whole childhood being mercilessly exposed in print as well!'

'That's great. I can see why you're so thrilled for her.'

'Obviously not great for *her*,' Flora conceded. 'But

it was so nice to meet someone who understands just how mortifying it is. Her mum still writes about her— only now it's all about how she wishes she would stop travelling, settle down and pop out grandkids. At least mine hasn't gone there—yet.'

'No, but leave it more than five years and she might do a whole show about women who leave it too late to have babies.' His mouth quirked into a wicked smile.

'If she does I'll get her to do a companion show about aging sperm count and use *you* as her patient,' Flora countered sweetly and was rewarded by an embarrassed cough.

Silence fell, a silence as dark and impenetrable as the night sky. They were both sitting as far apart as possible, almost clinging onto the side rails, but it was no good; every move of the sleigh slid them back along the narrow bench until they were touching again.

It was all too horribly, awkwardly, toe-curlingly romantic. From the sleigh bells tinkling as the proud-necked white horses trotted along the snowy tracks, to the lanterns the hotel had thoughtfully placed along the paths, the whole scenario was just begging for the lucky passengers to snuggle up under the thick blankets and indulge in some romance beneath the breathtakingly starry sky.

Or, alternatively, they could sit as far apart as possible and make the kind of stilted small talk that only two people who very much didn't want to be romantic could make. Remarks like, 'Look, aren't the stars bright?' and, 'The mountains are pretty.' Yep, Flora reflected after she had ventured a sentence about the height of the pine trees that stretched high up the mountainside, they were definitely reaching new depths of inanity.

If things were normal then they would be curled up laughing under the blankets. She would tease him about the women who had been clustered around him at the reception; he would try and cajole her to be a little more open-minded about her first ski lesson. They would probably refresh themselves from a hip flask. Completely at ease. But tonight the memory of that almost-kiss hung over them. It was in the clip clop of the horse's hooves, in the gasp of the sharp, cold mountain air, in the tall ghostly shadows cast by the lantern-lit trees.

'I feel like I should apologise,' she said after a while. 'And I *am* sorry for being drunk and silly, for putting you in a difficult position with Camilla. I am really sorry that you are having to sleep on the narrowest, most uncomfortable sofa I have ever had the misfortune to sit on in my life. And I'm sorry I kissed you.' She swallowed. 'I should have taken the hint when you stopped me all those years ago. But I've wanted to know what we'd be like most of my life. And when you told me I couldn't live in fear of rejection I just had to try, one more time...'

'And?' His voice was husky, as if it hurt him to speak. 'Was it worth it?'

'You tell me.' Flora shifted so she was sitting side on, so that she could see the inscrutable profile silhouetted against the dark night by the lantern light. 'Because I think actually that you wanted to as well. Maybe you have always wanted to. Even back then.'

He didn't answer for a long moment. Flora's heart speeded up with every second of silence until she felt as if it might explode open with a bang.

'You're right. I did. And it was...it was incredible.

But you and me, Flora. It would never work. You know that, right?'

Her heart had soared with the word incredible, only to plummet like an out-of-control ski jumper as he finished speaking.

She wasn't good enough for him. Just as she had always known. 'Because I don't have aspirations?' she whispered. 'Because I mess up?'

'No! It's not you at all.'

The denial only served to irritate her. Did he think she was stupid? 'Come on, Alex. I expected better from you of all people. You don't have to want me, it's okay, but please respect me enough not to fob me off with the whole "It's not you, it's me" line. Do you know how many times I've heard it? And I know *you* trot it out on a regular basis.'

'But this time I mean it. Dammit, Flora. Do you really think I'm good enough for you? That there's anything in my soulless, workaholic, shallow life that could make you happy?'

'I...' Was that really what he thought? 'You do make me happy. You're my best friend.'

'And you're mine and, believe me, Flora, I am more grateful for that than you will ever know. But you've been saving me since you were eight. Now it's my turn to save you. From me. Don't you think I haven't thought about it? How easy it would be? You're beautiful and funny and we fit. We fit so well. But you deserve someone whole. And I haven't been whole for a long, long time.'

How could she answer that? How could she press further when his voice was bleak and the look in his eyes, when the lamp highlighted them, was desolate?

She took in a deep breath, the cold air sharpening her focus, the icy breeze freezing the tears that threatened to fall.

'I break everything I touch, Flora,' Alex said after a while. 'I can't, I won't break you. I won't break us. Because if I didn't have you in my life I wouldn't have anything. And I'm just too selfish to risk that.'

What about me? she wanted to ask. Don't I get a say? But she didn't say anything. Instead she slipped her glove off and reached her hand across until she found his, looping her cold fingers through his, anchoring him tightly. 'I'm not going anywhere,' she whispered, her head on his shoulder, breathing him in. 'I promise, you don't get rid of me that easily.'

He didn't answer but she felt the rigid shoulder relax, just a little, and his fingers clasped hers as if he would never let her go. Maybe this would be enough. It would have to be enough because it was all he was offering her.

CHAPTER SIX

'YOU ARE NOT seriously expecting me to get down there?' Flora pushed up her goggles and glared at the ski instructor.

He shrugged. 'It's the only way down.'

'Yes, but I thought we would stay on the nursery slopes until I could actually ski! This is a proper mountain. With snow on it.'

'Flora, you were too good for those within an hour and you nailed that blue. You are more than ready for this. Come on, it's an easy red. End the day on a high note.'

'Red!' She stared down the icy slope. Easy? It was practically vertical. Her palms dampened at the thought of launching her body down there. She glared at a small group of schoolkids as they enthusiastically pushed off. They were smaller, more compact. Had a lot less further to fall...

A figure skied easily down the higher slopes towards them and pulled up with a stylish turn, which made Flora yearn to push them right over.

'Having trouble?' Alex. Of course. He was annoyingly at home on the slopes. Although, she reflected, he had an unfair disadvantage; after all he'd gone skiing with his school every year since he was eight. After he had left home and put himself through college and then university, his one extravagance was skiing holidays—although a host of rich school friends with their own chalets helped keep the costs down.

'She won't go,' her instructor explained. 'I tell her it's more than doable but she refuses.'

'So how are you planning to get down, Flora? Bottom first?'

She glared at the two of them, hating their identical, idiotic male grins. If only this particular slope had a nice cable car, like the one that had brought them up to the nursery slopes from the hotel. Then she could have just hopped back in and had a return ride. But no, it was a one way trip up in the lift and no way back down apart from on two plastic sticks.

Or she could wait here until spring and walk down in a nice sensible fashion.

The surprising thing was that she *had* been doing okay, that was very true. Surprisingly okay in fact. But not so okay that she wanted to take on such a big run. Not yet.

'The only way to improve is to test yourself,' Alex said, still annoyingly smug. 'And this looks far worse than it is. Really it's just a teeny step up from a blue.'

'Stop throwing colours at me. It's not helping.' The truth was she had barely slept again. An early start and an entire day of concentrating on a new sport had pushed her somewhere beyond tiredness to exhaustion. Muscles she hadn't even known she possessed ached, her feet hurt and all she wanted was a long, hot bath.

But she wouldn't be able to relax even once back in

the room. Because Alex would be there. Their conversation from last night had buzzed around and around and around in her head until she wanted to scream with frustration. It had told her so much—and yet it had told her nothing at all. Why did he think he was broken?

'Look, I'll take it from here,' Alex told her instructor. 'Why don't you get going and you can start again tomorrow? I promise to return her in one piece.'

The instructor regarded her inscrutably from behind his dark lenses. He was tall, tanned and had a lithe grace that at any other time she would have had some pleasure in appreciating but it had been absolutely wasted on her today—she had been far too tired to attempt to flirt back.

'Tomorrow morning,' he said finally. It didn't sound like a request. 'You will be begging to try a black slope by the end of the week.'

'Never,' but she muttered it under her breath, just holding up a hand in farewell as he launched himself down, as graceful as a swallow in flight.

'So, you know another way down?'

Alex shook his head. 'It's on your own two skis only. And we need to hurry up. It's getting late.'

Flora bit her lip. She shouldn't be such a wuss but staring down that great expanse made her stomach fall away in fear. It was the same reaction she'd had when Alex took her abseiling. She and mountains were not a good mixture. From now on she would stick to flat surfaces only. Like beaches; she was good with beaches.

'Okay.' She inhaled but the action didn't soothe her at all, her stomach still twisting and turning. Did people really do this for fun?

'I'll be right next to you,' he said, his voice low and comforting. 'I'll talk you through every turn.'

'Right.'

She pulled her goggles back down. Alex was right. It was just after four p.m. and the sun was beginning to disappear, the sky a gorgeous deep red. The slopes had been getting quieter so gradually she had barely noticed, but now it was obvious as she looked around that they were almost alone. Ahead of her the last few skiers were taking off, leaving the darkening slopes, ready to enjoy the huge variety of après-ski activities Innsbruck had to offer.

'It's a shame I didn't know you were here earlier.' Alex adjusted his own goggles. 'A couple of the hotel lodges are on this shelf. I'd have liked to show them to you.'

'It is a shame you didn't because I am never coming back here again.'

But he just laughed. 'You wait, when you've done it twice you'll wonder what all the fuss was about and be begging me to let you try something harder. Okay, count of three. One…two…three.'

Flora gritted her teeth and pushed off as he said three. The slope had been completely deserted as Alex began his countdown but as he reached the last number a group of snowboarders appeared from the slope above. Impossibly fast, impossibly spread out and impossibly out of control. Flora saw them out of the corner of her eyes and panicked, losing control of her own skis almost immediately as they swarmed by her, one of them catching her pole with his stick and spinning her as he sped by. She shouted out in fear and grappled for her balance, falling heavily, her ankle twisting beneath her.

'Oi!' But by the time Alex had caught her and yelled out a warning they were gone, their whoops and yells dissipating on the breeze. 'Are you okay?'

'I think so.' But Flora couldn't quite stop the little shivers of fear as Alex pulled her up. 'I thought they were going to run me right over.'

'I'll be putting in a complaint as soon as we get back down.' He retrieved her ski and handed it to her. 'Here you go, you're fine. I hate to hurry you, Flora, but it's getting pretty late. I don't want to guide you down in the dark. That *would* send you over the edge.'

'I know...' How long would it take? Her instructor had said that it was a ten-minute run but if Alex was going to talk her through it surely that would add on a few crucial minutes. She looked anxiously at the sky; the red was already turning the purple of twilight. Did they have fifteen minutes?

She put the ski down and slid her foot into the binding, wincing as a spasm of pain ran across her ankle. 'Ow!'

'What's wrong?'

'I must have twisted my ankle as I fell. It's not too bad. I should be able to walk it off...'

'But you can't ski on it.' His mouth tightened. 'Those damned idiots.'

'Can't we ask for help?'

'We could. But I hate to ask the rescue guys to come out in the dark for a twisted ankle—especially as we took so long to get started. We're going to look pretty silly.'

'But we can't stay here all night.' Or did he still

think she was going to make it down while they could still see? Flora swallowed. She was not going to cry.

Alex grinned. 'Panic not. I have a solution. Remember I said the ski lodges were on this shelf? This kind of situation is exactly what they're for. They should be completely kitted out because I know Camilla is hoping that some guests will try them out. It's hard to get permission to build anything up here so they're pretty special. Warm, comfortable and there should be food.'

'You built them for guests who got stranded on the slopes?' Now she thought she really might cry. Salvation! If the lodge only had running hot water then she would never ever complain about anything ever again. Her ankle was beginning to throb in earnest now and, standing still, Flora was all too aware of the chill bite of the wind.

'Really they're for people who want privacy or to spend time with nature. But this is as valid a reason as any. They're about half a mile this way. Can you manage?'

Half a mile? Through the snow? But if it was a choice between that and skiing down then Flora guessed it wasn't much choice at all. She nodded as convincingly as she could. 'Let's do it'

By the time they reached the first cabin the sun had disappeared completely and the twilight was moving rapidly from a hazy lilac grey to the thicker velvety purple that heralded night. Luckily both Flora and Alex had phones with torch apps on, which provided some illumination against the encroaching dark.

'Here we go,' Alex said with more than a hint of relief as they approached the pine grove. 'Good to know my memory hasn't forsaken me.'

The Alpine shelf was much narrower than the wide, buzzing nursery slopes and empty apart from the ski-lift way station. There wasn't even a *gasthaus* to serve up beer, hot chocolate and snacks, which meant that once the ski lifts had stopped running the guests would have total privacy.

'We built them in a pine grove, which means they have the advantage of shade in the much hotter summer months,' Alex explained as he guided her along the path. 'There are two in this grove and two even higher up. It makes them easier to service in pairs. But we've spaced them apart so guests should get the illusion of being all alone. In a fully catered, all-whims-pandered-to way.'

'I like the idea of being pandered to,' Flora said as Alex led her into the trees and down a little path. 'Oh, it's like a fairy tale cottage, hidden amongst the trees like that! A kind of sci-fi fairy tale anyway.'

It was a futuristic design, more of a pod than a traditional lodge with a low curving roof, built to blend into the landscape. 'They're so well insulated,' Alex said as Flora stopped still, trying to take it in fully, 'that they're warm in winter and cool in summer—although there's a stove in there to make it cosier.'

'It's gorgeous.'

It was, however, a little eerie arriving as darkness fell. Flora felt like a trespasser as they stamped their way through the snow to the door, discreetly situated at the side. 'It's as if we are the only two people in the world,' Flora whispered, not waiting to break the absolute silence with the sound of her voice. 'Like there's been some kind of apocalypse and we're all that's standing between the world and the zombies. Or the aliens.'

Alex shone his torch onto the keypad and punched at the buttons. 'Which would you rather?'

'Which would I rather what?'

'Zombies or aliens?'

This was so like their teen conversations that for one moment Flora forgot the cold, the ache in her ankle, the awkwardness of the last few days and was transported back to the roof of her house, accessed reasonably safely—although not with parental permission—from her attic window. She and Alex had spent many a summer night up there, staring up at the stars, discussing the Big Questions. Would you rather be eaten by a tiger or a shark? What would you do if you had twenty-four hours left to live? Were invisible? Could travel anywhere in time?

'Depends on what the aliens want, I suppose,' she said as she watched Alex swing the keypad open and extricate a key.

'If everyone's wiped out it can't be anything good.'

'No, but they might be allergic to something like salt water so we could do a mass extermination. With zombies you have to destroy their brains. That's quite a long process. Unless there were other pockets of survivors around. You?'

'Aliens would be cool. I always think zombies must reek.' He pushed the door open. 'Welcome, my lady.'

The door led into a spacious cloakroom with a flagstone floor. Hooks and shelves awaited, ready to dry out ski clothes or hiking jackets. Flora sank onto the nearest bench with a moan of bliss as she worked her boot off her sore ankle. It was a little swollen but not as bad as she'd feared and when she poked it nervously it didn't hurt too badly. She put her bare foot on the floor and squeaked in surprise. 'It's warm!'

'Underfloor heating. No expense spared here—and it means everything should dry out for tomorrow.' Alex was stripping off without any sense of embarrassment, his padded trousers and jackets neatly hung up, his boots put onto the bench provided, his socks stretched out ready to dry.

Flora's mouth dried. He was still decent—just—in his tight-fitting, thermal trousers and a T-shirt. But they fitted him so well it was almost more indecent than if he had been half naked, highlighting every muscle. Alex was so tall, so rangy he seemed deceptively slight when in a suit but the form-fitting material made it clear he was in perfect shape.

The last thing she wanted to do was parade around in leggings and her T-shirt, the wide straps of her sports bra visible beneath the neckline. But neither could she stay bundled up in her padded clothes any more. The pod was beautifully warm.

She reluctantly pulled down the zip and shrugged off her jacket. Alex had already taken her boots and socks and when he turned back she handed him the jacket as if it were fine, as if she were as comfortable as he seemed to be. But she couldn't help noticing how his eyes fastened onto the generous curve of her chest, made far more prominent by the light, tight material, or how they lingered there.

'I don't suppose there's anything I can change into?'

He looked away, a faint colour on the high cheekbones. 'As a matter of fact I think they are keeping some spare clothes here for guests. I'll...er...go and see.' He backed towards the door that led into the rest of the pod, opened it and backed out, looking anywhere but at her.

What had he been doing? Staring at Flora's chest like, well, as any red-blooded male would. She might and did bemoan her curves but they were pretty magnificent—and, showcased by the tight black stretchy material, had been even more magnificent than usual.

Or was it just that he was more aware of her than he usually was, than he allowed himself to be? Of the way her hair waved around her face, of the sweetness in her eyes, the humour in her mouth?

'Did you find anything yet? Oh, my goodness. Alex, this is sensational!' Flora appeared at the door and looked around the room, her mouth open in admiration. The main room *was* sensational. It was also pretty intimate. He had designed the pod for romance. To allow the guests complete privacy, to make them feel as if they were the only people in the world. The skylights were the only windows, allowing the occupants to look up and see the night sky as they slept, although summer guests could slide open the back wall and enjoy the outside from the wooden terrace attached to the back of the pod if they wished.

A small kitchen area curved around the front wall; just a hob, a microwave, and a sink, the large, well-stocked fridge was back in the drying room. On the opposite side a second door led into the bathroom and a wood-burning stove was cosily tucked into the corner, a love seat, rugs and cushions heaped before it. But the main focus of the pod was the huge bed. It dominated the room; covered in throws and fake furs, it was big

enough to fit several people. Flora's eyes settled on the
bed and she swallowed. 'Very discreet.'

'Let me just look for some clothes and I'll let the
hotel know where we are. They'll need to organise a
cleaning crew to come up tomorrow. I know that Camilla is making sure every couple gets a night up here.
She's hoping these pods will be a big hit with honey-
mooners.'

'Yes.' Flora's gaze was still fixed on the bed. 'I'm
sure they will be.'

Alex ducked out of the room and into the quiet of the
bathroom. Not that it was much better, the huge oval
bath, designed for two, taking up most of the central
space and the walk-in shower dominating the wall opposite. What had he been thinking? If they had set off
down the mountain straight away they could have got
back okay. Now here they were. Together. In a place
designed for seduction. It made their hotel suite seem
positively chaste.

Normally they would have laughed about it—and
goodness knew that bed was big enough for them both
to sleep completely sprawled out and never touch.

But these weren't normal times.

The cupboards, built in around the sinks, held fluffy
towels and, he was glad to see, a selection of warm
clothes. He pulled out one of the hotel-branded track-
suits for himself and looked for something for Flora.
There was another tracksuit, an extra-large that would
swamp her, or a couple of white silky robes. Grabbing
one of the robes, he handed it to her as he walked back
into the main room. 'Why don't you…? There's a bath
or a shower. I'll just get the stove lit and see what's in
the fridge.'

She took the robe with a self-conscious smile of thanks and walked into the bathroom. Alex tried, he really did try, but he couldn't help watch her walk out of the room. The sway of her hips, her deliciously curved backside perfectly displayed in the tight leggings.

He stood there and inhaled. *Get a grip, Fitzgerald,* he told himself.

Ten minutes later the hotel had been contacted, the stove lit and Alex had raided the fridge for supplies. It wasn't hugely promising—unless he was bent on seduction. The fridge held several bottles of champagne, some grapes and cheeses. The freezer was stocked full of hotel-prepared meals ready to pop into the microwave: creamy risottos, rich beef casseroles, chicken in white wine sauce. All of it light and fragrant. He'd have given much for a decent curry or a couple of bloody steaks. Substantial, mates' food, full of carbs and chilli, beer and laughter.

'I'm all done if you want the bathroom...' Flora stood by the bathroom door, her eyes lowered self-consciously. She had washed her hair and it was still damp, already beginning to curl around her face. The robe was a little too big and she had tucked it securely around her and belted it tightly. But no matter how she swathed herself in it, no matter how she tied it, she couldn't hide how the silky material clung to her curves, how the ivory set off the dark of her hair, the cream of her skin, the deep red of her mouth. She looked like a bride on her wedding night. Purity and decadence wrapped in one enticing package.

'If I want...' he echoed. His pulse was racing, the beat so loud it echoed through the room. Twice in the last twenty-four hours he had walked away. Twice he had done the right thing.

He didn't think he could manage it a third time because when it came down to it he was only a man, only flesh and blood, and she was goddess incarnate.

He couldn't move. All he could do was stand and stare. She took a faltering step and then stopped, raising her eyes to meet his. 'Alex?'

'I want *you*.' There it was said. Words he had first thought at sixteen. Words he had never allowed himself to say, words he had made himself bury and forget. 'I want you, Flora.'

Her mouth parted and he couldn't take his eyes off it. Couldn't stop thinking about how it had felt under his, how she had tasted, how they fitted so perfectly he could have kissed her for ever.

'If I say yes...' Her voice was low, a slight tremble in it betraying her nerves. 'If I agree will you back out again? Because I'm not sure I can take another rejection, Alex.'

'I can't make you any promises beyond tonight,' he warned her. Warned himself.

She raised her eyebrows. 'I'm not asking for an eternity ring.'

'This will change everything.'

She nodded slowly. 'I think everything has already changed. We opened Pandora's box and now it's out there.'

He held her gaze. 'What is?'

'Knowledge.'

That was it. That was it exactly. Because now he knew. Knew how she felt, how she tasted, how she kissed, how her hands felt when they slid with intent.

He knew the beginning; he had no idea how it ended. And oh, how he wanted to know.

And now that they had started they couldn't just pretend. Maybe this was what they needed, one night. One night to really know each other in every way possible. What was it Flora had said just two nights ago? That they should have done this in their teenage years?

He begged to disagree. He knew a lot more now than he did then. No less eager, a lot more patient.

She still hadn't moved although her hands were twisting nervously and her eyelashes fluttered shut under the intensity of his gaze, shielding her expressive eyes as he watched her. 'You're so beautiful, Flora.'

Her eyes opened again, wide with surprise. 'Me? No, I'm too…' She gestured wildly. 'I'm too everything.'

'No, you're perfect.' He took a step nearer, his eyes trained on her, the small room narrowing until he could see nothing else, just damp, dark curls, ivory silk and long lashes over velvet dark eyes. Another step and another until he was standing right there. Within touching distance. 'Like a snow princess, hair as black as night…' He twisted a silky curl around his finger and heard her gasp. Just a little. 'Skin as white as snow.' He brushed her cheek lightly. 'Lips as red as rubies.' His finger trailed down her cheek and along the wide curve of her mouth.

She stared at him for one second more, her breath coming quick, fast and shallow, and he could hold back no longer. He held her gaze deliberately as his hands moved caressingly down her shoulders, her arms until he reached her waist. He held them there for one moment, the heat of her flesh burning through the cool silk and then, in one quick gesture, he pulled at the knot holding her robe together. The belt fell away and as it did so the delicate ivory silk slithered back off first one white shoulder and then the other.

Flora reached out automatically to pull it back and he put out a hand to stop her.

'No, let it go.'

Her face flushed a fierce rose but she stood still in response to his words and allowed the robe to fall away, allowed herself to be unveiled to the heat of his gaze. She stood like the goddess she was named for, fresh as the spring.

Alex sucked in a breath, his stomach, his chest tightening as he saw her, really saw her. She was all softness and curves, all hidden dips and valleys, ready for an explorer's touch. He reached out reverently, to follow the curve of one breast. 'Let me worship you, Flora.'

She nodded. Just the once but it was all he needed as he took her hand and led her over to the bed. They had all night. He hoped it would be enough.

CHAPTER SEVEN

'I AM ABSOLUTELY STARVING.' Flora sat up, wrapping the sheet around her breasts as she did so. How could Alex parade around stark naked so unconsciously? It must be that public-school upbringing.

Not that she was complaining. Her eyes travelled across his finely sculpted shoulders, down the firm chest, the flat stomach and, as he turned, dwelled appreciatively on a pair of buttocks Michelangelo would have been proud to carve. No, she wasn't complaining at all.

'It's all that exercise,' he said as he disappeared through the cloakroom door, reappearing with a bottle of champagne, so chilled she could see the frost beginning to melt on the bottle.

'Mmm, the skiing was hard work,' she replied as demurely as she could and laughed at the affronted look he gave her.

'Minx,' he muttered. 'It'll serve you right if I let you go hungry.'

'Did I say skiing? Slip of the tongue. Oh, thank you...' She took the glass handed her and sipped it appreciatively. 'This is delicious.'

Don't be too happy, she warned herself. *Don't be too comfortable. This isn't real.* But it was hard not to be. It just felt so…so right. She should be embarrassed. This was Alex. Her oldest and bestest friend. They had just done things that definitely went against any friendship code but it wasn't awkward. It was horribly perfect.

He touched her as if he knew her intimately, as if he knew instinctively just what she wanted, what she needed, and she had wanted to touch every inch of him, nibble her way across every square inch of skin. No inhibitions—just want and need and giving and taking and gasping and moaning until she hadn't known where he stopped and she started.

Flora took another hurried sip of the champagne as her body tingled with remembered pleasure.

And now she could sit there, her hair tumbling down, her lips swollen and tender, muscles aching in ways that she was pretty sure had nothing to do with her earlier exertions on the slopes, clad only in a sheet and, although she might not feel confident enough to wander around in the buff, she was comfortable. Usually she jumped straight back into her clothes after lovemaking but with Alex she didn't feel too tall or too curvy. He'd made her feel fragile, desirable.

'Look how tiny your waist is,' he'd breathed as his hands had roamed knowledgeably across her body. 'Perfect,' he'd whispered as he'd kissed his way down her stomach. And that was how she'd felt. Perfect.

He sat down on the edge of the bed with that lithe casual grace she envied so much. 'I could heat up one of the frozen meals or, if you don't want to wait, there's cheese, biscuits and grapes?'

'Oh, cheese, please. That sounds perfect. Are you sure you don't want me to help?'

His eyes flashed with wicked intent. 'Nope, I don't want you to get out of that bed. Ever.'

'Sounds good to me.' How she wished this could *be* for ever, this perfect moment. The fire blazing in the stove, the stars bright in the skylights, she blissfully sated, lying in bed sipping champagne watching her man prepare dinner.

But he wasn't her man. And she needed to remember that.

'Alex, are you awake?' They had dozed off some time after midnight, blissed out after an evening of champagne and lovemaking. Flora had no idea what time it was now; the cabin was completely dark except for a faint reddish-gold glow from the stove.

Alex rolled over, throwing his arm across her as he did so, and she lay there, enjoying his weight on her, the skin against skin, the smell of him. 'Mmm?'

'Nothing,' she said. 'Go back to sleep.'

'Are you okay?'

'Yes, more than okay.' But she wasn't. The reality of what they had done was bearing down upon her. 'Are we?'

'Are we what?'

'Okay?'

He moved, propping himself up on one arm so that he could look down at her, a dark shadow in the dim room. 'Second thoughts, Flora?'

'No. I mean, it's a little late for that.'

He smoothed her hair back from her face, a tender gesture that made her chest ache and her eyes swell. 'Good. I don't know what tomorrow will bring, but right now I don't want to change a thing. Except wonder why we didn't do this a long time ago.' His hand trailed a long, languorous line down her face, down her throat, down and down. It would be so easy to let it continue its slow tortuous journey.

But his words reminded her of her vow. Her vow to try and help him. To make things right, somehow. She caught his wrist as it moved to her ribcage and held it. 'What happened, Alex?'

He laughed low and soft. 'Do you need me to explain it to you?'

She couldn't help smiling in response but she clasped his wrist, her fingers stroking the tender skin on the inside. 'Not tonight. Then.'

He froze. 'Don't, Flora.'

But she knew. If she didn't ask him now he would never tell her. After all he had kept his secrets through the long, boozy university years, through long walks and bonfire heart-to-hearts. Through backpacking and narrow boats and noisy festivals. But tonight was different. Tonight there were no rules.

'You came home from school,' she remembered. 'I had finished my GCSEs and you had done your AS Levels. I thought we would have another long summer together. But you were different. Quieter, more intense. More buttoned up. I had the most ginormous crush on you, which I tried to hide, of course. But that summer there were times when you looked at me as if...' Her voice trailed off.

'As if I felt the same way?' he said softly.

'We would be somewhere, just the two of us. On the roof talking, or lying on the grass, and I would look at you and it was as if time would stop.' Their eyes would meet, her stomach would tighten in delicious anticipation and she would find it hard to get her breath. 'And then nothing…' She sighed. 'I tried to kiss *you* that time. When we were watching that ridiculous horror film where all the teenagers died. I thought you would kiss me back but you didn't. You looked so revolted…' Her voice trailed away as she relived the utter humiliation, the heartbreak all over again.

He pulled his hand away from her gentle grasp, pushing the hair out of his eyes. 'Sometimes I wonder what would have happened if we had got together then. Do you think we'd be the friends we are now, our past relationship something to look back on nostalgically? Or maybe we would have ended badly and not speak at all. Or maybe we would have made it. Do you think that likely? How many people get together in their teens and make it all the way through college and university?'

'Not many,' she conceded. But *they* might have. If he'd wanted it.

'You changed that year.' He was still propped up on one arm, still looking down at her. She could smell the champagne on his breath, feel each rustle as he moved. 'Boys watched you all the time—and I watched them watching you. But you didn't even notice. I nearly made a move that New Year but I was away at school and we both had exams. So I told myself to wait. Wait till the summer.'

'What changed?' She hadn't imagined it; he had felt it too.

'My dad blamed me for my mother's death.' He said it so matter-of-factly that she could only lie there, blinking at the sudden change in conversation. 'Did I ever tell you that?'

'No.' She moved away, just far enough to allow her to sit up, hugging her knees to her chest as she tried to make out his expression in the dim light from the fire. 'I don't understand. How? I mean, it was suicide, wasn't it? Awful and tragic but nobody's fault.'

'He didn't want children. All he wanted was her, just her. You know my father. He's not the caring, sharing type. But she wanted a baby so much he gave in. He said it was the biggest mistake he ever made. That I was the biggest mistake… He was never really explicit but I think she suffered from fairly severe postnatal depression.'

A stab of sorrow ran her straight through as she pictured the lonely motherless little boy alone with an indifferent father. Allowed to grow up believing he was the cause of his mother's death. 'Oh, Alex. I'm so sorry.'

He shifted, sitting up beside her on the bed, leaning back against the pillows. 'She hid it from him, from the doctors, from everyone. Until I was two. Then she just gave up. She left a note, saying what a terrible mother she was. That she couldn't love me the way she was supposed to. That I would be better off without her…'

Flora touched his face. 'That doesn't make it your fault. You know that, right?'

'My father thought so.' His voice was bleak. 'That's when he began to work all hours, leaving me with a series of nannies, packing me off to boarding school as soon as he could. He told me it was a shame he had to wait until I was eight, that he would have sent me at five if he could have.'

Flora hadn't thought it was possible to think any worse of Alex's father. She had been spectacularly wrong. 'He's a vicious, nasty man. No wonder you came to live with us.'

He carried on as if she hadn't interrupted. 'He married again. I didn't really see much of him then, or of that particular stepmother, but apparently she wanted kids, wanted me around more and so the marriage broke up. He blamed me for that as well. I guess it was easier than blaming himself. And then that year, when I was seventeen, he remarried again.'

'Christa.' Oh, Flora remembered Alex's second stepmother with her habit of flirting with every male within a five-mile radius. She had made Flora, already self-conscious, feel so gauche, so huge like an over-sized giant. 'Horry had a real crush on her. Do you remember how she used to parade around in those teeny bikinis when we came over to swim?' She laughed but he didn't join in and her laughter trailed off awkwardly.

'It was so nice at first to have someone care. Someone to bring me drinks, and praise me and take notice, as if I were part of a real family. It didn't even occur to me that other people's mums didn't ask their teenaged sons to rub suntan oil onto their bare back or sunbathe topless in front of them.'

Flora's stomach churned and she pressed her hand to her mouth. 'Alex...'

'She started to drop by my room for a chat when I was in bed. She'd stroke my hair and rub my shoulders.' His voice cracked. 'I was this big hormonal wreck. This woman, this beautiful, desirable woman, was touching me and I wanted her. I wanted her to keep touching me. But at the same time she revolted me, she was married to my *father*. And there was you...'

'Me?' Flora didn't know at which point her eyes had filled with tears, hadn't felt them roll down her face, it wasn't until her voice broke on a sob that she realised she was crying. Crying for the little boy abandoned by his father, for the boy on the brink of adulthood betrayed by those he trusted to look after him.

'I was falling in love with you that summer. But how could I touch you when at night…when I didn't turn her away…when I lay there waiting and didn't say no.'

'You were a child!'

'I was seventeen,' he corrected her. 'I knew what I was doing. I knew it was wrong—on every level. But I didn't stop her. I let her in my room, I let her into my bed and in the end I didn't just lie there…'

Flora swallowed, clutching her stomach, nausea rolling through her. That woman with her tinkling laugh and soft voice and Alex? And yet it all made a hideous kind of sense. How withdrawn he had become, the way he would look at her as if something was tearing him apart but Flora couldn't reach him. The knowing smile Christa would wear, the possessive way she'd clasp his shoulders. How had she been so blind?

She made an effort to sound calm, to let him finally relieve himself of the burden he'd been carrying. 'What happened next?'

'By the end of the summer she had stopped being cautious. I didn't want… It was one thing at night, with the lights out—that was more like a dream, you know? As if it wasn't real. I would be back at school soon and the whole thing would just disappear. But Christa didn't want that. She started to try and kiss me in the house, run her hand over my shoulder in front of people. She wanted to make love in the pool, in the kitchen. The more I tried to pull away, the more determined she became. I was just a pet, her toy. She didn't want me to have any say in where or when or what. She was in control. And she was out of control. It was inevitable, I guess, that we'd be found out. My dad came home early one day and caught us.'

'He blamed you.' It wasn't a question. She'd seen the aftermath. Alex, white-faced, all his worldly possessions in one bag, determined to make his own way in the world.

'He told me I tainted everything I touched.'

'That's not true,' but he was shaking his head even as she protested.

'My mother died because she couldn't love me. My father hates me. My stepmother…there's something rotten at the heart of me, Flora.'

'No. No, there isn't.' She was on her knees and holding onto him. 'I love you, my parents adore you, for goodness' sake even Minerva loves you, in her own way. There *is* a darkness in your family but it's not you. It was never you.'

But she wasn't getting through; his voice was bleak, his face as blank as if it were carved out of marble. 'I saw you look at me, back then, so hopeful. As if you were expecting something more. But I had nothing to give. Christa took it all, like some succubus, taking another piece of my soul every time we had sex. All those girls at the ice rink, and the girls I date now. I felt nothing. I am incapable of feeling anything real. That's why I warned you to steer clear of me, Flora. There's nothing real inside me.'

She kissed him, his eyes, his cheeks, the strong line of his jaw, tasting the salt of her tears mingled with the salt on his skin. 'You are real,' she whispered as she pressed her mouth to his cold lips. 'I know you are.'

He didn't respond for a long moment and then, with an anguished cry, he kissed her back; hard, feverish kisses as if he were drowning and she the air. Flora held on and let him hold on in return. She didn't know who was saving who. And she wasn't sure that it mattered.

Alex knew the exact moment Flora woke up. She didn't move, didn't speak, but he knew. He had kept watch over her through the night. A lone knight guarding his lady. Her breathing, so slow and steady, quickened. Her body tensed. Was she wondering what would happen in the harsh light of day? What reality would mean after the passions, the confidences, the outpourings of the night before.

He wondered that too. He knew what had to be done but how he wished things were different. That he were different. 'Lukewarm left-over champagne or coffee?'

'Hmm?' She sat up unsteadily, brushing the long tangled curls from her face and scrubbing her eyes like a small girl, her eyes widening as she looked at him. Was she surprised that he was out of bed? That he was already dressed in jogging bottoms and his own top, showered, shaved and ready to go? 'You're not serious about the champagne?'

'It seems a shame to throw it away,' he teased, deliberately keeping his tone light. 'No. If it was chilled then that would be a whole different matter. There's eggs. We could make breakfast or would you rather have some back at the hotel? There's time. I texted your instructor to arrange a later meeting time.'

'A later time?' She sank back down onto her pillows dramatically. 'I was planning to spend all day in the spa today. I have barely slept…' She stopped, her cheeks pinkening in an interesting way. He wondered just how far down her blush crept—and then pulled his mind resolutely back to the matter at hand.

'Don't forget you have to get down the mountain first,' Alex said helpfully and was rewarded with a glare.

'Can't we just stay here for ever?' There was a plaintive note in her voice. He knew with utter certainty that it wasn't just the skiing she was thinking about. It was the aftermath. Of course she was.

His chest squeezed in sudden longing. *Stay here for ever.* Just Flora and Alex and a large bed and a supply of champagne. No facing the real world, no dealing with any situation. He inhaled long and deep, pushing the enticing vision away. 'What would we do when the food ran out? Hunt squirrels and roast them on the stove?'

'Not much meat on a squirrel.'

'Then we'd better return to real life. Sorry, Flora.'

She put out her hand. Part of him wanted to pretend he hadn't seen it, the other part was drawn to her, could no more walk away than he could stop breathing. He paced himself as he walked towards the bed, slow, unhurried steps, seating himself on the edge, deliberately not touching her.

'So, we pretend this hasn't happened.' She made it sound like a statement but he knew she needed an answer. Was she hoping he'd change his mind?

'That's best, isn't it? No need to complicate things further.' All he had to do was reach across, across just a few centimetres of rumpled white sheet. But it might as well have been metres, miles, oceans. Would she see a casual touch as encouragement? As a declaration?

Would he mean it as such?

He couldn't. He mustn't. If he allowed the slight torch she had always carried for him to blaze into brightness then all would be lost. He didn't know which would be worse—if it flickered and died when she discovered how hollow he really was for herself. Or if it continued to flame until he did something stupid, something unconscionable and broke her heart.

And he would.

His father's voice echoed through his mind. Mocking him. *You taint everything you touch. Nobody could care for you. You disgust me.*

He couldn't cope if he lost Flora.

She touched his arm, a small caress. 'What are you thinking?' Ah, the million-dollar question and one he had always hated. He never got the answer right.

But he was compelled to tell the truth. 'I don't want you to hate me.'

She rounded on him, eyes blazing. 'I could never hate you. Why? Because of last night? You were very clear it was a one-night deal and I understood that. Don't make this into some kind of melodrama. It was just sex.'

But her eyes fluttered as she said the words and she couldn't look him in the eye.

'Good sex,' she amended. 'But, you know, I'm not planning to join a nunnery because there won't be a repeat.'

Alex didn't feel quite as comforted by her words as he should have done. This was the result he wanted, wasn't it? There was a little part of him that had always wondered *what if* about Flora Buckingham and, sure, he had pointed out last night that a teen grand affair was bound to crash and burn, but still. He had wondered.

Now he knew. And even better she had no expectations beyond a cup of coffee and that he guide her safely to the bottom of the ski slope. By the time they got back to her parents' they would be their old selves. Only better. No more moments when he would look up and see a hopeful yearning in her face, no more watching her covertly as she walked across a room.

They had scratched that itch and it was satisfied. Let Flora move on to someone who deserved her. As for him? Well, maybe he would date a little less widely, date a little more wisely.

The thought made his chest feel as hollow as his heart.

Flora scrambled to her knees, the sheet held high against her chest, a thin barrier of cotton yet as effective as a cast-iron chastity belt. *You have no rights here.* 'We just need to get through the rest of this week. What do you want to do, tell Camilla that we quarrelled and get your room back? I mean…' as he raised an eyebrow at her '…you don't want to spend the next three nights on that sofa, do you? Unless…'

'Unless?' His pulse began to pound at the spark in her eye.

'We *are* meant to be dating, after all.'

'Flora…'

'Same rules,' she said hurriedly. 'No expectations, no protestations. What happens in Innsbruck stays in Innsbruck but, seriously. You can't stay on the sofa.

We don't want to make Camilla suspicious. As long as we're both clear about the rules, what's the harm?'

'We get back on Christmas Eve,' he reminded her. 'Straight to your parents'. Won't they guess?'

'How? We promised not to let anything change our friendship and it'll be finished by then. Finished the moment we get into the taxi to drive to the airport. Maybe you were right, we would have had a mad teen thing, all drama and lust, and it would have been glorious—and it might have ruined us for ever. But we're older now, we're far more sensible. It doesn't have to ruin anything. But I reckon we're owed just a few days of crazy fun. We owe it to our younger selves.'

It was a convincing argument—if he didn't examine it too closely. 'I suppose we do at some point. Guess it's either now or when we're in the nursing home.'

'We might be married to other people when we're in the nursing home,' she pointed out. 'Plus right now I'm still reasonably pert and have all my own teeth. You might not be so keen when we're finally retired.'

His mouth dried. Did she know what she was offering? The rest of the week as a no-strings, full-fun affair. He didn't deserve it; he didn't deserve her. But he wasn't strong enough to turn her down.

You've always been weak. He thrust the insidious thought aside. They were supposed to be dating, they were sharing a room and they had just spent the night very much together.

'May as well be hung for a sheep as a lamb.'

Her mouth curved into an irresistible smile. 'You do say the most romantic things. I can see why the girls love you. What's the very latest we have to be out of here?'

'We have about an hour if you want to eat, shower and change before your hot date with your dashing instructor. Why?'

'Well…' she let the sheet fall, just a little, not nearly enough '… I thought we might seal our deal with a kiss.'

CHAPTER EIGHT

'CAMILLA SEEMED IMPRESSED with your ideas.'

Flora put her hairbrush down and turned to look at Alex, admiring the lithe grace as he sprawled on the bed, completely at his ease as he looked through her sketchbook. 'It was like being summoned for an audience with the queen,' she said, her palms damp at just the memory. 'It's a good thing she can't actually raise those eyebrows of hers, she made me feel about six as it was.'

'That's just her way. I don't think she meant to question you quite so closely—she knew you would have no real idea of cost at this stage. We're still at the initial concepts.'

'How can I even think about putting costs in when she hasn't even decided which of your ideas she wants? Plus I have no idea of what I can actually source there—or what her actual budget is.' At least when she had worked in-house she hadn't had to worry about any of this part. She had been given a task, she'd completed it, easy—even if it had been dull and monotonous and about as creative as granola.

He turned another page, nodding as he looked at her carefully drawn plans. 'Relax. No one expects you to know any of this yet. Once Camilla gives us the go-ahead we can do a reconnaissance trip out there. We'll need to talk about money as well. The interior design is all subcontracted through my firm. Lola charged for each project as a whole but I could take you on as a contracted member of staff if that makes things easier.'

Flora froze. It would make things a *lot* easier. She had no idea about how much to charge if she free-lanced, nor how often she could invoice, when she would get paid—or how she'd live until she did. But working with Alex? Travelling to Bali with him? It wasn't going to be the kind of cold turkey she thought she might need…

Because four nights in and she was already getting a little addicted to his touch. To the way his eyes seemed to caress her. To the way his hands most definitely did. To his mouth and the long, lean lines of his body.

She was in way over her head, barely graduated off the nursery slopes and yet heading full tilt down a black run and she didn't even care. 'Do we have to go on this evening's jaunt?' She allowed her eyes to travel suggestively over his body. 'I've seen the Christmas markets.'

'Not at night, you haven't, and yes, you do. Three-line whip. But we don't have to hang around in the bar after we get back if you would rather get some rest.' He smiled like the big bad wolf eyeing up Red Riding Hood.

'I do need a lot of rest,' she agreed solemnly. 'All this mountain air is exhausting me. I may also need a really long hot bath.'

'I was thinking about a bath too,' he said softly and she shivered at the intent look in his eyes as he slowly

glanced from the large tub to her. 'I do feel particularly dirty this evening.'

A jolt of pure lust shot through her and Flora gripped
the top of the dressing table, her knuckles white. What
was she doing? How on earth could they ever return
to their old, easy camaraderie after this? How would
she manage when his hand was no longer hers to hold,
when she couldn't run her fingers over the soft skin
on the inside of his wrists, when she couldn't kiss her
way along the planes of his face and down his neck?

She had dreamt of this for so long that it all felt completely right, completely fitting. Stepping back again?
That was going to hurt. But she had promised him that
it would all be fine, that she would be fine, they would
be fine and she couldn't let him down. She would just
have to keep smiling and pretend her heart wasn't shattering into millions of little pieces.

'Okay.' She turned back to the mirror and outlined
her mouth with the deep red lipstick. She'd almost got
used to the striking colour over the last few days. It sent
out a statement of confidence that she might not feel
but that she could fake. She caught up a silk scarf, a
midnight blue patterned with abstract snowflakes, and
knotted it around her neck, the accessory adding some
much-needed style to the cream jumper and blue velvet
skinny jeans she'd chosen for their warmth. 'I'm ready.'

Alex caught her hand as they left the hotel room,
an easy gesture. She fought to keep her hand loosely
clasped in his, not to curl her fingers tightly around
and hold on, never letting him go.

'You can help me choose Christmas presents,' he
said as they made their way along the wide corridor to

the stairs. 'I haven't managed to buy any yet. I expect yours were all done and dusted by September.'

'This year's fabric was designed and printed by then,' she agreed. Twice a year Flora got several of her designs printed up into silks and cottons, which she then used to make the cushions and scarves she sold online. She also combined her own designs with vintage fabrics to create quilts, which she made to order. 'I've made both Mum and Minerva clutch bags. I hope they like them. I don't think Minerva has ever worn last year's skirt.'

'Strawberries and cream isn't particularly Minerva,' he pointed out. 'But it was a beautiful design. I'm sure she really appreciates it. Apron for your dad?'

'Of course.' Every year she made her father a new apron and a selection of tea towels and he always made sure they were prominently displayed in every tutorial and photoshoot. 'I've bought dolls for the twins and made them entire wardrobes.' She had also made shirts for Horry, Greg her brother-in-law and Alex in the same pattern as the scarf she was wearing this evening. Flora always made her presents; she suspected Minerva at least would rather she stuck to scented candles and bath salts but Flora loved to create things, especially for the people she cared about.

'As we're in Austria I'm thinking glass all round, animals for the littlies, crystal glasses and bowls for the adults. Too obvious?'

'No, they'll love them. It's unfair how you always manage to pull the perfect present out of the bag last minute when some of us plan all year round.' She squeezed his hand in mock protest and he grinned.

'Not unfair, it's because I have good taste.'

And money to spare, she wanted to retort—but she didn't. After all, he'd always managed to find the right thing, even when he was at college and working three jobs in order to pay his way, refusing to allow the Buckinghams to house and feed him rent free. This man who didn't think he was worth loving.

'I was thinking,' she said hesitantly. They hadn't discussed anything personal since the night at the ski lodge, a tacit agreement to keep the week as carefree as they could.

'Careful…'

She elbowed him. 'Ha-ha. Don't you have any grandparents? Uncles, aunts?'

'Trying to get rid of me, Flora?'

'Never. It just seems odd, that's all. There must be someone.'

But he was shaking his head. 'As far as I know my father's parents died before I was born and he was an only child—not that he'd tell me if there were a hundred relatives out there, I suppose. As for my mother, I did see my grandmother when I was much younger but she gave up. Either my father frightened her off or I…'

Flora squeezed his hand. 'Don't even go there with the "or I". If she disappeared I would bet all my Christmas presents your father was behind it. You should try and track her down. She might have some answers.'

'Maybe.' But he didn't sound convinced and she didn't want to push any further.

Flora was surprised by how at ease she felt as they approached the hotel lounge. It was busy; the guests buzzing as they discussed their impending visit to Innsbruck's famous Christmas markets, sampling the food and drink on offer and purchasing some last-minute gifts. Normally she'd find such a noisy and full room intimidating, hang behind Alex as he strode confidently in, let him be the one to mingle, she following where he led. But over the last couple of days she had struck up a few acquaintances and greeted her new friends with pleasure when Alex disappeared over to the other side of the room to charm an influential broadsheet journalist who was considering a magazine feature on Alex's work.

'I hear you skied down several red runs today,' Holly, the travel journalist Flora had met on the first evening, teased her. Flora was the only learner in the entire hotel and many people were watching her progress with encouragement and interest. 'We'll have you out on the blacks before we leave.'

'Not this trip.' Flora shook her head emphatically. 'But, I have to say—and I am amazed I am about to admit this—I think I'll come back and ski again. It has been sort of fun. Although I still prefer the hot-chocolate, hot-tub part of the proceedings most!'

'If I was sharing a hot tub with your boyfriend I think that would be my favourite part of the evening too.' Holly looked over at Alex, a wistful expression on her face. He was casually dressed: jeans, a dark green cashmere jumper, hair characteristically tousled. There were more obviously handsome men in the room, more famous men—richer men—but somehow he stood out.

Or maybe it was just that Flora instinctively knew where he was at every moment. Her north star.

Flora stood back to let one of the other women pass by. Although she recognised her they hadn't spoken during the week; the celebrity guests, mostly socialites and gossip-magazine staples, tended to keep to their own tanned, designer-clad selves and only a few people like Alex passed from one group to the other with no hint of unease. Bella Summers was gossip-magazine gold—an ex-model, TV presenter and extremely keen skier, she had been invited to bring the launch week a sprinkle of glamour and help create a buzz around the hotel.

'Oh, my goodness.' To Flora's amazement Bella stopped dead in front of her, staring at her neck in undisguised envy. 'Your scarf! Isn't that the same one Lexy Chapman is wearing in this week's *Desired*?' Her eyes flickered to Flora's face, curiosity mingling with undisguised surprise. 'Where on earth did you get it?'

'This scarf.' Flora touched it self-consciously. 'No, it can't be the same. It must be a coincidence.'

'It is exactly the same. That abstract snowflake print is unmistakeable,' Bella Summers insisted. 'Mitzy, come here. Isn't this the same scarf Lexy wore on her date with Aaron? The one in *Desired*?'

Another tall, skinny, elegant girl loped across to join them. The two of them stood there gazing at Flora's neck like a couple of fashion-hungry vampires. 'Yes, that's the one,' she said. 'Hang on. I think I left the magazine on the shelves over there. It only came out yesterday. Luckily a shop in Innsbruck stocks it.'

It can't be the same. It's just a coincidence, Flora told herself. It was always happening, designers inspired by the same things coming up with similar designs. Or of course work got plagiarised; small solo outfits like hers were particularly vulnerable.

Unfortunately it was a much more likely scenario than the other—It girls and style icons just didn't buy from small solo nobodies like her. She didn't even have a brand name or a website of her own, using an Internet marketplace to sell the handful of items she produced each year.

'Yes, I knew it.' Mitzy and Bella came back waving the latest copy of *Desired* triumphantly. 'Here you go. Flora, isn't it? Look.'

Flora took the glossy magazine from them. *Desired* was an upmarket weekly combining fashion, gossip and lifestyle in easily digestible sound bites and pictures. It was already open at the page they wanted, the street-style section. Photos of fashion-forward celebrities out and about, their outfits and accessories critiqued. Girls like Lexy Chapman were staples on this page—as were girls like Bella and Mitzy, although neither had the cool kudos of Lexy Chapman.

Normal people didn't have a hope of appearing on the hallowed pages, no matter how stylishly they dressed. And Flora was too awkward for style.

But maybe, just maybe she had some influence after all.

She sucked in a deep breath as her eyes skimmed over the photo. Lexy Chapman was casually dressed for her date with her on-off rock-star boyfriend in tight-fitting skinny jeans and a cream, severely cut silk shirt visible underneath an oversized navy military coat. The starkness of the outfit was softened by the scarf, tied around her slender neck with a chicness Flora could only envy.

She skimmed the brief wording, her heart thumping.

How does she do it? Once again Lexy Chapman strips back this season's must-have styles

*to their bare essentials combining masculine tai-
loring with military chic.*

*A clever touch is the snowflake motif scarf,
which adds a feminine twist and is a clever nod
to the season.*

The article was followed by a list of the clothes
and accessories, with price, designer and website. Sure
enough, right at the bottom…

Scarf, Flora B, £45

It was followed by her website address.

'Hang on.' Mitzy snatched the magazine back off
Flora and read the article again. 'Flora B? Is that you?
Oh, my goodness, you have to let me have one of your
scarves. What other designs do you have? Do you have
any on you?'

'I…' Flora tried to think. What did she have in stock
and ready made up? 'Sure. When we get back from
Innsbruck I'll show you my web shop. I only make
up a couple of patterns a year so it does depend on
what's left.'

'Exclusive.' Mitzy nodded in satisfaction. 'Good.'

'If you could just excuse me…' Flora tore her eyes
away from the page, her head giddy. What if the photo
had generated more interest? She hadn't checked her
orders since she had arrived in Austria. It wasn't as
if they usually came flooding in—more than three a
week would be a rush—and she had designated the
Friday of last week the last day she could guarantee
Christmas delivery. 'I just need to check on something.'

Flora was glad to escape from the noisy room. The

mood had changed as the news flew through the room. People—especially the celebrity clique—were looking at her differently, actually seeing her. Or seeing her value to them. One scarf in one picture. Was that all it took to go from zero to person of interest?

With this lot it appeared so.

She hurried upstairs, back to their recently vacated suite. It looked different, smelt different with Alex's belongings casually strewn around. His laptop was set up on the desk in the corner, a pair of his shoes left by the door. His book on the side table—not that he'd been doing much reading. Or work. Neither of them had. She liked it. Liked the casual mingling of their belongings.

Flora's phone was in a drawer along with her charger. She hadn't wanted it on, hadn't wanted to be in contact with the outside world, to be reminded that this short idyll was temporary. She switched it on, her mind whirling while it powered up. Would this mean a run on her small amount of stock? If so would it be worth investing in more fabric? How would she fund it? How could she make and store decent amounts of stock in her small rented room? What if she did invest and demand dried up?

She shook her head. Talk about counting chickens! She might find that Mitzy and Bella were the only people who had even noticed the scarf—and only because she was wearing it.

Her phone sprang into life, pinging with a notification—and another and another like a much less musical one-note version of the sleigh bells. Social-media notifications, emails, voicemails. Flora stared at her buzzing screen and felt her head spin. She had only started the social-media accounts for her business to stop her sister, Minerva, nagging her but rarely used them. She didn't know what to say to her tiny handful of followers.

'Flora?' The door had opened while she watched the notifications multiply. 'We're heading off.' Alex paused, waiting for her to answer but she couldn't find the words. 'What is it?'

She handed him the phone and Alex stared at it incredulously.

'What? Have you just won a popularity contest?'

'I don't know. I think it's about a scarf but I don't know where to start.'

'A scarf? Is this the same scarf that has half the women downstairs frothing at the mouth?'

She nodded, the surrealism of the situation disorientating her. 'Either that or I've won the lottery, been photographed kissing a boyband member or I am a long-lost princess. There are over fifty voicemail messages and I don't know how many emails.'

The phone beeped again. 'More than fifty...' he peered at the phone '...although it looks as if at least half are from Minerva. Hold on.' He put the phone back down a little gingerly, as if it were an unexploded bomb. 'I am going to make our apologies to Camilla and I'll help you sort this out.'

'Your glass animals...'

'Can wait. I'll pop down tomorrow before the Christmas Ball. Wait here. Don't touch anything.'

Flora sank onto the sofa, almost too distracted to notice just how uncomfortable it was. Her phone beeped a few more times and then it was mercifully silent. She unlooped the scarf from around her neck and passed it from one hand to the other, the silk cool under her fingertips. A midnight-blue silk with her snowflake design on it. She had only printed one roll of fabric. It was destined for the central square and edging for a handful of quilts, as the cuff lining on the shirts she had made Alex, Greg and Horatio, the lining of a few bags, some cushions and twenty or thirty scarves.

Her fabric design and sewing were a hobby that barely paid for itself. It took up time she should be spending trying to get her talents noticed so she could work in-house again or at least pick up some freelance contracts in her own field and leave the world of temping far behind.

She didn't do it for money or fame. The truth was it just made her happy.

Just…

'Right.' Alex appeared back, the magazine in his hands and open at the fateful page. 'It looks like this *is* the cause of all the fuss. I've just been asked by at least ten people if I can get them one of these scarves and they are all prepared to pay a great deal more than forty-five pounds.' His brow wrinkled as he looked at the photo. 'Who is this woman?'

'You know who she is. That's Lexy Chapman.'

He looked blank. 'Nope. What does she do?'

That was a good question. What did she do apart from look cool and date famous people? 'Right now she's making my scarves sought after.'

He took the scarf from her loose grasp and held it up to the light, turning it this way and that. 'I didn't know you sold them. I just thought it was a hobby.'

'It is a hobby.' She turned away from his scrutiny, jumping to her feet and retrieving her phone from the side. 'I have a little online shop, to help fund my projects, that's all.'

'Is it?' But he didn't probe any further. 'Okay, this is how we're going to play it. You listen to your voicemails and make a note of all the names, messages and numbers and we'll see who you need to call back and when. I'll log onto your email and social-media accounts, put a holding message on them and see if there's anything really urgent. What do you think?'

Flora nodded. 'Thanks, Alex.' It was what she would have done but having some help would make it easier—and a lot faster. 'I really appreciate it.'

'Come on, what else are friends for?' But he didn't quite meet her eyes as he said it. Worry skittered along her skin, slow and sure as a cat on a fence. Had grabbing a few days' pleasure meant the end of everything? Like a gambler staking everything on one last spin and losing. Was the thrill of watching the wheel turn and the ball hover on first red and then black worth it? That moment when anything was possible worth the inevitable knowledge that nothing was?

He opened his laptop. 'I hope you can remember your passwords. Right, where shall I start?'

It didn't take too long for Flora to open up each of her accounts for Alex, averting her eyes from the dozens of messages and multitudes of new followers. She retreated to the bed with a notebook, a pen and her phone ready to start listening to her messages. Alex was right; Minerva had been calling consistently all day. Flora steeled herself and began to listen.

Minerva, a fashion buyer from Rafferty's, one of London's most exclusive department stores, a couple of magazines, Minerva, Minerva—Minerva again. By

JESSICA GILMORE   125

the time she got to her sister's seventh message Flora knew she'd better call her back.

'At last!' Her sister didn't bother with formalities like 'Hello' or 'How's Austria?'

'Evening, Merva,' Flora said pointedly. But the point, as always, was lost.

'I'm glad you've decided to emerge from hibernation. I couldn't get hold of you or Alex.'

'We've been working.' Minerva hadn't been able to get hold of Alex either? It was most unlike him not to have one phone in one hand and the other in front of him—although now Flora thought about it she had only seen him check his work phone and emails a few times—and she hadn't seen his personal phone at all. Not since the ski lodge. Maybe he was enjoying living off grid just as she was. She glanced over at him. He was tapping away, frowning with concentration. Her entire body ached at his nearness.

Minerva's tart tones recalled her to the matter at hand. 'Working? Whatever. So who is handling this for you? I've asked around but no one has admitted it. Not surprisingly, I would never let you disappear at such a crucial time in a campaign. Unless that's part of the plan, to drum up more interest? Too risky, I would have thought.'

Handling, campaign? It didn't take too long for a conversation with her sister to feel like a particularly nasty crossword where the clues were in one language and the answers another. 'Minerva,' she said patiently. 'I have no idea what you're talking about.'

'Of course it didn't take too long for people to work out who you were, thanks to Dad's aprons. Another serious misstep. You really need him in the latest designs in this crucial period while you're establishing yourself, although I do think the whole apron thing is a bit saccharine myself. Still, it establishes you as part of that quirky routine he has going on. But you should be here, not drinking schnapps and frolicking on mountains.'

Flora froze. How did her sister know? 'I haven't been frolicking,' she said, hating how unconvincing she sounded. Alex looked up at her words and his mouth curved wickedly.

'I beg to differ,' he said, too quietly for Minerva to hear, and Flora's whole body began to simmer in response.

'Look,' she said hurriedly, wanting to get Minerva off the phone, everything else replied to and Alex back here, on the bed, while she was still allowed to want that. 'You are going to have to speak in words of one syllable. What are you talking about?'

Her sister huffed. 'Who is handling your PR for the Lexy Chapman campaign? I hope you know how humiliating it is for me that you didn't even ask me to pitch.'

Her what? 'Merva, there isn't a campaign.'

Disbelieving silence. 'You expect me to believe that the most stylish woman in Britain was photographed in your scarf by a complete coincidence?'

'I know you too well to expect anything, but yes. That's what happened. Goodness, Merva, as if I would ever not ask you in the highly unlikely event I was going to run a campaign. My inbox is full, my social media is insane, I have voicemails from scary influential people I don't dare call back and I'm terrified even thinking about logging onto my shop because I

don't have enough stock to fulfil half a dozen orders.'
She could hear her voice rising and took a deep breath.
'Come on, even I know enough not to launch a campaign like that.'

Minerva was silent for a moment and Flora could
picture her as if they were in the same room, the gleam
of excitement in her eyes, the satisfaction on her cat-
like face. Her sister loved a challenge—and she always
won. 'I need you,' she added.

'I know you do,' but Minerva's voice wasn't smug.
She sounded businesslike. 'Leave everything to me.
I'll take care of it all. Right. I need to know who has
left you a message and why, all your social-media
account details and you need to forward me every
email. Oh, and let me know your current stock list.
You won't be able to supply everyone so let's make
sure you only focus on the people who matter. When
are you back?'

'The day after tomorrow.' *Too soon.*

'Christmas Eve? The timing is really off. We'll lose
all momentum over the holidays.'

'Yes, well, next time I inadvertently sell a scarf to
a style icon I'll make sure she only wears it at a more
convenient time.'

'Luckily…' it was as if she hadn't spoken '…I am a
genius and I can fix this. Right, I want all that information in the next half-hour. Do not speak to a single
journalist without my say-so, do not promise as much
as a scrap of fabric to anyone—and, Flora? Keep your
phone on.' Minerva rang off.

'Goodbye, Flora. It was nice speaking to you. The
kids send their love,' Flora muttered as she put the
phone down, her head spinning. 'Alex, it's okay. Mi-

nerva is going to save the world armed with a few Tweets and her contact list.'

'Thank goodness.' He pushed the chair back. 'There are some hysterical women out there—and some even more hysterical men who think they will never have sex again if they don't produce one of your scarves on Christmas morning. No pressure.'

She flopped back onto the bed, her phone clutched in her hand. 'I just need to get all this information to Minerva and then we can head into Innsbruck—if you still want to go, that is?'

'We could.' His voice was silky; that particular tone was the one that always made her blood heat up, her body ache. 'Or we could use our time far more productively.'

Flora propped herself up on one arm and looked at him from under her lashes. 'Productive sounds good. What do you have in mind?'

He picked up the scarf and twisted it into a slim rope, pulling it taut between his hands before looking back at her, a gleam in his eye. 'Such a versatile material. I'm sure we'll think of something.'

CHAPTER NINE

'HERE YOU ARE. I was beginning to think you'd got yourself stranded in a ski lodge again.' Alex allowed the hotel door to swing closed behind him and leaned against the wall, watching her appreciatively. 'Room in there for a little one?'

'It's not that sort of bath,' Flora told him, slipping a little further into the bubbles so that all he could see was her hair piled into a messy knot on the top of her head. Little tendrils had escaped and were curling in the heat; his hands itched with the need to touch them.

'What other sort is there?' It was hard to make conversation knowing that she was naked and wet. Totally exposed and yet completely veiled. Whose idea was it to put a bath in the middle of the bedroom? Probably Lola's. If he weren't so angry with his ex-designer's lack of professionalism he would track her down and offer her a bonus. It was genius. That was it; every building he designed from now on would have a bath in the middle of a room. Even if it was supposed to be an office. Or a shopping centre.

Flora moved and the water lapped against the side of the bath, the sound another tantalising reminder of her undressed state. 'This is a ball-preparation bath.

It involves all kinds of depilation, exfoliating, filing and moisturising.'

'Sounds serious.' He took a step closer to her, then another. Each step unveiled a little bit more, the tilt of her face, rosy from the hot water, her long neck a delicate blush pink. Then bubbles, clothing the rest of her, although if he craned his neck and looked really hard there were a few intriguing gaps in the white suds revealing hints of interesting things.

'It is. Deadly serious. Did you find everything you wanted at the Christmas markets?'

'Yep. Eventually. I had a long hard morning on the slopes first. Gustav was desolated that you missed your last day's lessons. He had a particularly challenging slope ready for you. So what have you been doing while I was skiing and shopping?'

'Ugh.' The sigh was long and heartfelt. 'I have spent most of the day sat at my laptop video-calling Minerva. Although you'll never guess what she was wearing...'

Alex's mouth curved into a slow smile. He knew Minerva. 'Last Christmas's skirt.'

'*And* a scarf I gave her a couple of years ago in her hair. Nice to know my presents suddenly have value. Not that I should complain. She has sorted everything. Although she's set up a couple of interviews for next week.' She sounded apprehensive. 'Face to face and photos, which is not good news after all the *Kaffee* and *Kuchen* I've had—especially the *Kuchen*.'

'Don't forget your dad's five-course Christmas dinner,' Alex reminded her helpfully and laughed as she groaned.

'Don't—you know how upset he gets if we skip

anything—and he thinks that seconds is the only real way of gauging a dish's success. But I *am* really grateful. She's taken over the social media and created waiting lists, replied to all the emails and soothed every fashion editor's ruffled feathers. Her poor staff, two days before Christmas, and she pulled a three-line whip. I almost feel guilty that I'm luxuriating in this bath—and then I remember that this too is work.' She sank a little further into the steaming water with a small purr of pleasure.

'How much is she charging you?'

'That's the best bit. It's my Christmas present. She's keeping the exorbitantly expensive scented candles she *had* bought me, which are far more her bag anyway, and is giving me her staff's toil instead, nicely wrapped with a big bow on top.'

Alex bit back a smile. 'How very generous of her, although a cynical person would point out that it's not doing her any harm. You're the one in demand. She's handling the buzz, not creating it.'

'It's two days before Christmas and I'm about to go to a ball. No cynicism allowed.'

Alex perched on the edge of the bathtub and looked down at her. 'How are you feeling about your designs being out there?'

Her eyelashes fell. 'Half excited, half terrified. Naked—and not just because I am.'

'That's how it should be,' he told her. 'Even when you're working to a brief there should be a little something of you in there. You should be exposed, otherwise you haven't gone as far as you could have.'

She raised an eyebrow. 'Always? Even when I had to rebrand the Village Inns wine bar chain and they wanted pinks and lime greens and bits of fruit everywhere?'

'Especially then. Otherwise what's the point? That's why I struck out on my own so early. I wanted to be able to pick and choose my own work—that doesn't mean I don't listen to my clients though. There has to be a balance. I wonder…' He paused, not wanting to push too much when she was still adjusting.

'Wonder what?'

Oh, well, in for a penny… 'At your degree show it was obvious your passion—and a huge amount of your talent—lay in textile design. It shows every Christmas, with every gift you make. But you've never tried to make it your career. You set your sights on interior design and took the first job you were offered even though you hated their whole brand.'

'Hate's a bit strong…' she protested. 'Wholeheartedly disliked maybe. That's why it would never have worked with Finn. Even if he hadn't been a golf-obsessed workaholic, he really loved the branding.'

'It wouldn't have worked with Finn because he was an idiot.' Alex's teeth began to grind just at the thought of Flora's ex. How a girl with such good taste had such bad taste in men he would never know.

Not that he was any improvement. Actually that was untrue. A warthog was an improvement on Finn.

'Good point.'

'So why haven't you tried to sell your designs before? Into shops or to fashion designers? It seems like the perfect path for you.'

'I guess because I don't design fabric to make money. I do it because I love it.'

'Exactly. Why shouldn't you do what you love? I do. Your whole family does. Don't you deserve to as well?'

She slithered further down into the water, as if she were hiding from the question. 'It's different for you. You know what you want. You don't let anything stand in your way. That thing you said, about having a piece of you in everything you do? I see that in your work. In this hotel, in your designs for Bali. And it's wonderful. But it's so exposing.'

'And that frightens you?'

'If people hate the neon limes, and they mostly will, then that's fine. It's not *my* creatives they hate. I'm just following the brief. But if they hate my scarves or my quilts or my bags, things I've poured love and attention into? That feels like I've failed—again. Like I've been rejected again. I don't want the things I love tainted.'

Alex reached out and twisted one of the piled-up tendrils of dark silky hair around his finger. 'Everything worthwhile comes with a price, Flora.'

She sighed. 'Sometimes the price is too high. I don't want to feel that exposed. I've spent my whole life being judged. Noticed because of my height, leered at because I was a teenager with big boobs, every teacher pointing out how unlike my siblings I was. My parents dragging me onto TV. I just want to be anonymous.'

His voice softened as he pulled at the curl. 'But you're out there now. You need to harden up, think about the next step.'

'It's not that easy though, is it? I need money to expand—to buy fabric, a better machine, a studio, somewhere to keep stock. Even if I stay small and exclusive I don't think keeping my stock in boxes under my bed is going to cut it—or make me enough to live on!'

'That's where I have good news. Camilla caught me on the way in. She very much wants you to work on the next three hotels and is prepared to pay for the privilege. Do you trust me to negotiate you a good deal?'

Flora sat up, the water sloshing as she did so. It was so deep she was still respectably covered, just her shoulders rising from the white foam like Aphrodite. As enticing and tempting as Aphrodite. 'A good deal? Does she know that my previous experience pretty much consisted of that awful pink fruit décor and the teapot theme for those cosy retro cafés? And let's not forget the chintzy bedding range. This is a massive step up. I should be paying her!'

He grinned. 'All she's heard for the last twenty-four hours are her guests desperate to get hold of your work. If she can announce right now, while the buzz is still big, that you're the designer for her next three hotels then that's quite a coup for Lusso Hotels. I told you she likes to work with people who have a marketable story and right now that's you. It's a great way to get publicity for both here and for her future plans.'

She bit her lip. 'I suppose. And she was already considering me so nothing much has changed.'

'Nothing much but the price tag. If you subcontract to me then I can pay you monthly—which will give you some stability while you step up your own designs as well. Like all projects there will be weeks when you don't need to do much for Lusso Hotels and other weeks when it will be frantic. But the subcontract could include studio space at my office for the length of the contract and if you use it for your other work then that's fine. It'll be yours.'

'That would be great. At least that's the space issue sorted.'

Alex had saved the best bit for last. 'And she would like to see a touch of your own style in your plans for the Bali hotel, so I guess I was wrong when I said to watch the whimsy.'

Her eyes sparkled. 'Really? You were wrong? Can I have that in writing?'

'Watch it.' He dipped a hand in the bath and scooped up a little bit of water.

'Don't you dare…this is a serious bath. I already told you.'

'Don't I dare what? Do this?' He trickled the water slowly onto the exposed part of her chest, his heartbeat quickening as he watched the silvery drops trace a trail down her skin until they disappeared into the deep vee between her breasts.

'Or this?' she countered sweetly and before he could move away she grabbed the front of his shirt and hauled him into the bath, laughing as he landed on top of her. 'Mind my hair. I don't want to get it wet!'

Alex raised himself onto his hands and knees. 'Now look what you've done. My clothes are all soaking.' He rocked back onto his heels, ignoring the splash of the water as it sloshed over the side of the bath. 'I'm going to have to take them off. You wanted a serious bath, Flora Buckingham? You've got one.'

Her eyes didn't leave his as he pulled the sopping-wet shirt over his head, or as he began to unbutton his trousers. 'Bring it on,' she said, her voice breaking huskily, belying the tough words. 'If you think you're man enough.'

'Oh, Flora,' he promised her as his trousers and boxers followed his shirt over the side of the bath. 'I'm more than man enough. Just wait and see.'

'Come on, what's taking so long?' Alex sounded impatient as he rapped on the bathroom door. Again.

Flora rolled her eyes at her reflection. 'It's not my fault I had to redo my hair,' she called back. 'I told you not to get it wet.'

He didn't answer for a moment, then: 'Regrets, Flora?'

'That my hair got wet? It might have been worth it.' That didn't mean she was entirely regret free but she wasn't going to admit that to him. Or to herself. Not tonight. It was their last night, they were going to a Christmas ball and she looked, even if she said so herself, pretty darn smoking.

The dress she had bought from the vintage shop in Innsbruck was deceptively demure. The chiffon cap sleeves revealed just a hint of her shoulder and the neckline hugged the tops of her breasts, the bodice narrowing at her waist before flaring out again, the full skirt finishing at her calves. She saw more revealing outfits every day in the offices she temped in.

Deceptively demure. It covered everything and yet…was it the bright red, a shocking contrast to the paleness of her skin? Was it the fit, the way it clung like a second skin? Or was it the way it defined and enhanced every curve so that, despite the modest neckline, Flora felt more exposed than if she was venturing out in just her bra?

Maybe it was because she was so obviously and evidently dolled up? Her hair tumbled free in carefully arranged curls, her lips were red and her eyes outlined in dark, dark kohl and, for once, she had slipped her feet into heels, which would make her taller than most of the men in the room.

But Alex would still top her.

'Flora…'

'Okay, okay, I'm coming.' She took one last look. Yes, she was definitely smoking—either that or she looked like a pin-up version of Mrs Claus but either way she had no choice. She had nothing else even remotely suitable for a Christmas ball. Inhaling deeply, Flora opened the bathroom door.

And stared. It was so unfair. Here she was. Two hours later. Hair washed, curled, sprayed and teased. Body plucked free of each and every stray hair, moisturised and buffed, face artfully painted, nails filed and polished, dress squeezed into, shoes forced on. And what had Alex done? Showered, shaved and shrugged himself into his tux.

She swallowed, her mouth dry. The stark black, relieved only by the crisp white of his shirt, suited him, brought out the auburn glints in his hair, made his eyes greener than grey. He looked like a stranger; a powerful, imposing and hot stranger.

A powerful, imposing and hot stranger who was staring straight back at her, mouth slightly open and a dazed expression on his face.

'Will I do?'

He didn't answer straight away, just nodded. 'Yes,' he said, clearing his throat. 'You look incredible.'

Heat flooded her cheeks at the expression in his

eyes. 'Fine feathers,' she said a little unsteadily. 'Put anyone into a dress like this and they'll scrub up okay.'

'No.' His eyes were so intent, heat smouldering in their depths, that she felt completely exposed, naked. 'The dress is...' His gaze travelled over her, burning a trail onto her, marking her, claiming her. 'The dress is sensational. But it's all you, Flora. You'd look just as amazing in a sheet.'

'Thank you.' She blinked, unexpected tears filling her eyes at the raw want in his voice. 'You don't look too bad yourself.'

They stood, caught in time just staring at each other, the pressure in the room intensifying until it was just the two of them, caught in a spotlight. Flora cleared her throat. 'Shall we go?' She didn't want to prolong the moment. Not tonight. Not when tomorrow meant moments such as this would be finished for ever.

Flora waited for him to open the door but he just stood there. 'I...er... I got you this. I know Christmas isn't for another couple of days but, well...' He held out a black velvet jewellery box.

Flora froze. He had never bought her jewellery before. Alex was usually a generous and perceptive gift buyer but jewellery buying was too intimate, a line he had never crossed before. Still, they were crossing all sorts of lines this week. Why not this one?

'For me?' She was aware how stupid the words were as she uttered them and he nodded, a faint smile playing on his lips as he did so.

'For you. Don't you want to open it?'

She reached out cautiously. 'I'm not sure,' she confessed. 'There's not a trick snake in there, is there?'

'One time, Flora, one time. And I was ten!'

'Okay, then.' The box was solid, heavier than she expected and she turned it around in her hands, the velvet soft against her skin. It wasn't new, she knew that at once; the hinges were tarnished and the velvet rubbed in places. She smiled over at Alex, her heart lifting with the discovery; she wasn't much of one for new, she preferred her possessions to have a history, a story.

She found the clasp and sprung it before carefully opening the lid and let out a little anticipatory breath she hadn't even been aware that she was holding. A necklace sparkled on the yellowing white satin cushion. Flora stole a quick look up at Alex. His face was impassive, as if he were waiting for her to comment on the weather or ask the time, but the strained set of his shoulders showed that he was waiting for her reaction. Slowly she hooked the necklace onto one newly manicured finger and drew it out of the box.

It was a two-tiered circlet of large, crystal beads designed to fall just below the neck, nestling on the collarbone. 'It's…' She shook her head, searching for the right words. 'It's perfect. How?' She couldn't complete the question.

'I knew where you bought the dress from so I popped in and said I wanted something to go with it. They remembered you quite clearly.' He took the necklace from her unresisting hand and moved behind her. She felt the cool heaviness of the beads settle around her neck, his fingers brush against the nape of her neck as he swept her hair aside, his breath on her skin as he leaned forward and clasped the necklace.

'It's nineteen fifties, like your dress, and made of the local Austrian crystal.' He let her hair fall back and stepped away. She instantly felt colder.

'It's absolutely gorgeous.' Flora put her hand up to her neck and fingered the chunky beads. 'Thank you, Alex. It's very thoughtful of you.' She turned around and rose on her tiptoes, pressing a kiss onto his cheek, inhaling his freshly washed scent as she did so. It *was* thoughtful—and it finished her dress off perfectly—but part of her wished that he hadn't bought it. That he'd stuck to books, or tickets or any of the usual gifts. Because each time she saw it she would be reminded of this night, of this trip. Each time she saw it she would be reminded of him. Not of Alex Fitzgerald, best mate and partner in crime, but of *this* Alex. The one who made her stomach turn over, her legs tremble and who made all good sense go flying out of the window.

The one she would say goodbye to in the morning. She put a hand up to her necklace and touched the central bead, the truth hitting her with brutal force. It wasn't going to be easy because she didn't want it to end. She wanted him to look at her with that mingling of desire and need and appreciation and humour for ever. But she'd made him a promise and she was going to keep it. No fuss, no repercussions, nothing was going to change. But, oh, how she wished it would.

'Come on.' She stepped back and turned to the door, her voice as artificially bright as her lipstick. 'We don't want to be late. Camilla has invited some local dignitaries and that means that you, my friend architect, have some schmoozing to do.'

'Oh, my goodness.' Flora stopped dead at the entrance to the dining room and stared, open-mouthed, at the décor within. 'This is…'

'Like the ghost of Christmas kitsch just threw up in here?' Alex murmured in her ear.

'No!' She gave him a little shove. 'Well, only a little. It's very pretty though.'

Lights hung in the windows encircling the rooftop room; lit, dazzling, heavily bedecked Christmas trees stood to attention between each window like an army of greenery guarding the room. More lights were draped from a centre point in the ceiling, creating a marquee-like effect.

The lighting was all blues and whites, giving the illusion that they were standing in a particularly gaudy ice cave. The same colours were repeated on the tree decorations, on the tables that were dotted around the room, on the huge snowflakes and baubles that hung from the ceiling. A small band in the corner played a waltz, the music soaring over the glamorous guests as they stood chatting in small groups throughout the room.

'I hope the colour scheme isn't reflected in the drinks,' Flora whispered. 'I haven't drunk blue curaçao since university but I don't think it agrees with me.'

'It could be white drinks. What about advocaat?'

She shuddered. 'Now you're being mean. I thought we'd promised never to mention that New Year ever again.'

Luckily, before too many more embarrassing memories could be dredged up, a waitress stopped before them with a tray of kir royales, topped with raspberries. Flora took the glass Alex handed to her, thankful it was nothing more dangerous. 'Happy Christmas,' she said and raised her glass to him.

'Happy Christmas, Flora.' He toasted her back but

the expression in his eyes was completely unreadable; his face wore the shuttered look she hated. It made him seem so far away. They only had tonight; she couldn't say goodbye early. She wasn't ready…

'Dance with me?'

He looked up at that, surprised. 'What? No one's dancing. It's still early.'

'So? If I can ski a red run on my second day you can be the first person onto the dance floor.'

'First couple,' he corrected her. 'There is no way on earth I would face that alone.' But he didn't demur any longer, holding his hand out to her and leading her to the centre of the room. There was a sudden hush as the other guests saw them step out but it was brief; the chatter starting up again as quickly as it had stopped.

Alex pulled her closer, one arm settling around her waist, the other clasping her hand. 'If we must do an exhibition dance then I am, for the first time, thankful that Minerva insisted that the whole wedding party needed to learn to dance properly.' It was a few years since the mandatory dance lessons but as he adjusted to the beat of the music it all began to come back. He could hear the teacher marking out the time as he had attempted to steer a mutinous Flora around the floor.

It was all so different now. She was pliant in his arms, letting him lead, her feet following his, her body at one with his—even if she did keep looking down at their feet.

'I don't remember you saying thank goodness at the time,' she pointed out, pausing to count under her breath. '*One* two three, *one* two three. It's a good job Minerva didn't want us all to salsa though.' She raised her eyes to his. They were luminous in the low light. 'Can you imagine how we'd look trying to salsa to this? We'd have to just do that slightly awkward shuffle instead.'

He tightened his arm, enjoying the feel of her so close to him, knowing that she was completely compliant, allowing him to take control. 'Did you know that the waltz was once considered scandalous?'

'Was it? Why?'

He lowered his voice. 'Just two people, a man, a woman, moving so closely together there's barely any space between them. His arm holding her to him, her hand clasped in his. He can feel her breasts pressing against his chest, smell the shampoo in her hair. If he wanted to...' He paused and looked directly into her upturned face, her mouth parted. 'If he wanted to kiss her then all he has to do is bend his head.'

'What if she didn't want him to kiss her?'

'Doesn't she?'

'Well...' Her lips curved into an enticing smile. 'Not in the middle of the dance floor. That really would cause a scandal. He would have to marry her if that happened.'

Alex blinked and she squeezed his hand reassuringly. 'In olden times I mean, silly. Don't worry, that wasn't a proposal.'

'Of course not.' But the words echoed round and round in his head. *Then he would have to marry her.*

The evening passed by in a quick blur as if someone had pressed fast forward. Alex lost Flora soon after their dance. Camilla whisked him away to meet, greet and act merry with the local dignitaries and influential industry movers and shakers while Flora was absorbed into a laughing group of revellers. The band switched to covers of popular songs and the dance floor was full.

But he could always find Flora; she stood out. Not just because of her height and her vibrant dress, but because she glowed as she moved across the floor.

He envied her even though he knew she deserved a carefree evening. He, on the other hand, was on his best behaviour, projecting the right image as he chatted to the VIPs Camilla needed him to impress.

Tomorrow it would all be over. This dazzling throng would pack away their finery ready for their trips home. He would return to Kent with Flora ready to resume their old friendship. Would it be enhanced by this week or tarnished? Maybe now they had given way to that old thrill of attraction they could move on—properly. She deserved a good man, someone to worship her, love her properly.

Alex folded his hands into tight fists, jealousy burning through him at the thought. How would he be able to stand there and smile as she held hands with another man, laughed up at another man, kissed another man?

There was only one way to bear it—to start thinking of his own future. A future beyond work and the need for success and recognition that had driven him so far, so fast. Was it so unthinkable that he too could have a long-term relationship? Maybe even marriage? Plenty of people had satisfactory, even successful lives together based on mutual respect and shared goals rather than passion and romance. Why not him?

He took another glass of kir royale from a passing

waitress, mechanically nodding and smiling as the conversation around him turned to families and Christmas. His least favourite subject.

It wasn't that he didn't love spending the festive season with the Buckinghams. It wasn't as if they ever treated him as anything but one of the family. They didn't. He had been expected to muck in with the rest of them long before he'd started living there, peeling potatoes, setting the table, chopping logs for the fire—whatever was needed. Yes, they treated him like one of the family. But he *wasn't* family.

His own family had cast him out and one day the Buckinghams would too. Not on purpose but time wouldn't freeze. They wouldn't all return to the small Kentish village for the festive season for ever. One day Minerva would want to host Christmas, or Horry, if he ever looked up from his scalpel long enough to have a relationship. Or Flora would. Would there be a place for him in the family then? In ten years? In twenty?

He downed his drink. The solution was simple. It was time he thought about creating his own place. His own traditions and memories. Somewhere he built so he couldn't be cast out. The problem was he couldn't imagine anyone beside him but Flora.

And she deserved more…

He took another glass from a passing tray. And he watched her, trying to ignore the unwanted leap his heart gave when she smiled over at him. A secret smile of complicity.

Yes, she deserved more. But would she get it?

The thing was, he decided as he finished one glass and swapped it for another, that good things didn't always come to those who waited. After all, Flora hadn't had much luck with her past boyfriends. Just because he was prepared to do the right thing and stand aside didn't mean she would end up with someone who deserved her. It was all such a lottery. *He* could offer stability, space, affection. These were all good commodities in the trading place that was marriage. In return he would get a home. A place that was his.

It was a good trade.

Marriage.

Was he seriously thinking about it?

The room had darkened, the music quietening back to the classical waltzes so typical of Austria and the dance floor was now occupied by couples, the English swaying together awkwardly, the Austrians waltzing with the same grace he had admired on the ice rink and on the slopes.

Flora stood on the opposite side of the room, leaning against a chair and watching the dances, yearning on her face. Alex put his glass down and weaved his way over to her. He had drunk more than he usually allowed himself to; everything felt fuzzier, softer. Sweeter.

'Hi, have you been released early?'

'Time off for good behaviour. Having fun?'

'You know what...' she blinked at him, owlish in her solemn surprise '... I have. There are some really lovely people here.'

'Dance with me.' It wasn't a request and she obediently took his proffered hand, allowing him to lead her back onto the floor. She sank in close, her hand splayed on his back, and he could feel where every part of her touched him as if they weren't separated by layers of material but as if they were back in the ski lodge, learning each other anew.

Her head was on his shoulder, nestled in trustingly. They had trust. They had friendship.

They had passion.

It was a lot.

Alex stopped. 'Flora?'

'Mmm…why aren't we dancing?' She looked up at him, her mouth curved invitingly, and that was all he needed. Alex dipped his head and kissed her, a sweet, gentle caress.

She smiled up at him. 'That was nice. What was that for?'

'I wanted to.' He began to move again, slowing the steps down so that they were out of time with the music, dancing to their own private beat, their lips finding each other again, a deeper, intoxicating kiss. He was dimly aware that they were still moving, that the violins were soaring, the lights were low, but none of it was real. Only they were real. Just the taste of her, the feel of her, the scent of her. He wanted to sink deeper and deeper, to be absorbed by her, into her.

Only she was real. She made him real.

'Not here.' Flora's breath was ragged as she broke away. 'Not like that.'

He stared at her uncomprehendingly, still lost in the memory of her warmth.

'I mean…' She squeezed his hand, running her thumb over his palm, trailing fire with her touch. Fire that threatened to consume him. 'We're in the middle of a dance floor. I think we should take this back to our room.'

Of course. How could he have forgotten? How could he have been so swept up in the moment that he had lost track of where they were, forgotten that they weren't alone?

He swallowed. 'I warned you that the waltz was a scandalous dance.'

'You did,' she agreed. 'Am I quite compromised?'

''I think so...' His earlier thoughts came back to haunt him. Peace, stability, a family of his own... 'Unless we marry. What about it, Flora? Will you marry me?'

CHAPTER TEN

THE WALK BACK to the room seemed to take for ever. Every few steps they bumped into a group of Flora's new friends wanting to drag her off to the bar, to after parties, for midnight walks out in the snow.

She turned each of them down with a laughing non-committal reply but the whole situation didn't seem real. Her voice was too bright, her smile too wild and there was a buzzing in her ears as if she were in a waking dream.

Alex didn't say anything at all. His hand clasped hers tight; his eyes burned with that same strange intensity she had seen on the dance floor.

And his words echoed round and round in her head. *Will you marry me?*

Of course he had been joking. Of course. There was no doubt. Just because his fingers were gripping hers tightly, just because she had daydreamed a similar scenario more times than she had imagined winning the lottery didn't make it real.

Only…he had sounded serious.

What if he was serious?

No. Of course he wasn't because dreams didn't simply just come true. A dance floor, a waltz, beautiful lighting, champagne; that was the stuff of fairy tales, not real life. Not Flora's life.

But he *looked* serious.

She had been so desperate to get him back to the room but as they approached the door an unexpected caution hit her. Whatever was done and said when they got inside couldn't be unsaid, couldn't be undone. And his face was so very set. The passion and laughter wiped clear as if they had never been.

Flora took a deep breath as they walked into the room. It was her imagination, that was all, working on his words and twisting them into something more serious than intended. She needed to lighten up, enjoy these last few hours before it all changed back and she was back in her rags clutching a pumpkin.

Okay. Lightening up. 'Alone at last.' She smiled provocatively at him but there was no answering smile on his face.

'I meant it, you know. Marry me.'

Flora reached up to unclasp her necklace but at his quiet words her hands dropped helplessly to her side. 'No bended knee, no flash mob, no ring in my ice cream?' She tried to tease but the joke was flatter than one of her father's failed soufflés, and Alex didn't acknowledge it with as much as a flicker of an eyelid.

She walked over to the window and stared out. Ahead was darkness but if she looked up then the stars shone with an astonishing intensity, unfamiliar to a girl used to London's never fully darkened skies. Below Innsbruck was lit up like a toy town. Not quite real.

Like this moment.

'Why?'

She held her breath, hope fluttering wildly in her

chest. Would he say it? *Because I love you. I have always loved you.*

He didn't answer, not straight away. She heard him pace back and forth, imagined him shrugging off the tuxedo jacket, undoing his bow tie, running his hands through his disordered curls.

'Does it matter why?' he asked at last.

She still couldn't turn to face him but at his words hope's flutters became feebler and nausea began to swirl in her stomach.

'I think so, yes.' *Tell me, tell me,* she silently begged him. *Tell me what I need to hear and I'll believe you.*

Even though she knew it wouldn't be true.

'No one knows me like you do. You know everything, all the darkness, and you're still here.'

'Of course I am.'

'We know we're compatible. I think we could lead very comfortable, happy lives together. The sex is good—more than good. And marriage would tick other boxes too.'

Flora swallowed. Hope finally gave up and withered away. Her stomach still twisted with nausea but most thought and feeling drained away to a much-needed numbness. 'Great,' she murmured. Marriage as a box-ticking exercise. Just what she had always dreamed of. Maybe they could make a list and follow it up with a presentation on the computer.

'It would make things a lot easier for you as you change focus. I know money has been tight. That wouldn't be an issue any longer, and there's plenty of space at my house for a studio and storage.'

'Money, storage...' she repeated as if in a dream,

the practical words not quite sinking in. 'And what about you? What's in it for you, apart from good sex?'

He didn't seem to hear the bitterness in her last words, just continuing as if this were a completely sane conversation. 'For me? No more dating, trying to be someone I'm not. Freedom to work—you wouldn't mind when work took me abroad, wouldn't expect me to check in every five minutes. There wouldn't be any misunderstandings, any expectations—you wouldn't want more than I can give.'

'No, I suppose I wouldn't.' Not now anyway. It wasn't as if he hadn't warned her, was it? She had chosen not to listen. Not to guard herself against this.

She wasn't numb now, she was cold. A biting chill working its way up from her toes, bone deep.

He hadn't noticed, was still listing soulless benefits as if it were next week's shopping list. 'And there would be no real adjustment. We know each other's bad habits, moods, and I get on with your family. Think about it, Flora. It makes perfect sense.'

'Yes, I can see that.' She turned at last. He had discarded his jacket and his tie, his shirt half untucked and unbuttoned, his hair falling over his forehead. He looked slightly dangerous, a little degenerate like the sort of regency rake who would kiss a girl on a dance floor and not care about the consequences.

And yet here he was offering a marriage of convenience. If she said no—*when* she said no—then everything really would change. They might be able to sweep a week of passion under the carpet. They wouldn't be able to sweep this away.

Especially when every traitorous fibre of her wanted to say yes.

'I can't...' she said before she allowed herself to weaken.

His eyes blazed for one heartbreaking moment and then the shutters came down. 'Right. I see. Fine. Silly of me to think you would. Let's not mention it again.'

'I need more from marriage.' The words were tumbling out. 'I want love.'

A muscle worked in his cheek. 'I do love you, you know that. As much as I can.'

'But are you *in* love with me?'

She couldn't believe she'd asked that. The last taboo, more powerful than the kisses they had shared, the whispered intimacies. This, *this* was the big one. But she had to know. She took a deep, shuddering breath and waited. Would he? Did he? All he had to do was tell her he loved her and she would be in.

He ran a hand through his hair. 'Do I care about you? Yes. Desire you? Absolutely. Like your company? You know I do. Isn't that enough?'

Flora shook her head. 'I wish it was,' she whispered. 'But I want more. I want the whole crazy, passionate, all-consuming love. I want to be the centre of someone's world and for my world to revolve around them.'

But he was shaking his head, a denial of her words, of her hopes and dreams. 'That's not real love, Flora. That's a crush at best, obsession at worst,' and with those calm words Flora felt something inside her crack clean in two.

'Oxytocin, serotonin. Hormones telling you lies. Love? It's unstable, it can't be trusted. But you're right. Marriage between us is a bad idea.' He stepped back and picked up his jacket, shrugging himself into it. 'I'm sorry I embarrassed you. If you'll excuse me, then I am going to get a drink. I'll see you later. Don't wait up.'

The plane was buzzing with festive spirit. Bags stuffed into the overhead lockers filled with brightly wrapped presents, people chatting eagerly to their seatmates— even strangers—about their plans for the next few days. Even the pilot made some flying reindeer jokes as he prepared them for take-off.

But the buzz didn't reach their two seats. They were ensconced in roomy first-class comfort. There were free drinks, legroom, food—but Alex and Flora sat stiffly as if they were crammed into the most cramped economy seat.

Flora was sleeping—or, Alex suspected, she was pretending to—and he was looking through documents as if the fate of Christmas depended on his memorising them by heart. If that had been the case then Christmas was in trouble; no matter how often he skimmed a sentence his brain could not make head or tail of it, his brain revolving round and round and round.

She'd said no. Even the person who knew him best, who he thought loved him best, didn't want to risk her happiness on him.

And now he'd done exactly what he had sworn he would never do. He'd broken Flora's heart, tainted their friendship, ruined his relationship with her family. Because how could he possibly turn up there tomorrow ready to bask in Christmas cheer when he couldn't even look at Flora?

Especially as she couldn't look at him either. Oh, she was trying. She made stilted conversation, her smile too bright, her voice too cheery, but her eyes slid away when they reached his face, her body leaning away from his whenever they were close. Luckily his monosyllabic replies hadn't seemed too out of character when other people were around—most of the departing guests were similarly afflicted, suffering the effects of overindulgence the night before.

It wasn't a hangover that affected him, although heaven only knew he'd tried his best. Sitting in the bar until three a.m., drinking alone at the end, trying to block out the voices from his head.

You taint everything.

I can't marry you.

I want love.

What could he answer to that when he didn't even know what love was? The twisted obsession his father had had for his mother, so jealous he didn't even want to share her affection with their child? The grateful desperation he had shown towards his stepmother for deigning to notice him and the dark turning that had taken?

He didn't want or need that selfish emotion. There was a time when that made him feel invincible, as if he had an invisible armour protecting him from the follies that befell so many of his friends.

Now he just felt lost. Stuck in a labyrinth he didn't have the key for—only there was no princess holding a ball of string ready to guide him out. And there was no monster. *He* was the monster.

How could he return to Kent with her now? It was her home, not his. The only place he belonged to was the house he had designed in Primrose Hill. But he didn't want to return there alone, to spend Christmas alone in a house without a heart.

Maybe it wasn't too late to grab a last-minute flight and head out again. He looked around the plane at the bland décor, the packed seats filled with strangers, the almost soothing signs telling him to sit back, switch his phone off, keep his seat belt on. He could spend Christmas Day on a flight. It almost didn't matter where to.

'Do you have to pick up presents and things before you head back home?' His throat scratched as he forced the words out, as if unaccustomed to speaking.

Flora's eyes opened a fraction. 'Yes, if that's okay.'

'I've ordered you a car. It'll run you back to yours and wait for you, as long as you need, then take you home to Kent.'

She sat up at that, any pretence at sleep forgotten. 'You're not coming back with me?'

'Not tonight, I have too much to do.'

'Too much to do on Christmas Eve? Everything's shut for the next few days. What on earth can't wait? But you are driving down tomorrow?'

He couldn't answer.

Her eyes flashed. 'We promised, Alex, we promised that we wouldn't let things change.'

Had she really believed they wouldn't? Had he? He closed his eyes, exhausted. 'We lied.'

There was no more to be said. Not for the last hour of the flight, not during the tedious business of disembarking, immigration and baggage collecting. Not as he saw the sign with his name on it and steered a mute Flora towards it.

'Can you drop my bags and skis off at my house on your way out?' he asked. 'You have your key?'

She turned to look at him, her face paler than usual, the white accented by the deep shadows under her eyes.

'You're not even travelling with me? How are you getting home?'

He shrugged. 'Train, Tube. My own two feet.'

'You're getting on the train? On Christmas Eve? It'll be packed!'

He couldn't explain it, the need to wander, to be anonymous in a vast sea of people where nobody knew him, judged him. 'I'll be fine. I just need some space.'

She stared at him sceptically and then turned away, the dismissive movement conveying everything. Hurting far more than he had expected. 'Suit yourself. You always do.'

He stood and watched her walk away. 'Merry Christmas, Flora.' But she was too far away and his words fell unheard.

The train was as unpleasant as Flora had forecast. Alex was unable to get a seat and so he stood for the fifteen-minute journey back into London, barricaded into his spot by other people's suitcases and bulging bags of presents. The carriage stank of sweat, alcohol, fried chicken and desperation, the air punctuated by a baby's increasingly desperate cries and the sounds of several computer games turned up to a decidedly anti-social volume.

No wonder he rarely travelled by public transport. Alex gritted his teeth and hung on; he deserved no better.

Not that anyone else seemed to be suffering. His fellow travellers seemed to be as full of Christmas Eve cheer as those on the plane, upbeat despite the conditions. But once he had finally got off the train and stood under the iconic glass curved roof of Paddington Station the last thing he wanted was to disappear underground and repeat the experience on a Tube train full of last-minute desperate shoppers, Christmas revellers and people freed from work and ready to celebrate. It was a couple of miles' walk to Primrose Hill but half of that was through Regent's Park and he could do with clearing his head.

Besides, he didn't want to risk bumping into Flora when she dropped his bags off. For the first time in his life he had no idea what to say to her.

It was hard not to contrast the grey, unseasonably warm day with the crisp air and snowy scenes he had left behind. Hard not to dwell on the fact that for the first time in a week he was alone.

Hard to face the reality that this was his future. He'd always thought of himself as so self-sufficient. Hardened.

He'd been lying to himself.

Alex bought a coffee from one of the kiosks, curtly refusing any festive flavourings, and set off, the last week replaying through his head on repeat, slowing down to dwell in agonising detail at every misstep. He shouldn't have kissed her. He shouldn't have allowed her to kiss him.

He shouldn't have proposed.

It shouldn't hurt so much that she said no…

He wandered aimlessly, not caring much where his feet took him. The back streets were an eclectic mix of tree-lined Georgian squares, post-war blocks and newer, shabbier-looking business premises. Like all of central London, the very wealthy rubbed shoulders with the poor; wine bars, delis and exclusive boutiques on one street, a twenty-four-hour supermarket and take-away on the next.

It wasn't until he hit Russell Square that Alex realised just how far he had walked—and how far out of his way he was. He stood for a moment in the middle of the old Bloomsbury square wondering what to do. Head into a pub and drink himself into oblivion? Keep walking until he was so exhausted the pain in his legs outweighed the weight in his chest? Just sit here in the busy square and gradually decompose?

Or run home, grab the car and head off to Kent. He'd be welcomed; he knew that. Flora would try her best to pretend everything was okay. But he didn't belong there, not really. He didn't belong anywhere or with anyone.

So what would it be? Pub, walk or wither away in the middle of Bloomsbury? He leaned against a bench, unsure for the first time in a really long time which way he should go, looking around at the leafless trees and railings for inspiration when a brown sign caught his eye. Of course! The British Museum was just around the corner. He could while away the rest of the afternoon in there. Hide amongst the mummies and the ancient sculptures and pretend that it wasn't Christmas Eve. Pretend he had somewhere to go, someone to care.

Pretend he was worth something.

His decision was made; only as he rounded the corner and hurried towards the huge gates shielding the classically inspired façade of the famous museum he was greeted, not by open gates and doors and a safe neutral place, but by iron bars and locks. The museum was closed.

Alex let out a deep breath, one he hadn't even

known he was holding, gripping the wrought-iron bars as if he could push them apart. No sanctuary for him. Maybe it was a judgement. He wasn't worthy, no rest for him.

He stared at the steps, the carved pillars, the very shut doors. It was strange he hadn't visited the museum in the eleven years he'd lived in London; after all, it was visiting this very building that had first triggered his interest in building design. The neoclassical façade built to house the ancient treasures within. He used to come here every summer with his grandmother.

With his grandmother...

When had that stopped? When had he stopped seeing her? Before he was ten, he was pretty sure. She took him out a couple of times his first year at prep school, had visited regularly before then, although he had never been allowed an overnight stay. And then? Nothing.

No cards, no Christmas presents. Nothing. He hadn't even thought to ask where she had gone—after all, his father had made it very clear that it was Alex who was the problem. Alex who was innately unlovable.

But it wasn't normal, was it? For a grandparent to disappear so completely from a child's life? If she had blamed Alex for her daughter's death then she wouldn't have been around at all. And surely even his father would have told him if she had died.

There was something missing, something rotten at the heart of him and he had to know what it was, had to fix it. Fix his friendship with Flora.

Be worthy of her...

He couldn't ask his mother why she couldn't love him, why she'd left him. He couldn't expect any mean-

ingful dialogue with his father. But maybe his grandmother had some answers. If he could find her.

He had to find her. He couldn't go on like this.

Christmas Eve was usually Flora's favourite day of
the year. All the anticipation, the air of secrecy and
suppressed excitement. The rituals, unchanging and
sacred. They were usually all home and unpacked by
late afternoon before gathering together in the large
sitting room to admire the tree and watch Christmas
films. The last couple of years they had pretended that
the films were to amuse the children—but the children
usually got bored and wandered off leaving the adults
rapt, enthralled by stories they had watched a hundred
times before.

Then a takeaway to spare Flora's dad cooking for
this one evening, before stockings were hung. Milk
and carrots would be put out for the reindeers, home-
made gingerbread and a snifter of brandy for Father
Christmas himself and then the children were bundled
off to bed. The last few years Minerva and Flora's
mother had stayed behind to babysit the children and
put the last few touches to presents but the rest of the
family would disappear off to the pub for a couple of
hours, finishing off at Midnight Mass in the ancient
village church.

She loved every unchanging moment of it.

But this year it would all be different.

What if she had said yes? Right now she and Alex
could be walking into the house hand in hand to congratulations, tears, champagne.

But it would all have been a lie.

Flora took a deep breath, trying to steady her nerves

as the car Alex had ordered for her rolled smoothly through the village towards the cottage her parents had bought over thirty years before, but her hands were trembling and her stomach tumbling with nervous anticipation. They must never know. Alex thought they would blame him but she knew better; they would blame her for driving him away.

She needed some air, time to compose herself before the onslaught of her family. 'This will be fine, thanks,' she said to the driver as they reached the bottom of her lane. 'I can walk from here.'

Flora stood for a moment gulping in air before shrugging her weekend bag onto her back and picking up the shopping bags full of presents. The bags were heavy and her back was aching before she had got more than halfway down the lane but she welcomed the discomfort. It was her penance.

The cottage stood alone at the end of the lane, a low-roofed half-timber, half-redbrick house surrounded by a wild-looking garden and fruit trees. Her father grew most of his own vegetables and herbs and kept noisy chickens in the back, although he was too soft-hearted to do more than collect their eggs.

The house was lit up against the grey of a late December afternoon, smoke wafting from the chimney a welcome harbinger. All she wanted to do was curl up in front of the fire and mourn but instead Flora pinned a determined smile onto her face and pushed open the heavy oak front door.

Game face on. 'Merry Christmas,' she called as the door swung open.

'Flora!' 'Aunty Flora!' 'Darling.' She was almost instantly enveloped in hugs and kisses, her coat removed, bags taken from her aching arms, drawn into the sitting room, a mince pie put into one hand, a cup of tea into the other as the chatter continued.

'How was Austria? Did you see snow?'

'Your scarf looked lovely in that picture. Congratulations, darling.'

'We need to talk strategy.' Minerva, of course. 'Boxing Day you are mine. No running off.'

'Nice journey back, darling?'

And the inevitable: 'Where's Alex?' 'Didn't Alex travel with you?' 'Did you leave Alex in Austria?'

If she had come back to a quiet house. If it had just been Flora and her dad, she sitting at the wide kitchen counter while he bustled and tasted and stirred. Then she might have cracked. But the tree was in the corner of the room, decorated to within an inch of its life and blazing with light, her nieces were already at fever-pitch point and for once nobody was asking when she was going to get a real job/move out of that poky room/get a boyfriend/grow up.

So she smiled and agreed that yes, the scarf looked lovely; yes, Minerva could have all the time she needed; yes, there was plenty of snow and guess what, she'd even been on a horse-drawn sleigh. And no, Alex wasn't with her, he had been delayed but he should be with them tomorrow.

And if she crossed her fingers at that last statement it wasn't because she was lying. It was because she was hoping. Because now she was here she couldn't imagine Christmas without him. She couldn't imagine a life that didn't have him in it.

And even though she wished that he loved her the way that she loved him. And even though she would have given everything for his proposal to have come from his heart and not his head, she still wished he were here. Even if it was as friends. Because friends was still something special. Something to cherish.

She needed to tell him. Before he sealed himself away. Before he talked himself into utter isolation.

'I'm just going to take my bags upstairs. No, it's okay, thanks, Greg,' she assured her brother-in-law. 'I can manage. Besides…' she looked mock sternly at her giggling nieces '…I don't want any peeping.' She kissed her still-chattering mother on the cheek and went back into the hallway to retrieve her bags and hoist them up the wide carpeted staircase that led to the first floor and then up the winding, painted wooden stairs to the attic. There were just two bedrooms up here, sharing a small shower room. To the left was Flora's room, to the right a small box room they had converted into a room for Alex.

His bedroom door was ajar and Flora couldn't help peeking in as she turned. The bed had been made up with fresh linen and towels were piled onto the wicker chair in the corner. An old trunk lay at the foot of the bed—his old school trunk—a blanket laid across the top. A small bookshelf held some books but otherwise it was bare. Spartan. He had never allowed himself to be too at home here. Or anywhere. No wonder he was such an expert packer.

Flora's room was a stark contrast. It was more than twice the size of his with a wide dormer window as well as a skylight. Old toys, books and ornaments were still displayed on the shelves and on the white, scalloped dressing table and chest of drawers she had thought so sophisticated when she was twelve. Old posters of ponies and boy bands were stuck to her walls and a clutter of old scarves, old make-up and magazines gave the room a lived-in air.

She dropped her bags thankfully in a corner of the room and pulled her phone out of her pocket. The message light flashed and Flora's heart lurched with hope as she eagerly scanned it, but, although she had received at least a million emails urging her to buy her last-minute Christmas gifts Right Now, been promised the best rate to pay off her Christmas debts by several credit-card companies and a very good deal on sexual enhancement products, there was nothing at all from Alex.

Swallowing back her disappointment, she stared thoughtfully at her screen. Call or text? Texting would be easier, give her a chance to phrase her words carefully. But maybe this shouldn't be careful. It had to be from the heart. She pressed his number before she could talk herself out of it and listened to the dial tone, her heart hammering.

She was so keyed up it didn't register at first that the voice at the other end wasn't Alex but his voicemail message. 'Darn it,' she muttered while his slightly constrained voice informed her that he wasn't available right now but would get back to her as soon as he could.

'Alex,' she said quickly as soon as it beeped. 'It's me. Come home. Please? It's not the same without you. We all miss you. We'll be okay, I promise. Just come home. Come home for Christmas.'

She clicked the hang-up icon and let the phone drop onto her bed. She had done all she could. It was up to him now.

CHAPTER ELEVEN

HOW HE REMEMBERED the address, Alex had no idea. He must have written it on enough letters that somehow he had retained the information, lying dormant until his need unlocked it once again. It took less than an hour of research to ascertain that his grandmother was still alive and living in the same house. But as he drove along the leafy, prosperous-looking road it was all completely unfamiliar and doubts began to creep in.

What if he had got the name and address wrong?

Or worse, what if he had got them right and she didn't want to see him?

He pulled up outside a well-maintained-looking white house and killed the engine. What was he doing? It was Christmas Eve and he was about to drop in, unannounced, on a long-lost relative who probably didn't want to see him. He must be crazy. Alex gripped the steering wheel and swore softly. But then he remembered Flora's face as she walked away from him at the airport. Disappointed, defeated. If there was any way he could put things right, he would.

And this might help.

The house looked shut up. Every curtain was drawn and there was no sign of light or life anywhere. The driveway was so thickly gravelled that he couldn't step quietly no matter how lightly he trod, and the crunch from each step echoed loudly, disturbing the eerie twilight silence. Any minute he expected a neighbour to accost him but there was no movement anywhere. It was like being in an alternative universe where he was the last soul standing.

The door was a substantial wooden oval with an imposing brass door knocker. It was cold and heavy as he lifted it, making far more of a bang than he expected when he rapped it on the door. He stood listening to the echo disturb the absolute silence, shivering a little in the murky air.

Alex shifted from foot to foot as he waited, straining to hear any movement in the house. He was just debating whether to try again or give up, half turning to walk away, when the door swung open.

'Oh, you're not the carol singers.' He turned back, words of explanation ready on his tongue when he found himself staring into a pair of familiar green-grey eyes, eyes growing round, hope and shock mingled in their depths. 'Alex? Is it really you?'

'You're not watching the films?' Flora's dad looked up from the pastry he was expertly rolling out and smiled at her. 'It's *The Muppet Christmas Carol.*'

'I know.' Flora wandered over to the oak and marble counter where her father practised his recipes and slipped a finger into the bowl of fragrant home-made mincemeat, sucking the sweet, spicy mixture appreciatively. 'Mmm, this is gorgeous. What's the secret ingredient?'

'Earl Grey and lemon.' He nodded at her finger. 'Dip

that again and I'll chop it off. I thought the Muppets were your favourite?'

'They are.' Flora slid onto a high stool and leaned forward, propping her chin in her hands as she watched her father work. The pastry was a perfect smooth square as he began to cut out the rounds. 'Only I peeped in and Minerva, the twins and Greg are all curled up on the sofa. They looked so sweet I didn't want to disturb them.'

'They wouldn't have minded.'

'I know, but it's not often I see Minerva so relaxed. She might have wanted to start talking marketing strategy or buzz creation and then the film would have been ruined for everyone.'

'That's very thoughtful of you.' Her mother bustled into the kitchen, her phone in her hand. 'Great news, darling. Horry's colleague wants to work Christmas, bad break-up apparently, so she'd rather work. Awful for her but it means Horry can come home this evening after all. Now we just need Alex and the whole family is together again.'

Guilt punched Flora's chest and she resisted the urge to look at her phone to see if he'd responded. 'I'm sure he'll be here as soon as he can.'

'We're all very excited about your scarves.' Her mother filled the kettle and began to collect cups from the vast dresser that dominated the far wall. The kitchen used to be two rooms but they had been knocked into one and a glass-roofed extension added to make it a huge, airy, sun-filled space filled with gadgets, curios and the bits and bobs Flora's dad couldn't resist: painted bowls, salt and pepper pots, vintage jugs and a whole assortment of souvenirs. Saucepans hung from a rack on the ceiling, there were planted herbs on every window sill and the range cooker usually had something tasty baking, bubbling or roasting, filling the air with rich aromas.

'It doesn't seem quite real.' Flora grimaced. 'I'm sure Minerva will change that. She was hissing something about Gantt charts earlier.'

'She's right, you should take this seriously.' Her mother added three teaspoons of tea to the large pot and topped it with the boiled water. No teabags or shortcuts in the Buckingham kitchen. 'I don't know why it's taken you so long. It's obvious you should have been focusing on this, not wasting your talents on that awful pub chain. Those disgusting neon lemons…' She shuddered.

Flora stared at her mother. 'I thought you wanted me to have a steady job.' She couldn't keep the hurt out of her voice. 'You're always asking me when I'm going to settle down—in a job, a relationship, a place of my own.'

'No,' her mother contradicted as she passed Flora a cup of tea. Flora wrapped her hands around it, grateful for its warmth. 'I wanted you to have direction. To know where you *wanted* to go. You always seemed so lost, Flora. Vet school to compete with the twins, interior design to fit in with Alex. I just wanted you to follow your own heart.'

'It's not always that easy though, is it? I mean, sometimes your heart can lead you astray.' To Flora's horror she could feel tears bubbling up. She swallowed hard, trying to hold back the threatening sob, ducking her head to hide her eyes. She should have known better. Nothing ever escaped Dr Jane Buckingham's sharp eyes.

'Flora?' Her mother's voice was gentle and that, combined with the gentle hug, pushed Flora over the edge she had been teetering on. It was almost a relief to let the tears flow, to let the sobs burst out, easing the painful pressure in her chest just a little. Her mother didn't probe or ask any more, she just held Flora as she cried, rubbing her back and smoothing her hair off her wet cheeks.

It was like being a child again. If only her mother could fix this. If only it *were* fixable.

It took several minutes before the sobs quietened, the tears stopped and the hiccups subsided. Flora had been guided to the old but very comfortable chintzy sofa by the window, her tea handed to her along with yet another of her father's mince pies. She curled up onto the cushions and stared out of the window at the pot-filled patio and the lawn beyond.

'I won't ask any awkward questions,' her mother promised as she sat next to her. 'But if you do want to talk we're always here. You do know that, I hope, darling.'

Flora nodded, not quite trusting herself to speak. She didn't often confide in her parents, not wanting to see the disappointed looks on their faces, not to feel that yet again she was a let-down compared to her high-flying siblings.

But she wasn't sure she could carry this alone. Not any more.

'Alex asked me to marry him.'

She didn't miss the exchange of glances between her parents. They didn't look shocked, more saddened.

'I wondered if it was Alex. You've always loved him so.'

She had no secrets, it seemed, and there was no point in denying it. She nodded. 'But he doesn't love me. He thought marriage would be sensible. He said I would have financial stability and storage for my designs.'

'Oh.'

'I mean, I didn't expect sonnets but I didn't think anyone would ever suggest storage as a reason for marriage.' Flora was aware she sounded bitter. 'How could I say yes? It would have been so wrong for both of us. Only now he's not here and I miss him so much…'

Her mother patted her knee. 'Have I ever told you how your father and I met?'

Flora stifled a sigh. Here it came, the patented Dr Jane Buckingham anecdote filled with advice. 'You were flatmates,' she muttered.

'For a year,' her father said, standing back to survey the trays of finished mince pies.

'And then you went out for dinner and looked into each other's eyes and the rest is history.' Perfect couple with their perfect jobs and a perfect home and nearly perfect children. The story had been rehashed in a hundred interviews.

'I think I fell in love with your mother the moment I saw her,' her father said, a reminiscent tone in his voice. 'But I didn't think I was good enough for her. I was a hobby baker and trainee food journalist and there she was, a junior doctor. Brilliant, fierce, dedicated. I didn't know what to say to her. So I didn't really say anything at all.'

Flora's mother picked up the tale. 'But when I came off shift—exhausted after sixty hours on my feet, malnourished after grabbing something from the hospital canteen—I would walk in and there would be something ready for me. No matter what time. A filo pie and roasted vegetables at two in the morning, piles of fluffy pancakes heaped with fruit at seven a.m. Freshly made bread and delicious salads at noon.' A soft smile curved her mother's lips. 'Do you remember when I said I missed falafel and you made them? They weren't readily available then,' she told her daughter. 'It was just a passing comment but I got home two days later to find freshly made falafel and home-made hummus in the fridge.'

'You old romantic.' Flora smiled over at her dad.

'I still barely spoke to her,' he admitted. 'I didn't know what to say. But I listened.'

'And then on Valentine's Day I came in, so tired I could barely drag myself in through the door, and waiting for me was the most beautiful breakfast. Home-made granola, eggs Benedict, little pastries. And I understood what he'd been telling me for the last year. Not with words but with food, with his actions. So I slept and then I took *him* out for dinner to say thank you. We got married six months later.'

'If you want to be wooed with flowers and lovely words, then Alex is never going to be the man for you, Flora,' her father added. 'And maybe he really does think storage and stability is enough. But *maybe* those words mask something more. You need to dig a little deeper. See what's really in his heart. A pancake isn't always just a pancake.'

Flora bit into the mince pie. The pastry was perfect, firm yet melting with a lemony tang, the filling spicy yet subtle. When it came to food her dad was always spot on. Maybe he was right here as well.

'Thank you,' she said, but she couldn't help checking her phone as she did so. Nor could she deny the sharp stab of disappointment when she saw that Alex hadn't replied.

Was her father right? Was Alex's matter-of-fact proposal a cover for deeper feelings and if so would she be able to live with someone who would never be able to say what was in their heart? Live with the constant uncertainty? Flora sighed; maybe she was clutching at straws and there was no hidden meaning. Maybe storage was just that. The question was how willing was she to find out and what compromises was she willing to make?

And if a practical marriage was the only way to keep him, then could she settle for that when the alternative was losing him for ever?

'That's you and your mother. You must have been about eighteen months.'

Alex stared at the photo, lovingly mounted in a leather book. It was one of several charting his mother's brief life from a smiling baby to a wary-looking teen, a shy young bride to a proud mother.

'She looks…'

'Happy?' his grandmother supplied. 'She was, a lot of the time.'

Alex struggled to marry this side of his mother with the few pieces of information his father had begrudgingly fed him. He put the album back onto the low wooden coffee table and stared around the room in search of help.

Alex had never really known any of his grandparents but he had always imagined them in old, musty houses filled with cushions, lace tablecloths and hordes of silver-framed photos. The light, clean lines of his grandmother's sitting room were as far from the dark rooms of his dreams as the slim woman opposite with her trendy pixie cut and jeans and jacket was from the grey-haired granny of his imagination.

'My father said she cried all the time. That she hated being a mother, hated me. That's why…' he faltered. 'That's why she did what she did.'

His grandmother closed her eyes briefly. 'I should have tried harder, Alex. I should have fought for you. Your father made things so difficult. I was allowed a day here, a day there, no overnight stays or holidays and I was too scared to push in case he locked me out completely—but he did that anyway. In the end my letters were returned, my gifts sent back. He said it was too hard for you to be reminded of the past, that he wanted you to settle with your stepmother.'

Letters, gifts? His father hadn't just returned material items. He had made sure that Alex would never have a loving relationship with his family.

His grandmother twisted her hands. 'If I had tried harder then I could have made sure you knew about your mother. The colours she liked, her favourite books, the way she sang when she was happy. But most importantly I could have told you that she loved you. Because she did, very, very much. But she wasn't well. She didn't think she was a good enough mother, she worried about every little thing—every cry was a reminder that she was letting you down. Every tiny incident a reminder that she was failing you. In the end she convinced herself that you would be better off without her.'

Alex blinked, heat burning his eyes. 'She was wrong.'

'I know. I should have made her get help.' She closed her eyes and for a moment she looked much older, frailer, her face lined with grief. 'But she was good at hiding her feelings and she was completely under your father's control. He couldn't admit that she wasn't well; it didn't fit with his vision of the perfect family. And so she got more adept at denying she was struggling but all the time she was sinking deeper and deeper. I knew something was wrong but every time I tried to talk to her she would back away. So I stopped trying, afraid that I would lose her. But I lost her anyway. And I lost you.' Her voice faltered, still raw with grief all these years later.

Alex swallowed. 'Can you tell me about her now?'

His grandmother blinked, her eyes shiny with tears, and glanced up at the clock on the mantelpiece. 'Goodness, is that the time? My son—your uncle—will be collecting me soon. I always spend Christmas Eve at their house. You have three cousins, all younger than you, of course, but they will be so excited to meet you.'

Christmas Eve, how could he have forgotten? 'I'm sorry, I didn't think…'

His grandmother carried on as if he hadn't spoken. 'I'm just going to ask him to collect me in the morning instead. You will stay for dinner? There's a room if you want to spend the night. We have a lifetime of catching up to do. Unless, there must be somewhere you need to be. A handsome boy like you. A wife?' Her eyes flickered to his left hand. 'A girlfriend?'

Alex shook his head. 'No,' he said. 'There isn't anyone.' But as he spoke the words he knew they weren't entirely true.

Alex wasn't sure how long his grandmother was

gone. He was lost in the past, going through each album again, committing each photo to heart. His mother as a young girl on the beach, her graduation photos, her wedding pictures. There was a proud, proprietorial gleam in his father's eyes that sent a shiver snaking down Alex's spine. Love wasn't meant to be selfish and destructive; he might not know much but he knew that. Surely it was supposed to be about support, putting the other person first. Shared goals.

Pretty much what he had offered Flora.

And yet it hadn't been enough...

His brooding thoughts were interrupted as his grandmother backed into the room holding a tray and Alex jumped to his feet to take it from her. 'Thank you,' she said. 'There's not much, I'm afraid. I'm at your uncle's until after New Year so rations are rather sparse.' She directed him to the round table near the patio doors and Alex placed the tray onto it, carefully setting out the bowls of piping-hot soup and the plates heaped with crackers, cheese and apples.

'It looks perfect. Thank you for rearranging your plans. You really didn't have to.'

'I wanted to. Everything's arranged and your uncle has asked me to let you know that you are welcome to come too tomorrow—or at any point over the holidays. For an hour or a night or the whole week. Whatever you need. There's no need to call ahead, please. If you want to come just turn up, I'll make sure you have the address. Now sit down, do. I tend to eat in here—I don't like eating in the kitchen and sitting in sole state in the dining room would be far too lonely. I rarely use it now.' She sighed. 'This house is far too big but it's so crammed with memories—of my husband, of your mother—that I hate the idea of leaving.'

'When did my grandfather die?' Another family member he would never know.

'When your mother was eighteen. It hit her very hard. She was a real daddy's girl. I sometimes think that's why she fell for your father. He was so certain of everything and she was still so vulnerable. Your grandfather's death had ripped our family apart and we were all alone in our grief. I still miss him every day. He was my best friend. He made every day an adventure.'

The soup was excellent, thick, spicy and warming, but Alex was hardly aware of it. Best friends? So it *could* work.

'That's the nicest epitaph I ever heard. He must have been an amazing man.'

How would Alex be remembered after he died? Hopefully as a talented and successful architect. But was that enough?

No. It wasn't. He wanted someone to have that same wistful look in their eye. That same mingled grief, nostalgia, affection and humour. No. He didn't want just *someone* to remember him that way.

He wanted Flora to. He wanted every day to be an adventure with his best friend. Not because it was safe and made sense. No. Because he loved her.

CHAPTER TWELVE

FLORA WOKE WITH a start, rolling over to check her phone automatically. Five a.m. and still no answer from Alex.

She rolled onto her back and stared at the luminous green stars still stuck to her ceiling. It had been a typical Christmas Eve; Horry had turned up during dinner, ready to hoover up all the left-over rice, pakoras and dahl, and then Greg had insisted on babysitting so that Minerva and Flora's mother could join the rest of their family for a couple of drinks before they all trooped to the ancient Norman church for the short and moving celebration of Midnight Mass. It wasn't often they were all together like this, but it just made Alex's absence all the more achingly obvious. Flora had tried not to spend the whole evening checking her phone. She had failed miserably, barely taking part in the conversation and mouthing her way through the carols.

Still no word. She just needed to know he was okay.

No, she was kidding herself. She wasn't that altruistic. She wanted to *know*, to look deeper, to see if somewhere, deep inside, he cared for her the way she so desperately wanted him to.

And if not to ask herself if that was all right. If all

he was capable of offering was friendship mixed with passion, then should she agree to marry him anyway—because she would still be with him? Was it settling or being pragmatic? Selling herself short or grabbing the opportunity with both hands?

Although it was rather moot; having said no once, she wasn't sure how to let him know if she did change her mind. It wasn't exactly something you could drop into conversation.

Flora turned her pillow over, plumping it back up with a little more force than was strictly necessary, and attempted to snuggle back down; but it was no use. She was wide awake. Not the pleasurable anticipatory tingle of a Christmas morning but the creeping dread that nothing would ever be the same again.

Well, she could lie here and brood or she could get up, make coffee and make a plan. She reached for her phone again and the sudden light illuminated her room and the bags of presents still piled in the corner. It was an unwritten law that all presents had to be snuck under the Christmas tree without the knowledge of anyone else in the household. Flora and Alex usually spent most of the early hours trying to catch the other out—a heady few hours of ambush, traps and whispered giggles because it was also a sternly enforced law that nobody could get up before seven a.m., the edict a hangover from her childhood.

She swung her legs out of the bed, feeling for her slippers in the dark and shrugging on the old vintage velvet dressing gown Alex had bought her for her sixteenth birthday, before padding quietly across the room to retrieve the bags. The house was in darkness and, not wanting to wake anyone else up, she switched on the torch on her phone to help guide her down the windy stairs. Alex's door was still ajar, the empty room dark.

Her bags were bulky and it was all Flora could do to get them quietly along the landing and down the main stairs. Every rustle of paper, every muffled bang as the bag hit the bannister made her freeze in place, but finally she stepped over the creaky last step and into the hallway. Not for the first time she cursed her mother's decision to furnish the wide hall as a second sitting area. Not only did she have to dodge the hat stand, umbrella stand and the hall table, but she also had to weave around a bookcase and a couple of wing-backed chairs before she reached the safety of the sitting-room door.

Flora froze, her hand on the handle as she clocked the faint light seeping under the door? Another early riser? She could have sworn she had heard all her family make their stealthy present-laying trips soon after she had gone to bed, and it was far too quiet to be either of her nieces.

One of them had probably left the light on, that was all. She turned the handle and nudged the door open with her hip as she lugged the two bags into the room, turning to place them next to the tree…

Only to jump back when she saw a shadowy figure already kneeling under the tree. Grey with tiredness, hair rumpled and still in the clothes she had seen him in yesterday morning, on his knees as he added his own gifts to the pleasingly huge pile. 'Alex?'

He rocked back onto his heels. 'Merry Christmas, Flora.'

Her throat swelled and she swallowed hard, so many things to say and she had no idea which one to start with. 'You're here?' Great, start with the blindingly obvious. 'I tried calling…'

'I know. I got your message, thank you.'

'Where have you been?'

'That's a long story.' He nodded at the bags lying forgotten at her feet. 'Shall I pretend I haven't seen those and go and put some coffee on?'

She blinked, trying to clear her head, take in that he was actually here, that he had come home. 'Yes. Coffee. Thanks.'

The corners of his mouth quirked up in a brief smile. 'Good. I could kill for one of your dad's mince pies as well.'

Normally Flora took her time placing her gifts, making sure they were spread out, tucked away, but right now she didn't care, chucking them onto the pile haphazardly with no care for the aesthetic effect. She switched off the lamps and sidled out of the room, closing the door quietly behind her before turning into the kitchen.

The scent of coffee was as welcome as the sight of Alex. Really here, reassuringly here, leaning against the counter, a mince pie in one hand, a mug in the other. 'Nothing says Christmas like your dad's baking.'

'That was the title of his last interview.' Flora leaned over and stole a crumb off his plate. 'It's good to see you, Alex.' It didn't feel like less than twenty-four hours since they had parted; it felt like a lifetime.

'I'm sorry I just took off but I needed some time, some space. I took your advice. I looked up my mother's family.'

Whatever Flora had been expecting, it wasn't this. 'You did? I thought you didn't know where they were?'

'I didn't. Only since you mentioned them the idea was niggling away at the back of my mind. You were right, there had to be someone out there. And then I remembered, when I was a little boy I used to see my grandmother sometimes—and I wrote to her a lot. I remembered enough of her address to be able to track her down.'

'What it is to have a photographic memory.'

'Turns out it comes in useful.'

'So.' Flora felt unaccountably shy. 'What was she like? Did you meet her?'

To her surprise Alex laughed. 'Nothing like I expected, very chic, rather cool and very lovely. You'll like her, Flora. And it was as if all the missing pieces just slotted together. She had answers and photos and she knew.'

'Knew what?'

His voice broke. 'That my mother loved me. She didn't kill herself because she hated me. She killed herself because she thought she was letting me down. It was her illness that was to blame, not me.'

Tears burned the backs of her eyes, her throat. How could he have lived all these years believing it was his fault? How could his father have allowed him to? All awkwardness, all restraint disappeared as Flora reached over to grab his hand, her fingers enfolding his. 'Of course it was—and of course she loved you. How could she not have?'

'She hung on for two years after I was born, terrified and so unhappy, but she tried. She really tried. If she'd got help it would all have been so different but she was in denial and my father thought that she was weak. He didn't want her talking to anyone but him.'

'If anyone's to blame he is. For all of it. For your mother, for taking your stepmother's side, for allowing you to leave home.'

'I think I know that now. The stupid thing is I have spent my whole life wishing I had a family and a home and yet I had one all along.'

Flora looked down at the counter. 'With your grandmother.'

'No.' His voice softened. 'With you.'

She looked up, startled at his words. Her eyes locked onto his and her pulse began to thump at the look in his eyes. It was more than the desire she had enjoyed over the last week, more than the candid friendship of the last twenty years. It was new, unknown and so intense she could barely breathe. 'I'm glad you know that. No matter what happened with you and me your home is here...'

'I know that but that's not what I mean. I mean that wherever you are, Flora, that's where I belong. London, Kent, Bali, Austria. My house, your room or a tent in the pouring rain. I could lose everything tomorrow and as long as you were with me I wouldn't mind. You...' His voice cracked. 'You make every day an adventure, Flora, and I was too blind or too scared to see it before.'

The blood was rushing in her ears and she had to grip the counter tightly, afraid that she might fall without its solid support. 'Me?'

'I think I've always known it—from the very first day when you helped me make a den. Remember? I was running away but I wasn't scared because I'd found someone to be with. But I didn't want to face it. I didn't want to taint you. My father said I ruined everything and everyone I touched and, oh, Flora, I didn't want to ruin you.'

'You won't, you couldn't.'

'When I asked you to marry me I was a fool. I thought I meant those things, those sensible reasons, the list of positives, but really I was a coward. I was too afraid to tell you what I really meant. I wanted to tell you that you were the most beautiful woman in the ballroom, that I couldn't take my eyes off you all night, that you were my best friend and that I loved you and didn't want to spend a single second of my life away from you. That's what I should have said.'

Flora blinked hard, willing the tears not to fall. 'It's a little more convincing than storage.'

'If I'd told you all this then, would you have said yes?'

She nodded, unable to get the words out.

'And...' he stepped around the counter so that he was right next to her, turning her unresisting body so that she faced him, cupping her face in his hands and looking down at her, tenderness in his eyes '...if I ask you now?'

Flora smiled up at him, her voice scarcely more than a whisper. 'Why don't you ask me and see?'

Laughter flashed in his eyes as he took her hand in his. 'No flash mobs, no rings in ice cream, no sonnets. Just you and me, Flora. Just like it's always been.'

She nodded, her chest so swollen with happiness she thought she might drift away.

'Flora Prosperine Buckingham, would you do me the incredible honour of being my best friend, my companion, my lover, my confidante and my partner in adventure every day for the rest of my life?'

'I can't think of anyone I'd rather spend my life with.' Flora looked at him, at the ruddy, disordered curls, the freckles, the long-lashed eyes, and her heart turned over with love. 'Of course I'll marry you. I think I fell in love with you too, that day in the lane. You were so determined and so brave. I just wanted to make it all better.'

'You did, you do. It just took me far too long to notice.'

'Look.' She pointed upwards to the beam overhead. 'Mistletoe.'

'I don't need mistletoe to tell me to kiss you, not any more.' Alex leaned forward and brushed her mouth with his. 'Merry Christmas, Flora.'

'Merry Christmas, Alex.' She could finally say the words she had been holding in for so long. 'I love you.'

He looked over at the grandfather clock in the corner. 'We still have ninety minutes before the household's allowed to get up. Can you think of any way to spend it?'

Flora rose onto her tiptoes and allowed herself to kiss him properly, deeply, lovingly. Her fiancé, her man, her best friend. 'I'm sure we can think of something...'

* * * * *

THE PRINCE'S CHRISTMAS VOW

JENNIFER FAYE

To my readers…
I am so blessed to have the most amazing readers,
some who have become dear friends.
I greatly appreciate your friendly notes, unfailing
support and daily company on social media.
Thank you.

You all are amazing!

CHAPTER ONE

THE PLAN WAS in motion.

Though suddenly, it didn't sound like such a good idea.

Demetrius Castanavo, the Crown Prince of the Mirraccino Islands, shrugged off the worrisome feeling as he stepped out of the air-conditioned black limousine. Nothing was going to go wrong. He glanced at the clear blue sky, appreciating this last bit of good weather before it cooled down in the weeks leading up to Christmas.

Demetrius buttoned his charcoal-gray suit jacket, gave each sleeve a tug and then straightened his shoulders. Today he must look his best. It was imperative.

A bright camera flash momentarily blinded him.

He blinked, regaining his focus. The media coverage had begun. He restrained a sigh. Instead he lifted his chin and forced his lips into a well-practiced smile.

Demetrius, the royal playboy, was no more. His days of nonchalance and bucking the system were over. Now he was intent on becoming a proper and worthy heir to the Mirraccino throne. It was, after all, his birthright—whether he desired it or not.

And now he was about to participate in a very important interview that would help shape his new, improved public image—one he hoped would sway the residents of the Mirraccino nation to support his inevitable rise to the throne.

His gaze settled on an impressive set of steps that led to a historic mansion. At the top was an expansive landing with large, white columns amid the backdrop of blue shuttered windows. The place was a timeless beauty. He was glad they were going to save this building by revitalizing it.

There was just one snag in his well-thought-out plan—Zoe.

His estranged wife.

But that situation would be resolved soon—very soon.

The head of his security detail leaned in close and whispered, "The reporter is waiting for you on the landing, Your Royal Highness."

Demetrius shoved the disturbing thoughts of his estranged wife to the back of his mind. He'd deal with her tomorrow. "Good. As soon as I meet with him, we have to get moving if we're going to stay on schedule today."

"Sir, the reporter, it's a woman."

"*Sì*. I remember now." Demetrius needed to keep his head in this game instead of wondering how Zoe would react when she saw him again.

Demetrius swiftly climbed the steps that fanned out, covering a large area while adding to the building's charm. He'd definitely made the right decision by insisting the all-access ramp be constructed on the side of the building, readily accessible yet not losing the building's aesthetic appeal.

His vision was to marry the building's beauty with functionality. They were doing well with the functionality. The beauty would be Zoe's area of expertise. And tomorrow would be her first day on the job.

Off to the far side of the landing stood a short, slender brunette. Her makeup was a bit heavy for his tastes, but he reasoned that it must have something to do with spending so much time in front of the television cameras. Interviews were one of his least favorite tasks, but at times they were a necessity—like now.

When his advisors had unanimously agreed this was the best way for him to overhaul his scandalous youthful past, they had also assured him that agreeing to the one-on-one interview would be the best way to give the citizens access to him—to let them know that he was serious about being a caring, involved ruler. Though he'd rather keep his distance from the paparazzi, Demetrius had to admit that in this one particular instance, they may in fact come in handy—quite handy indeed.

He reached the landing and turned to the reporter. Greetings were quick and formal. Demetrius had every intention of keeping things moving along at a brisk pace. He knew the more time he spent with the media, the more they'd learn. And in his experience, that was never a good thing. He wanted to control the flow of information, not the other way around.

Ms. Carla Russo, the face of Mirraccino's entertainment news, held a microphone. "Before we begin, I wondered if you might have an announcement for our viewers."

"I do have news—"

"Oh, good. We've been hearing all sorts of rumors, and the viewers would really like confirmation that you've decided upon a princess."

What?

The cameraman moved closer. Demetrius's throat constricted. They knew about Zoe? No. Impossible. The reporter was on a hunting expedition. Pure and simple. Anything for a sensational headline. Well, he wasn't about to give her anything to chase. Nothing at all.

With practiced skill, Demetrius forced his lips into a smile. "I can assure you there is no princess in my near future."

"That's not what we've heard. There are rumors floating about that someone special has caught your attention. Could you share her name with us?"

Maybe the reporter did know something about Zoe, after all. Though the palace employees had all signed confidentiality agreements, there could still be a leak. A delivery person? A guest? There was always room for someone who'd slipped through the cracks. But obviously, whatever this woman knew wasn't much or she'd be throwing out names and facts.

He couldn't lose control of this interview. It wasn't just the building that was about to get a fresh lease on life. If his plan succeeded, their futures would both have makeovers. After all, he'd been putting off getting on with his royal duties long enough now. He'd grown. He'd learned. And now he was becoming the man he should have been all along.

With his twin brother, Alexandro, now married and spending a lot of time abroad in his wife's homeland, more responsibilities had befallen the king. But the king was not in the best of health. The physicians kept warning him to slow down. And that's why Demetrius's plan just had to work. He didn't want his father to have a heart attack or worse.

The first part of his plan included gaining the public's trust. The second part was a bit more delicate—getting his estranged wife to quietly sign the annulment papers. The question that needed answering was why had she ignored the papers for months now?

By the time the revitalization project had finally gotten off the ground, so had Zoe's career as an interior designer. She'd worked on some of the most notable buildings here in Bellacitta, the capital of Mirraccino. With the public enthralled with her work, he knew he needed to hire her. His advisors, knowing his history with Zoe, said he was foolish. But Demetrius insisted he had reasons for this unorthodox approach.

His first reason was that she had a flare with colors and arrangements—a way to make people sit up and take notice without it being over-the-top. And the second reason was to be able to get close to her without arousing the press's suspicions. With her close at hand, he'd be able to work the answers out of her that he needed to put his short-lived marriage to a very quiet end.

Demetrius struggled to maintain his calm and easy demeanor. "Today, I'd like to focus on Mirraccino and in particular the South Shore redevelopment. It's very important to me and to the king. It promises to bring new homes and businesses to the area as well as create new job opportunities for the local residents."

"So the rumors of a new princess are false?"

Drawing on a lifetime of experience of dealing with the media, he spoke in a calm, measured tone. "You will be my first call when I have a marriage announcement. But I believe right now the viewers would like to hear more about the project."

The reporter's brows rose and her eyes filled with unspoken questions, but he met her gaze head-on. If she dared to continue this line of questioning into his personal life, he'd wrap up this interview immediately. It wasn't as if she was the only reporter on the island, though she did host the nation's most popular entertainment show.

Color infused her cheeks as she at last glanced at the camera. "The South Shore project is going to benefit quite a number of people. How exactly did you come up with the idea to revitalize this area?"

"This endeavor is something that has been of interest to the crown for some time now. However, it wasn't until recently that we were able to gain the last of the property deeds in order to push ahead with the plans."

The loud rumble of an engine caught his attention. He sought out the source of the noise. It was a taxi that had pulled to the curb near his limo. A tall, willowy brunette emerged from the blue-and-white taxi. She turned and leaned in the passenger window as she handed over the cab fare. If Demetrius didn't know better, he'd swear that was his wife. But he refused to let his imagination get the best of him and upend this interview.

He turned back to Ms. Russo. "Residenza del Rosa is our first project. We will have it up and running by the beginning of the new year."

"So you have plans for more than just the mansion?" Ms. Russo sent him an expectant look.

"*Sì.*" Demetrius swallowed hard and forced his thoughts back to business. "Residenza del Rosa is already well underway. As soon as we have the necessary funding secured, we will start on phase two, which will be to build affordable housing." The clicking of heels caught his attention. He refused to be distracted. Security would handle it. "We intend to make the South Shore accessible to both the young and the young at heart. This area will once again be a robust community."

The head of his security detail approached him. Demetrius held up a finger to pause the interview. The bodyguard leaned over and whispered in his ear. "It's a Ms. Sarris. She has a pass and she says she works here. Should we let her through?"

"Oh, look." Ms. Russo's face lit up. Too late. She'd caught sight of Zoe. The reporter's eyes sparkled as though she'd been given a special treat. "Isn't that the interior designer, Zoe Sarris?"

Before answering the reporter, Demetrius gave an affirmative yet reluctant nod to his man to allow Zoe to join them. That woman certainly did have bad timing—first when she walked out on him just hours after saying "I do"—and now. How did she do it?

He could feel the reporter's gaze on him. He cleared his throat. "Yes, it's Miss Sarris."

"I wonder what she's doing here?" The reporter sent him a speculative look. "Did you arrange this?"

He resisted the urge to frown at the reporter's fishing expedition as well as the fact that his estranged wife was about to crash his very important interview. "No. It appears she's here to work. We've been lucky enough to obtain Ms. Sarris's exclusive services to create a welcoming yet relaxing environment for the future residents of Residenza del Rosa."

"And what features will it provide?"

"This long-term care home will be able to accommodate different levels of care from assisted living to skilled nursing."

"And Ms. Sarris is here to make this mansion into the beauty it once was?"

"We're hoping she'll be able to take what is here and give it a fresh feel."

"I'm sure she will. Is Miss Sarris signed on for the other buildings in the revitalization project?"

"Not at this point. We want to see how this first building goes and then we'll reevaluate, figuring out what works and what doesn't."

Ms. Russo nodded in understanding. "How splendid that she can join us and give our viewers an idea of what she has in mind for the place. I've seen her work before and it's fantastic. In fact, we can do before and after shoots of the mansion, both inside and out, with your permission of course."

"That sounds like a good idea."

Demetrius followed Ms. Russo's gaze to the woman in question. Zoe's clothing choice was nothing out of the ordinary, a short black skirt and a pink blouse. But on her, it looked fantastic as it nestled her curves perfectly—curves that he still knew by memory. She lifted her black sunglasses and then shook out her long dark curls before resting her shades atop her head like a hairband.

No matter what had gone down between them, there was

no denying the obvious—she was a knockout. He should glance away—check his phone—continue the interview—anything but continue to stare at her.

Her legs were long, toned and tan. He couldn't have turned away even if he'd have tried, which he had no inclination to do. It'd been months since he'd laid eyes on her. Visions of her in his dreams didn't count—they couldn't hold a candle to the real thing.

Zoe moved one strappy black high heel in front of the other. The classic ZZ Top song "Legs" started playing in his head. This girl definitely knew her strongest attributes and she worked them—no wonder he'd fallen for her hard and fast. Was it possible that she was even more gorgeous now than she had been when they'd met more than a year ago?

"It's warm standing here in the sun. Perhaps we should move to the shade." Ms. Russo signaled to her cameraman to take a break. "Prince Demetrius, are you all right?"

The concern in the reporter's voice startled him out of the trance he'd fallen under. He drew a breath of air into his straining lungs. With effort, he turned his gaze from Zoe to the reporter who wore an inquisitive expression.

Not good, Demetrius. Not good at all. Stay focused.

He cleared his throat. "Sorry. I just remembered something that needs my attention. Let me just make a note of it." He pulled out his phone and made the pretense of typing something while he got his brain screwed on straight.

The same question kept playing over and over in his mind. What in the world was Zoe doing here? Surely she hadn't come to see him. No. That was impossible. His schedule was kept under wraps for security purposes. Even Ms. Russo had not been alerted to the location for this interview until this morning. So that still left the question of why Zoe had crashed this important interview?

Demetrius slipped his phone back in his jacket pocket. "Okay. Where were we?"

"I thought we might want to wait for Ms. Sarris to join us."

Her comment had him instinctively turning back to the woman who'd gained the reporter's attention. Zoe climbed the last two steps in those sky-high black heels that made her legs look as though they went on and on forever. His mouth grew dry and his palms became moist.

He should have had his men turn her away. How was he supposed to concentrate on the interview when all he wanted to do was confront Zoe?

He only had one question: Why?

Okay. So maybe he did have a couple more questions. Like, when did she start dressing like that? Were her skirts always so short? How was a man to make intelligent conversation when all he could think about was her bare, tanned legs?

Concentrate on the business at hand.

Every muscle in his body tensed. He couldn't continue to stare at her. He didn't want anyone to notice that he was affected by Zoe's presence.

"Excuse me." Zoe's gaze didn't quite meet his. "I didn't know anyone would be here today. If it's okay, I'll just go inside and make some notes."

"No problem." Demetrius backed up to let her pass by.

"Wait." Ms. Russo stepped in Zoe's way. "Ms. Sarris, would you have a couple of minutes to speak with us?"

Zoe shook her head. "I don't want to intrude."

"You aren't. In fact, I'd like to get a few quotes from you. But first I need to go track down my cameraman. He wanted to film a few frames of the mansion under construction."

Demetrius waited until the reporter was out of earshot before turning to Zoe. "What are you doing here?"

"I already told you. I came to take notes." Her steady gaze met his. "What are you doing here?"

Leave it to Zoe to question a prince. She never was one to be awed by someone's position or power. To her, everyone put on their pants one leg at a time just like everyone else. Then again, that was one of the things he'd always admired about her. But suddenly, it wasn't so admirable— suddenly she made him uncomfortable having to explain himself.

Though his family thought he'd only known Zoe for a few weeks, the truth was that they'd been involved for six months before taking the plunge. When his family found out about their elopement, chaos had ensued, so he never got a chance to correct them. Besides, what difference would it have made? His family had already determined that he was impulsive and foolish to rush into marriage with someone so unfitting for the role of princess.

But that was then and things had changed a lot since then. Now Demetrius was cautious and he thought out his actions before he acted. In fact, he'd planned out what he would say to Zoe when they first met up again, but he hadn't expected it to be here on these steps—in public— in front of a television camera.

Not about to get into anything personal right now, he settled on, "I'm the prince and I have every right to be here. After all, this project is under the direct supervision of the Crown."

"Of course." Her cheeks took on a pink tinge. "I should have known. I was just caught off guard by your presence."

"Listen, there's something you should know—"

"Sorry about that." Ms. Russo smiled as she rejoined them.

Demetrius cleared his throat. It was time to put this all to an end before it blew up in his face. Instead of gaining the public's trust, he might just damage his reputation beyond repair if they unearthed the truth about his very brief, very rushed marriage.

Demetrius stepped forward. "Ms. Sarris just informed me that she won't be able to stay."

CHAPTER TWO

SO MUCH FOR thinking Christmas had come early.

There appeared to be a lump of coal in her stocking.

Zoe arched a brow at Demetrius. Question after question crowded her mind. Like what exactly was her ex-husband really up to? Then again, their marriage had been annulled so technically he wasn't her ex. So what did that make him? Her fairy-tale past? Her delicious mistake?

Not that any of it mattered.

They were history. That part was undeniable.

"The prince is correct. I just stopped by to check on something." Zoe made sure to wear her friendliest smile. "If you'll excuse me."

She stepped past Demetrius and kept walking. The murmur of their voices resumed. It wasn't until she'd reached the other end of the landing that she paused and glanced over her shoulder.

Her gaze scanned over Demetrius's tailored charcoal-gray suit and polished dress shoes. He looked quite smart in his designer clothes. His hair was a little shorter and styled. So much for the laid-back, not-worried-about-his-looks prince. The tide had most definitely turned. The man standing in front of the camera definitely had a serious persona about him.

What had happened to turn Demetrius into the focused prince standing before her? The question teetered on the tip of her tongue, but she knew that it was no longer any of her business. The thought settled as a lump in her stomach. She'd done what she thought was best at the time by walking away—even if she had loved him.

When his dark gaze met hers, the breath hitched in her throat. It was abundantly clear that she was the very last person he'd expected to see today. And he was none too happy about it. Her fingers fidgeted with the material of her skirt. Would he have her replaced?

Zoe's stomach dipped. This job was not only impressive but it also paid well—quite well. It'd certainly improve her declining bank account and give her the funds necessary to continue helping her ailing mother. Without it, she didn't know how she'd make do.

She'd lingered too long. It was time to slip inside the mansion away from the paparazzi, away from the questions—away from Demetrius's accusing stare. She was just about at the front door of the mansion when a man stepped out from behind one of the columns.

"Smile for the camera, sweetie." He snapped a picture of her.

The flash momentarily blinded her. She stood rooted in the same spot. What in the world?

The man was short and had a paunch. He hadn't seen a razor recently and his hair was greasy with a long, stringy comb-over. His eyes narrowed in on her. "They're going to love you."

"Who are you? What do you want?"

"I'm the man who's going to learn your secrets."

There was no way he was with Ms. Russo. Zoe started to back up. Not realizing there was a step behind her, she tripped and a scream tore from her lungs.

"Zoe?" Demetrius called out.

Her hands flailed about as she struggled to regain her balance. And then suddenly there was a steadying hand clutching her arm, pulling her to safety. Once she was on level footing, her gaze met Demetrius's concerned look.

"Are you all right?" His voice was gruff with concern.

"I'm fine." She glanced around but the man who'd startled her was gone.

"Did you see that man?"

Demetrius shook his head. "Was it one of the construction workers?"

"I don't think so. He had a camera."

Demetrius called over one of his security detail, and in hushed tones they spoke. Then he turned back to her. "Don't worry. If he's still here, they'll find him. Do you know what he wanted?"

Zoe shook her head.

Ms. Russo rushed over. "Is everything okay?"

"There was a man here," Demetrius explained. "He startled Miss Sarris."

The reporter lowered her microphone. "I caught a glimpse of him just as he turned to leave."

Zoe was so relieved to know that someone had seen him. "Do you know who he is?"

"I don't know his name." Ms. Russo's dark brows drew together. "I've seen him before. I think he may be a stringer, selling whatever dirt he digs up on celebrities to the highest paying publication. He doesn't look it, but he's very good at sniffing out the scandalous stories." Ms. Russo's gaze moved from Zoe to Demetrius. "So Prince Demetrius, do you know why he's investigating you?"

Demetrius frowned. "I have no idea."

Wanting to diffuse this line of questioning, Zoe spoke up. "What will happen if they catch him?"

Demetrius's gaze met hers. "Did he hurt you?" When she shook her head, he continued. "He'll most likely be questioned and released."

It wasn't exactly a comforting thought to know that man would soon be loose. But Demetrius was right. They couldn't lock him up just because he'd scared her.

"Don't look so worried." Demetrius's voice was low and comforting. "He was interested in me, not you."

Zoe wasn't so sure about that. The man's beady eyes had been staring right at her when he'd spoken. Goose bumps raced down her arms. She'd prefer to never see him again.

"Are you all right?" The reporter sent her a worried look.

Zoe nodded. "I should be going."

"Please don't rush off." Ms. Russo gestured to her cameraman to start filming. "Since you're here, can you give us some idea of what to look forward to with the mansion?"

Zoe wanted to leave—to get as far away as fast as possible. But how would that look? Talk about giving credence to that creep's allegations that she had secrets. She refused to let him or anyone else run her off.

With every bit of willpower she could muster, Zoe flashed the camera a smile. "Sure. As long as Prince Demetrius doesn't mind."

He made a pretense of checking his Rolex watch. "I suppose we have time. But it will have to be quick. I have another meeting shortly."

"Certainly." The reporter's eyes gleamed with victory.

The woman started rambling off questions about the project as the cameraman filmed the whole session. It was bad enough running into her ex, but now to be filmed with him for primetime television made her want to groan. Could this day get any worse?

"Now, how did you two meet?"

"What?" When all three people turned inquisitive eyes Zoe's way, the heat of embarrassment inched up her neck. "Sorry." She searched for the easiest way out of this mess. "I got distracted. What did you ask?"

"I was wondering how you and the prince met."

Zoe waited, hoping Demetrius would speak up and put an end to this interview. But instead he remained silent, letting the awkward silence grow. Zoe improvised. "We don't really know each other."

The reporter's brow arched. "That's interesting. I'd have sworn you two seemed to know each other. Are you sure there wasn't another project? Or a social engagement?"

"We don't move in the same social circles," Zoe said with utter honesty.

At last, Demetrius found his voice. "This is actually our first project together and Miss Sarris might not remember, but we met ever so briefly at the opening of the DiCapria corporate offices. She'd done such an excellent job with its design that when the Residenza del Rosa project came up, her name immediately came to mind."

Of course Zoe remembered that moment. It had been the night her whole world changed. So then how could he just stand there and talk about their very first meeting at the DiCapria party as though nothing had come of it? It had been the precipice of her heart tumbling and careening into his.

"The DiCapria office is beautiful." Ms. Russo turned to her. "That project brought you a lot of public attention. Would you say it was a turning point in your career?"

"Definitely." Zoe was very proud of that project. They'd given her a lot of freedom with the design and she'd ended up impressing everyone. "It was and still is one of my favorite projects."

"I'll make a note to get some photos of the DiCapria offices to include in this exposé." The woman keyed a note into her phone. "And if we could just have one more photo of you two together for our website, we'll be done."

Zoe's cheeks ached from smiling so much. *Don't they already have enough footage?* But when she glanced up the cameraman had gone to exchange his filming equipment for a digital camera.

While the reporter spoke to the camera guy, Demetrius

leaned close and spoke in her ear. "Hang in there. Doing what she asks will be a lot faster and easier than trying to duck out."

His crisp, fresh cologne teased her memory. She remembered all too clearly what it was like to lean into him and press her mouth to the smooth skin of his neck. His quickening pulse would thump beneath her lips as she'd leave a trail of kisses from his jaw down to his chest—

She groaned as she drew her thoughts up short.

That was then. This is now.

Demetrius sent Zoe a warning look as her groan reached his ears.

She had to hang in there just a little longer.

This interview couldn't fall apart now.

If he failed to gain the nation's confidence, there was a very good chance that anarchy would ravage this very beautiful island nation his father had spent his whole life protecting. Demetrius would do all he could to keep that from ever happening to his much-loved homeland.

Most of all, he couldn't let down his father. He knew in the grand scheme of things that it shouldn't weigh so heavy on him, but his father hadn't had the easiest life despite his position. When Demetrius was fifteen, his mother had been murdered in an assassination attempt. It'd fractured their family.

His twin, Alexandro, blamed himself for the murder and had assumed the role of protector. Their father had grown quiet and reserved, spending all of his time working. Demetrius had gone a bit wild, living life to its fullest. He never thought any of them would be happy again.

Then last year, his brother had led the paparazzi on a wild chase to the United States to divert attention from Demetrius's elopement to Zoe. And his brother's daring plan had worked...sort of. While in the States, Alex had fallen in love and married an American. Somewhere during all of this, they'd started to act like a family again—sharing meals and catching up on each other's lives. And he couldn't lose that. Not again.

But now being here with Zoe, he realized he'd made a huge mistake by thinking they could work side by side. His gaze strayed to her. She was answering some more questions about her profession for the reporter.

His gaze skimmed down over her, noticing on closer inspection that her clothes hung a bit loose. Had she lost weight in the time they were apart? She had been slender when he knew her. The fact that she'd lost weight was worrying. He hoped she wasn't sick. He studied her face. She didn't look ill.

As he continued to stare at her, he felt the draw of attraction as strong now as it had been back when they were together. Was it possible she was even more beautiful today than she had been when he'd pledged his heart to her? His gaze slipped to her full lips—

Realizing the direction of his straying thoughts, he jerked them to a halt. No matter how tempting he still found her, he refused to fall for her charms again. His foolish behavior had already cost him so much.

"We're almost done." The reporter clasped her hands together. "I just need a couple more candid shots for the website. Could you both move to the edge of the steps?"

While they moved into the designated positions on the top step, he chanced another glance Zoe's way. Her lips lifted at the corners. However, her smile didn't quite reach her brown eyes. He wasn't about to complain. At least she was playing along.

"Can you shake hands?"

With anyone else, the request would have been simple, but Zoe was not just anyone. She was most definitely someone—someone he was over. His jaw tightened. So then why was he making such a big deal out of this?

He extended his hand to her.

There was a moment's hesitation. Her gaze met his, but he couldn't read what she was thinking. When her hand slipped into his, there was a jolt—no, it was more like a lightning bolt—of awareness that coursed between them.

It means nothing.

She means nothing.

It's all in my imagination.

"Hold that pose." The reporter turned and frowned at the camera guy. "What's the problem? Don't keep the prince waiting."

The photographer waved over the reporter. With a flustered look on Ms. Russo's face, she uttered an apology and rushed down the steps to straighten out the problem.

"Are you really planning to oversee this project personally?" Zoe's gaze was hard and cold.

He lowered his voice to a whisper. "Why wouldn't I? This is my project. Surely you know that."

"I know that they were bandying your name about when I was hired, but I figured they were just trying to impress me. I had no idea you could actually be persuaded to take part in this venture."

He wanted to take offense. He wanted to assure her that he was always on top of things. But then again, not so long ago, he'd had his priorities all turned around. Back then, he'd only been worried about his personal happiness. Even as a teenager, he'd known that once he stepped up and took his rightful place in the monarchy that his life would not be his own. So he'd put off the inevitable as long as possible.

He kept his voice low. "Things have changed since you knew me."

"You act like we were just strangers that passed in the night."

Demetrius cleared his throat. Using the same voice he used when his advisors didn't agree with him, he whispered, "This revitalization project is important. There's a whole lot more at stake than just my reputation—"

"Sorry about that." Ms. Russo joined them again. "My cameraman had a problem with the equipment. We need to film the part where you shake hands again." Hesitantly they joined hands while Ms. Russo smiled. "This is great! The viewers will love it. This will definitely add a sense of hands-on attention by the prince."

Hands-on. The words conjured up the memory of Zoe in his arms. Demetrius schooled his facial features to keep the unintended meaning of the reporter's words from showing. He didn't dare look at Zoe. He didn't want to do anything to bring about a reaction in her. After all, how was he supposed to smile and relax while standing next to the one woman that he thought he could trust above all others?

"Can you look at each other?"

Demetrius reluctantly gazed at Zoe. Her gaze was closed and guarded. She was none too excited about this unexpected reunion, either. Well, good, he was more than willing to share the discomfort, although it didn't come close to the agony he'd experience after she'd run out on him.

"Good. Good." The reporter's voice held a happy tone. Obviously she was the only one happy about this encounter. "Now could you continue to shake hands while talking about the project? We need a sound bite—one showing you two working together. A team effort."

Demetrius cleared his throat. "*Grazie*. Your presence is appreciated."

There was a pause and Demetrius tensed, waiting and wondering what Zoe would say.

"I'm honored to have been chosen for this very special project."

"We are the lucky ones to have your talent to create a

stunning retreat for the residents of this facility to forget about their lives—their problems—and just relax in the common rooms of this historic building."

There was the slightest flash of emotion in Zoe's eyes, but in a blink it was gone. "I hope to live up to your expectations."

He'd give her credit. She was keeping this professional. Then again, he could never fault Zoe for acting anything but mature and professional. Otherwise they'd have never been able to maintain a relationship that was out of sight of the paparazzi. Which left him with a question that had been nagging him since she'd left him—why hadn't she sold her story—their story—to the tabloids?

His gaze narrowed in on the woman standing before him. He didn't understand her any more now than he did before. Perhaps he understood her even less. His advisors had insisted she was holding out for a bigger payday— bigger than the check he'd insisted on sending with the annulment papers. Was that why she'd never signed and returned the papers?

He withdrew his hand and turned to the reporter. "Ms. Sarris needs to get on with her work."

Zoe thanked both of them and turned away. Then instead of leaving, she headed inside the building. The fact she didn't use the opportunity to make a hasty escape surprised him. Then again since the night she'd walked out on him, everything she did surprised him.

CHAPTER THREE

THIS CAN'T BE HAPPENING.

It must be some sort of nightmare.

Zoe seriously considered pinching herself, but before she could put her thought into action, she heard footsteps behind her. Her pencil paused over the rough sketch she'd been making of the ballroom with notes for a tentative design.

She didn't even have to turn around to know who was behind her. It was Demetrius. What did he want now? The sure, steady steps of his dress shoes clicked over the marble floor, growing louder as he grew nearer. The footsteps stopped. He cleared his throat as though to gain her attention. Her entire body tensed.

The truth of the matter was that she owed him an explanation. It was long overdue. But this was not the time nor the place for this reunion. She didn't even know what to say to him. "Sorry" just wasn't enough. Regardless, there was no chance of ignoring him.

She leveled her shoulders and turned. "Did you need something, Your Highness?"

"You can stop with the 'Highness' bit, we're alone."

Zoe's gaze darted around the room, just to be sure. She took a calming breath. "I honestly didn't expect to find you here."

"Obviously. Your start date isn't until tomorrow. What are you doing here early?"

The easiest solution would be for her to hand in her resignation here and now. The words teetered on the tip of her tongue. But the artistic part of her didn't want to walk away from this amazing opportunity. This mansion was steeped in Old World charm and beauty. However, her feet were poised to run from the one man in this world who could make her heart flutter with excitement with just one dark, mysterious gaze.

Fight or flight? Fight or flight?

Her spine stiffened and her chin lifted. "I wanted to be prepared for tomorrow when I meet with Mr. Belmonte."

"Your meeting isn't with him."

"What do you mean?"

"I mean that your meeting is with me. I requested you for this job."

Zoe's stomach lurched. None of this made any sense. Why would he hire her with their messy history?

"By the time this job is completed, this mansion is going to be restored to its former glory. It'll start outside with the sweeping steps and the large, white columns and continue inside with its vintage style. In this section, I want people to forget that it's a care home and instead feel as though they've been transported to a tranquil place. Do you think you can deliver something like that?"

She glanced around at the peeling paint and the chipped plaster. The mansion had been downright neglected. It was hard to imagine the building being transformed into one of beauty. But she knew that it could be done.

"Of course I can do it." Her unwavering gaze met his. "But you knew that or you wouldn't have hired me."

"True enough."

"What are you really up to? And don't tell me that you hired me out of the goodness of your heart. I won't believe you."

Demetrius's dark brows rose. "If I didn't know better, I'd swear you just implied that I'm heartless."

"I don't want to play word games with you." She took a

second to pull herself together, because it felt as though her world had just slipped off its axis. "What are you up to?"

"I would think that is obvious. This is a royal project and I am overseeing it from start to finish."

"Not that. I want to know why you hired me of all people."

"Does it matter?"

"It does." There was something more—something he wasn't saying.

The man standing before her wasn't the same man she'd married—the man who'd swept her off her feet was sweet and fun. His biggest worry back then had been wondering what he'd do for entertainment the next day. She didn't understand how someone in his position could have lived his life so carefree, but obviously it'd all caught up with him. Because this man with his lips pressed together into an uncompromising line while staring directly at her meant business—of that she was certain.

He crossed his muscular arms. "Perhaps hiring you was a mistake—"

"No—" She bit back her next words but it was too late. Demetrius's brows lifted at her sudden outburst. "I mean, we have an agreement. Or at least I do with Mr. Belmonte."

"Agreements are made to be broken."

"But it's in writing."

"And you didn't think that I would leave myself a loophole—a way out if the need arose?"

Who is this man? And what had happened to the laid-back Demetrius?

Her gut told her to get out now. That she was getting in far too deep with a man who still had a hold on her heart. But what kind of daughter would that make her? This was her chance to make the remainder of her mother's life better.

And to complicate matters further, she had no job to return to. She'd already resigned from her position as interior designer for the island's most prominent and discriminating furniture store. And most important, this job paid well—well enough to pay her mother's bills.

Zoe was stuck.

"You still haven't answered my question. Why did you hire me?" She watched him carefully, not sure what sort of reaction to expect.

"I wanted the best for this job. And you are the best on the island."

Was he serious? He thought she was the best? A warmth swirled in her chest and rose to warm her cheeks. Their gazes connected and held. Her heart thudded harder, faster. She refused to acknowledge that his words meant anything to her. She was over him. Past him.

"So you just expect us to work together like…like nothing ever happened?"

A loud bang echoed through the expansive ballroom.

Demetrius's body tensed.

"What was that?" Zoe whispered.

He didn't know but he certainly intended to find out. He peered around the various drop cloths, plaster buckets and scaffolding. "Who's there?"

A movement caught his attention. Across the room, a worker in a yellow hard hat straightened from where he'd dropped a load of lumber. He glanced their way. "Hey, you aren't supposed to be in here. This is a designated hard hat area."

Demetrius nodded his understanding. "We were just leaving."

"See that you do. I don't want to have to throw you out." The man turned and walked away.

Obviously the man hadn't recognized him with the shadows and the distance. That was all right with Demetrius. Sometimes he got tired of being the prince, of posing for pictures and answering questions. Sometimes he just wanted to be plain old Demetrius. He'd been able to pull that off not so long ago when he was partying and showing up in places most inappropriate for royalty. But those times were over and not to be repeated.

Zoe laughed. The sound startled him. It'd been so long since he'd seen her happy. In the beginning, their relationship had been an easy and relaxed one. He missed those times. He hadn't relaxed like that since—

No. He wasn't going down memory lane. That was then. This is now.

Everything had changed over the past year. He refused to be swayed by the way the gold specks in her eyes twinkled when she smiled or how her cheeks filled with color when she was paid a compliment. He was immune to it all.

Zoe turned her attention back to him. "I guess he didn't realize who he was threatening to toss out of here."

"The man was just doing his job and making sure that no one is injured on his watch."

"Then I guess we better hurry." She turned and snapped a couple more pictures of the room with her phone. "I've already been given the dimensions of the rooms as well as the architectural drawings." She glanced around again. "And now with these photos, I should be able to get started. We should get going before that man comes back."

Demetrius stepped in front of her. "Not so fast. We need to establish guidelines for our working arrangement."

"That's easy. When I have some sketches, I'll contact you."

When she once again started around him, he reached out and grasped her wrist. "That won't work. I want a more hands-on approach."

She yanked her arm away and glared at him. "Surely you aren't proposing to look over my shoulder?"

"That's not how I would have worded it, but so be it."

Zoe planted her hands on her hips. "I don't work well under close supervision. I need room to do my research and then I start sketching and playing with colors. It isn't going to be an overnight project. It will take me time."

"I understand that. As long as you understand that you'll need to keep your design plans a secret from everyone—even your family and friends. The big reveal will be the week of the Royal Christmas Ball. Large contributors will be invited to wow them into donating more funding for more renovations in the neighborhood. The following day, Ms. Russo will be airing another segment on her television show giving viewers before and after shots of the mansion."

Zoe nodded her understanding. "Trust me. No one will see my designs. When I have something ready for you to see, we can meet in the village at the *caffè* house."

"That's impossible. My daily presence in the village, as well as the security detail, would be far too disruptive to businesses."

A frown pulled at her beautiful face. "Fine. What do you suggest?"

Demetrius glanced over, noticing the workman had yet to return, but his gut told him the man would be back soon. They had to make this brief. "I think our best solution is to work at the palace."

"The palace?" Zoe's face noticeably paled.

"Offices have been set up there for the architect, the PR consultant and others. It will be very handy having all of the key people under one roof."

"But I don't have a car."

He hadn't thought of that, but if that was her only objection, he'd find a solution. "I'll send my car for you."

Her mouth opened, but then she closed it as though she'd run out of protests.

Good. Another problem solved. "Now that we have that

straightened out, let's get out of here before that guy comes back. I don't relish the idea of facing him down."

The worry lines smoothed on Zoe's face. "You don't have anything to worry about. I remember how you'd visit the gym each morning, not to mention your evening run along the beach. I'm guessing you still do both."

"I do. When time allows." Demetrius's shoulders straightened. Had she just paid him a compliment? "Still, I prefer to keep a low-key presence."

"Since when? You used to love to be the playboy and you didn't care who photographed you."

"Things certainly have changed since those days."

She glanced away. "I guess they have."

Everything had changed, apparently for both of them. And the more time he spent with her, the more he wondered about those dark smudges under her eyes that her makeup didn't quite cover. Something was keeping her up at night. But what?

CHAPTER FOUR

WHAT HAD SHE been thinking?

Agreeing to work side by side with her ex.

And at the royal palace of all places.

The next morning, Zoe muttered to herself as she tried on outfit after outfit. The pile of discarded clothes on her bed was growing. What did one wear to the palace? Business attire? Nah, too stiff. A summer dress? Too casual. Nothing seemed fitting for the occasion.

And then she recalled that she wasn't an invited guest. She was the help. She'd probably be ushered in the back entrance and kept out of sight. With that in mind, she dressed as she normally would for a consultation—a short purple skirt, a white blouse and a pair of heels.

Up until now, she'd carefully avoided Demetrius. In some ways, it seemed like forever since that horrible day at the palace when her whole house of cards had come tumbling down, and in other ways it seemed like just the other day. Demetrius had no idea how much that decision had cost her—she'd sacrificed her heart that night. And her life had never been the same since then.

Leaving had been the only way she'd known to care for her mother and to protect the prince. With Zoe gone from his life, he could move on. He could find someone else to be his perfect princess—someone whose DNA didn't have a fifty-fifty chance of inheriting the blueprint for early onset familial Alzheimer's disease.

In the beginning, she'd let herself get so caught up in his attention—in the belief that their love could overcome anything. In the end, she'd learned the harsh reality of life.

Love couldn't fix everything.

If it could, her mother wouldn't be ill. Her mother wouldn't be fading away right before her very eyes.

As it was, her mother had just gone to stay with a family friend who had a house by the sea—the community where her mother had grown up. Her mother insisted that she wanted to go. She'd referred to it as her final vacation as the sea had always brought her mother great peace. The trip couldn't have come at a better time. It provided Zoe with a chance to make the most of this amazing opportunity.

The buzz of her phone drew Zoe out of her thoughts. The number was blocked. She could only figure that it must be the driver sent to pick her up. She stabbed her finger at the keypad and an unfamiliar male voice came over the line. It was indeed the driver. He was waiting for her in the back alley. It was obvious Demetrius didn't want to draw attention to her comings and goings. That was fine with her.

Most people in the building walked to work, making it possible for her to slip down the back stairs unnoticed. She entered the alley to find an unmarked black sedan with heavily tinted windows.

The driver opened the door for her. She climbed inside and leaned back against the cool leather seat. It was hard to believe that once upon a time this lifestyle had been hers. Sure it'd been brief—quite brief. But for a moment, it had been magical.

As the sedan rolled through downtown Bellacitta, she stared out at the colorful city. Though it was only November, the shops were already decked out in festive red and silver decorations. The lampposts were adorned with colorful wreaths. A sense of kindness and compassion was in the air. Zoe and her mother had always enjoyed this time of the year. Any other year, their Christmas tree would already be trimmed, supplies would be on hand for Christmas cookies and carols would fill their home.

A deep sadness filled Zoe because the Christmases she once knew were now nothing more than memories, and the future looked bleak.

When the car rolled to a stop at an intersection, Zoe got the strangest feeling that someone was staring at her. She glanced out the window. She didn't see anyone at first. Then at last her gaze rested on a man—the creepy reporter from the mansion. She froze.

He was standing on the sidewalk not more than a few feet away. He was staring at her. His dark eyes narrowed. Heavy scruff covered his squared jaw as his thin lips pressed into an unyielding line. The little hairs on Zoe's arms lifted. When he raised his camera, Zoe ducked back in her seat before realizing that the dark tint on the windows would shield her. It wasn't until the car was in motion again that she let out a pent-up breath. She rubbed her arms, easing away the goose bumps. At least she was going someplace he wouldn't be able to follow—of that she was certain.

As the car exited the city, she wondered what the reporter was after—something specific or was he just digging for a juicy nugget. She told herself to relax. Sooner or later, the man would give up and move on to another story. She just hoped it was sooner rather than later.

Zoe glanced out the window as they passed by the outskirts of the historic village of Portolino with it stone walkways, quaint shops and renowned craftsmen. It was a much slower pace than the city life of Bellacitta, but it held its own charms. Caught up in the throes of life, she hadn't been there since she was a child. If there was time someday after work, she wanted to visit the village, but the only way to do that was on foot. She'd have to remember to bring more sensible footwear.

The car slowed as it made a right turn. They wound their way along the long palace drive with its colorful foliage and the shadows of the palm trees. The last time she'd been driven up this driveway, it had been under the guise of moonlight. Today the sunshine was bright and cheery. This time it felt so different. Good in some ways. But then she glanced to her right, noticing the empty seat next to her. And not so good in other ways.

When the enormity of the palace came into view, the breath caught in her throat. Sure, she'd seen pictures of it all her life, but with it being tucked back in away from public view, she'd never had an opportunity to view it in the daylight. It was so impressive—reminding her once again that Demetrius didn't come from the same world as her.

She sat up straighter, taking in the palace's warm tan, coral and turquoise tones. The place was simply stunning. The palace's subtle curves and colorful turrets reflected an island flair that was Mirraccino. Sure the island nation had evolved with technology and such, but they also kept with traditions as much as possible. And she loved that Demetrius wanted that Old World feel for the mansion.

To her utter surprise, the car rolled to a stop at the front entrance. An enormous wooden door with brass fixtures swung open. An older gentleman in a black-and-white tux strode toward the car. She was so struck by this surreal moment as he opened the door for her that she failed to move. She'd never expected to be welcomed back here after things had ended badly between her and Demetrius. And though they weren't rolling out the red carpet for her, this was more than she'd ever imagined.

The butler stood aside. "Welcome, Miss Sarris."

Coming to her senses, she stood. "You were expecting me?"

The man nodded. "Prince Demetrius asked that you be escorted to the suite of offices reserved for the South Shore project. He said to tell you that he has been delayed, but he will catch up with you shortly."

She tried to ignore the disappointment that consumed her. It wasn't like Demetrius had invited her to the palace to relive the good old days. No, this was business, pure and simple. Then again, nothing was simple when it came to her ex—nothing at all.

She was guided inside where her heels clicked on the marble floor of the spacious entryway. The sound reverberated off the ornate walls and high ceiling. There were a couple of ladders and a tall pencil Christmas tree. Boxes of decorations littered the floor. It appeared she and her mother weren't the only ones to decorate early.

Zoe would have loved a bit of time to look around, but she was briskly ushered away—down a long hallway, around a corner and down a flight of steps. They turned another corner where the palace sprang to life in a flurry of activity. There were people holding electronic tablets, *caffè* cups and papers, hustling through the hallway. Everyone smiled and greeted her. They were definitely a very friendly bunch.

A smile tugged at Zoe's lips. Maybe this working arrangement wouldn't be so bad, after all. Especially if Demetrius was off attending to his princely duties. In that moment, she realized she'd been worried about nothing. As busy as this place was, she doubted she'd see Demetrius much at all.

"You'll be working in here." The butler stood aside to let her enter.

"Grazie."

"You are welcome, ma'am. I'm sure someone will be along to answer any questions you might have. Do you need anything before I go?"

She shook her head. "No."

"Very well, ma'am."

Alone in the room, she glanced around impressed by the enormity of it. The walls were painted a warm cream white. Detailed crown molding framed the ornate ceiling with a crystal chandelier. This was all for her?

She'd never been in an office so steeped in history. She glanced at one of the garden paintings on the wall. She'd bet it was older than her and worth far more than she earned in an entire year.

"You must be Zoe," came a young female voice.

Zoe spun around to find a pretty blonde standing in the doorway, wearing a friendly smile. "Hi. That's me. Did you ever see an office like this? It's amazing."

"I guess so if you like old stuff."

Old stuff? Try antiques. Heirlooms. Rare treasures. "Are you part of the palace staff?"

The young woman shook her head and her bobbed hair swished around her chin. "I was hired to work on the South Shore project." She stepped farther into the room. "My name's Annabelle."

"Nice to meet you. Looks like we'll be working together."

"I'm looking forward to it. If you have any questions, feel free to ask. I probably won't know the answer, but I'll be able to point you toward the right person to ask."

"You're here. Good." Both women turned at the sound of Demetrius's voice.

"I'll let you get to work." Annabelle made a hasty exit.

Zoe wished she could follow her new friend. Suddenly, this very spacious office seemed to shrink considerably. Thankfully Demetrius appeared to be a very busy man. So once he welcomed her, he'd be off to another meeting, she hoped.

Demetrius cleared his throat. "Sorry I'm late. I didn't mean to intrude."

"You didn't." She couldn't help but notice he looked immaculate with his short hair combed into submission and his tailored suit hugging his muscled shoulders and broad chest. Her heart kicked up its pace a notch or two. She assured herself that it was nothing more than nervousness. She swallowed hard. "We were just introducing ourselves. Annabelle seems really nice."

Demetrius's brows rose as though her admission caught him by surprise. "Annabelle's great. She's the daughter of the Duke of Halencia."

The news that Annabelle was an aristocrat dampened Zoe's excitement over having an ally behind the palace walls. For some reason she'd been thinking her newfound friend was just like her—a commoner.

"I'm surprised she'd want to work here." Zoe uttered her thoughts without realizing how it might sound.

Demetrius cleared his throat. "It's an arrangement between the duke and my father."

An arrangement? Could it be a marriage arrangement? Jealousy swift and sharp stabbed at Zoe's heart making the breath catch in her throat. Not that she had any right to feel anything about Demetrius moving on with his life. Now that their marriage had been annulled—erased—wiped clean—he was free to do as he pleased. This is what she wanted, wasn't it?

Forcing herself to act as though this bit of news didn't bother her, Zoe said, "I look forward to working with her."

"Good." He walked over to the larger of the two desks. When he noticed that she'd followed him, he stopped and turned. "Um. This is my desk. Yours is over there."

"You mean we're sharing an office?"

His dark brows rose. "Is that going to be a problem?"

The professional part of her knew the answer was supposed to be no, but her scarred heart said otherwise. It sounded like she had a frog in her throat when she choked out, "No. No problem at all."

A puzzled expression came over his face. "We ran out of offices. And with you being the newest member of the team, it was either fit you in here or move you to another wing by yourself."

She swallowed hard. "If I'm in your way, I don't mind working elsewhere."

He shook his head. "I'm hardly ever in here, so it won't be a problem."

She supposed his frequent absence was some small consolation.

Zoe moved to the other side of the room and settled her laptop and day planner on the desk where she noticed a vase of fresh cut flowers. Red, white and purple blossoms beckoned to her. She leaned forward and inhaled their perfumed scent.

All the while she could feel Demetrius's gaze following her every movement. She needed to show him—show herself—that she was over him. She could be just as professional as him—even if his mere presence could still make her stomach shiver.

She stepped around the desk and crossed the great divide. She stopped in front of his massive carved cherry desk and laced her fingers together.

He glanced up from his computer monitor. "Did you need something?"

"I wanted to thank you for this opportunity. I won't let you down." His eyes reflected a mixed reaction. Perhaps she could have worded it better. "I also wanted to tell you that I won't let the past come between us."

His dark brows drew together as he shushed her. With long, swift strides, he moved to the door. He noiselessly pushed it closed before turning back to her. "If I didn't think you could be professional, you wouldn't be here."

She didn't know whether to be complimented or insulted. "*Grazie.*"

"As for the other matter, we do need to talk. We have some unresolved business to address. But I don't want to get into it here. It'd be too easy to be overheard. And I don't want rumors to start."

"Neither do I." But obviously for different reasons than him. "You don't have to worry, Annabelle won't hear anything about the past from me."

"I hope not. Now if you'll excuse me, I have a meeting with the contractor." And with that he swung open the door and set off down the hallway, leaving her to wonder what his cryptic comment had meant.

What unresolved business?

CHAPTER FIVE

"HOW'S IT COMING?"

Demetrius strolled into the office late the next afternoon. He couldn't help but notice how Zoe jumped. He hadn't meant to startle her.

"Good." Her voice said otherwise. "Well, as good as can be expected at this stage."

"I just visited the work site and the construction of the residential rooms on the backside of the mansion is moving ahead of schedule. Soon you'll be able to get in there and do your thing."

A frown pulled at her full, lush lips, but she didn't say anything. Things definitely weren't going as well as she'd like him to believe. Maybe she wasn't up to the task, after all. There were still those dark smudges beneath her eyes. Something was most definitely keeping her up at night. But what?

His immediate instinct was to go to her—to rectify whatever was troubling her. He took a step forward, then hesitated. What was he thinking? Obviously he wasn't—at least not clearly. Her problems were no longer any of his concern. And that had been her choice. Not his.

She glanced up at him, peering over her laptop. "Did you need something else?"

He cleared his throat. "I'd like to see what direction you're taking the project."

Her mouth gaped, but nothing came out. He couldn't help but notice the pink gloss shimmering on her lips. His thoughts rolled back in time, remembering how her kisses were always sweeter than berries. His body stiffened. With determined effort he focused his mind back on the only thing that mattered—the only thing he could count on—work.

"Perhaps I could see what you've been able to do so far on the computer." His words eased the awkward silence.

"I...I don't have anything but some rough outlines."

"That's okay. It's just with all of my meetings, we haven't been able to talk much."

There was a rebuttal reflected in her eyes, but in a blink it was gone. With a shrug, she stood up. "Be my guest."

He wasn't sure by the stilted tone of her voice whether she would be open to his feedback or if she'd just give him lip service and then disregard his input. He wanted to believe they could set aside their differences in order to make this important project a success. They were, after all, both professionals.

He took a seat, surprised that she was doing all of her work on the small laptop when he'd provided her with a computer and a large-screen monitor, which was much easier on the eyes. Then he noticed that she had specialized software. He should have expected that, but he'd noticed how his thoughts became severely distracted around her.

She stood off to the side. "You have to realize that what you're looking at are some rough sketches. There are no details. I haven't had a chance to refine them."

"I understand."

She showed him how to navigate the software. As she leaned over his shoulder, he caught a whiff of her perfume. The alluring scent was the same as what she wore when they were together.

Concentrate on the pictures.

Minutes passed, and then she asked, "Well, what do you think?"

"I don't know." It was the truth.

"Don't tell me you hate all of the themes."

He flipped back and forth between the three layouts of the mansion's ballroom that she'd done up. The first screen cobbled together garden-themed pictures with lots of greens, pinks and yellows. The second screen contained images more in line with ancient Roman ruins utilizing the idea of the large columns on the front porch as well as adding some Greek and Roman statues. The last screen pulled together various Mediterranean aspects from the blues of the sea to the green of the palms.

"Say something. The suspense is torture."

He'd never seen her so anxious. Under different circumstances, he might have turned this into a bit of fun, but the time for teasing and light banter had long passed them by.

"They all have aspects that I really like." He flipped through the images once again. "Can you combine them?"

"What?" She moved to stand on the other side of the desk in order to face him. "You're not serious, are you? They're too different. It would be a mess."

He raked his fingers through his hair. "I never said that I was any good at decorating. That's what I have you for."

She crossed her arms and leveled a steady stare at him. "And you're the one who insisted that we work on this together. You went on and on about how you had to approve everything."

He got to his feet. "Fine. I pick the garden theme. Wait. No. The sea one."

She waited as though sensing he would change his mind yet again. "You're sure about the sea setting?"

He thought for a moment and then nodded. "I think it's the most relaxing of all them. If the residents aren't capable of making an outing to the seaside, then we can bring it to them."

"Okay. Then we need to pick out a color scheme." She pulled up a few color combinations. "I'd like to get some samples up on the walls as soon as possible to get a real feel for the shades before we commit to a color scheme."

However, as she leaned over his shoulder to type something in the computer, one of her barrel-roll curls landed on his shoulder. A driving need grew in him to wrap her silky strands around his finger. If he were to turn ever so slightly—if he were to reach out to her and draw her closer—she'd land in his lap.

As though in a trance, he reached out. His fingers slid down over the soft, smooth strands. What would it hurt to taste her sweetness again? He started at the end of her curl. His finger and thumb worked together wrapping her hair inch by inch around his digit.

Her surprised gaze met his. His heart pounded in his chest. But there was something more in her gaze. Interest. Excitement. Desire.

The fact that he could still turn her on sent the blood roaring through his veins, drowning out his common sense. Long-denied desire drove him onward. One thing that couldn't be denied was that they had chemistry. They should have a warning sign—combustible when mixed.

With each twist of her hair, her face moved closer. He would show her what she'd given up. He'd remind her that all of this could have been hers if only she'd believed in them—if only she'd loved him.

A noise in the hallway caused her to jump back. He reluctantly relinquished his hold on her hair, allowing her to straighten. He tried to tell himself that it was for the best, but a sense of regret churned in his gut.

He cleared his throat as he tried to remember where they'd left off. "What about this gray-blue color? I like it."

There was an unmistakable pause before Zoe spoke. "That is a bit dark and you have to realize the darker the shade, the smaller the space will appear. Why don't you see what you like on this page?" She adjusted the computer so that it displayed dozens of much lighter shades of blue. "Trust me. They'll appear darker on the wall."

This time instead of hovering, she stepped back, giving him space. Though he knew it was for the best, he missed that brief moment where they'd recaptured a bit of the past. He'd have to be more alert going forward. Things were already complicated enough between them.

For the next hour, they went over the various shades, mixing and matching. There was even a slick computer software program that let her slip the colors into the basic layout of the common rooms. It gave them a better idea of what it would look like in real life. But Zoe insisted there was nothing like seeing it in person with the natural light bouncing off the walls. He took her word for it. They agreed to wait until then to make the final decisions.

Two full days had passed. And she still had a job.

Zoe smiled.

This arrangement, though a bit bizarre working with her ex, just might work out in the end.

After a long day at the palace offices, Zoe had Demetrius's car drop her off at the market so she could pick up some food for dinner—not that she had much appetite these days. It seemed her stomach was forever filled with the sensation of a swarm of fluttering butterflies. She hoped a salad might pique her appetite.

Armed with fresh fruit, vegetables and some still-warm-from-the-oven bread, she walked toward her apartment. Ever since she'd left the market, something hadn't felt right. Zoe glanced over her shoulder.

Nothing out of the ordinary.

Still, the little hairs on Zoe's arms remained lifted.

She picked up her pace. At an intersection, she paused and glanced back. Her gaze met a set of dark, menacing eyes. The creepy reporter. Her heart lurched.

Though he didn't approach her, there was something threatening about the way he looked at her. There was no point calling for help. What would she say? He looked at her the wrong way?

The best thing she could do was keep moving. It wasn't much farther to her apartment. Hopefully she'd lose him. Her feet moved rapidly along the sidewalk. She refused to glance back again. She was making too much of seeing the reporter. Still, she recalled his eerie words about finding out her secrets. What secrets? About her mother? Demetrius?

Zoe rushed across the street. Her apartment building was in the next block. Though she'd promised herself she wouldn't, she paused and glanced back. The street was busy as people rushed home to their families. She didn't see any sign of the reporter. She breathed a sigh of relief. Perhaps it'd just been a coincidence.

Once safely in her apartment, she did something she didn't normally do—locked her door. She rushed to the kitchen window and peered out. She searched up the street. Nothing. Down the street. Nothing.

Get a grip. You're imagining things.

And then she saw him across the street. He emerged from between the buildings. The breath caught in her throat. He leaned back against the bakery and pointed his camera up at her. She ducked out of sight. Hastily, she closed the kitchen curtains.

What do I do now?

She rushed to put her groceries in the fridge, having lost any bit of hunger she may have had. She thought of calling Demetrius, but what would she say? Some guy was following her? Would Demetrius believe her? And after the way she'd walked out of their marriage, why should he care?

Knock. Knock.

Zoe jumped.

She moved to the window and peeked out. The reporter was gone.

Knock. Knock.

Or was he?

It was time they talked.

And Zoe had given him the perfect excuse.

Demetrius glanced down at her leather-bound day planner. She always had it close at hand, marking every meeting and deadline in it. She impressed him with her attention to detail. He knew that he could have left the planner on her desk till the morning, but he liked having an excuse to visit her at home—especially if her mother answered the door.

He'd knocked twice but still no one answered the door. That was strange. He'd thought he'd overheard her mention to Annabelle that she was planning to stay in and make a salad—not that he'd stuck around eavesdropping. Perhaps she'd decided it was easier to eat out. That would be just his luck.

Unwilling to give up the thought of seeing her—of finally gaining some answers about the annulment—he knocked one last time.

"Go away!"

What?

"Zoe? Open the door."

"If you don't leave, I'm calling the *polizia*."

The *polizia*?

What is going on?

"Zoe, it's me. Demetrius. Open up."

There was the sound of footsteps. Then a pause as he felt her gaze through the peephole. Followed by the click of the lock. At last the door swung open. A pale-faced Zoe stood there.

"I...I wasn't expecting you." Her gaze didn't quite reach his.

"Obviously. Who did you think I was?"

She shook her head and waved away his question. "It's nothing."

"It is quite obviously something. I insist you tell me." Her face was devoid of color. Her eyes were filled with worry. He wasn't leaving until he got to the bottom of what had her scared.

"Remember that reporter from the interview at the mansion? You know, the creepy one?"

He nodded, not liking the direction this conversation was going. "What did he do to you?"

She shook her head again. "Nothing."

"You look awfully worked up for nothing. Tell me and let me be the judge."

"It's just that he's been lurking around here, watching me and taking photos."

Demetrius's gut tightened. "And just now you thought he was knocking on your door?"

She shrugged.

"When's the last time you saw him?"

"He followed me home from the market. I...I saw him out the kitchen window, standing across the street. He tried to take my picture, but I think I ducked before he could."

Without waiting to be invited inside, Demetrius strode past Zoe toward the aforementioned window. This was his fault for thrusting her into the media spotlight. Now that she was working closely with him, the media would want to know everything about her. They would dissect her life, looking for a juicy piece of gossip.

Demetrius swept aside the curtain and peered out at the busy roadway. He didn't see anyone acting suspicious. "Do you still see him?"

She moved to his side and gazed out at the numerous faces. "No. He disappeared just before you arrived. That's why I thought you were him."

Demetrius let the curtain fall back into place. He glanced around, noticing the quietness. "Are you here alone?"

She nodded. "My mother is visiting a friend at the coast."

"Well, you can't stay here alone. Pack a bag. Tonight you're staying at the palace."

Her eyes grew round. "No, I can't. I won't."

Why was she being difficult? This was for her own welfare. "You can and you will. I'm not leaving you here."

"I'll be safe. I'll keep the door locked." Her lips pressed into a firm line as her gaze took a defiant gleam.

He wasn't going to let her have her way. Not this time. Not with her safety at stake. "Why are you being stubborn? It's not like I'm asking you to return to the palace as my wife."

Her chin lifted. "So far I've been lucky enough to avoid the king and his advisors. I won't be able to do that if I'm living there. And...and I don't want to deal with them. I didn't exactly leave on the best of terms."

Demetrius couldn't argue that point. The king's advisors were certain that she was a gold digger, but surprisingly the king had been quite reserved with his thoughts about Demetrius's failed marriage. Maybe his father thought that he'd suffered enough without adding an "I told you so."

Still, there had to be an alternative. A way to assure himself of her safety until the media set their sights on a new target. He rolled the options around in his mind.

"I have the perfect alternative." Why he hadn't thought of it in the first place was beyond him.

Her eyes widened with interest. "You do? What?"

"You'll see. It's not far from here."

CHAPTER SIX

Just as Demetrius had promised, his chauffeured car ushered them past the palace gates, beyond the palace itself and down a narrow lane Zoe didn't even know existed. Unspoiled green foliage and wild flowers lined both sides of the roadway. They were heading far, far away from any curious eyes. It sure was a good thing that she knew Demetrius as well as she did. Otherwise, she would be wary of their isolated destination.

"Where are we going?" She turned to Demetrius as he continued to type response after response into his phone.

His fingers paused as he glanced out the window. "We're almost there."

"That doesn't tell me anything."

"Stop worrying. I'm certain you'll approve."

"And if I don't?"

There was a moment of silence. "Then we'll go back to your apartment."

She didn't believe it'd be that simple. Nothing was ever simple when it concerned this particular prince—this very sexy prince. "What's the catch?"

"There isn't one." When she arched a brow at him, he sighed. "You don't believe me?"

"Let's just say I know you well enough to expect you not to give up so easily."

Like when he'd proposed to her on a starlit night along the seashore. He refused to take any answer but her acceptance. Not that accepting a marriage proposal from a prince had been a hardship. In fact, in that moment, it had been quite the opposite.

Demetrius slipped his phone in his pocket. "There's no catch."

"I don't believe you."

Their gazes met and held as though in a struggle of wills. Demetrius was the first to turn away. "Before we go any further with this argument, see if this will calm your worries."

When she turned to the window, her gaze landed upon a beautiful white beach house. It was like something out of a glossy magazine. The door and some of the trim was done in a light teal. The appearance was refreshing and welcoming. Was this part of the royal estate?

"It's amazing."

"I'm glad you like it." A smile lifted his lips and eased the stress lines marring his face.

The car pulled to a stop and the driver got out to open her door for her. "If you want to go inside, ma'am, I'll bring in your luggage."

"*Grazie.*" She turned back as Demetrius alighted from the car. "Is there anyone here?"

He shook his head. "It's all yours for as long as you need."

Zoe made her way down the stone walkway, passing by a garden full of exotic foliage and blossoms from bright yellow and orange to pink and deep red. It was impossible not to fall in love with this place.

Anxious to see if the interior was as impressive as the exterior, she grasped the brass door handle and swung open the teal door. She stepped inside, greeted by a light-gray tiled foyer. The house had an open floor plan with a spacious kitchen that could be closed off by some teal shutters. The interior decor was of white walls and teal trim like the outside.

An abundance of open windows let the sea breeze filter through the house. She'd never been to such a charming place. When Demetrius said he'd take care of her, he hadn't been kidding. This was her idea of paradise.

She moved to the wall of windows facing the Mediterranean. It was absolutely gorgeous. It didn't matter how many times she looked out over the sea, she never tired of it. It would appear her mother wasn't the only one having a seaside holiday of sorts.

Zoe heard footsteps behind her. "You can just set the bags by the door. I'll get them—"

"Are you sure?"

That deep, rich voice sent a wave of delicious sensations coursing up her spine. It was most definitely not the driver. She spun around, finding Demetrius standing there holding her bags. "Sorry. I thought you were the driver."

"I hope you're not disappointed. I sent him away."

"What? But why?" Being alone with the one man who could send her heart pounding with just a look was not a good thing. "I mean, I'm sure you have work to do."

"I do. But first we have to talk."

Talk? About what? She got the distinct impression from his serious expression that she wasn't going to like what he had to say. Was he going to blame her for the nosy reporter sniffing around for gossip?

Demetrius cleared his throat. "But first, do you approve of your accommodations?"

"It's absolutely amazing." Zoe moved to his side and retrieved her luggage. She glanced up at him and her stomach quivered with excitement. They may no longer be a couple, but that didn't mean she was immune to his charms. "I owe you an apology. I should have realized that you would have the perfect place in mind. *Grazie.*"

"You're welcome. It's the family's escape from the palace life. A place where we can just be ourselves without the constant expectations that go along with royal life."

"I feel safe here." She glanced all around. "I can already imagine that I'll be spending a lot of time out on the deck."

"I've spent many hours there. It's great for clearing your mind."

"I'm sure it is." Not anxious for the ominous talk, she said, "Well, I know you have things to do and I have to unpack, so I won't keep you."

"Not before we talk."

Something told her that this much-changed prince didn't normally have lapses in his schedule. Whatever he wanted to speak to her about must be important. Had something happened with the renovation?

She hoped not, for more than one reason. The South Shore revitalization project was a hard-fought-for and long-awaited improvement. And somehow, someway Zoe planned to get her mother a spot at the Residenza del Rosa. The doctor had warned that finding her mother appropriate accommodations needed to be a priority. The time for hesitating had passed.

Zoe set down her suitcase next to the couch. "What's the matter? Has something happened at the mansion?"

Demetrius's brows scrunched together. "Why would you think that?"

"It's your tone and…and your demeanor. You have something serious on you mind."

"You're right. I do. This conversation is long overdue."

Her stomach churned. She forced her gaze to meet his. "What conversation?"

Demetrius raked his fingers through his hair. "I've been waiting for you to say something about it, but I'm so tired of playing these games with you."

"What games? I haven't been playing any games with you."

"Sure you have. Why else wouldn't you have signed the annulment papers?"

The whites of her eyes widened and her mouth gaped. Was she really going to try and act surprised? What did she hope to gain by acting all innocent?

All of his pent-up frustration came rushing to the surface. "Don't look so shocked. I'm certain it comes as no surprise to you that we're still husband and wife."

"What? But...but that can't be."

"It can be when you don't sign and return the annulment papers."

"No, that isn't right." She pressed her fingers to her forehead as though she were trying to piece everything together.

Was she angling to garner his sympathy? Well, it wouldn't work this time. Demetrius's wounded pride refused to accept anything but a reasonable explanation. His ego hadn't just been pricked. It had been slashed to ribbons. This had to stop. And it had to stop here.

He was on a roll now and he couldn't stop. Not until she admitted what she wanted from him. Did she want more money? Or did she regret the way she'd trampled over their wedding vows on her way out the door? Did she want him back? The wondering and the not knowing had been nagging at him for months now. "Were you hoping for a bigger payday?"

"No!" Her gaze narrowed. "You know me better than that. I ripped up the check and mailed the papers back to you."

"I don't know what you did with the check or the papers, but I never received them."

Her eyes filled with confusion. "Then...then that means we're still married?"

He nodded. For the first time since the dreadful day when she walked out on him, he witnessed that same anguished look on her face. What was he supposed to make of it?

Don't trust her. She already hurt you once.

The little voice in his head continued to issue warnings. But his heart longed to hear her out. There was something more here—something he was missing.

But could he afford to take another chance on her?

Before either of them could say a word, his phone buzzed. He retrieved it from his pocket and stared at the screen. It was the king—a man who didn't go near a phone unless it was urgent.

Demetrius wanted to ignore it. He wanted to finish this conversation, but his royal duties trumped his personal life—just like he'd seen the king do time and again.

He took the call. All it amounted to was a few short, clipped sentences. There was an emergency at the shipping port. A car had been dispatched to pick him up.

When the call was concluded, he turned back to Zoe. "I have to attend to this."

Her face was completely washed out as she nodded but said nothing.

"We aren't finished with this. I'll be back." He strode for the front door.

He wanted to believe that her surprised expression was legitimate. In fact, he'd never wanted anything more in his life, but he couldn't risk it. He couldn't let himself become vulnerable again. Every time he let himself get close to someone—really close—they faded out of his life. First, his mother. Then his wife. And the last blow had been his twin who was now an ocean away with his beautiful bride—not that he could blame him.

But the truth of the matter was Demetrius had given Zoe a chance—he'd given her everything. And in the end, she'd rejected him. How was he supposed to trust her again?

* * *

That can't be right.

We're still married?

Zoe leaned against the back of the couch. Her knees had turned to gelatin.

Thankfully Demetrius had been called away. She needed time to make sense of what he'd said. They were still married? How was that possible?

Once her legs felt a bit steadier, she retrieved her suitcase and moved back through the hallway just off the kitchen. She entered the first spacious bedroom. It was decorated with sunny yellows and perky pinks. The exact opposite of her mood right now.

Demetrius had to be wrong. She was certain she'd signed the papers. She didn't understand. Papers didn't just disappear. What had happened to them?

It was obvious Demetrius wasn't any happier about this development than she was. And now more than ever she needed to make peace with him. He not only held her future in the palm of his hand but also that of her mother. A contract to work on the rest of the revitalization project would make a huge difference in the type of care that Zoe could provide for her mother.

Speaking of her mother, she needed to check in with her. Zoe grabbed her phone and pulled up the number of their friend she was staying with, Liliana. The woman had been their neighbor most of Zoe's childhood. Liliana hadn't just been a friend, she and her husband had quickly become family. Watching Zoe when needed. Sharing holiday meals. And being there for any emergencies.

After a quick greeting, Zoe dove into the reason for her call. "Liliana, how's my mum doing?"

"She has her good days and her bad days. I'm sure you know how that goes."

"I do." It was heartbreaking to watch the confusion that would come over her mother's face—the utter lack of recognition. But thankfully for now the good times outweighed the bad. "I just wanted to let you know that work has me away on a short trip. So you won't reach me at the apartment, but you can always reach me on my cell phone."

"I'm glad to hear that you're getting out and about. You need to do that more often. Too bad the trip is business. Maybe you can squeeze in some fun time."

Demetrius's face flashed in her mind. "I don't think that will be possible. There's a lot of work to do."

"Does this have something to do with that South Shore project?"

"*Sì.*" Zoe knew she had to handle this carefully. Liliana was an astute woman. If Zoe wasn't careful, her friend would add two and two. And there was no doubt about it, Liliana would get four. "I'm doing some research. It appears this project is bigger than I was anticipating."

"Really? That's a good thing, right?"

"It's very good. I just need to be on top of my game."

"Well, don't you worry. Your mother is fine here. She can stay as long as you need."

"Thanks so much. I really appreciate this. Did…did Mum tell you she's moving into assisted living as soon as the arrangements can be made? The doctor suggested that sooner was better than later." The thought that things had deteriorated to that point made Zoe's heart ache.

"I'm so sorry, Zoe. You know I'm just a phone call away."

"*Grazie.*" Liliana was like a second mother to her. "It means a lot."

"This is one of your mother's good days. Would you like to talk with her?"

"I would." Zoe missed her mother dearly. It'd always been the two of them against the world. But lately their roles had started to be reversed and the strong woman that Zoe had always known her mother to be was becoming less and less sure of herself. *Damn disease.*

After a brief talk with her mother, Zoe stowed her unpacked suitcase in the walk-in closet. Not sure whether she was coming or going, she'd deal with it later. Right now, the fresh air beckoned to her. Hopefully a walk on the beach would give her the peace needed to make sense of Demetrius's claim. *They were still married. Husband and wife.* She stared down at her bare ring finger. There had to be an explanation, but what?

Zoe moved to the deck. A long set of wooden steps led her down to the pristine beach. It was so hard to believe that this was all private property—property of the Crown. And she had it all to herself.

The thought brought her no joy. All she could picture was the accusing stare that Demetrius had leveled at her. Why would he think she had something to do with the missing papers when she was the one to end their marriage?

CHAPTER SEVEN

"ZOE, WHERE ARE YOU?"

Demetrius stood in the living room of the beach house and raked his fingers through his hair. It'd taken him longer at the palace than he had anticipated. With his twin brother, Alex, in the States with his wife's family, the responsibility for Mirraccino's shipping port fell to Demetrius.

He'd hoped Zoe would have made herself at home, but there was no sign of her. "Zoe!"

Again there was no answer.

Where was she? His mind spun back in time. This wasn't the first time that he'd searched for her, only to find her gone. The last time he'd found a brief note and tracked her down in the palace driveway—where she'd told him that she was leaving. If he hadn't gone after her, she would have left without saying one single word to him. Is that what she'd done again? Had she left?

He rushed back the hallway, checking each bedroom for any sign of her. Each room was empty and there was no sign of her suitcase. His gut churned. Why did he think this time would be any different?

He strode to the deck where he rested his palms on the railing and leaned forward. His gaze stretched out over the crystal-blue water. Gentle swells rose and fell. Usually he could find solace in the water, but not today. All he could think about was how once again she'd skipped out on him. This time there wasn't so much as a note.

His palm smacked the top of the railing. This was it. He was done trying to play nice with her. If she didn't want to deal with him, she could hash it out with the palace's team of attorneys.

Just then a movement on the beach caught his attention. He turned and focused in on the person strolling up the beach. But how was that possible? This beach was protected as part of the royal estate. As the figure drew closer, he quickly recognized the dark ponytail and the purple jacket.

It was Zoe. He stood up straight. She hadn't left after all. He suddenly felt foolish for jumping to conclusions.

She glanced up at him and waved, but she didn't smile. He raised his hand and waved back. He told himself that she didn't still get to him. This whole arrangement was just a means to an end. That was all.

"I thought you'd left," he said as she joined him on the deck. His voice came out gruffer than he'd intended.

Her eyes widened. "Is that your way of telling me to leave?"

"No." He rubbed the back of his neck. "That isn't what I meant."

"Did you get your problem resolved?"

He nodded. "It's dealt with for the moment. Now it's time to deal with our problem."

"You make it sound like your life is a series of problems." She leaned back against the deck rail. "Since when did you get so serious? Weren't you the one that said life is for enjoying?"

He sighed. "That was a long time ago."

"Not that long ago."

A frown pulled at his lips. "I'm fine just the way I am."

"You aren't the same happy guy I used to know."

"I'm happy." Wasn't he? In all honesty, he'd been so focused on living up to people's expectations that he'd dismissed what was important to him.

"But you rarely laugh or smile. It's like you're afraid

your face will crack if you let your guard down and enjoy yourself."

He shook his head, refusing to hear what she was saying. "I enjoy myself...when there's time. I have a lot of things that need my attention. And right now I don't have time to be irresponsible."

"So you decided to take your royal responsibilities seriously?"

"I did. It was time." His work was a refuge from the pain of yet another person he loved disappearing from his life. When Zoe had walked out on him, it'd nearly crushed him.

After his mother's death and the disintegration of his family, Demetrius thought he'd finally found what he'd been searching for when he met Zoe. Warmth, happiness and most of all, love. Life couldn't get any better—or so he'd thought. If only she'd have stayed, he would have moved heaven and earth to make her happy.

"What are you thinking about?" Zoe studied him.

He turned and gazed out over the blue sea. "Us."

There was a noticeable moment of silence. "What about us?"

He wasn't about to admit that he was thinking about their failed marriage. About how his world had crumbled after she'd left. Nor would he admit to how he had to rebuild himself in the aftermath. She didn't deserve to know the damage she'd caused.

He faced her. "I want to know why you walked out on me and yet you refuse to sign the annulment papers." His gaze narrowed in on her. "What's your agenda?"

All of the pain came rushing back to him. He wasn't about to let her plead innocence. He wasn't going to let her run away again—not until he got the answers that had been alluding him this past year.

"Are you holding out for more money?"

"No! How could you think that?"

He left her question unanswered. He had his own questions and they took priority right now. "Are you sure you aren't holding out for a moment in the spotlight? A chance to sell your story to the highest bidder?"

"No. No. No." Hurt reflected in her eyes. "Would you quit with the accusations. I never wanted your money. I wanted—" She pressed her lips together.

At last they were getting somewhere, and he wasn't going to let it drop now. "You wanted what?"

Silence was his only answer.

He stepped forward. She lowered her gaze. Maybe her reason for not signing the papers was something he hadn't considered—not until now. Did she have regrets? Was she hoping for a reconciliation? If so, she was going to have a very long wait.

As though she could read the direction of his thoughts, her head rose. Their gazes caught and held. An old spark of attraction flared to life. This shouldn't happen. He was over her. But the longer she stared into his eyes, the harder it became to remember why this was a bad idea—a very bad idea.

He reached out to her. His fingers traced her cheek. Her skin was soft and subtle. "Is this what you wanted?"

"No." But her voice lacked conviction.

"I think it is. Remember how good we used to be together?"

Her gaze never left his as his fingers trailed down her jaw to trace her lips. Her eyes dilated as she inhaled a swift breath. The little voice in his mind that said he shouldn't be doing this became more and more distant—like the night he insisted they elope. He'd ignored that little voice then and he ignored it now. He had to prove to her that she'd made the biggest mistake of her life when she'd walked away from him. This time he'd be the one doing the walking.

His free hand wrapped around her waist, pulling her voluptuous curves snug against him. Her soft jasmine scent teased his senses. Every time he detected that scent, he thought of her—of her body next to his. It had been so long—so terribly long since he'd been this close to her. She wanted him, too. The passion was there in her eyes.

Buried emotions, desires and longings bubbled to the surface. He needed her—wanted her. The breath hitched in his throat. His head dipped, replacing his fingers with his lips. Her mouth didn't move at first. His touch was gentle, holding back the powerful rush of desire raging through his veins. His heart hammered against his chest.

His mouth brushed over her petal-soft lips. Just as sweet and tempting as he remembered. He wouldn't scare her away—not again. She just needed a moment to remember how amazing they'd been together. No one could forget that—not even him.

The next thing he knew her hands slipped up over his chest and wrapped around the back of his head. Her nails scraped up over his scalp as she pulled him closer. A moan swelled in the back of her throat as their kiss intensified.

He knew it. She still wanted him. If there was one thing they always had going for them, it was chemistry. The distance they'd endured had done one very obvious thing— it'd intensified the sparks arching between them, making them combustible.

Her lips moved with frantic need under his. Her excitement only aroused him more. Somewhere along the way the kiss became less about teaching her a lesson and more about him filling that empty spot in his chest. How had he lived so long without her? Her kisses were like a wellspring of life. They sealed the hollow spots in his scarred heart.

Not about to let this moment end, he scooped her up in his arms. Her hands braced on his chest. She pulled back. Her eyes were filled with a mixture of rousing desire and confusion.

"I thought you might want to continue this inside." His voice came out deeper than normal.

"*Sì*...um, no." She struggled against his hold on her. "Put me down."

"But, Zoe—"

"I mean it. Put me down."

With great regret, he did as she asked and lowered her feet to the ground. His jaw tensed. His back teeth ground together.

The moment had slipped through his fingers just like the whirlwind marriage had slipped past him. One minute they were whispering sweet nothings to each other in their palace suite—the next he was returning from a meeting with the king to find their rooms empty except for a note on his pillow that said, "Sorry. This was a mistake." A blasted note! That was all she had felt it necessary to leave him.

"That shouldn't have happened." Her fingers pressed to her lips.

His gaze challenged her. "You certainly seemed to be enjoying it."

This time she didn't turn away. "I did, but it wasn't right. We can't recapture the past."

How was he supposed to argue when she was the only one making sense right now? He was the one who was supposed to be saying these things. All it'd taken was one kiss and everything had become mixed up and turned around.

He raked his fingers through his hair. They needed to finish this here and now. This time he wouldn't let himself get distracted, no matter how sweet her kisses may be.

"You're right. We can't go back in time." He mentally kicked himself for trying such a stupid stunt. "But that doesn't mean you don't owe me an explanation for running out on me—on our marriage."

"It's too late to get into all of that."

"No, it isn't."

"Fine. If you want to know the truth, it's simple. I left because I'm not right for you. I never was and I never will be."

Frustration churned in his gut. "That isn't an explanation. That's an excuse."

"Trust me. It's all you need to know."

Her unwillingness to be forthcoming only irritated him more.

"Fine. Keep it a secret. You seem to be good at holding things back. It really doesn't matter anymore. But you will explain why you didn't sign and return the annulment papers. So if you don't want money and you obviously aren't interested in a reconciliation, why else continue our marriage?"

CHAPTER EIGHT

HE WAS RIGHT about one thing.

Zoe had been holding back but not for the reasons Demetrius was suggesting.

She never imagined how it might look to him. At the time, she'd been so caught up in her fear for her mother's safety to think clearly. A call from the *polizia* had burst the illusion of happily-ever-after. That long-ago call had made her face reality—accept the graveness of her mother's illness.

Until the *polizia* had found her mother wandering the streets in her nightgown, lost and confused, Zoe had been living in a state of denial—unable to accept the harsh sentence this disease was exacting on her mother. It had been all too easy to get caught up in the rush of love— of the promise of a fairy-tale ending—rather than to acknowledge that she was on the verge of losing the one person who meant the world to her. But Zoe didn't have that excuse now—not when Demetrius thought the absolute worst of her.

Her gaze moved to the steps. An escape was so close and yet so far away. The sandy beach looked so inviting. But she couldn't. Not yet. Not until she got to the bottom of this mess.

She rolled back the memories. Though it had all taken place less than a year ago, in so many ways it seemed like a lifetime ago. She clearly remembered the day the annulment papers had arrived. They'd been messengered to her apartment. They'd nearly destroyed her to read, but somehow she found the strength to pen her name on them. As for the check, she just couldn't accept the money, especially after the way things had ended. She clearly recalled ripping it into itty-bitty pieces.

At the time, things had been so hectic. Her mother's situation had been in flux. There were doctors' appointments. And with her mother's rapidly declining condition, lots of tests. But Zoe was certain she'd taken care of the annulment papers.

Her head started to pound. "I know I signed the papers. I...I don't know what happened to them after that. A clerk must have misplaced them because I don't have them."

"And that's it? That's your only explanation?"

"*Si!* Do you really find that so hard to believe?"

He paused as though really giving some thought to the possibility there could have been a clerical snafu. "I'll check into it."

"Your words say one thing but your eyes say another." She frowned at him. "Why do you find it so hard to believe that I'm not behind the missing papers?"

"Because it wouldn't be the first time you lied to me."

She pressed her hands to her hips and lifted her chin. "What's that supposed to mean?"

"It means you lied when you married me. You said you loved me, yet when our marriage hit a few snags, you cut and ran—"

"That's not true. I had to. I..." Realizing that he was in absolutely no frame of mind to comprehend what she was about to say, she pressed her lips together and turned away.

"You didn't have to run away. I told you numerous times that we'd work it out with the king and his counsel. We'd have found a way to sway the public's support."

"I know you tried. And...and I wanted to believe you. I desperately wanted to believe that everything would fall into place. But it didn't. Don't you understand, my leaving was for the best?"

"The best for whom? Me? Not hardly. You knew that I loved you. So it must have been best for you. Did leaving make you happy?"

She didn't say anything. She really did owe him an explanation but not now—not with him tossing around blame. He was justifiably angry. She knew all too well about anger. She'd spent the past year angry at the entire world. In the end, the anger had been easier for her to deal with than the acceptance of what was happening to her mother and the fact that Demetrius would be better off without her.

"Well?" he persisted.

"No. It didn't make me happy. But I did what I had to do. I didn't have a choice."

Demetrius's dark brows rose. "Wait. Are you saying that the king forced you out?"

Her temples throbbed. "I…I…"

"What? I need to know. You owe me that much."

"Not now. I can't do this." Her feet barely brushed over the steps as she made her escape from the disappointment and hurt reflected in Demetrius's eyes. She knew that she'd put it there, and she couldn't stand it. And it didn't matter what she said now, it wouldn't fix it.

Sometimes it didn't matter how much power or money a person had, they couldn't fix everything. There was no reversing her mother's condition and there was no way to change the fact that most likely her own DNA was corrupted with the devious disease that would slowly steal away a lifetime of memories and worse.

"Zoe! Wait!" Demetrius's agitated voice called out to her. "Zoe, don't run away again!"

She couldn't stop. Her knees pumped up and down. Harder. Faster. Her bare feet moved over the now-cold sand. She had no destination in mind. No finish line. She just had to keep going—putting distance between herself and Demetrius.

But it didn't matter how far she went, his words followed her. They dug inside her, poking at all of her tender spots. Was he right?

Was she running away?

She stopped. Her heart pounded. She drew one deep breath after another into her straining lungs. And still Demetrius's words were all she could hear over and over in her mind.

Don't run away again.

She'd never thought about it before. She'd never stopped to even consider her actions. She dropped to her knees, covering her face with her hands. He couldn't be right. Could he? Was that what she did? Run away?

Her mind started to replay the events since she'd met him. First her mother's diagnosis—the diagnosis that Zoe refused to accept. And what had she done, she'd run into Demetrius's arms.

And just after the royal counsel pointed out that she wouldn't live up to the king's expectations for a princess, there was the urgent phone call from the *polizia*. They'd found her mother wandering the streets—proof that she really wasn't fit to be princess. Not wanting Demetrius to pity her—to stay with her out of obligation—she'd run.

Later, she'd told herself that it was the shock and the fear for her mother that had her dashing off a note to Demetrius before she disappeared into the night. But the truth was that it was easier to run than to stand her ground—to face the pain she'd caused him.

Why hadn't she seen this before? Why did Demetrius see her biggest weakness so clearly when she'd been blind to it? It seemed she was more like her absentee father than she'd ever imagined.

Because of her mother, Zoe had finally stopped running. Zoe was doing her best to be steady for her ailing mother. Now it was time that she stood still and faced the problems with Demetrius—her husband. After all, if her mother could face Alzheimer's with dignity, Zoe could deal with her broken heart.

She got to her feet.

It was time she spoke openly and honestly with her husband.

When she made it back to the beach house, it was dark. "Demetrius." She turned on the lights in the living room. No sign of him. "Demetrius, are you here?"

No answer.

He'd left. Disappointment assailed her. She couldn't be upset with him. It was no less than she'd done to him. Twice now.

In and out of meetings all of the next day, Demetrius finally arrived at the palace offices to find Zoe gathering her things together. He glanced at his watch. "I guess it is time to call it quits for the day."

She glanced up as though she wasn't aware he'd entered the room. "I'll be out of the office most of tomorrow. In fact, probably all of it. I need to go to the mansion for photos and measurements. And then I need to do some shopping—"

He held up his hand, stopping her gush of words. "It's okay. You don't have to tell me your every move. And please feel free to use the car I've put at your disposal."

Surprise flashed in her eyes. "*Grazie*." She zipped her computer case and headed for the door. As though it were an afterthought, she turned back. "Good night."

"Zoe. Wait." She hesitated in the doorway, eventually turning around to face him. He wasn't sure how to say this, but he'd give it his best try. "About last night. I handled it poorly. I guess I'm not as over it as I thought."

Her eyes grew shiny and she blinked repeatedly. "I'm so sorry for everything."

After Zoe had hedged around the fact that his father

might have had something to do with her leaving, he just wouldn't—couldn't—leave it alone. Unable to harness his emotions, he'd gone to his father and laid out the stark facts. His father, confronted with these allegations, had aged right before Demetrius's eyes. The king admitted that he hadn't handled the news of the elopement as well as he should have, but he swore on all that was precious to him that he hadn't run off Zoe.

Before Demetrius could tell Zoe what had happened, she turned and disappeared down the hallway. Part of him said to let her go, but another part of him knew that this thing between them had to be resolved. They couldn't continue to work together in this emotionally charged atmosphere.

She'd told him what she knew about the annulment papers, now he needed to stop pushing her for an answer about what happened to their marriage. It hadn't been his father. It hadn't been anything but the fact that she hadn't loved him enough to take on this intimidating life of royalty. And he had to stop blaming her for that—for refusing to live a lie.

He dropped his tablet on the desk and headed down the hallway. The only problem was the palace was a maze of hallways. Zoe could have gone in any direction.

"Are you looking for Zoe?" Annabelle stopped next to him.

At that particular moment, he didn't care what rumors he might start, he had to find her. "Did you see which way she went?"

Annabella pointed toward the front staircase. "She was in a hurry. I don't know if you'll catch her."

He took long, quick strides until he was in the driveway. The car he'd put at her disposal was still parked. Well, that was a good sign. He still had a chance of finding her.

The young driver came rushing over. "Sir, may I help you?"

"Did you see Ms. Sarris?"

He nodded. "She said that she wouldn't need a ride this evening, sir. She said she wanted to walk."

"Which way did she go?"

The young man pointed toward the beach.

Demetrius set off after her. Still in a suit and tie, he wasn't exactly dressed for a stroll on the beach, but that didn't stop him. He was intent on setting things straight. He told himself that it was purely a business decision. The strain between them wasn't conducive to productivity.

He set off down the long set of steps at the back of the palace. They stretched down the cliff to the pristine beach below. He paused midway down the stairs and searched the shoreline. He immediately spotted her standing at the edge of the water, staring off into the distant horizon where the setting sun hovered low in the azure sky.

As he rushed down the remaining stairs, he wondered what was going through her mind. At one point he'd been able to read her thoughts or so he liked to think. Back when they were together there had been times when a deep sadness was reflected in her eyes. It seemingly came from nowhere and when he asked her about it, she brushed it off and changed the subject. He never wanted to be responsible for causing her such pain, but last night he'd done just that and he'd witnessed that same look of pain again—pain he'd inflicted.

He stopped behind her. "Zoe."

She didn't move, but he knew that she'd heard him. Maybe it'd be easier this way. "I wanted to apologize. I was out of line last night. I'm not going to make excuses. I just want you to know that it won't happen again." Still, she didn't move. He deserved her cold shoulder. "You should know that I confronted the king. He feels bad about not being more welcoming. I also initiated an investigation into the missing annulment papers."

Zoe spun around.

"Why would you do that? Does Annabelle know?"

Why did she keep worrying about Annabelle? Had they become that good of friends so quickly? Was she worried that Annabelle would stop talking to her if she knew they were married? He had to admit that he didn't know much about the ways of women's minds, but Annabelle didn't strike him as the petty type.

"You don't have to worry. Even if Annabelle knew the truth about us, she'd still be your friend."

Zoe shook her head. "I don't think so. Although I'm surprised you haven't confided in her. Don't you think she should know?"

"No, I don't." He and Annabelle were acquaintances at best.

"If I was planning to marry you, I'd want to know that you already have a wife—"

"Marry?" What? Had he heard her correctly? "Annabelle and I?"

Zoe nodded. "She's perfect for you. An aristocrat's daughter. Your country will have a strong ally in Halencia."

"Stop!" The unintentional boom of his voice had Zoe's eyes opening wide. He made a point of lowering his voice. "Annabelle and I are not getting married."

"But after the annulment is resolved—"

"Not then. Not ever."

Zoe's brow wrinkled. "I don't understand."

"Neither do I. Annabelle isn't in Mirraccino to get married. Her father didn't approve of her globe-trotting, partying ways. He thought a job would teach her some responsibility. Her father and my father put their heads together. In exchange for Annabelle being the face of the South Shore revitalization project that includes advertisements and billboards, her father agreed to be a large investor in the project. He will be attending the Royal Christmas Ball."

"He's one of the people you need to impress?"

Demetrius nodded. "Now do you understand? Annabelle has nothing to do with you and me."

"But you can't launch a search for the annulment papers. People will talk. Rumors will start. What if the media finds out about you and me?"

He rubbed the back of his neck. The muscles were tense and giving him a headache. "Honestly, I'm surprised the paparazzi hasn't found out by now."

"But you've worked so hard to change your public persona—to get the people to respect you—"

"And I have no intention of smearing my name. Everything will be done hush-hush under the direction of counsel." He was struck by her genuine concern. If there was any doubt whatsoever of whether she'd signed the annulment papers or not, he had his answer now.

"I hope they find them before someone else does."

"I do, too. But we'll deal with that issue if we have to."

"So you believe me? You believe I wasn't going to use the papers against you?"

He shifted his weight from foot to foot. "I still have questions, but no, I don't think you were planning to blackmail me or anything."

"I guess that will have to be enough."

He wasn't sure where that left them, but he'd take it as a good sign. After all, there was no reason they had to be enemies. There were plenty of exes who were friends. Weren't there?

"It's a nice evening for a walk. How about I walk you back to the beach house?"

Surprise lit up her eyes. He thought for sure that she'd turn him down. He still wasn't so sure he could pull off this friend thing, not when he remembered vividly the sweetness of her kisses. But he wanted to give it a try. They'd done the fighting thing and it wasn't working for him. It was time for a change.

Zoe nodded. "I'd like that."

"So would I."

Side by side, they strolled down the beach as the sun sunk lower on the horizon and the water rolled farther up the beach. When a strong breeze rushed past them, Zoe rubbed her arms and he realized she wasn't wearing a jacket. He slipped off his suit coat and placed it over her shoulders.

After all, that's what friends do—look out for each other. With a little practice, he just might be able to pull this friendship off. And it felt so much better than arguing.

CHAPTER NINE

A PEACEFUL COEXISTENCE had formed.

Dare she call it a friendship?

Zoe had her hands full traveling between Residenza del Rosa, the palace and the beach house. Days turned into a week and then two weeks as rush orders were placed for state-of-the-art office furniture. The pieces were needed for the administrative suite on the second floor of the mansion. Those offices needed to be smart looking as well as functional. That was the easy part.

The common rooms on the first floor would take more effort—more creativity. They would have a different function and hopefully portray a more relaxed mood.

Today, the painting should be underway. She was anxious to see if the shades they'd settled on were the same calming colors once it covered the entire wall. She crossed her fingers for luck. They were running out of time to have additional colors specially mixed and delivered.

The royal sedan pulled right up to the front of the mansion. She immediately noticed that the construction equipment had been removed. New sod had been laid on the front lawn. The end was in sight. When she stepped out of the vehicle, she could still hear some smaller machines as they worked on the back of the building. If she had to guess, she'd say they were working on the landscaping.

Suddenly she got the feeling she was being watched. The hairs on the back of her neck lifted. She looked around as she started up the steps to Residenza del Rosa.

This time, there weren't any reporters or photographers waiting, but there was something different—the royal security detail was out and about. She was quite certain they weren't there to secure her safety.

Demetrius was there. Somewhere. Her stomach fluttered with nerves.

She reached the landing at the same moment he stepped out of the front door. He stood there in the early morning sunshine looking quite regal in his navy suit. The top buttons of his shirt were undone giving the slightest hint of his tanned, muscular chest. She knew that chest inch by inch, and she recalled how he had this one ticklish spot on his right side—

She jerked her meandering thoughts to a sudden halt. She couldn't go there. No way. Not even now that she knew they were legally husband and wife. She didn't want to jeopardize this brand-new friendship.

Demetrius strode over to her. "Are you that disappointed at seeing me?"

"What? Um. No. Just surprised is all."

"Well, if you keep frowning like that when we're together, rumors are going to start."

"Oh." She immediately smiled.

"That's much better."

He was so handsome. Her gaze moved from his strong jaw, to his kissable lips and up to his eyes that were staring back at her. Her heart tip-tapped. *Remember to keep things light. Don't ruin things.*

She swallowed hard. "What's brought you here this morning?"

"I was just notified that all of the invitations for the Royal Christmas Ball have gone out to the select group of guests. I need to make sure that everything here is progressing as planned. Are there any problems I should be aware of?"

Again, she had the feeling she was being watched. She glanced around. Who was it? She grew frustrated, not being able to locate anyone. Maybe she was just being paranoid after her run-ins with that persistent reporter.

"Zoe, did you hear me?"

"Um, what?" She didn't want to mention anything and sound paranoid. After all, it was just a feeling. Thankfully, she hadn't seen the creepy reporter in a few weeks, not since the night Demetrius showed up at her apartment. Surely by now he'd given up.

Demetrius's brows drew together. "Zoe, what's the matter? You haven't heard a word I've said."

She gave the area one last glance before turning her full attention back to Demetrius. "The progress of the mansion is on schedule. As of right now, the administrative suite upstairs is painted and scheduled to be carpeted tomorrow. The furniture is being shipped express. The staff will be able to move in shortly. I know that's a priority." She started for the entrance. "As for the common rooms, I've been in daily contact with the various contractors. In fact, today the paint is already going up on the walls."

Demetrius stopped just outside the front door and turned to her. "Listen, I've been meaning to tell you that you've done a really good job with this project so far."

"Really?" His compliment made her heart do the tip-tap-tap rhythm again. "But you haven't even seen it yet."

"I've seen the progression of your sketches and I know that you've been on top of the whole project. I'm certain that it's going to turn heads."

"*Grazie.* And I don't just mean for your kind words. I mean for giving me this great opportunity."

"It wasn't altruistic. I needed the best, and you are it. A rising star."

It felt so strange to talk to him like this, but she eagerly welcomed the friendly words. "Shall we go inside and see how the color scheme is panning out?"

He nodded. He pulled the door open for her.

She stepped inside the foyer and was immediately greeted by the serenity of blue walls with a cloud-white trim. It all blended beautifully with the white marble floor woven with a gray-and-brown mineral pattern. She smiled. So far so good.

A gentle breeze rushed past her carrying with it the scent of fresh paint. She loved the smell. It meant that one of her many sketches was being brought to life. Her hands clenched as a mixture of excitement and worry collided. There were times when projects didn't turn out quite as expected. *Please don't let this be one of those times*.

She couldn't wait to see the ballroom. It was to be the shimmering jewel of this entire project. She turned in that direction when she heard Demetrius clear his throat.

She stifled a sigh and turned. "Did you have someplace in particular that you wanted to start?"

He nodded in the opposite direction. "I thought we'd take a look at the garden. I know you weren't in charge of it, but your vision for the interior greatly influenced the approach they took."

She had to admit that she was anxious to see the garden. Her mother had a fondness for them. In fact, Zoe thought her mother would approve of Residenza del Rosa. Now, if only Zoe could figure out how to get her mother a room in the exclusive and expensive center. She had a feeling a deep and honest conversation was on the horizon between her and the administrator of the facility. She wasn't above begging if that's what it took.

She followed Demetrius down the hallway to a doorway that led to the courtyard surrounded in the distance by a low wall. They stepped out onto the freshly laid mosaic tiles. They were of earthy red tones offset by a bright blue-and-white pattern.

The walkway led to a center patio with an old fountain that had been lovingly restored. The tiles there contained seashell outlines. Someone had the foresight to continue the theme by surrounding the edge of the patio with crushed shells.

Demetrius pointed to the edge of the patio. "There will be benches added so people can come out here to enjoy a bit of the day or to entertain company."

"I love it." Her gaze met his. Her heart picked up its pace. "They're doing a fabulous job."

"I'm so glad you approve. I told the gardener that the courtyard would have to be extra special so it didn't detract from the interior design."

Heat warmed her cheeks over his compliment. She turned away, glancing around as a few men were hard at work digging spots for a variety of plants, from olive trees to medium palms and citrus trees. There was other foliage that Zoe couldn't name. But she liked it…a lot.

Zoe's gaze lingered over the potted plants with brilliant red, lemon yellow and spicy-orange blooms. All were waiting to be transplanted into the rich soil. She could already envision the garden completely finished. It would be wonderful. She would definitely spend some time here if given the opportunity. She hoped the residents would find it just as appealing.

Demetrius turned to her. "I take it you approve of the decision to refurbish the fountain."

She nodded. "You can't find that sort of detail these days. And the fish and seashell design will go splendidly with what I'm doing with the inside."

"I thought you might approve. There's still quite a bit of work they need to do out here, but it should be completed in time for the big reveal."

"Good." She glanced up. His gaze met hers causing her heart to thump rapidly.

Ever since she'd learned that he was still her husband, it was as if she was seeing him differently. He was no longer the impulsive guy that she'd initially fallen for. There was so much more to Demetrius than she'd noticed before. And she found herself falling for him all over again.

He had quite a brilliant head for business. He was a natural at taking control of not only his emotions but also emotional situations. He thought before he acted. This was a man she felt confident would one day be a good leader for their nation.

He was also good for her—whether she wanted to admit it or not. Though he could make her heart race like no other, he could also put her at ease as though nothing in this world was insurmountable, which was ridiculous considering her mother's irreversible diagnosis. But somehow, he still made her want to believe in dreams and the power of love.

She knew she was setting herself up for a fall. Sooner, rather than later, this unconventional marriage would end—for real this time.

She dreaded that quickly approaching day.

Demetrius escorted Zoe around Residenza del Rosa, paying her more attention than the restoration work being done on the historic mansion. But he couldn't help it. Zoe kept sending him strange looks. He wanted to stop her and ask what was on her mind. Was she thinking about the fact they were still secretly married?

He couldn't tell if that knowledge came to her as good news or bad news. Not that he cared. Well, maybe he was just a bit curious. Okay, a lot curious.

After inspecting the shell pink paint in the sunroom and the sandy shades in the library, they made their way back to the reception area. He'd asked the foreman to gather the workmen together. He wanted to give them a word of encouragement.

While waiting for everyone to be assembled, a few of the men approached him to discuss the revitalization project.

The men were friendly and thankful for the work. Demetrius promised to do all he could to keep the revitalization project alive.

When it came time for the talk, Demetrius motioned for Zoe to join him. She stepped forward. As strange as it sounded, it felt natural having her next to him. Dare he admit it, he liked having her back in his life.

He cleared his throat. "Ms. Sarris and I would like to thank you all for doing such wonderful work. This place looks amazing. I know this isn't the sort of place people want to end up, but I'm hoping Ms. Sarris's vision will give the place a fresh and easy air. I know that we don't have much time until the Christmas ball and the official opening in the New Year, but I personally appreciate all of the extra time and effort you've put into this very special project. Give yourselves a round of applause."

Demetrius started clapping. Zoe joined him and then one by one the men started clapping and smiling.

When silence fell back over the room, Demetrius had one more announcement. "I'm so impressed that each of you will be receiving a Christmas bonus if the project is brought in a week early."

Another round of clapping. Cheers and whistles went up.

"Okay, men, let's get back to it," the foreman said.

"Kiss. Kiss. Kiss." A soft chant started.

What in the world? Demetrius's first thought was to glance at Zoe to see if she had any clue what they were talking about, but he didn't dare look in her direction. He didn't want anyone to read anything in his expression.

"Kiss. Kiss." The chant grew louder and some started to clap. There were smiles all around.

Demetrius turned a questioning look to the foreman. The man pointed upward. Demetrius tilted his head back, already suspecting what he'd find. Mistletoe.

Something told him that the workers had a bit of holiday

mischief going on as he recalled how they'd pointed out where he should stand to give this talk. He tried to figure out which man had suggested this particular spot. Demetrius was unable to locate him in the crowd.

And still the chanting continued.

Not seeing an easy way out of this awkward spot, he turned to Zoe to see if she'd been wise enough to make a hasty exist. This time he wouldn't blame her for running away. But much to his surprise she was still standing there frozen. Worry, or was it panic, reflected in her eyes. A kiss certainly wasn't going to help his resolve to keep their relationship on friendly terms.

Still, he didn't know how to just walk away without turning this awkward situation into a big deal. He glanced out at the sea of smiling faces. Their jolly moods were good for business. And if he walked out now, he knew there would be a distinct shift in attitude. Too bad he'd thrown out the Christmas bonuses before this mistletoe scene. He'd lost a very effective distraction.

"Kiss. Kiss. Kiss."

This wasn't a good idea. And yet…

"Kiss."

This was a really bad idea. But still…

"Kiss."

Demetrius leaned toward her and her eyes opened wide, but it was her glossy lips that beckoned to him. He wanted—no—he needed to once again feel her lips beneath his. He longed to taste her sweet kiss again. In fact, he'd never wanted something so much in his life.

But at the last second, he moved, letting his lips land on her cheek. It definitely wasn't what he'd had in mind, but it was for the best. The crowd went crazy. Applause made any attempt at conversation nearly impossible.

The quick and simple kiss was over in a heartbeat. When Zoe's gaze met his, his heart thumped hard. In fact, it was beating so loud that he was sure she could hear it. How was it that a woman who'd hurt him so deeply could have such a tremendous effect on him?

Perhaps he'd been working too much—for far too many hours. That had to be it. Because he was over Zoe. He'd put her in his rearview mirror that dark, overcast night when she'd left without an explanation. They were friends now. Nothing more.

He turned away from her. It was then that he noticed a number of phones pointed in their direction. So their little bit of fun had been photographed. That was a complication he hadn't anticipated. It seemed that when Zoe was around, there were quite a few things that slipped his mind.

But he didn't have to worry. His security team was all over it. Demetrius breathed an easy breath as phones were confiscated and photos of himself and Zoe were deleted. Apparently the men had forgotten that upon being hired for this very special project—a project that he planned to oversee personally—that they'd signed confidentiality agreements.

The part of this whole scenario that alarmed Demetrius was that after everything, Zoe still got to him. He'd have to be careful in the future. Keep more of a distance in their friendship.

He wouldn't give her a chance to hurt him again.

CHAPTER TEN

TIME TO MAKE a hasty exit.

Zoe didn't even wait for Demetrius as she moved away—far away from the mistletoe. Her heart was still hammering. She'd thought for sure he was going to lay a real kiss on her—in front of everyone. And the truth was, she wouldn't have stopped him. Did that make her desperate? Or was she just plain pathetic?

She gave a shake of her head as she rushed past the newly erected registration desk toward the grand ballroom. She didn't need any distractions right now—even if it was from the sexiest prince on the planet. She needed to concentrate on her work. Everything had to be perfect for the Royal Christmas Ball. She wouldn't let Demetrius down this time. She owed him that much.

Before she reached the ballroom, she felt a hand on her shoulder. She paused and turned, not quite ready to discuss what had happened back there.

Demetrius stood before her with a frown on his face. "What are you running from?"

"I wasn't running." Was she?

"It sure looked like it to me."

Drat. She wanted to show Demetrius that she was changing. That she wasn't the same person he used to know. She was done running. She was working hard at facing her problems head-on. At least most of them.

"Well, you are mistaken." She wondered how many people had the nerve to say that to the prince. "I was excited is all." Then realizing that her words could be misconstrued, she added, "Excited to see how the ballroom turned out."

His eyes reflected disbelief. "You know, you don't have to worry."

"Who said I was worried?" She forced a smile to her lips.

"No one has to say it. It's written all over your face. The thing you don't know is that all of the people on this job site signed a confidentiality agreement. They can't share any photos of me or talk to the press about what they witness here. In fact, my security team confiscated their phones and deleted the photos."

"Really?"

He nodded. "Do you feel better?"

"*Sì.*" The worry of the paparazzi spinning one innocent holiday kiss out of control slid off her shoulders. "Come on. Let's go see it." She reached for his hand to pull him along with her.

Her fingers slid over his warm palm. Her fingertips curled around his hand and she started toward the ballroom. Then she realized that she couldn't be this familiar with the prince in public. Not unless she really did want people to talk. With much regret, she loosened her grip, but when she tried to withdraw her hand, he held on.

Her pulse quickened and her heart raced. In her imagination, she envisioned turning to him. He'd gaze into her eyes just before his head dipped and he kissed her properly. This time there'd be no anger. Instead, there'd be a sweetness to it—a yearning for two souls to blend as one.

A frustrated sigh passed her lips.

"What's the matter?"

He had heard her? She'd have to do better at concealing her thoughts. "Nothing. Nothing at all." He sent her an I-don't-believe-you look, but before he could say more, she added, "Let's go see the ballroom. When I checked on it yesterday, I thought it was coming along wonderfully."

The oversized, white doors with gold trim were propped open and she rushed past them. The breath caught in her throat as she took in the massive changes to the room. The Roman pillars she'd insisted Demetrius splurge on lined both sides of the room. On the far side, between the pillars, were two sets of French doors. They led to a private terrace.

She turned to find Demetrius standing directly behind her. "What do you think?"

"I think you are very good at your job."

A smile pulled at her lips. *He liked it. He really liked it.*

"And best of all, after the ball is over there is furniture ordered to make this an all-purpose room. Couches will be added on the side with the French doors. A group of tables will be added at the far end for card or board games. And over at the other end will be a bunch of armchairs and end tables for families to get together and visit."

"It seems you've thought of everything."

"I doubt it, but I've really tried to make this place as comfortable for everyone as possible."

"I'm sure they'll appreciate all of your hard work."

"But there's something missing." She stepped into the middle of the room and turned all around. The smile slipped from her lips. She turned around again. This time slower. There was definitely something missing.

"What has you frowning? Is it the pillars, because I have to admit that you were right about them? They are exactly what a room this size needed."

She shook her head. "It's not the pillars. It's something else."

"Maybe it's the paint. I think they only have up the first coat."

"No. That's not it, either." She turned in a circle again. This time her gaze stopped on the interior wall. It was blank. Empty. Boring. "That's it."

"What's it?"

"See this wall." She moved to stand directly in front of it. "It needs something."

"What do you have in mind? A group of paintings?"

She shook her head. "That would be a waste of the space."

"Then what?"

And then it came to her like someone had just switched on a lightbulb. "A mural."

"A what?"

"You heard me. A mural would be perfect here."

He stepped next to her. "Are you sure?"

"Of course I'm sure or I wouldn't have said it." Her mind conjured up all sorts of scenes to fill this blank canvas.

"I guess you do know what you're talking about. But where would we find an artist at the last minute capable of doing such work?"

"I think I know someone who can do it."

"You do?" He turned and looked at her. "Are they available?"

She shrugged and didn't meet his gaze. Maybe she shouldn't have mentioned it. Demetrius would probably find her idea preposterous when she told him the name of the artist.

"Zoe, are you trying to tell me that you want to paint it?"

This was her chance to put her artwork out there—to spread her wings so to speak. Besides, this was about the people who would eventually live here. They needed a welcoming, relaxing atmosphere, and she was convinced a mural would be just the ticket to pull the whole design together. "*Sì.*"

He rubbed his jaw as though seriously considering her proposal. That had to be a good sign, right? She willed him to go with the idea. Her mother for one would love it—if only Zoe could get her a room in the upscale residence.

Unable to take the silence any longer, she uttered, "Well, what do you think?"

* * *

Zoe pleaded with Demetrius with her eyes.

How could he deny her this?

He could feel any reservations he might have folding like a house of cards. "I think it'll be perfect."

She clapped her hands together in excitement. "Great! I can't wait to start."

Demetrius stared up at the big blank wall. A mural certainly would turn heads. But it was a huge task. The interior design already had Zoe so busy. He didn't want her to wear herself out. "Are you sure you're up for an additional project?"

Her face glowed with happiness. "I'm positive. The design is done. The color combinations work. The furniture is ordered. There's nothing pressing at this point that requires my constant attention."

"Okay. You've sold me on the idea."

"You won't be sorry. This is going to be fantastic."

Her enthusiasm was contagious. He'd seen a little of her artwork in the past from her sketch pads. And she'd also shown him pictures of some paintings, mostly landscapes. They were colorful and captivating.

There was still one thing nagging at him—the time element. He stared up at the big blank wall. It was a wide-open space and he couldn't help but wonder how long it'd take to paint a mural. He honestly didn't have any clue.

"What's bothering you?" Zoe's voice drew him out of his thoughts.

"I was wondering how long it'd take to paint a mural."

The light in her eyes dimmed. "You don't think I can do it—"

"That isn't what I said—what I meant. I know that you're very talented and you can do anything you set your mind to. But do you have enough time for such a large project? Do you even know what you'd paint?"

She glanced up at the wall as though giving his words serious consideration. "I know you're hesitant to add something new to the mix at this late stage, but I have a proposition for you."

His ears immediately perked up. So did other parts of him. "What exactly do you have in mind?"

Her eyes widened at the sound of his deep, sultry voice. "Not what you have going on in that dirty mind of yours."

A deep chuckle rumbled in his chest. "Hey, now you're the one throwing around propositions."

She smiled and shook her head. "I'm glad to see there's still some of the Demetrius I used to know lurking about."

She was right. The new Demetrius—the proper one—wouldn't be flirting and playing with innuendos. Maybe he'd taken the role of crown prince too seriously. He rubbed the back of his neck. "About the mural, what are you suggesting?"

"I have some sketches I'd like to show you. They're at my apartment. I have one in particular of the beach that I think would be perfect. But I'll let you pick which sketch I paint."

"Okay. Let's go get them."

"What?" She looked at him as if he'd just spoken in a foreign language.

"We'll pick up your sketch on the way back to the beach house."

She shook her head. "No. Never mind."

He didn't understand the problem. He was willing to entertain her idea and now she was changing her mind. What in the world had he missed?

His gaze met hers. "You no longer want to do the mural?"

"I want to do it."

"Good. But if you think you're going back to your apartment alone with that reporter snooping around then you're mistaken. It's my fault that he's bothering you—"

"No, it isn't."

He arched a brow. "We both know it is. He wants a scoop on the crown prince. The more scandalous, the better. And I'm not going to let him near you."

"You can't always be there to protect me."

She was right and he didn't like it, not one little bit. "But I'm here now."

Her unwavering gaze met his. "Are you sure you have time?"

"I'm sure. Let's go."

CHAPTER ELEVEN

IT WILL ALL work out.

That was what Zoe kept telling herself.

She sat next to Demetrius in the same unmarked black sedan that had escorted her to Residenza del Rosa. Demetrius wanted to stir the least amount of public attention as possible. Although with his security detail in the lead with another black car and an additional black car following closely behind, they stood out even here in the capital of Mirraccino. She tried to reason with him to delay the trip, but he was insistent they move on this immediately.

Frantically, she tried to remember what condition she'd left the apartment in when she'd rushed out the door. Sure he'd been there before, but only for a few minutes, most of which he'd spent standing in the hallway. And then he'd been so concerned about the creepy reporter that she doubted he'd noticed much of anything as he rushed off to speak with his security detail.

Had she put away the dishes? Was there still some lingerie on the drying rack? And that basket of laundry—was it still sitting in the living room? Or had she put the clothes away?

She'd always been able to keep him away from her apartment when they were dating. That hadn't been too hard considering their relationship had been kept on the down low. If her mother had known she was dating the prince, her mother never would have been able to keep the exciting news to herself. Not that Zoe could blame her. At times, she'd felt like she would burst, holding in the fact that she'd found her very own Prince Charming.

"Are you feeling okay?" There was a note of concern in Demetrius's voice.

"Sure. I'm fine. Why wouldn't I be?"

He studied her intently. "You know that you can talk to me about whatever is on your mind?"

Why did things have to be so complicated between them? She longed for a normal life. One where her mother was healthy and could live on her own. One where her mother didn't get confused and frustrated with aspects of life that so many people took for granted.

"Why does life have to be so unfair?" Zoe muttered under her breath.

"Sometimes I wonder the same thing. Being a prince doesn't give me a pass on painful and unhappy moments." Demetrius reached out and wrapped an arm around her shoulders. "I am here if you need me."

At first, she resisted the pull of his arm, but needing to feel his strength and the comfort of someone being on her side, she gave in. Her head came to rest against his shoulder. The scent of his spicy cologne taunted her, reminding her of all the things in life she'd had to give up in order to do right by the people she loved. And now, she had to be content with this platonic touch.

All too soon the car rolled to a stop behind Zoe's apartment building. She reached for the door handle. "Stay here. I'll be right back."

"Not so fast." Demetrius followed her out the door. A bodyguard leaned over and whispered something in Demetrius's ear. "We're clear to go up."

"How do you know?"

He sent her a knowing smile as though he was always two steps ahead of her. "Some of my men were sent ahead to secure the area."

"It must be tough always having to be so careful where

you go and having to be surrounded by your own private army." She truly meant it. She might not be rich, but she did have her privacy and the freedom to come and go as she pleased.

He shrugged. "It is what it is. I'm sorry that it bothers you."

"I...no, it doesn't. It's just so different from my life."

He truly didn't seem fazed by it. Even when he'd been living life to its fullest as the playboy prince when they'd first met, he'd still been surrounded by bodyguards. Demetrius insisted that the men dress to fit in with the crowd. These days, those same bodyguards wore dark suits and dark glasses. There was no missing the fact that they were part of his security detail, and the expression on their faces said that they meant business.

When Zoe stepped into the darkened hallway of the older building, she paused and turned to him. "You really don't have to come with me. I'm sure you have phone calls and other things to do."

His brows rose and for a moment he didn't say anything. "I promise you that you have my undivided attention."

Any other time, she would have loved to be the center of his attention, but not right now. Knowing no other way to deter him from following her to the humble little apartment she shared with her mother, she mounted the steps to the second floor.

All the while, she kept telling herself that it didn't matter. Once this project was done...once the annulment papers were recovered...she'd never see Demetrius again, aside from the photos in the newspaper and the television appearances. Still, she'd have her memories for as long as they lasted. She could only hope they weren't snatched away like her mother's—only to be replaced with confusion and uncertainty.

* * *

Her discomfort was palpable.

Demetrius followed Zoe up the stairs. Her shoulders were rigid. She didn't say a word. He wished she would relax. She didn't have to be self-conscious about the apartment building. Sure it was older and there was nothing fancy about it, but there was an air of hominess—a warmth that at times was lacking from the glamor of the palace now that his mother was no longer around.

Zoe paused outside a brown wooden door. Gold numerals read 213. She turned to him, her gaze not quite reaching his. "My place…it's nothing fancy."

"It's okay, Zoe. Remember, I've been here before." Without thinking of the implications, he reached out and stroked his fingers over her silky smooth cheek. "Stop worrying. It doesn't matter what it looks like. Not everyone is born into a palace. Sometimes, I think you ended up with the better end of the deal."

She sent him a disbelieving look. He couldn't blame her. He realized looking from the outside in that it was hard to believe that life within the palace walls was anything but perfect and worry free.

Sometimes he wondered if part of the problem was that the palace was just so massively big that as a child he sometimes felt as though he got lost amongst the statues and paintings. His mother and father were always hosting an event or entertaining a dignitary. As a kid, he'd promised himself that when he had his own family that he'd always have time for them.

The head of his security detail approached Zoe and requested the key to her apartment. She hesitantly handed it over. With instructions to wait in the hallway with two other bodyguards while the apartment was searched, Zoe crossed her arms and stared at the floor.

"I forget that you aren't used to these security procedures." Feeling as though he owed her a better explanation, he went on. "Lately, there has been a spike in chatter about a revolt. That's why my brother took it upon himself to keep our…" he lowered his voice "…our marriage a secret. He didn't want to give the rebel rousers any help with their cause until the palace figured out how best to present our marriage to the people."

"I didn't know. No one told me."

"No one wanted to worry you." He almost added that he'd warned everyone to keep this from her because he hadn't wanted to scare her off, but it didn't matter. She'd run off anyhow.

The bodyguard reemerged from the apartment. "All clear, sir."

Zoe pushed open the door that led into the modest living room. She stepped inside and waited for him. "Welcome to my place." She rushed over to the radiator and grabbed some shirts and a black lacy bra. They'd been laid out to dry since clothes dryers weren't common in the region. "Sorry about the laundry." She moved the articles of clothing behind her back. "I wasn't expecting company."

"Don't worry. I'm the one who is intruding. I'll admit I've always wondered about your home life."

Her eyes widened. "You did?"

He nodded. "You always kept this part of your life such a mystery. I never even had the opportunity to meet your mother. I would have liked that. Maybe she could have told me some stories about you when you were a kid."

"She would have enjoyed that. Mum loved to tell stories."

He repeated Zoe's words in his mind. "You said that in the past tense." He stepped closer to her, wondering if he'd solved the reason for the smudges beneath Zoe's eyes and the pained look reflected in her eyes when she didn't think he was watching her. "Did something happen to your mother? Did...did she pass on?"

"What? No. Of course not."

"But the way you talked about her—"

"It was nothing. A slip of the tongue."

She snatched up a bed pillow from the old wooden framed couch with a yellow-and-blue-checked pattern. "It's my mother's. Sometimes she falls asleep out here."

"Will she be home soon?"

"Uh, no. She won't be home until the week of Christmas."

"I'm surprised you still live with her." He thought back to the numerous conversations they'd had when they were dating and how Zoe was anxious to move out on her own— that is until he swayed her to marry him. "What happened to your plan to get your own place—somewhere closer to the sea?"

"I...um, changed my mind." Her gaze lowered and her face took on a pale, pasty tone. "Let me put this laundry away, and then I can get you something to drink."

"No need." He didn't want to make her any more uncomfortable. "Go ahead and do what you need to. I'll be fine here."

"I...I'll be back with those sketches." She gave the area one last glance as though making sure everything was in its place before moving off down a hallway.

The apartment was tiny—much tinier than he'd been imagining. The living room consisted of a couch, a small white table for magazines and a simple wooden stand with an old television atop of it. The living area was directly connected to the kitchen. The space was one long, narrow room.

There was nothing fancy about any of it. Everything was clean, but almost everything had seen its better day. He never imagined that Zoe struggled to get by. When he saw her snappy clothes, he'd just assumed that she had a comfy life. But it looked like she, too, was a master of appearances.

He moved over to a group of framed pictures hanging behind the couch. There was one of Zoe as a little girl. She was so cute with her long braids. And there was another of her and who he assumed was her mother on the beach. Zoe looked so happy—so full of dreams. He wondered what happened to those dreams.

He turned around, taking in the white paint coating the wall behind the framed family photos. Even the kitchen was white except for the tan and aqua tiles serving as a backsplash. When he turned fully around he noticed the wall behind the television was anything but white. In fact, it was quite intriguing.

He stepped back against the couch to get a better look. It was a mural. Pastel colors blended to create a giant conch shell resting in the sand with the foamy sea in the background. Blue skies with a couple of puffy white clouds reached up to the ceiling. Wow!

He couldn't tear his gaze from this humongous masterpiece. Zoe was so much more talented than he'd ever imagined. What was she doing hiding her talent by sorting through paint chips and picking couches? She should be creating artwork for the world to enjoy.

"I've got it." Zoe rushed back into the room. "We can go now."

"Not so fast. When were you going to tell me about this?" He gestured to the wall.

She shrugged. "It's just something I did for my mother."

"Well, she's one lucky lady." He noticed Zoe's lack of response. He assumed that she was just being modest. "Don't be shy. Why aren't you painting full-time?"

Zoe's fine brows scrunched together as she shot him an

are-you-serious look. "Because painting doesn't pay the bills. I need a steady paycheck, especially now."

Now? What did that mean? There was definitely something he was missing and he fully intended to find out what. "Zoe, tell me what's going on with you. I know that you aren't telling me everything."

"I don't want to talk about it. I've got the sketches. Now we can go."

"No, we can't. I don't understand. Why won't you talk to me?"

"I am talking. And I'm telling you that if you want to get this mural done in time for the ball, I need to get started." She turned toward the door.

"Not so fast." He crossed his arms. "There's something I want to go over with you."

She sighed and then turned. "Does it have to be right now?"

"*Sì*." When she frowned, he continued. "I'd like you to walk me through exactly what happened with the annulment papers."

"I told you I signed them."

"And so far my advisors haven't found any trace of them. I thought since they were last seen here that this visit might jog your memory—something that you've forgotten."

Her mouth gaped open as pain reflected in her eyes. "You really think that I'd forget something that important?"

He raked his fingers through his hair. "I don't know what to think. That's the problem. You keep sidestepping things. Sometimes you stop in the middle of sentences and you leave me wondering what you're working so hard to hide from me."

"Why should I be hiding something?"

Frustration balled up inside him. He struggled to keep it at bay. "Because I was always able to read you before."

"You don't think I've changed since then?"

She was doing it again. She was dodging his questions by supplying questions of her own. "Zoe, stop with the questions. Just walk me through what happened to the annulment papers and the check."

Her gaze narrowed and her lips pressed into a firm line. Seconds passed and at last she spoke. "Fine. You want to know. Here it is. I had the papers. They were over there on the kitchen counter. I signed them. I put them in the envelope to drop in the mail. And then I ripped up your check into tiny pieces which I dropped in the garbage."

"Is it possible you accidentally dropped the papers in the garbage, too?" When she frowned at him, he said, "Okay. I just had to ask."

"I can assure you the check was the only thing I trashed."

"Why would you do that?"

"What? You don't think this place lives up to your standards and that I was foolish to toss away the money?"

"No, that isn't it." He clenched his jaw. He wasn't going to fall in that rabbit hole with her. What he needed to do was concentrate on the whereabouts of the annulment papers. "So you ripped up the check. What did you do with the papers? We need to make sure they didn't end up in the wrong hands."

"If they did, I didn't do it."

He believed her. It was highly doubtful, because by now he'd have been contacted for blackmail or it would have been sold to the paparazzi. Demetrius had a feeling the papers were right here in this apartment.

"Where did you last see the papers?"

"I…I don't know." Her shoulders slumped. "I've tried to remember ever since you told me they are missing, but I can't remember what I did with the envelope after I signed the papers."

"Think hard."

"I am. I must have posted it. That's the only reasonable explanation. They must have lost it."

"You didn't send it by special courier?"

She shook her head. "You have to believe me. I did what you wanted."

What he wanted? He never wanted this annulment. The only reason he'd issued the papers was because she'd walked out on him. He was about to say as much when he noticed her eyes grow shiny. Were those tears in her eyes? *Please don't start crying.* He was never good with women when they became emotional.

He moved to the counter. "Is this where you signed the papers?"

"*Sì.* That's the last place I remember having them." She paused as though she remembered something—something important. "I remember signing them and slipping them in the envelope. Then my phone rang. It was an important client."

"And?"

Zoe worried her bottom lip. Her gaze didn't meet his. "I had to go into the office early."

"Think hard about what you did with the papers."

Her eyes widened. "My mother offered to post them."

"Your mother? She knows about us? I thought you were waiting to tell her?" This could be a complication he hadn't anticipated.

"I swear I didn't tell her about us. She didn't have a clue what was in the envelope."

"So what do you think happened?"

"I think I know." Zoe rushed out of the room and down the hallway.

Demetrius followed. Zoe entered a small, modest bedroom. She stepped up to an old chest of drawers and pulled open the top drawer. Frantically she started flipping through papers and envelopes.

"Zoe, what are you doing?"

She didn't stop to look at him as her search continued. "This is where my mother keeps her important papers." Zoe grasped a large manila envelope and held it up. "It's here."

Demetrius raked his fingers through his hair. A mix of relief and worry rushed through him. Was he really supposed to believe her mother was hiding annulment papers for a marriage that she wasn't supposed to know about?

Zoe smiled. "Isn't this great?"

"Great?"

"Yeah, you know, because no one else has the papers. The media doesn't know. Your reputation as a reformed, reliable prince is intact."

"Until you mother finds the papers missing and does something about it."

"That won't happen. She couldn't tell anyone even if she wanted to." There was a certainty in Zoe's voice, but he wasn't so sure. He didn't even know her mother except for what Zoe had told him about the woman.

"Why won't it happen?" When Zoe averted her gaze, he stepped closer to her. "Zoe, stop with the cryptic comments. Tell me what is going on. I need to understand."

CHAPTER TWELVE

THIS WAS GOING to be the most difficult conversation of her life.

Where did she even start?

Demetrius stepped closer. "Zoe, whatever it is, just say it. I'm listening."

She glanced up, meeting his unwavering stare. Within his eyes she found a steadiness that she craved. She could do this. She would get through this confession just like she'd endured all of the doctors' visits, the testing and the trying times with her mother.

"It all started before you and I met. My mother started forgetting little things at first, like not going to the market. And then I started to notice her cooking had changed. Instead of the big, traditional meals, she would heat up ready-to-serve food. And sometimes it was burned. My mother never burned food in the past. She was amazing in the kitchen." Zoe blinked, keeping her tears at bay. "I didn't want to see what was happening to her, and she was so busy trying to cover up her lapses that she was too embarrassed to ask for help. So we both ignored the telltale signs—signs I didn't even know I should be watching for."

Demetrius reached out to her, but Zoe backed away. If she gave in to the tears now, she'd never get this out and she'd kept it bottled up for too long. He had to realize that a future with her wasn't possible. He already had an entire nation's troubles to handle. He didn't need hers, too.

She drew in an unsteady breath. "By the time I met you, my mother was no longer able to keep up with her job and was let go. That's when we couldn't ignore her problem any longer. The doctors told us it was Alzheimer's. But I was in denial. I couldn't accept that I am going to lose my mother one agonizing piece at a time until she no longer knows me." A sob caught in Zoe's throat. She choked it down. "My mother's going to forget everything."

"I had no idea."

"You weren't supposed to know. I couldn't cope with the diagnosis. The last thing I wanted was sympathy. I just wanted to pretend everything was normal."

"And I was the perfect distraction."

She nodded. "I let myself get swept up in the romance, and I did my best to block out the problems at home. I tried to keep everything as routine as possible. But as time went on, my mother's condition got harder and harder to ignore. When we were out with friends, my mother grew quiet and withdrawn, only talking when spoken to and answering with short, vague answers. Her gaze would dart around the group watching for other peoples' facial responses to certain comments and then she'd respond accordingly." Zoe blinked repeatedly. "I am watching my mother disappear and there's nothing I can do to stop it."

Sympathy reflected in Demetrius's eyes. "And the night you left the palace."

"That was the night that I could no longer ignore what was happening to her and by extension my life. That night she got lost and the *polizia* picked her up. She couldn't remember where she lived. Luckily, she remembered her name."

His voice was soft and soothing. "Why didn't you tell me?"

"Tell you what? That my mother needed me, and I didn't have time to be a princess?"

Demetrius frowned. "I'm being serious. I would have helped you."

"I know. And that's why I didn't tell you. I didn't want

you looking at me like you are now." She took off down the hallway.

He followed her to the living room where he stopped in front of her. "And how am I looking at you?"

She stared at the floor. "With pity in your eyes."

He placed a finger beneath her chin and lifted until their gazes met. "No, that's compassion you see. I can feel compassion, can't I?"

She shrugged, not exactly sure what to say.

"You shouldn't have to go through all of this alone."

The truth is she'd never felt more alone. Her gaze met his. She yearned to reach out to him, to feel his reassuring touch. Her fingers tingled, longing to slip around his hand—to feel that human connection.

She staved off the desire. "I…I'm not alone. I still have my mother."

He had never seen this coming.

Demetrius felt totally at a loss.

Witnessing Zoe's pain tore at him. He wanted to make it all better for her, but not even a prince could solve her misery. All he could do was let her know that he'd be there for her. Right now, he'd do almost anything for her.

She was, after all, his wife. Maybe they hadn't realized exactly what that meant when they'd made their vows, but he'd done a lot of reflecting since then. Being married meant being there for each other through the good and the bad. He wouldn't abandon her. She needed him, even if she refused to admit it.

He gazed deep into her eyes while feeling a tug in his gut. "And you've got me should you ever need a friend. After all, you're still my wife. My very amazing, compassionate wife."

"And you are still my husband." Her voice wobbled.

"Which gives me the right to do this." He pulled her

closer. She didn't resist as her hands came to rest upon his chest.

At last, he could do what he'd been thinking about since they'd kissed at the beach house. His hold on her tightened. Her hands slid up over his shoulders and wrapped around his neck.

His head dipped, seeking out her petal-soft lips. His mouth brushed over hers, sending a jolt of awareness zinging through his whole body. His heart ached for her and everything she'd endured on her own. He wanted her to know that she wasn't alone.

Her lips moved hungrily under his as her fingernails raked through his hair. Her soft curves pressed up against the length of him and a moan swelled deep in his throat. They'd been apart for far too long. He was still her husband, and he had every right to comfort his wife.

Their kiss grew in intensity and it no longer mattered that they were standing in the center of her living room. All that mattered is that they were together and they weren't arguing. They definitely weren't arguing. At last, they seemed to be on the right page and he wasn't about to let her go. Not now when he'd just got her back in his arms. There was plenty of time later to figure out where they went from here. It wasn't important now.

In the background there was a sound. He tried to listen but when Zoe caught his bottom lip between her teeth and sucked, his thoughts spiraled in a totally different direction. She was as turned on as he was. He moaned. It'd been so long—so very long.

There was that sound again. This time it was louder. And it didn't stop.

The annoying sound was a knock on the door, followed by someone calling out his name.

The moan in his throat turned to a groan of frustration. *Damn.*

With the greatest regret, he pulled back from Zoe. Her eyes fluttered open, showing her utter confusion. Her lips were rosy red and slightly swollen. And her cheeks were flushed. A smile pulled at his lips knowing that he was responsible for putting that freshly loved look on her face.

"I'll be right there." He called out to his bodyguard to keep him from intruding on his last few moments alone with Zoe. "I'm sorry. But we have to get moving, and I'm sure your neighbors will be relieved not to have my detail littering their hallways."

The disappointment was evident in her eyes and he hated that he couldn't erase it, but he had a job to do. There was always something that needed his attention. Since he'd assumed his proper role as crown prince, the constant meetings had never bothered him.

Those busy activities had been just what he'd needed after Zoe had left him. It had kept him from getting lost in his loneliness. The back-to-back meetings kept him from dwelling on where things had gone wrong in his brief marriage. But now, with Zoe back in his life, he wanted time to stop. He wanted to talk to her—to comfort her—to help her.

He scooped up the envelope with the annulment papers and then glanced at his watch. If they didn't get moving, he'd be late for his meeting with the king. And there was one part of the meeting that Demetrius was anticipating. At long last, he could tell the king and anyone else that cared to hear that their suspicions about Zoe were totally unfounded. His grip tightened on the papers. He was holding the proof in his hand.

While Zoe gathered her sketch pads and a few clothes, he pulled the papers from the envelope. They were indeed signed. This knowledge dampened his excitement over the passionate kiss they'd just shared. Zoe hadn't lied. She did indeed want out of their marriage. Disappointment settled heavy in his chest. There was still so much to discuss. He wasn't sure exactly what to do with the papers. For now, he would keep them safe.

"I'm ready." Zoe, wearing a pair of big black sunglass, came to a stop by the front door with a floral canvas bag slung over her shoulder. She lifted her hand and placed a pink ball cap on her head and eased her long ponytail through the opening in the back. "I wanted some stuff to wear for the times I walk on the beach."

He followed her out the door and down the steps. Once they were next to the car, Zoe came to an abrupt stop. Demetrius bumped into her. He instinctively reached for her shoulders to steady her.

"Zoe, what's the matter?"

Her head was turned to the right, staring down the alleyway. "Did you see that? There it is again."

He glanced around, not noticing anything out of the ordinary. "What is it?"

"A flash. Over there." She pointed between a couple of buildings across the street. "In the shadows."

Just because he hadn't seen it didn't mean it wasn't there. He nodded to the head of security who was standing by his side, hearing everything that was said. A couple of men took off to investigate.

Demetrius rushed her into the idling car. "Don't worry. You're safe."

He would do whatever it took to protect her. He remembered how they'd hounded his mother. She'd handled it with such grace—until that fatal day. On an outing, the paparazzi had gotten out of control, blocking the royal processional. And when his twin had grown bored and taken off into the crowd, mayhem had ensued. Security tried to move the paparazzi out of the way, but before they could a shot rang out. Demetrius's body stiffened at the memory of his mother being shot.

"Are you okay?" Zoe sent him a worried look.

"I'm fine." He patted her hand.

Whoever this stalker was, they'd find him before he did anything to Zoe. Demetrius vowed to keep her safe at all costs.

CHAPTER THIRTEEN

A VERY LONG day had passed and Zoe was still confused.

What does one say to the man who is officially your husband—an estranged husband at that—a prince—the man she'd made out with in the living room of the apartment she shared with her mother?

Well, the answer was simple. Nothing.

Or at least, as little as possible.

Not until she had her head screwed back on straight and her thoughts were actually coherent.

When Demetrius had dropped her off at the beach house the day before, she'd told him that she had a headache. It hadn't been a lie. Her head had ached from the constant tug-of-war between the will of her heart and the common sense of her mind.

She'd spent most of the night staring into the dark, trying to make sense of where things stood between her and Demetrius. Luckily, it was now Saturday and she didn't have to go to the office. She could spend the whole day at the beach house. She'd intended to complete her sketch for the mural, but she couldn't sit still long enough—especially not after Demetrius called to say he was stopping by because they needed to talk.

Talk? Talk about what? The South Shore project? Or the unforgettable kiss?

She glanced at the clock on the wall. A frown tugged at her mouth. It'd been almost two hours since he had called. Where was he?

As though in answer to her thoughts, there was a knock at the door. When it swung open, Demetrius strode in with a reserved look on his face. "Sorry I'm later than I planned. I had something to deal with."

"Uh, no problem." She wasn't about to admit that she'd been dying of curiosity to know what he wanted to discuss. A glance at the clock revealed that it was approaching lunchtime. "Would you like something to eat?"

"Before we get to that, I have something to show you." His face was devoid of emotion, but his voice held a serious note.

"Is something wrong?"

He paused as though trying to choose his words carefully. "Depends on how you look at it."

Her whole body tensed. "Quit dragging it out. Just tell me."

He pulled a folded piece of paper from his pocket and held it out to her. "This appeared in this morning's paper."

She hastily unfolded the clipping. There in color was a photo of her and Demetrius getting into his car outside her apartment building. The breath trapped in her lungs. Her mind raced with all of the ramifications.

"Zoe, relax. It's not as bad as you're thinking. Between your sunglasses, your cap and having your head lowered, no one can make out that it's you. Most of your face is hidden."

Zoe let out the pent-up breath. "What are we going to do?"

"Nothing."

"What? But we have to do something otherwise people will think—they'll think—"

"Nothing. There's nothing going on in the photo except I am helping someone into my car. Your name was not mentioned. Just a blurb about me being out and about in the city."

She turned to him, searching his face for answers. "This was taken by that creepy reporter, wasn't it?"

Demetrius rubbed the back of his neck. "That's my suspicion, but so far the paper is guarding their source. Don't worry. Now that you've moved in here, we shouldn't have any further problems with that photographer. But when we are out in public, we're going to have to be extra careful."

She nodded. "I understand."

He hesitated. Then deciding that he'd made his point, he changed the subject. "Now about lunch, I'll give the kitchen staff a call and have them send over something. What do you want?"

"Actually, I was thinking of making a salad." When he reached for his phone, she added, "You don't need to call anyone. The fridge is fully stocked. There's even some fresh shrimp."

"Sounds good." His facial expression said otherwise.

"If you want something else, that's fine."

He shook his head. "It's not the menu."

"Are you sure?"

He nodded. "It's just that I'm not exactly good in the kitchen. I haven't had much experience there."

"No problem. You can watch."

He started to roll up his sleeves. "And have you do all of the work? I don't think so. You just tell me what needs done and I'll do my best."

They moved to the kitchen and raided the refrigerator of all the fresh vegetables. Demetrius washed while she chopped. The truth was Zoe didn't have an appetite, no matter how colorful the vegetables or plump the already cooked shrimp.

Demetrius wasn't the problem—not exactly. It was what had happened a couple of nights ago that was bothering her. It'd be so easy to get caught up in more kisses, in more of this domestic bliss. But she knew the truth—the fact that she had a fifty-fifty chance of ending up like her mother. And she couldn't—wouldn't—put Demetrius through that. A sharp pain started in her finger and rushed up her arm.

"Hey, you're bleeding."

Zoe glanced down to see she'd nicked the tip of her thumb. She muttered under her breath as she moved to the sink to rinse it off.

"I'll get a bandage." Demetrius rushed out of the room. He quickly returned and played the concerned doctor as he applied antibiotic cream and a bandage. "Now sit down and I'll finish."

Grudgingly, she did as instructed.

He grabbed a tomato and started to slice it. "Were you able to work on your sketch?"

Really? He thought she'd be calm enough to be creative. "Umm…no."

"You know, I never did get to see any of your sketches. And you did say I'd get to choose one."

"And you will. But I don't want anyone seeing them until I do some more work on them." Cutting him off before he could launch into a rebuttal, she asked, "Did your meeting with the king go well?"

"It went as well as could be expected." Demetrius scraped the tomato pieces into the salad bowls. "I told him about all of your wonderful work at Residenza del Rosa. He's quite impressed. He'd like to meet with you sometime."

The king wanted to meet with her?

She didn't respond, not exactly sure what to say. She knew that she was supposed to be honored and tripping all over herself to accept, but her one and only encounter with the king had been anything but impressive. The king had been skeptical about her intentions as far as her marriage to his son.

The king had never insisted that she leave Demetrius, but he did make it clear if she were to stay what would be expected of her. He pointed out how she would be under constant scrutiny by the press. In her mind, all she could think about was her mother's disease being documented in the tabloids. How could she do that to her mother who was already struggling? And how could she do that to Demetrius?

"I don't think it'd be a good idea for us to meet."

"You worry too much. I told you I fixed things. He understands about the mix-up with the papers—"

"You told him about my mother?"

Demetrius stilled the knife and turned to her. "I wouldn't do that. I know how hard it was for you to tell me. When you're ready, you can tell people."

She breathed easier. "*Grazie*."

"You don't have to thank me. I wouldn't intentionally hurt you by breaking your trust."

But she was going to hurt him unless she cleared things up about the kiss. "Demetrius, we need to talk."

"I'm listening."

She took a deep, steadying breath, held it a second and then released it. "About yesterday—the kiss. It was a mistake." Was it her imagination or did his body tense? "It... it was an emotional moment for me and you were comforting me—"

"And things got out of control. Don't worry. I didn't read anything into it. That's actually what I wanted to talk to you about."

"You did?" When he nodded, she added, "So we're still good?"

There was a slight pause. "Don't worry. We're still friends. Now let's eat this amazing salad."

Knowing they were still friends should have made her feel better, but she couldn't help but think about what she was missing. Her gaze followed Demetrius as he carried their lunch to the table next to the windows. If only her life were different.

* * *

Just stay focused.

Zoe stifled a yawn.

Instead of reporting to her shared office at the palace each day, she now spent her days at the mansion. Piece by piece her vision for a relaxing atmosphere where family members would feel comfortable visiting with residents was coming together. When she wasn't pointing out where things went, she was painting her vision of a serene beach on the ballroom wall—the drawing Demetrius had finally settled on from her sketch pad.

However, Zoe had cut her day short and returned to the beach house. She'd thought of something she wanted to add to the mural, but she needed to do some research before she sketched it out.

For the umpteenth time, her fingers paused over the keyboard as her thoughts drifted away. Memories of the steamy lip-lock she'd shared with Demetrius played over and over. Even though they'd both agreed that it had been a mistake, she had a hard time defining that passionate, toe-curling kiss as a mistake. And she wanted more. Lots more.

The chirp of a bird out on the deck drew her out of her daydream. No matter how amazing that kiss had been, it couldn't be repeated. They were wrong for each other. After all, he was a royal prince bound by duty to produce the next healthy heir to the throne. And she, well, she was a mere commoner with no nobility in her past, no prestigious connections, nothing to offer the crown except some faulty genes.

Stirring up the burning embers between them would only lead to trouble.

The chimes of the doorbell rang through the beach house.

She rushed to the door. A smile lifted her lips in the

hope it'd be Demetrius. But he didn't normally ring the bell or wait to be greeted at the door. So who else could it be?

She swung open one of the expansive teal doors and there stood two uniformed men from the palace staff. Each held a cardboard box.

The older of the two men was the first to speak. "I believe you inquired about some extra Christmas decorations."

"I did. I want to surprise De—erm… Prince Demetrius. I thought he might enjoy a bit of holiday cheer."

When she'd passed the butler in the hallway the other day, she'd mentioned that the palace looked lovely. And she might have added that it'd be nice to have some of the extra decorations for the beach house. To be honest, she hadn't thought the man was paying her a bit of attention. Obviously he'd heard every word she'd said. She made a mental note to thank him.

"Where would you like these?" the younger man spoke up.

"I'll take them." She held out her arms for the box in his hands.

"It's okay, ma'am. We've got them. There are more in the truck—"

"More?"

"Sì. Lots more."

"Oh my. I didn't expect so much."

"You did ask for the extras, didn't you?"

"Um… I did. Come on in." She stepped out of their way. Luckily the beach house was quite spacious. "You can place them in the living room."

It took a few minutes for the two men to haul in boxes of all shapes and sizes. After Zoe saw the men off, she walked back into the living room and her mouth gaped open. What was Demetrius going to say when he saw all of this?

She smiled, thinking of the old Demetrius. He would

have thought it was great. He loved to find reasons to celebrate. He'd have popped some bubbly, turned on some
festive music and been the first one to explore the boxes.
Boy, she missed that part of him.

This new Demetrius had her stumped. She never knew
what to expect from him. Just like that kiss that had come
out of nowhere. What did it mean? Did it mean that he
wanted them to start over? Or had it just been a fleeting
thing?

Not wanting to dwell on those troubling thoughts any
longer, she started opening boxes. There were ornaments,
table decorations and wall hangings. But when she came
to a pencil tree, she stopped. It was perfect. Now she just
had to find a spot for it.

Zoe set to work. She placed the seven-foot Christmas
tree next to the fireplace. The tree was adorable with a real
bark trunk that was anchored in a red bucket. The short
limbs were lined with white lights. All she had to do was
plug it in. The twinkle lights lit up, sending a soft glow
through the shadows now filling the room.

In another box, she found candles, which she lined along
the mantel. After some digging in the kitchen, she found a
lighter. With a chill in the air, she decided to go ahead and
burn the logs in the fireplace. The apartment she shared
with her mother didn't have such a luxury. And Zoe did
love how the light from the fire danced upon the walls while
the wood snapped and popped.

Onward she went digging through the boxes, amazed
at the variety and quantity of decorations. No expense had
been spared. She pulled out her cell phone and selected
some Christmas music. She started singing along as she
continued to create a holiday retreat.

"What's going on here?"

CHAPTER FOURTEEN

ZOE JUMPED, ALMOST dropping the glass ornament in her hand. She turned to find Demetrius propped against the wall. His arms were crossed while his facial expression was unreadable.

"I...I didn't hear you come in."

"Obviously. Do you want to explain all of this?"

Zoe retrieved her phone and switched off the music. "With Christmas just around the corner, I thought you might enjoy some holiday cheer."

"I had no idea that you planned to redecorate the beach house."

"I didn't. I mean, I'm not." She glanced down at the ornament in her hand. She turned to put it back in the box. So much for surprising him.

He glanced around. His gaze paused on the pile of boxes.

"Sorry about the mess. I'll make those boxes go away." Zoe worried, biting her bottom lip.

Demetrius turned to the fireplace. Now that the sun had sunk below the horizon, the flames of the fire flickered and cast a warm glow over the room. As the temperature rose, Demetrius discarded his suit jacket and rolled up the sleeves of his blue Oxford shirt.

Feeling a need to explain, she said, "I thought a fire would be nice."

He stepped up to the tree. He reached out and touched a glittery silver star ornament.

She swallowed hard, feeling like a kid with her hand in the proverbial cookie jar. "I can get rid of the tree, too."

When he turned, he was wearing that serious expression—the one that created lines between his brows. She laced her fingers together while wishing he would say something. She didn't deal well with the silent treatment.

Rushing to fill the awkward silence, she said, "I just got caught up in the excitement of the season. When I inquired at the palace about decorating, they sent over their extra ornaments. I never expected them to send so much stuff."

Demetrius glanced around at the opened boxes. "I think we need to do something about this."

In all honesty, it was rather a mess. It looked a little like Santa's workshop except instead of toys there were decorations. She really didn't want to take down the festive ornaments, but this wasn't her house. "I'll have everything put away tonight."

"Could you hand me that box?"

He was going to help her take down the tree? She thought of putting him off, hoping he'd change his mind. But she didn't want to push her luck. She quietly handed him the designated box. His fingers brushed over hers as he took it. Her pulse raced. Their gazes met but Zoe glanced away. Things were already complicated enough without making it worse.

In the silence where there once had been festive music, she started closing up the boxes. Perhaps she could fit them in a spare bedroom until she figured out exactly what to do with them.

"I could use a little help over here."

"Um. Sure." She closed the lid on another box before turning around. "What do you need?"

"You to help me." He waved her over to where he was standing near the Christmas tree. "Don't you think you've missed something?"

She was confused. "Oh, you want the tree taken down first?"

He shook his head. "That isn't what I mean. The tree is

only half-decorated. I think you better bring some more of those ornaments over here."

She stopped, her mouth gaping. He didn't want to take it all down? Instead, he was going to decorate the tree with her? Really? Maybe somewhere inside him there was still a little bit of the Demetrius she used to know—the one she'd fallen in love with.

A tempting thought crossed her mind. Would it be possible to find that smiling, fun-loving guy again? With a little bit of encouragement, would he let down his guard?

"Why are you looking at me like that?" His dark brows drew together. "Do I have a bit of garland or something in my hair?"

She smiled and shook her head. "Do you really want to help me decorate?"

He shrugged. "Why not? I'm always up for trying something different."

She grabbed the box with some ceramic ornaments. "You mean you've never decorated a Christmas tree before?"

"Not since I was a kid. Professional decorators come in to do the palace decorations. Everything has to be just right for photo ops."

She tried to envision a life where there were people that decorated your Christmas tree for you. It was so far from her modest lifestyle that it was a difficult concept. Right now, she didn't even have enough money to get her mother around-the-clock care.

"I guess when you're the richest man on the island, you can afford to have people do those sort of things for you."

He straightened. His shoulders took on a rigid line. He didn't say anything, but he didn't have to. She knew that she'd misspoken. She didn't mean anything by her comment. She'd just let her guard down and done some thinking out loud. She'd have to be careful going forward.

"I'm sorry. I didn't mean anything—"

"Could you hand me that candy cane ornament?" His gaze didn't meet hers.

"Um, sure." She moved to the couch.

She bent over to untangle the red ribbon looped around another ornament. After a bit of maneuvering, she freed it. She straightened and turned in time to find Demetrius staring at her. He quickly averted his eyes, but not before she realized that he was still attracted to her.

"Why don't you turn on the music you were playing when I interrupted you?" Demetrius hung the candy cane on the tree.

"You mean the Christmas carols?"

He nodded. "Then you can sing some more."

"Oh, no." Then she got an idea—a delicious idea. "Not unless you sing with me."

He waived off the idea. "I don't sing."

"Why not?"

He paused as though not quite sure. "It's not proper."

"Proper? Who's worried about proper? This is just you and me. And you know that I'm not proper most of the time. So let's hear it." She grabbed her phone and found the music app. With festive carols filling the silence between them, she sent him an expectant look. To her surprise and delight, his mouth started to move.

"I can't hear you." She grinned at him, excited to see the fun side of him. "Lip-synching doesn't count."

To her utter amazement and delight, he belted out a verse of "Santa Claus Is Coming to Town." Zoe clapped her hands. She hadn't had this much fun since…since Demetrius was a part of her life.

They added a variety of exquisite ornaments to the tree. None of them were like the common ornaments that Zoe and her mother hung on their little tree. These decorations were the best of the best. But then again, she supposed that was to be expected when they came from the royal palace—only the best for the king. Still, it felt weird to handle such valuable items.

As the evening progressed, they laughed and smiled more than they sang. At one point, they both took a few steps back to inspect their handiwork. Zoe loved their tree. Her gaze moved to Demetrius.

"Not too bad." He turned to look at her.

Unable to turn away, she added, "We do good work together."

He nodded. "My mother would have enjoyed this. She loved the beach house. It was her escape from the protocol of palace life." He strode over to the window overlooking the sea with the last bit of color in the darkening sky. "Did I ever tell you that my father built this house for her?"

"No. You didn't." Zoe glanced around the place, wondering what it'd be like to have someone love you enough to do all they could to make your dreams come true. Not that money and physical things can make a person happy. It's just the thought of the king going out of his way to make his queen happy was so romantic.

"My mother was the perfect queen. She was kind, thoughtful and beautiful. She was everything that my father could ever want. When the public was around she had the perfect smile, and when my brother and I were young, she made sure we looked and acted like the little princes the king could be proud of."

The love and awe was evident in Demetrius's voice. His love for his mother was as alive now as it had been all of those years ago. "She sounds amazing."

"She was. She would have liked you. I wish she'd have had a chance to meet you."

"I'm sure I would have liked her, too."

He turned around and glanced about the room. "She

would have loved what you've done with the beach house. Christmas was her favorite time of the year."

Zoe's gaze moved to the little tree that was still lacking something. She thought about it for a moment and then realized what was bothering her. "The angel is missing from the top of the tree."

"Grab it and we'll put it up there."

She rummaged through the boxes, finding the angel and something else—two tiny ceramic turtledoves. The artwork on them was quite detailed. She wondered if they were handmade.

"What else did you find?"

Zoe held out the ornaments, letting them dangle from the gold ribbon strung through each one. "Two turtledoves. My mother would love them." Zoe watched as the doves twisted back and forth. "They're her favorite birds as they represent true love since the birds mate for life."

"Really? I had no idea."

Zoe nodded. "When my father abandoned my mother, when she was pregnant with me—she lost her belief in love. She figured the only person she could count on was herself. But she said when I was born, she never felt such a strong love in her life. She said that with each smile, I healed her broken heart. She believed in love again...but sadly she's never found someone to share her life with."

"Don't look so sad. She has you. I'm sure watching you grow up made her very happy."

Zoe blinked repeatedly. "I guess you're right."

"Of course I am. I'm the prince." He smiled and winked at her, letting her see that lighthearted, teasing side of himself that she'd missed so much this past year. "Now, how about you find the perfect spot for those turtledoves while I put the angel on top?"

The best part of the evening was watching Demetrius let down his guard and enjoy helping her decorate. She glanced over as he climbed on a step stool to place the angel atop the tree. It was so easy to imagine that this was their first Christmas together as a real couple.

Just then he glanced over at her. Their gazes met and held. Her heart raced. She couldn't let herself get swept up in the moment. He smiled. This wasn't real. She smiled back.

Then again, there'd be enough time for reality tomorrow.

CHAPTER FIFTEEN

THIS WAS THE MOST amazing evening…ever.

Demetrius glanced over at Zoe. When they'd first been reunited on the mansion steps, he'd been prepared to despise the very ground she walked on. She was, after all, the woman who'd married him one day and then within forty-eight hours had ended their marriage. And now, he couldn't imagine holding such harsh feelings toward her.

Sure, she hadn't handled the situation with her mother very well, but he had no idea what he would have done if he'd been in her shoes. Maybe he'd been too caught up in his own problems with seeking his father's approval for his very hasty, very secretive wedding to notice her turmoil. Maybe if he'd made himself more accessible to Zoe, she might have turned to him—confided in him.

He'd never know. All they could do now was move forward. In the soft glow of the fire with the twinkle of the lights on the Christmas tree and festive lyrics filling the air, he couldn't be happier. And he had Zoe to thank for that. He glanced across the room, finding her busy organizing the empty boxes to be sent to storage.

As though she could sense him staring at her, she turned. Her gaze met his and she smiled, not a little smile but one that puffed up her cheeks and made her eyes sparkle like fine jewels. There was definitely no room here for anger or resentment over the past—not when her glowing smile filled him with such warmth.

If he could have one wish for Christmas, it would be this. Happiness, contentment and love—not that he had all of those things with Zoe. But maybe just for this one evening, he could pretend. After all, tomorrow would be soon enough for the sharp edges of life to pop their happy bubble.

He studied Zoe. What was so special about her?

Nothing.

Everything.

She had this way of disarming his strongest defenses and getting past his walls. Right now, when he looked at her as she sang some ridiculous Christmas tune, he no longer saw the woman who'd broken his heart, but rather he saw the woman who made his heart skip a beat or two with a mere touch or glance.

For a little while, he could have his one Christmas wish. Sure it was early in the year for presents, but maybe Christmas didn't have to occur on a certain day on the calendar. Maybe it was more about that special moment in one's heart when the pain and hurt melted away.

Maybe for tonight he could have what he wanted most of all—Zoe. When he was perfectly honest with himself, he'd never wanted to let her go. But after reading her note— seeing with his own eyes her desire to end their marriage, he'd had no choice but to accept the gut-wrenching fact that she didn't love him anymore.

Was it wrong to want to recapture a bit of the past? After all, at one point they had been happy. And they never did get to share Christmas together. They'd been cheated of one of the happiest times of the year. But not this year if he could help it.

"Hey, are you going to help me with these boxes before the palace staff shows up to haul them to storage?"

Zoe's voice snapped him out of his thoughts. "Sure. As long as you promise to share those chocolates."

"There are chocolates? Where?" Her whole face lit up. Then she started a mad search through the remainder of the boxes. She straightened with a triumphant look on her face. "And these aren't just any chocolates. They're the gourmet ones from Giovanni's Cioccolato."

Demetrius had to admit that he wasn't into chocolate, but he knew that it was one of Zoe's favorite indulgences. And Giovanni's was one of the finest chocolatiers in the Mediterranean. "Well, what are you waiting for?"

"Are you sure they meant to include them?"

"I might have mentioned they're your favorite."

"You did? Have I told you how amazing you are?"

"No, you haven't. Feel free to repeat that as many times as you like."

Right now, she could ask for the moon and he'd move heaven and earth to give it to her. He'd forgotten how powerful her smile was and how it radiated a warm, happy feeling within him.

Her fingers were a flurry of motion as she tore the wrapping paper from the box. Beneath the paper was a red ribbon, which she slipped off the maroon-and-gold box. And it wasn't a small box by any stretch of the imagination. Best of all was the look of excitement glinting in Zoe's eyes. If he had only remembered what joy chocolate brought to her, he would have had some ordered long ago.

She held out a chocolate to him. "Want some?"

"I'll have some later. Right now, I'll just watch you sample them."

"Are you sure?" When he nodded, she didn't waste any time slipping the chocolate between her raspberry-pink lips.

Demetrius couldn't help but stare as a look of ecstasy came over her. Zoe's eyes drifted shut in utter delight. The breath caught in his throat, unable to turn away from the sight of Zoe savoring the chocolate. When a moan of pleasure reached his ears, his heart slammed into his ribs. He definitely needed to buy this woman chocolate and often.

When her eyelids fluttered open, her gaze met his. The

tip of her tongue trailed over her lips. Her mouth lifted into a smile. She was doing this on purpose. His straining lungs insisted he blow out his pent-up breath. Blood pumped hard and fast through his veins. She had to know that she was driving him to utter distraction.

He watched her shimmery lips wrap around another piece of chocolate. This time, as she savored the candy, her gaze held his. Oh, she was a temptress. And it took every bit of willpower for him to keep his distance. But if he kept staring at her, he'd lose the battle. Second by second his common sense was slipping from his grip.

When she raised her fingers to her mouth, he intently watched. She popped one finger in her mouth. Her pink lips wrapped around it. Then she slowly withdrew it. A soft moan vibrated in his throat. Did she know just how crazy she was driving him?

She smiled at him. "That was amazing."

Indeed it was. Very much so.

"I suppose I need to finish with these boxes." Zoe replaced the lid on the chocolates and set them aside. She moved back to the boxes.

Seriously? After all of that tempting and teasing, she was going back to work?

He glanced around at all of the decorations. If she could act indifferent, so could he. Though it might be the most difficult feat he'd ever accomplished.

Zoe tried to slow the rapid beat of her heart.

Being here with Demetrius in his bare feet, jeans and his shirtsleeves rolled up, it was so hard to remember that they were no longer a couple. But that was the way things had to be. It was best for Demetrius. Sucking down the sadness in knowing that she could never have the only man she'd ever loved, she got back to work straightening up the mess of boxes.

For a prince, he surprised her with the way he didn't complain about cleaning up. He even knew where the vacuum was kept, and to her astonishment he knew how to work it.

When everything was sorted, she turned to him. "*Grazie*. I didn't expect you to do all of this."

"I enjoyed this evening." He yawned and stretched.

His shirt rode up giving a hint of the light splattering of hair on his abdomen. Zoe inwardly groaned, unable to turn away. His gaze caught hers and it glittered with amusement. Heat flared in her cheeks. He'd busted her checking him out.

"I...I'm glad we could do it together." There was a nervous quiver in her stomach. "You should probably be going. I know you're tired and you probably have a lot of meetings first thing in the morning."

He took a step closer to her. "I know why you're trying to get rid of me—"

"I...I'm not." Liar. Liar.

"Zoe, you can't deny the chemistry between us. It's always been there." He moved until he was standing in front of her. "But there's one thing I need to know."

She gazed up into his eyes. Her heart squeezed. Not so long ago, when she looked into his eyes, she saw nothing but love. These days it was as if he had a protective wall around himself, and she couldn't tell what he was feeling. "What is that?"

When he spoke next his voice was soft and she had to strain to hear him. "Did you ever love me at all? Or was it all just a lie?"

The backs of her eyes stung. She blinked repeatedly. "How could you think that?"

"How could I not? You left me."

"It...it wasn't like that. You have to understand that it was such a difficult decision."

"But still you did it. You made the decision to leave." The walls came down and pain reflected in his eyes. All she wanted to do was soothe it away. He reached out, gripping her shoulders. "Please tell me. Did you love me?"

With each word spoken, it was getting harder and harder for her not to blurt out that she did love him—that she'd always loved him. She looked everywhere but at him. Her gaze came to rest on the French doors. They beckoned to her. "I...I never meant to hurt you."

"There's something else. Something that you're not saying. What is it?"

She shook her head.

"Zoe, look at me."

She didn't want to. How could she look him in the eyes and continue to deny that she still had feelings for him?

"Zoe, don't do this. Don't avoid talking to me because it's easier. Don't run away from us."

"I'm not running. I'm standing right here."

"And you can't even look at me. You might not be running down the beach, but inside you're hiding from your feelings—from being honest with me."

She faced him. "What do you want me to say?"

"I want you to tell me what you've been holding back all of this time. I want you to admit that we have something special and it isn't all in my imagination. I want this—" He swept her into his arms.

The surprise of his actions had her dazed for a moment. He pulled her close and without a moment's hesitation, his lips sought hers out. Her lips moved hungrily beneath his. This kiss wasn't sweet and innocent. His actions were full of raw emotions. Love. Loneliness. Pain. All jumbled together.

And what surprised her most was that she was just as hungry for him. For almost a year she longed for him. And this past month, he'd been so close and yet so far away.

What would it hurt if they shared this one special moment? They both wanted it—needed it.

Tonight they would create a memory to keep her company on the long, lonely nights when he was no longer hers. That was what this was—a passionate goodbye.

CHAPTER SIXTEEN

WHAT HAD HE DONE?

Demetrius raked his fingers through his hair as he lay back on the couch. Zoe's head rested against his bare chest. When this whole affair had begun, all he'd intended to do was get some answers from her and then negotiate an annulment that would keep their past out of the tabloids. When had he lost control?

Tonight he'd abandoned his resolve to hold her at arm's length. He'd tossed aside the walls he'd worked so hard to build between him and Zoe. When her lips had moved beneath his, none of the reasons he'd been telling himself to keep his distance from her seemed so important.

Nothing had mattered in that moment but being with her.

In the end, the joke was on him, because somewhere during that frantic kiss and their mind-blowing lovemaking he'd realized he wasn't over her. Not by a long shot. He loved Zoe as much today as he had the day he'd married her. Okay, a lot more.

But how was that possible?

How could he trust her when he knew that when times got tough she'd rather run than talk?

"What are you thinking?" Zoe's soft, dreamy voice wound its way through his alarming thoughts.

"The truth?"

"Always."

"I was wondering how we ended up here—like this."

Zoe pulled back and slipped on his discarded dress shirt. He liked the look on her. The shirt definitely looked so much better on her than it ever did on him. He'd never met anyone as beautiful as her—both inside and out. She was a very special woman.

Once she finished buttoning the shirt and rolling up the sleeves, she curled her bare legs up on the couch. She turned a big worried look to him and sighed. "Are you implying this was a mistake?"

He hated that he'd ruined this moment for her. He would have to be more careful with his words going forward. He reached out to her, but she resisted. He needed to say something to fix this. After all, it'd been a year since their marriage had failed. They'd both done a lot of growing up. This time, things would be different. "No, it wasn't a mistake. It was fantastic. You're fantastic."

At last, she gave in to the pull of his arms and snuggled to his side again. "I think you're fantastic, too."

His fingers stroked her silky hair. "You know, we still have to do something about the annulment?"

"I know. I just don't want to think about it tonight. I want one last night with you. A night where we don't have to think about the future."

He didn't like the thought that he'd never get to hold her like this again. He'd already been down that road. And even with his busy schedule and countless meetings, it still didn't erase the empty spot in his heart where Zoe should have been. But now she was back, and he didn't want to let her go again. Holding his wife close was heaven—it was the way it should be.

He cleared his throat. "Why does this have to be our last night together?"

"You know it would never work. Surely by now, you can see that our lives are too different. We've already talked about this."

He scooted over to the edge of the couch in order to actually be able to see her face. "No, we didn't talk about it. You always make excuses or skirt around the issue."

"I do not." She paused as though considering his words. "Okay, so maybe I do. It's not easy to talk about."

"The important things in life aren't normally easy, but that doesn't mean you should run from them."

She sighed. "I'm trying to do better—to take things head-on. I never thought about it before you mentioned it, but I guess I've got some of my father in me."

"You never talk about him."

"That's because there isn't much to say. My mother used to say he was a dabbler. He dabbled with this or dabbled with that until something bigger or better came along. And if things got too tough, he ran. When my mum got pregnant, he ran."

"I'm sorry."

Zoe shrugged. "It's okay. My mum was enough for me. But the one thing he did give me was my artistic ability. I have a painting in my bedroom that he did of the snow-capped Alps. It's the only thing of value that I got from him."

Demetrius liked that she was letting him in. At last, she was letting down her guard. He settled back on the couch next to her. Her cheek once again pressed to his chest. He wondered if she could hear how hard his heart was pounding.

She played with a loose thread on the shirtsleeve. "Would you still want me if I had a secret?"

His body stiffened. "What secret?"

"Relax." She pressed a hand to his chest. "We're talking hypothetically. You know, what if I had a criminal past?"

His muscles eased upon accepting that they were playing a game of what-if. "I don't know what it matters because you don't have a criminal past."

"But if I did, would you still care about me? Would you have still asked me to marry you?"

He wrapped a lock of her long dark hair around his finger. "Of course. How could I say no when you look at me with those big brown eyes of yours?"

"Demetrius, I'm being serious. I want you to be honest."

His jaw tightened. He didn't know where this conversation was going, but he suddenly didn't like the direction—not one little bit. "Fine. I don't know what I'd have done. I guess it would have all depended on the secret. If you're an ax murderer, then probably not. If it's something else, we'd face it—together."

"How can you say that? There's no way you can marry someone who isn't perfect—someone who would be a princess and eventually your queen."

He wanted to change the subject. This conversation was making him exceedingly uncomfortable. "Why don't we talk about the mural? Do you think you'll have enough time to finish it—"

"Demetrius, this is important. Don't change the subject."

"Fine. I don't know what I'd have done if you weren't perfect, but you are. So it's a moot point."

"But you don't know that. We didn't know each other that long when we eloped. What if you found out after we married that I couldn't have children? That I couldn't give you any heirs to the throne?"

His chest tightened. He never would have guessed this was what she'd been holding back. "You can't have kids?"

"I can…at least I think I can." Her hand slid up over his chest. "Relax. Remember this is just a round of what-if."

"I don't like this game." A frown pulled at his lips.

"Humor me. If you knew I couldn't have kids, would you have stuck by me?"

"Of course."

"Out of sympathy?"

"Stop. I'm done with this game. I knew everything I needed to know when I married you."

He tickled her side, knowing all of her sensitive spots.

He was tired of all this serious conversation. He wanted to see her smile again.

The corners of her mouth lifted, but she swiped away his hand. "I'm not talking about that. I'm serious. How did you know that marrying me wouldn't be a mistake?"

"Fine. If you want to know, I had you checked out. I might have been a little reckless back then, but I did have to be cautious."

She sprang up off the couch. The parts of his body where she'd been snuggled quickly grew cold. But the fire in her eyes practically singed him. "What do you mean you had me checked out? You mean you had people spying on me? How could you?"

"Of course I didn't have people following you around. But a standard background check was imperative, especially if we were going to make things formal. I don't know what you're getting so worked up about. They didn't uncover anything. You didn't even have so much as a motor vehicle violation."

"Of course I didn't. I don't own a car. Public transportation is so much easier. But that's beside the point. You violated my privacy."

"Why are you getting so worked up? I didn't do anything that the paparazzi wouldn't have done when they found out about you and me."

Her mouth gaped as though she hadn't realized how intrusive the paparazzi would be in her life. That creepy reporter would be nothing compared to the numerous exposés about any little bit of juicy information the press could dig up. And if they couldn't dig up any dirt, they'd create some—of that he was certain since they'd done it to him. Although to be honest, after his mother died and his father had withdrawn from his family, Demetrius had given the press plenty of fodder to fill their front pages. But Zoe didn't need to know any of that.

"And you didn't find out anything about me that would stop you from marrying me?" Her big eyes searched his.

"Of course not." Was she trying to tell him that there was something there—something that the palace staff had missed? "Tell me, Zoe. What should they have found? Is this about your mother?"

"No." The little bit of color in her face faded away. "Um…it's nothing. I'm just rambling."

He wanted to believe her. Honestly, he did. But there was still something she wasn't saying—something that she was afraid of him learning. Still, he didn't think it was as big of a deal as she was making it out to be. His staff may have missed something small—something inconsequential—but there was no way they'd have missed something that would affect the royal family.

CHAPTER SEVENTEEN

TWELVE DAYS.

Twelve very fast days had passed.

This amazing fairy tale was almost over.

Zoe started down the steps from the administrative offices of Residenza del Rosa. Perhaps she should smile because at last she'd secured her mother's safety and care. And she'd done it without involving Demetrius. She'd negotiated with the center's administrator to get her mother a room there. The administrator realized that Zoe had the prince's ear, but to her relief, he didn't make a big deal of it.

However, the administrator did make a big deal of her completed mural. He was exceedingly impressed with it as well as her interior design. He offered that in exchange for Zoe teaching art classes to the center's residents, she would get a reduced rate on her mother's care. Zoe immediately jumped at the offer. Even with the reduction, the cost would stretch Zoe's budget. However, she would do whatever it took to see that her mother had the care she needed. And this move would retain as much of her mother's dignity as possible. That was very important to her mother. And her mother's happiness was very important to Zoe.

She had reached the last step when she noticed Demetrius stroll past the reception desk. He wasn't alone. There was the female reporter, Carla Russo, next to him with a mic and a photographer in front of them. Demetrius's manner was casual as though he lived in front of the camera all of his life. Then again, he pretty much had lived out his life with a camera following him around. She could never imagine being at such ease with the press.

This interview must be another push for publicity for the revitalization project. Zoe hung back. She knew that he was keeping certain parts of Residenza del Rosa under wraps until the night of the Royal Christmas Ball—rooms such as the library, the garden and the ballroom.

As though Demetrius could sense her gaze on him, he turned her way. "And here is the mastermind behind the mural."

The photographer focused in on Zoe. The flash practically blinded her. What in the world? She wasn't prepared for this. She wasn't even dressed appropriately for photos. Her hair was pulled back in a haphazard fashion while her makeup was almost nonexistent. What was Demetrius thinking?

Ms. Russo smiled at her. "Hello again, Miss Sarris. We're very anxious to see your mural. Prince Demetrius says that it's a sight to behold."

Zoe's gaze moved to Demetrius. He did? He said that about her—erm…about her work?

He smiled and nodded. "Ms. Sarris, will you please show them your masterpiece?"

Masterpiece? Wasn't he laying it on a bit thick? After all, she definitely was no Leonardo da Vinci or Michelangelo. Not even close. She just did her best and hoped other people would take pleasure from her efforts.

Zoe swallowed hard. "I'm very honored that His Royal Highness has enjoyed my work. I just hope you're not disappointed."

"I'm sure we won't be." The eager look on Carla Russo's face revealed her true interest in Zoe's work. "Is it possible to see it now?"

Zoe's gaze sought out Demetrius. He'd moved into the background, leaving her alone in the spotlight. She had no idea what he was up to and no way of asking him privately. The only thing she did know was that he'd been super kind to her these past couple of weeks, reminding her of all the reasons she'd fallen in love with him in the first place.

When Demetrius nodded toward the ballroom, she knew that he was giving her yet another gift. Her heart gave a fluttering sensation as his gaze held hers. He was giving her a chance to spread her wings as an artist and to make a name for herself. How would she ever repay him?

She turned back to Ms. Russo. "The mural is right this way."

As they walked, the reporter asked one question after the next. "Was the mural your idea or was it something the prince came up with?"

"Um…it was actually my idea. I wanted to give the residents a relaxing, calming atmosphere. My mother has a great love of the sea, having grown up in a seaside village. I recently painted a similar mural for her. Though not nearly as large, she has enjoyed it a lot. And…and I thought others might enjoy it, too." Zoe wondered if it was a mistake mentioning her mother, but it was too late to worry about it now.

"Your mother is one very lucky lady to have an artist for a daughter." Ms. Russo meant well, but her words dug at the tender spot on Zoe's heart.

"I've been fortunate enough to view both murals and they are amazing," interjected Demetrius. "We were very lucky to have Ms. Sarris sign on for this project. She's very talented."

"And has it been decided if she'll be working on the other buildings slated for renovation?" Ms. Russo held out the digital voice recorder for him to speak into.

Demetrius's gaze met Zoe's before turning back to the reporter. "That's my hope, but we're currently in negotiations."

He didn't disclose anything in his facial expression, but Zoe could tell he wasn't referring to the revitalization project any longer. Her heart fluttered. Try as she might, she just couldn't get him out of her system—even if it was the only way to protect him from his own good intentions.

When he found out about her chance of inheriting her mother's disease, he would stay with her for all of the wrong reasons—pity, obligation and honor. She couldn't let him fall on his sword for her. She loved him too much for that.

Ms. Russo turned to Zoe. "When Prince Demetrius called to tell me about your mural, he couldn't stop singing your praises. You've definitely won him over, which I hear isn't an easy feat."

"We should move along. Ms. Sarris's time is limited." Demetrius stepped up to Zoe's side. "She still has a lot of final touches to attend to before the ball."

Ms. Russo frowned, but she quietly continued toward the ballroom. When the reporter turned away, Zoe could at last take in a full breath of air. She turned to him and flashed him a grateful smile.

He smiled back and signaled for her to lead the way to the mural. After weeks of hammering, plastering and painting, it was time for the grand reveal of Residenza del Rosa. On shaky legs, Zoe moved into the lead.

Even Demetrius had yet to see the mural since she'd put the final touches on it. All it needed now was a clear topcoat to help keep the colors from fading as well as to protect it from fingerprints. She'd been worried about how it would be received, but now with Demetrius's encouragement and the administrator's praises, she felt confident enough to share it with others.

She swung the door to the ballroom open and stood back, letting the others enter. The reporter and the photographer rushed forward, but Demetrius hung back, refusing to enter until Zoe had done so. He was forever a gentleman. That was just one of the many things she loved about him. The truth was there was so much to love about him that if she wasn't careful, she was going to throw caution to the wind and forget why this relationship couldn't be a forever thing.

The small group stopped in front of the mural. Her stomach quivered with nerves. She gazed up at her greatest creation and hoped it would be well received. Her gaze settled on the deepening blue sky dotted with puffy white clouds. Midway down was the bright orange and yellow of the sun as it started its descent into the horizon. Brilliant shades of orange, pink and purple streaked out along the sea. The calmness of the dark blue water reflected the sun's rays as the tide gently rolled into a sandy shore. Upon the beach rested a maroon sailboat with a yellow stripe. She'd wanted to give the impression that it was waiting for someone to sail away in it—away from their troubles—to a place of peace and tranquility.

After answering countless questions, more about what it was like to work with the prince than her artwork or her interior design work, Ms. Russo and the photographer departed. Zoe sighed in relief. At last her lungs could fully expand as her tense muscles loosened up. She would definitely not make a good spokesperson like Annabelle. Not a chance.

Zoe turned to him. "I wish you'd have given a little warning about the interview. I'm a mess." She ran a hand over her hair. "Those pictures are going to be terrible."

"They will be beautiful, just like you." His gaze met and held hers.

Her heart pit-pattered faster.

"I don't know how you deal with the press day in and day out."

Demetrius walked over and opened the door leading to the veranda. "In all honesty, I don't like answering questions, but it's part of my world. I guess for the most part, I've grown used to it—at least as much as anyone can."

She followed him outside. "I want to thank you for this

amazing opportunity, but words don't seem like enough. I still can't believe you went to all of this bother for me."

"What bother?" He acted so innocent, but she knew he went out of his way just for her. "Oh, you mean arranging for Residenza del Rosa to get some additional coverage? I should be the one thanking you."

She shook her head. "Don't dismiss this. Admit it. This wasn't about the center. You didn't even mention it."

His dark brows scrunched together. "I didn't? Surely I must have."

She couldn't help but smile at his antics. "Afraid not. Maybe if you run after them, you can catch them."

"Hmm... I don't think so. I'd rather stay here." He gazed deeply into her eyes.

"You would?" Her voice came out much softer and sultrier than she'd intended.

He nodded, stepping closer.

"I don't know why you did what you did today, but *grazie*. You don't know what this means to me."

His hand slipped around her waist. "Does this mean that you're not upset about the impromptu interview?"

She lifted onto her tiptoes and leaned forward. "If I was mad, would I do this?"

Her lips met his. At first, he didn't move as though he were afraid of scaring her away. She slipped her arms up over his shoulders and moved her mouth over his. That's all it took for him to reach out and pull her close.

Her heart swelled with love. She knew that this thing—them together—couldn't last forever, but in that moment, it didn't matter. No one had ever done something so sweet, so thoughtful for her.

She reveled in the fact that he wanted her as much as she wanted him. The kiss went on and on. She didn't want it to end. She knew when it did that they'd crash back into reality. And indulging in a passionate kiss with the Crown

Prince of Mirraccino was not part of her reality—even if they were secretly married.

The sound of footsteps caused them to spring apart. Her gaze met his and she knew that if they'd been back at the beach house things wouldn't have ended there. And if she was honest, she didn't want it to end. The more of Demetrius she had, the more she wanted.

He straightened his shirt. "I'll go inside and see who that is."

"I'm going to stay out here for a moment." She just needed a second or two alone to gather her thoughts.

He gave her a quick kiss and walked away.

A deep sadness replaced the joy in her heart because she knew that just like Cinderella, when the ball was over, she would turn back into a pumpkin. Her life and that of the prince wouldn't—couldn't—intersect again.

The next evening, Demetrius's shoulders sagged.

He was exhausted.

And now he had to do something that would only succeed in upsetting Zoe. He clutched the day's newspaper in his hand as he knocked on the door. Accustomed to coming and going without any formality, he let himself inside.

He was immediately greeted by the most delicious aroma of butter and sugar. Was Zoe baking? His steps came a little quicker as he made a beeline for the kitchen.

Sure enough, Zoe was pulling a tray of cookies from the oven. She glanced in his direction and smiled. "You're just in time to help."

"Help? With what?" He sure hoped she didn't want him to bake anything. It'd end up burnt to a crisp. He sat down on a stool at the kitchen island and tossed the paper on a neighboring stool.

She slid another tray in the oven before turning to him. "Don't look so worried."

"What are all of the cookies for?" He'd never seen so many cookies decked out in red, white and green sprinkles.

"I thought I'd do something special for the workers at the mansion. They've really gone out of their way to make this whole project a success." Worry lines creased her beautiful face as she looked around the kitchen at the dozens of sugar cookies. "Do you think it's a silly idea?"

"Silly? Absolutely not. In fact, I'm jealous."

"No, you're not."

"Oh, but I am. In all the time I've known you, you've never baked me cookies."

"I did too." She paused as though searching her memories. "Didn't I? Surely I must have."

He shook his head, knowing he was right. He'd never forget having such a pretty young lady present him with homemade cookies.

"Hmm..." Her lips pressed into a firm line. "Well, maybe you won't even like them."

"Why don't you pass me one and I'll let you know."

She snatched up one in the shape of Santa with red and white sprinkles. She held it just out of his reach. "You can have it on one condition."

He arched a brow. "What would that be?"

"You help me decorate the rest."

He glanced at the two trays of bare cookies, then at the almost empty mixing bowl and at last he focused on that cookie in her hand—that very tempting cookie. "Okay, you've got a deal. Just don't expect them to be pretty like yours."

"Just do your best." She placed the cookie in his hand.

Their fingertips brushed and a current of awareness zinged up his arm. Suddenly, he didn't feel so tired. He eyed up Zoe, who was smiling at him. "Pass me one of those trays and some sprinkles."

"Not before you wash up."

"Of course." He returned her smile. The action felt so strange after he'd frowned most of the day.

For the next hour, they worked together on the cookies. He got in trouble numerous times for thieving one or two. He couldn't help it. They were the best he'd ever tasted. And it didn't hurt that the baker looked pretty tasty, too. Her pink lips beckoned to him.

"Hey, mister, you're supposed to be working."

"I'm done." He pushed the decorated cookies across the counter. "And now I take my payment in kisses."

She laughed. "I don't seem to recall that."

"Well come over here and I'll remind you."

She smiled and shook her head. "You come over here."

The invitation was too good to resist. He got to his feet and rounded the counter. When he stood in front of her eagerly anticipating her cookie-sweet kisses, she instead tossed him a dishcloth before turning to the sink full of dishes.

A frown tugged at his lips. "What about those kisses you owe me."

"You don't get paid until the job is done."

"That's not fair."

She lifted up on her tiptoes and planted a kiss on his lips. But alas it was far too short. Her twinkling eyes stared at him, promising more. "Consider that a down payment."

"Well, what are you waiting for? Let's get those dishes done."

An hour or so later, Zoe closed the lid on the last storage container of cookies. "Everything is boxed up and ready to go in the morning." She walked over to the couch next to the lit Christmas tree. She stretched. "*Grazie*. I wouldn't have made it through those last trays on my own."

"Glad I could help, but I think I ate as many as I decorated." He rubbed his full stomach.

She laughed. "I think you're right."

There was no point in putting off his news any longer. This concerned her as much as it did him. "Zoe, we need to talk."

The smile faded from her face. "Any time you say those words, whatever follows is never good."

He wanted to tell her not to worry, but he knew that it would be futile. He might as well get this over as quickly as possible. He retrieved the newspaper from the stool in the kitchen.

"You need to see this" He handed over the paper.

She held it in front of her. A gasp filled the air. A color photo of them kissing made the headline of the *Mirraccino Gazzetta*. This wasn't the innocent peck under the mistletoe. This was a full-on, passionate embrace and lip-lock.

When he'd been roused from his bed in the middle of the night because an informant had delivered an advance copy, Demetrius hadn't wanted to read the accompanying blurb. But it was like a train crash that you just couldn't turn away from. His gaze had panned down to the words…

THE CROWN PRINCE IS SMITTEN!
Prince Demetrius and the interior designer Zoe Sarris are creating a steamy scene of their own.
Is the Prince going back to his old partying ways? Or has Ms. Sarris stolen his heart?
You be the judge.

Zoe's pale face turned to him. "But how?"

"Apparently a photographer snuck onto the terrace at Residenza del Rosa yesterday without anyone noticing. It seems that we put on quite a show for him."

Her worried gaze moved to him. "Do…do you know who the photographer is?"

"Not at this point. The security cameras aren't hooked up yet."

"Was it that creepy reporter who has been lurking about?"

"I don't know. My men are working on it."

"So everyone has seen this." Her face turned a pasty white. She jumped to her feet. "I need to tell my mother."

"Calm down. No one has seen this. At least not the general public. The palace staff took great pains to get the print run stopped and the story replaced."

She pressed a hand to her chest and breathed out. "Maybe you should have led with that part."

"The thing is, people know about us. There's no putting this genie back in the bottle—"

"But the palace staff—"

"Only delayed the inevitable. They gave us time to figure out how to spin the story."

"Spin it?" Worry lines marred her face.

He knew this was a lot for her to take in at once, but they didn't have much time to figure out what they were going to tell the public. He'd already decided what he wanted. He swallowed hard, hoping she'd agree. "I think we should announce our marriage."

"What? No." She shook her head. "You can't. You've worked so hard to redo your public image."

"And if this news comes from you and me, people will be happy for us. They'll all want to know how soon we'll be having children."

"Children?" Zoe looked as though she was going to pass out.

He hadn't meant to throw everything at her at once. "It's okay. We can wait. There's no rush."

"The king...he won't be happy if we reconcile. Not at all. He wasn't pleased when you brought me home the first time."

"That's because I caught him off guard. This is different."

When her mouth opened again, he pressed a finger to her lips. "Don't say anything you'll regret. I know this comes as a big surprise. Think on it tonight and let me know tomorrow." He paused and though it pained him to say it, he added, "I'll accept whatever decision you make, as long as you think about it. Will you do that for me?"

She grabbed his finger and gave a squeeze. "I will."

CHAPTER EIGHTEEN

HE WAS LATE.

Zoe checked her watch again. What was keeping Demetrius? It was his idea to meet here in the courtyard. Before he'd left the beach house last night, he'd made her promise that she'd give him an answer about what to tell the press regarding their relationship.

She hadn't slept a wink last night. Not that she had anything to debate. She had to walk away—she had to do what was best for Demetrius. The last thing he needed was to have a country to run and a wife with Alzheimer's. She'd stared into the dark, thinking how much she'd miss him. This time walking away would be so much harder. Her heart already ached.

Footsteps behind her had her turning. "Demetrius, I'm over here."

The smile slipped from her face when the creepy reporter stepped out from behind a lush shrub. Uneasiness inched down her spine. What was he doing here? What did he want with her?

"Ms. Sarris, at last we meet again." His leering smile revealed stained teeth.

Zoe didn't say anything as her eyes darted around searching for Demetrius or any of his security detail. There was no one about. Her palms broke out in a cold sweat as the hairs on her arms stood on end. She was alone with this man who was standing between her and the door. Why was he stalking her? What did he want with her?

"Excuse me. I'm needed inside." She attempted to go around him.

"Not so fast." The man in a white polo shirt and a blue sports jacket stepped in her way. "Don't worry. I'm not going to hurt you. See, you and I, we're going to become good friends."

Zoe, in an attempt to keep the man from touching her, stepped back so quickly that her foot landed on the edge of the walkway. She stumbled. Her arms flailed as she struggled to regain her balance.

"Careful." He clicked his tongue. "We don't want you getting hurt."

Her gaze hesitantly met his. "I have to go. People will be looking for me."

He shook his head. "You aren't going anywhere until we talk."

"What…what do you want from me?"

"I want the truth, Ms. Sarris. Or do you go by Princess Zoe now?"

Her heart hammered in her chest. He knew the truth. How could he? Was he just fishing? If he did know, what did he plan to do with the information? And if he knew this much, what did he want with her?

"Answer me!" His voice echoed off the surrounding walls.

"What? Uh…no. I'm just Zoe Sarris. A nobody."

The man's beady eyes narrowed. "Come now. You surely didn't think the prince was going to keep your secret forever."

"I…I don't know what you're talking about."

"Don't play dumb with me." His face filled with color. "I'm warning you. This is my big break and you aren't going to ruin it for me."

"I…I won't." Her gaze darted between him and the door. There was only one way out of the courtyard and it was straight past him.

The wild look in the man's eyes shook her to the core. She had to get out of there. Now!

She set off running. She pushed him out of her way, but he was too quick for her. His meaty fingers bit into the tender flesh of her upper arm. She let out a scream.

He yanked her to him and placed his other hand over her mouth. His voice was menacing as his hot breath brushed over her cheek, making her sick to her stomach. "That wasn't very nice of you." She yanked at his hand, but he was too strong for her. "I thought we could have a friendly conversation. Now, why did you have to go and ruin it?"

Zoe struggled to calm herself. Her gaze searched the doorway, willing Demetrius to appear. Where was he?

The man's bad breath smelled of garlic and onions. "If I let you go, do you promise to be quiet and not run?"

She nodded while swallowing hard to keep her nausea at bay.

First, he removed his hand from her mouth. She sucked in a deep breath. Next, he released her arm. She didn't move, not yet.

"Good. I knew you'd cooperate. Now, we were talking about your new title of princess. You know these sorts of things shouldn't be kept from the public."

"What...what do you mean?"

The man's beady eyes narrowed. "Did you honestly think I wouldn't do some digging into your life?"

"I don't know what you mean." Her gaze moved to the doorway. If only she had something to throw at him—just enough of a distraction to get past him.

"You aren't getting away. Not yet."

She hated that he knew what she was thinking. It was time for a different tactic. No matter that her insides shivered with fear, she had to stand up to this guy. She dug deep for a bit of confidence, hoping to bluff this man until

Demetrius showed up or she figured out a plan to get out of there.

She pressed her shaking hands to her hips, lifted her chin and prayed her voice wouldn't betray her. "What do you want from me?"

His eyes lit with surprise. "That's more like it, Princess. I've seen your marriage license. I know that you and Prince Demetrius tied the knot."

"If you know that, what do you need with me?"

"The thing is, even though I paid the clerk good money to browse through his records, I was interrupted. Before I could snap a photo, I had to sneak away."

"That sounds like your problem, not mine."

The man's eyes narrowed and his voice lowered. "It's your problem now because I want a confession." He held out a voice recorder. "I want you to tell the world that Prince Demetrius, heir to the throne of Mirraccino, has been sneaking around behind everyone's back with you. Does the king even know what his son has been up to?"

"What are you implying?"

"The readers have a right to know." He stepped up to her, cupping her chin with his hand. "Don't try to lie your way out of this. I already know the truth."

"I...I won't." She knocked his hand away. Her skin began to crawl where he'd touched her. "You already know everything, why do you need my confession?"

He swore under his breath. "Without concrete evidence, no paper will touch this story, not when it involves nobility. No one wants to be on the wrong side of the king. But with your verbal confession, they'll be able to verify your voice with that television interview you gave for that revitalization project. At last I'll be able to name my price. I'll be able to live a rich life like all of these people that I've had to report on—those people who don't even know I exist. That will all change once this story breaks."

"If all you want is money, Prince Demetrius will pay you—"

"It isn't all I want! Haven't you been listening? This story is going to be huge—it will be award winning. I'll be famous and rich. You wouldn't begrudge me my moment in the spotlight, would you?"

She shook her head vigorously.

The tension in his face eased. "You know, I've been watching you this past month—getting to know you. You're a good person. Much too good for the likes of that playboy prince."

As the man rambled on, she couldn't help but think this guy had it all turned around. She was the one who was damaged goods, not Demetrius. But she wasn't going to argue with this man. He'd obviously lost a firm grip on reality.

"So, now you will confess that you are in fact married to Prince Demetrius." He held the voice recorder up to her. Her gaze darted to the door. "Don't try running again. You won't like what happens if you do." The man patted his pocket as though he were armed. "You're not getting away this time."

Demetrius's body tensed.

He took in the scene unfolding in front of him. The wide-eyed fear written all over Zoe's face and the short, stout man leering at her.

So this was who'd been stalking Zoe. Well, no more. Anger drowned out any other thought of protocol. Demetrius rushed forth. When the stalker turned, Demetrius's clenched hand connected with the man's jaw. The man went down to the ground in a heap.

Zoe let out a scream. The security detail that Demetrius had ordered to remain at the doorway so he could speak to Zoe in private came rushing into the garden.

Once the stalker was detained, Demetrius rushed over

to Zoe. He reached out to her. Her body trembled as he pulled her to him.

"It's okay. You're safe now."

His arms wrapped tightly around her. He pressed her head to his chest. He hadn't been that scared since—since his mother had been shot. He closed his eyes, willing away the painful memories.

"I have a right to be here!" the man yelled. "The people have a right to know what their future ruler is up to with his supposed interior designer. Care to add a comment about your secret marriage?"

"Take him away," Demetrius called out. "Charge him with everything you can think of."

The men moved toward the door with the reporter fighting them. "What? You don't have a comment. Too bad. This is all going to come out. You can't hide."

Once the man was gone, Zoe pulled away from Demetrius. When he reached out to her again, she said, "Don't."

"Zoe, relax. You're safe now."

She wrapped her arms around herself and shook her head. "This—you and I—we...we aren't going to work. I can't do this."

Her words struck like daggers to his heart. "You're wrong. This time around will be different, I'm different."

"But I'm not. I can't have my life on display for the world."

"You're in shock. You don't know what you're saying—"

"I'm speaking the truth." Her voice was eerily calm. "I can't be the kind of princess you need—you deserve."

Her words stopped him from reaching out to her. Through all of this, he hadn't stopped to consider what he'd been asking of her. Asking her to remain his princess would put her whole life under the media's microscope. They wouldn't leave any stone in her life unturned—including her mother's illness.

In the end, the title of princess would bring her more pain than joy. He couldn't—wouldn't—do that to her.

Though the thought of walking away from her killed him, he had to do it. He loved her so much that he couldn't risk letting anything happen to her like what had happened to his mother. He'd vowed to protect Zoe, no matter what it cost him.

Besides, Zoe already had more than enough issues with her ailing mother. He couldn't put it off. He had to walk away now—before he lost his nerve. With a heavy heart, he started for the exit.

He paused at the doorway. He couldn't bring himself to turn around and see the pain swimming in her eyes. Instead he called out, "I'm sorry. My security will see that you get home safely."

Tonight he wouldn't sleep. Tonight he needed a long run on the beach. A chance to pull himself together—to figure out how he was once again going to let go of the woman he loved.

CHAPTER NINETEEN

SUMMONED TO THE PALACE.

This couldn't be good.

What did the king want to speak to her about? The incident yesterday with the stalker? Or was this meeting about the prince? Did the king want an assurance from her that she'd go away quietly once the ball was over?

Zoe's stomach quivered as the butler guided her through the grand entryway that was bigger than the entire apartment she shared with her mother. Instead of going to the left toward the offices, she was guided to the right. The staccato sound of her heels over the polished marble floor echoed against the ornate walls. She found her mouth gaping open in awe at such beauty.

As she made her way down a wide hallway, it was impossible not to gawk at the stunning artwork. Classic paintings hung on the wall between each doorway. There were also a handful of sculptures on pedestals. She was drawn to one such sculpture of a mother and her child. Zoe was struck by the emotion on the mother's face. Sadness assailed Zoe that she would never know such happiness while holding Demetrius's child.

Noticing that the butler had kept moving, she rushed to catch up. She couldn't even imagine what it was like to live there. It was like a museum. At the end of the impressive hallway were French doors that the butler swung open and then stood aside for her to pass by him. She glanced around at the enormous veranda with enough lawn furniture to easily accommodate a large luncheon party, but today the area was deserted, which seemed a shame on such a sunny day.

Though the last thing in the world Zoe felt like doing was partying. Right now, all she wanted to do was get as far from here as possible. So if the king had called her here to kick her out, he need not have wasted his time. She'd already moved back to her apartment.

"His Majesty is this way." For a man of his advanced years, the butler was surprisingly spry. He set off at a brisk pace down one of the many meandering paths in the sprawling garden.

As impressive as the interior of the palace was, she found the gardens utterly breathtaking. Geometrically shaped hedges surrounded each section. Within each section, there was just one vibrant color whether it was a flower, a fruit or a vegetable. It was awe inspiring. This whole place was a true treasure, in every sense of the word.

The butler came to a stop. "Your Majesty, Ms. Zoe Sarris."

She wasn't quite sure how to greet the king as their one and only meeting had been strained at best. This time things weren't much different. They really needed to stop meeting like this.

For the lack of an alternative, she did a quick curtsy and waited until the king spoke first. "May I call you Zoe?"

She nodded, too nervous to speak.

"Zoe, thanks for coming. Please walk with me." She nodded and moved to his side. "I heard about your unfortunate encounter yesterday. I'm sorry that happened. Are you okay? Is there anything you need?"

Other than a bandage for her broken heart, there wasn't much anyone could do. "I...I'm fine."

The king sent her a speculative look, but he didn't say anything else about the incident. "My wife loved the garden. She'd spend a lot of time out here. She said that everyone should pause to smell the roses...and often."

"She...she must have been quite a lady."

"She was. I miss her dearly. She was so much better at handling our boys than I have ever been. I've made so many mistakes along the way."

Zoe wasn't sure what to make of this conversation. She laced her fingers together to keep from fidgeting. Was he trying to apologize? Or was he preparing to send her packing? She really hoped it was the latter. It'd make leaving so much easier. Not that any part of this was easy.

The king stopped walking and turned to her. "I have a question for you." When she went to say something, he held up his hand, silencing her. "But I need you to think carefully and tell the truth. Can you do that?"

She didn't want to. She had a feeling she knew what his question was going to be. And the answer was best left unspoken. But she nodded her head anyway.

"Do you love my son?"

She was right about the question. The truth was Demetrius's name was tattooed upon her heart. She didn't know where the king was going with this conversation, but she couldn't lie. Not about that.

She nodded. "I love him. I never stopped."

The king didn't look the least bit surprised. "I suspected as much. And so will anyone who sees that picture of you two."

"But—"

He held up his hand again. "I need you to listen carefully to me."

She wrung her hands together. If only the king knew the whole truth, he would banish her from the palace—banish her from his son. Guilt hung heavy on her shoulders.

"I've watched my son over this past year. I've seen how he's grown—how he's taken on his responsibilities. And I couldn't be more proud of him. But this change came at a horrendous price."

Zoe's chest tightened. She knew that the king was going to blame her for his son's unhappiness. But he was too late. She already blamed herself. If she could undo it, she would.

The king's gaze met hers. "When he first brought you home, I didn't believe my son had found his soul mate. Back then he was known for his rash decisions. And I must admit that I was quite leery at first. I thought that his elopement was just him acting out again. But I was wrong. Over this past year I've learned how much he truly loves you."

Zoe blinked repeatedly, keeping her tears at bay. "I never meant to hurt him."

"I know, my dear. And I've called you here because I owe you an apology. If I have played a part in keeping you two apart, I am sorry. Please excuse this old man's meddling. I only ever wanted what was best for both of my sons."

Zoe couldn't let the king believe he was the reason for her and Demetrius breaking up. Sure, at first she was overwhelmed and a bit intimidated with the skepticism from the king and his advisors, but that was to be expected. Her problem was that she had unrealistic expectations—hopes that life with a prince would solve all of her problems.

The truth was only she could solve her problems—by facing them head-on. And even then there weren't always solutions, sometimes there was only acceptance of the inevitable.

"Your son is a wonderful man. He will one day be a great leader."

"But will you be by his side?"

The backs of her eyes stung with unshed tears. She shook her head. "It's better this way."

"My dear, if I've learned anything in this life, it is that life is fleeting and true love should never be taken for granted. If you love my son as you say you do, trust in him and his love."

She wanted to do just that, but the king had no idea what he was asking. He didn't understand that she was not the proper match for Demetrius. She was flawed and she just couldn't put Demetrius through the same agony she endured day in and day out as she watched her mother slowly fade away.

"And now, my dear, I hate to bother you, but I have a most urgent request. Would you be willing to help out this old man?"

Zoe would never classify the vital man standing before her as old. She had no idea what he was about to ask of her, but she didn't have it in her to turn him down.

"Of course. Just tell me what you need me to do."

CHAPTER TWENTY

ZOE WAS ON a special mission—a royal mission.

She sat alone in the back of a limo.

The car pulled to a stop in front of the Mirraccino Royal Hospital. The driver opened the door for her. *Here goes nothing.*

Zoe stuck one shiny, red-heeled boot on the pavement. Then the other. What had possessed her to agree to this? Okay, so it wasn't every day the king asked her for a favor. Oh boy, what a favor.

Taking a deep breath, she stood up. She automatically reached down and gave a tug on the snug-fitting green velvet skirt with a jagged hem that stopped just above her knees. The neckline was scooped with red fringe and gold jingle bells. A red belt with a large gold buckle held everything in place. And a matching red velvet shrug sweater with three-quarter-length sleeves kept away the chill in the December air. The hat was really special in a unique kind of way. It was made of the same red-and-green material as the dress, but what was worse were the two or three dozen jingle bells sewn all around it. With every move she made, her head jingled and heads turned her way. Oh, the things the spectators must be thinking.

When she told the king that she'd do him this favor, she'd imagined handing out gifts in her normal street clothes. She didn't recall the king mentioning anything about dressing up like an elf. But then there'd been a special box delivered to her apartment that afternoon with her name on it. Inside she'd found the outfit and a note with the king's crest on the front. She'd opened the note card to find a hand-scrawled message that simply said, *"Grazie."*

The limo driver removed a red sack from the trunk. When he returned to her side, she said, "I can take it."

The driver's gaze moved from her to the sack. "It's my job."

It didn't look too heavy and the car was currently parked in the fire zone. "I insist." She held out her hand. "I've got it from here."

The driver looked torn. "You're sure?"

She nodded. "I appreciate the ride."

The man in the black suit and driver's cap handed over the Santa sack full of what she suspected were toys. And though it weighed a little more than she anticipated, she could manage on her own.

The driver cleared his throat. "They're expecting you on the fifth floor. Just follow the sound of excited voices."

Zoe thanked the kind man again, slung the pack over her shoulder and set off. *Jingle. Jingle. Jingle.* Women smiled. Men stared—some even winked. Thank goodness Demetrius wasn't here to witness her experience as an elf. She'd never live it down—then again, it was highly doubtful that he'd speak to her again.

The driver's directions were perfect. She easily found the Christmas party. The large room was filled with an army of wheelchairs holding excited children who were all chattering at once. At the front of the room sat a very plump Santa in a red velvet outfit with lush white fur trim. Santa's deep ho-ho-ho boomed across the room as he held a hand over his round belly that was strapped in with a wide black belt.

"She's here! She's here!" Cheers filled the room.

They were all waiting for her? As everyone turned her way, heat rushed to her cheeks. She'd be willing to bet if she checked a mirror that her face was as red as Santa's suit.

"Annabelle, we've been waiting for you." Santa's voice

was deep but there was a familiar tone to it. When she stopped next to Jolly Saint Nick and slung her load to the floor, he leaned over and said softly, "You're certainly not Annabelle. What are you doing here?"

Now Zoe knew why that voice sounded so familiar. Behind that bushy beard, gold-rimmed glasses and makeup was Demetrius. Her heart clenched. Had the king known his son would be here? Well, of course he had. He was the king.

"Your father sent me." She thought the explanation would put a quick end to his questions and they could get to work. Being so close to Demetrius and yet so far away was extremely difficult for her.

"Why would my father send you here?"

Zoe resisted the urge to sigh in frustration. "I think the kids want their presents."

"Not until you explain why he sent you."

"The king summoned me to the palace and explained how Annabelle had come down with the flu. He explained how delivering toys to the children's ward was a royal family tradition. And since he thought that Annabelle and I are about the same size, he thought that I could fill in for her."

Demetrius sent her a puzzled look. "But I just saw Annabelle this morning at the office. She looked fine. It was my father who told me he wasn't feeling well. Come to think of it, this is the first Christmas I can recall when he hasn't dressed up like Santa."

"Well, he looked fine when I talked to him." Zoe wasn't about to tell Demetrius what else they'd discussed such as her loving his son.

Demetrius's mouth opened but nothing came out.

"What?" Concern filled her. "Demetrius, what's the matter?"

"I think my father is playing matchmaker."

She'd gotten that feeling earlier at the palace, but she

never thought the king would take it this far. Her gaze lifted and met Demetrius's. Her heart pitter-pattered faster and faster. If only...

"Don't worry. I'll take care of this. I'll make it clear to my father that you and I are through." Demetrius's tone lacked emotion. And then he turned away. "Who's ready for some presents? Ho-ho-ho."

Demetrius was a far better actor than she. It took all of her determination to keep her eyes from misting up. If it wasn't for the hopeful faces and the excited voices, she'd have never made it through the afternoon.

They never had a chance to speak privately again. She told herself that it was for the best. The less contact they had the better it'd be.

But none of those excuses eased the pain. She loved Demetrius more now than the day she'd married him. And even if she didn't have the threat of that dreaded disease hanging over her head, Demetrius didn't want her. He'd finally realized she wasn't cut out to be a princess—his princess.

He couldn't get Zoe out of his thoughts.

Demetrius paced back and forth in his office. It was the only peaceful place in the palace. Tonight was the Royal Christmas Ball and he'd given the entire staff the day off in order to prepare for the big event.

"I thought I'd find you down here."

Demetrius stopped pacing and glanced up to find his twin, Alex, standing in the doorway. "When did you get back from the States?"

"Last night. I thought I'd see you at dinner—"

"I wasn't hungry." He'd barely eaten a bite since his relationship with Zoe had disintegrated right before his eyes.

"From the looks of you, I'd say along with giving up food, you've given up shaving and combing your hair."

Demetrius sent his brother a cold, hard stare. "Leave me alone."

"Not until you hear me out."

"I don't need a lecture. I need to be alone." If Alex wasn't going to leave, Demetrius would. He started for the door, but Alex moved in his way.

Alex gave him a wary look as though trying to decide if he was going to have to tackle him to the ground to make him stay in place. "It looks like I got back just in time. Someone needs to talk some sense into you."

Demetrius raked his fingers through his hair, not caring what he looked like. That was the least of his problems. "You don't know what's going on."

"Actually, I know a lot more than you think. Papa's very worried about you. He's filled me in on what he knows. What I don't understand is how a stalker reporter broke you and Zoe up."

"Do you really want to know?"

Alex nodded and Demetrius let it all spill out. His worry that the title of princess would bring more pain to Zoe's life than any joy he could give her. His fear that something would happen to Zoe like had happened to their mother. He just couldn't be responsible for any harm coming to Zoe.

Alex reached out and squeezed his shoulder. "It isn't easy. I won't pretend that love and marriage don't require putting yourself out there. If this Zoe is the right lady for you, you have to take the risk."

"But what if something happens to her? I'll never forgive myself."

"If you're looking for guarantees, there aren't any. But is it worth it to give up the woman you love over a what-if scenario?"

His brother had a point. But that wasn't the only thing eating at him. Zoe had a secret—a really big secret.

"But how am I supposed to open up to her about my

worries when she's afraid to tell me what she's most afraid of?" It tore him up that she wouldn't trust him with the information.

"It sounds like you already know what it is."

"I do. I've known for a while. She's afraid she's going to end up with Alzheimer's like her mother."

Alex didn't say anything for a moment as the news sunk in. "That's a really big deal. I can't blame her for being scared."

"But she doesn't seem to believe that part of our vows where it said 'for better or worse, in sickness and in health.'"

Alex arched a brow. "So you're saying that no matter what, you're going to love her?"

"*Sì.*" There was no hesitation in his answer—none whatsoever.

"Then go tell her what you just told me. Nothing important in life comes easily—at least not in my experience. Trust me. I almost let the woman I love slip through my fingers. The best approach is to be up-front and honest. You can't attempt to solve the problem until you both have it all out there in the open. Let her know that you love her and that you aren't going anywhere."

Demetrius knew that his twin was right. But would Zoe hear him out?

Alex cleared his throat, regaining Demetrius's attention. "Is winning Zoe back truly what you want?"

"*Sì.*" He'd never been more certain about anything. "She's the one and only for me. And if she'll have me, I plan to have our wedding vows renewed."

CHAPTER TWENTY-ONE

SINCE WHEN HAD Alex become a relationship expert?

Obviously Alex's wife had taught him some important lessons.

Demetrius rushed through the shower, shaved his three-day beard and threw on his tux. On his ride to the ball, he finally checked his messages. He found a text from Zoe saying she wouldn't be attending the ball. He redirected the car to her apartment.

It was his fault that she'd be missing her chance to shine like the star that she was both inside and out. She was amazing. And thanks to his brother, Demetrius realized that he'd been a fool to let her go.

Certain that she loved him, he just had to find her. It was past time they got everything out in the open, including her secret. Even if she'd been diagnosed with the Alzheimer's gene like her mother, it wouldn't change the way he felt about her. The thought of her being ill was painful but what was even more painful was the thought of wasting all of the good days they could have together—talking, laughing—just being in each other's company.

He rushed up the steps of her apartment building and stopped in front of her door. It was only then that he realized he shouldn't have showed up empty-handed. He should have brought flowers—roses—red roses. That's what women liked, wasn't it?

Oh, well, it was too late to worry about it now. Tomorrow he'd place an order with the florist to have flowers delivered to Zoe every month or every week, whatever made her happy. He clenched his hand and knocked. She just had to be there.

Almost immediately the door swung open. An older woman stood there with a very surprised look on her face. He'd seen that look on many faces when people recognized him. Her mouth opened but nothing came out. This must be the friend Zoe mentioned that was helping out with her mother.

He sent her a friendly smile, hoping to gain an ally. "Hello. Is Zoe at home?"

The woman smiled back at him and shook her head.

"Who is it? Who's at the door?" Another woman made her way across the living room to join them. The woman had gray streaking through her dark hair. She most definitely resembled Zoe. This had to be her mother. So this was what Zoe would look like when she got older. Still beautiful.

Lines creased between her brows. Zoe's mother studied his face as though she should know him, but she couldn't quite place his face. "Do I know you?"

"I don't think that I've had the pleasure. I'm Prince Demetrius."

The title didn't seem to faze Zoe's mother. "Are you a friend of my daughter?"

Demetrius's gaze moved to the other woman, looking for direction. She shrugged, leaving him on his own. He turned back to Zoe's mother. "*Sì.* She's very special to me."

"Don't you hurt my Zoe. You hear?" The woman sent him a no-nonsense look.

"I'll do my best not to." But he knew that he'd already failed that request.

Confusion clouded her eyes. "Who are you?"

"Prince Demetrius."

The other woman held up a finger, signaling for him to wait.

He nodded in understanding. The woman escorted Zoe's mother to the couch before returning to the door.

"Thanks for being so understanding. I take it you know about her condition."

"Zoe told me."

"Well, Zoe didn't tell me about you." The woman ran a hand over her hair. "Oh, my goodness. Where are my manners? I'm Liliana, a friend of the family."

"It's nice to meet you. About Zoe, do you know where she is?"

"She's at the ball. I insisted she go after how hard she worked. This is her night to shine—"

"*Grazie.* I'm sorry to rush off, but it's urgent that I speak with her."

The woman smiled. "Tell Zoe not to worry about coming home tonight. I have everything under control."

"I will."

Not about to let the princess of his heart get away, Demetrius set off after her.

She shouldn't have come.

Zoe was in no mood for a party. In fact, that afternoon she'd escorted her mother to a doctor's appointment. The doctor had urged her to get her mother situated in Residenza del Rosa as soon as possible. He assured her that it would be better for her mother in the long run. She'd feel more settled as the disease progressed.

Though Zoe wanted to argue with the doctor, she couldn't. Her mother had told her at the beginning of this journey that she never wanted to be a burden on Zoe. The day had just arrived far sooner than Zoe had expected. She wasn't ready to let go. But her mother had squeezed her hand and told her it would be all right. Next week, her mother would move in to Residenza del Rosa—her new home.

Zoe was set to cancel her plans and stay home tonight, but her mother and Liliana insisted they wanted to see her in the gown. She'd picked it out special with Demetrius in mind.

She tugged at her burgundy taffeta gown. She glanced down wondering if the strapless, sweetheart neckline embellished with delicate crystals dipped a bit too low. The problem was she just wasn't used to being all gussied up in an A-line gown that hugged all of her curves with a gentle ruching at her hips.

She hoped it didn't make her look fat. She sucked in her stomach a little more, hoping it would help. Her mother and their friend assured her that she looked wonderful, but she didn't trust either of them. They'd say that even if her face was breaking out and she was wearing an old sack.

"You showed up."

Zoe didn't even have to turn around. She recognized the voice. It was Demetrius. She hadn't seen him since they'd posed as Santa and his trusty elf.

She turned to him and was immediately struck by how handsome he looked in his black tux. His hair was perfectly styled. Her fingers tingled with the urge to reach out and stroke his freshly shaven jaw. She resisted the temptation.

She swallowed hard. "Bet you're surprised to see me here after the message I sent you."

"More like relieved."

Relieved? That was a good sign, wasn't it? She glanced around the crowded room, wondering if there were photographers lurking about just waiting to catch a picture of them together. "Do you think it's a good idea to be seen talking to me?"

"The first thing to learn about dealing with the paparazzi is not to let them dictate your life. Otherwise, I'd never leave the palace. If they want to create a story, they will with or without any help."

She supposed he was right, but that didn't put her at ease. The last thing she needed was the paparazzi digging around in her life. She already had too much going on with the pending annulment and her mother's care.

"Zoe, stop worrying. I made sure the press wasn't allowed into the ball tonight."

"You did?" Her eyes widened. "But I thought you wanted as much press coverage as possible for the project."

"Not at the expense of your happiness. I'll still make sure there's plenty of coverage, just not tonight." Demetrius moved closer and placed a finger beneath her chin, tilting it up. "Are you okay?"

"Um...*sì*." Definitely better now that he was there.

"You look a little pale. Did you eat anything today?"

She shrugged. "I had a little."

He sent her an I-don't-believe-you look.

The truth was she hadn't had more than *caffè* and toast that morning. She'd been worried about her mother's appointment and then the thought of fitting into her gown. And now with Demetrius standing before her looking like he'd just stepped off the cover of a glossy magazine, her stomach felt as though it were filled with a swarm of fluttering butterflies.

"That dress looks amazing on you." His smile succeeded in increasing the fluttering sensation in her stomach.

"You're the one who looks amazing. You were born to wear a tux."

"*Grazie*." He gave a tug on each sleeve. "It takes years of experience to properly pull off the look."

She grinned, enjoying the fact that he was in a good mood. After all of his hard work, he deserved to enjoy this success. "You shouldn't be wasting time with me."

"It's definitely not a waste of time. I can't think of any place I'd rather be."

"But you have important guests to entertain. You need their support to continue the project."

"Don't worry. There's plenty of time for all of that."

"Demetrius, I need to apologize. I want to explain—"

"Shh...we'll talk. We have all night. Liliana said she doesn't expect to see you tonight. She has everything under control."

"You saw Liliana and...and my mother?"

He nodded. "I went looking for you."

"But why?"

"Because you're my date for tonight. And now it's my turn to ask you a question. Can I have this dance?"

Heat rushed up her neck and warmed her cheeks. There was music playing? She hadn't noticed until he'd mentioned it. Demetrius held out his arm to her and suddenly she felt like Cinderella at the ball.

Oh, what would it hurt to enjoy herself for the evening in the arms of the most amazing man in the world? She accepted his arm. He escorted her onto the busy dance floor. She didn't even want to contemplate the number of women who would die to be in her place, much less be the wife of this amazing prince. She'd pinch herself to make sure this was all real, but she didn't want to remove her hands from him—afraid he might disappear again.

As the eighteen-piece orchestra played, Demetrius skillfully guided her around the dance floor. She'd swear that her feet never even touched the floor. She smiled and smiled until her cheeks hurt, and then she smiled some more.

Throughout it all, she didn't let herself think about what would happen when the clock struck twelve. The whole world slipped away, leaving just the two of them swaying gently to the music. She never wanted to let him go.

Demetrius stared deep into her eyes. "Close your eyes."

Instead of arguing and questioning him as she normally

would do, she simply closed her eyes, trusting him to guide her safely around the room.

Demetrius pulled her closer. "Now imagine that my lips are pressed to yours."

She could visualize his face and how he would lean over to her. She could imagine his lips pressed to hers. A wishful sigh crossed her lips.

"Imagine me pulling you close. Real close. Our bodies press together. My lips moving over yours. You taste sweet as *vino*. No. Sweeter." His voice was warm and soft, for her ears only. "I can't stop kissing you."

Was he really seducing her here on the dance floor? Because if so, it was working. Heat rushed up her neck, setting her whole face ablaze. Her eyes sprang open.

"Hey, no cheating. Close your eyes."

It was as though his touch and the deep tones of his voice had a spell over her. She once again did as he asked, eagerly wondering where this fantasy was to take them next. Her mind started to jump ahead quite a few steps. It was getting warm in there. Very warm indeed.

"My lips are still on yours." He pulled her closer. His lips were next to her ear. His breath brushed lightly over her neck. "My fingers work their way up your back until they are plucking the pins from your hair and letting your curls fall down over your shoulders."

The breath hitched in her throat as she waited for his next words. "And…"

He chuckled. "Anxious, aren't you?"

She smiled. "Definitely."

"My lips trail over your cheek and over to your ear where I whisper a few sweet nothings. And then I move down to that sensitive spot on your neck. You know, the spot that drives you wild."

Goose bumps trailed down her arms as she recalled the delicious sensations that he could arouse. "And then what?"

CHAPTER TWENTY-TWO

BEFORE HE COULD say another word, the music stopped. Zoe's eyes opened. *Not yet.* She resisted the urge to stomp her feet in frustration. Things were just getting good. Who knew that Demetrius could play out a seduction scene so smoothly?

"Quit pouting," he whispered in her ear as he led her from the dance floor. "We aren't finished."

"We aren't?" She knew that she shouldn't be so eager, but she just couldn't help herself.

"If you eat something, we'll continue this fantasy."

She still didn't have much of an appetite. "Does chocolate count?"

His lips pressed together as he considered her request. "How about some crackers and cheese with a side of chocolate?"

"If I must." Crackers actually didn't sound so bad, after all.

"Good. Why don't you go wait for me out on the terrace? We should have some privacy there and then I might do more than just talk."

"Promise?"

His eyes glittered with unspoken promises. "I do."

As he walked away, her feet came back down to earth. As much as it pained her to admit, she couldn't let this fantasy go on. It'd be too painful when it was over. When he returned, she steeled herself to be brutally honest with him. He deserved to know what he was getting himself into.

A couple of minutes later, he joined her in the cool evening air. Luckily, no one had decided to come outside to admire the stars. They had the whole terrace to themselves.

He handed her a plate of finger foods. "Here you go. Make sure you eat the crackers."

"But there's something I need to tell you first. Something I should have told you a long time ago."

The smile slid from his face. "If this is about you inheriting Alzheimer's, I know."

She set aside the plate. "You know?"

He nodded. "And it doesn't matter. I just wish you'd have told me sooner."

"I couldn't, because I knew you'd do this. You'd be a knight in shining armor and do the gentlemanly thing."

"Which is what?"

She pressed her hands to her hips and lifted her chin. "You'd say that none of this matters. That we can do anything as long as we're together."

He couldn't help but smile just a bit. "That is exactly what I'd say. And I'd be right."

She shook her head. "Stop being so gallant. You have more than yourself to think about. You're the prince. The future ruler of Mirraccino. You are expected to produce the next heir to the throne."

"And..."

"And I can't give you that heir. Don't you see, I have a fifty-fifty chance of inheriting the same disease? I can't— I won't pass that on to my children."

His brows drew together. "So you don't know if you have the disease?"

She shook her head. "There's DNA testing, but I haven't had it done yet."

"Why not?"

Her voice grew soft, hating to have to admit this to a man who never had to inquire about the price before purchasing whatever his heart desired. "I couldn't afford the tests.

My mother's medical expenses take everything I earn." But aside from the cost, she was afraid. "And I didn't know if I could deal with the results while I was watching what it was doing to my mother. She needed all of my focus and positivity."

"And this design job—"

"I needed it in order to pay for my mother's care. Her doctor has been warning us that the time was coming when she'd need more than I could give her while holding down a job. My mother insisted all along that she didn't want me caring for her to the end. I thought that if she could stay here at Residenza del Rosa that it would be close enough to the apartment that I could visit her every day."

Demetrius nodded as though at last the pieces of the puzzle were falling into place. "I just wish that you would have trusted me. I would have helped you through all of this."

She blinked repeatedly. "It isn't you I didn't trust. It was me. I'd been running so long, so hard that I didn't know if I could be the strong, sturdy person that my mother needs me to be."

"It looks to me like you're an amazing daughter."

"I'm doing my best. I was trying to protect you, too. I didn't want to become a burden to you. You have a country to run—people counting on you—"

He reached out, cupping his hands over her shoulders. "Don't you know by now that there's nothing and no one more important to me than you? I love you. I have since the day we met."

That was it. The dam broke. She lowered her head as a tear splashed onto her cheek. "I love you, too. But you would be better off without me. I'm all wrong to be a princess."

"I disagree." His thumb moved beneath her chin and lifted her head until he was looking into her eyes. "I can't think of anyone who would fit the position better."

"What? No. You can't be serious."

"I'm very serious."

He wasn't thinking this through. "What if I have this disease? What if I can't—won't—have kids?"

"Then my brother and his kids will inherit the crown."

This couldn't be happening. He really wanted her, flaws and all. "But I'm a commoner. I have no money, no influence, and no important ties to any foreign countries."

"You have something more important. You are the bravest person I know. You took on the world by yourself in order to care for your mother. You have a heart of gold—always putting the happiness of others ahead of your own. And you aren't afraid of hard work. Just look at this place, it's amazing."

"Really?" When he nodded, she continued. "You aren't just saying that to make me feel better? You thought about this?"

"I haven't thought of anything else. I mean every word I've said. I'm the luckiest man in the world."

Her heart swelled with the warmth of love radiating from Demetrius. "What does this mean?"

He gazed deeply into her eyes. "It means I love you with all of my heart. I can't imagine my life without you in it."

"I love you, too. I never stopped."

His hand moved, allowing the backs of his fingers to swipe away her tears. His head dipped, and then his lips claimed hers. She leaned into him. At last, she knew where she belonged. She didn't know how the next chapter of her life would end, but she now knew how it would start.

Demetrius stopped kissing her and leaned his forehead against hers. "Come inside with me so we can announce our marriage. I want everyone to know how lucky I am."

"What about the annulment papers?"

"Did I forget to tell you that I accidentally dropped

them? They landed in the paper shredder. So it looks like you're stuck with me."

Her vision blurred with tears of joy. "So we're still married?"

"That we are. You are now and always will be the princess of my heart."

EPILOGUE

A year later...

"You do know that you're breaking with tradition?"

Demetrius strode into the palace library, finding his wife standing on a step stool with a red shimmery ornament in her hand. He'd never imagined that he could fall more in love with her, but each day that passed, he found himself falling further and further under her spell. And he couldn't be happier.

Zoe glanced over her shoulder at him. "I just need to find a spot for this last ornament."

Demetrius's gaze reluctantly moved to the Christmas tree. White twinkle lights shimmered off the dozens of ornaments. "I don't think there's room for more."

"Sure there is." Zoe sounded so confident. "There's always room for more."

He smiled and shook his head at her determination.

Over the past year, so many things had changed. First, they had a splashy wedding to the thrill of the people of Mirraccino—and Zoe, who got to wear a white dress with a long train. After which Zoe decided to get the DNA testing done. There had been some long sleepless nights while they both waited for the results, but to everyone's relief, Zoe hadn't inherited her mother's early onset familial Alzheimer's.

And though they'd moved into the palace and Demetrius was fully immersed in matters of state, his father still refused to step down from the throne, even though his doctors had advised him that it would be best for his heart. Demetrius now knew where he'd inherited his stubborn streak. All he could do was be there to alleviate as much of the stress as he could until his father was willing to see reason.

Zoe held up the sparkly Christmas ornament, regaining his attention. She'd never been more beautiful. He'd swear she was glowing with happiness. She moved the decoration around, still trying to decide which limb to place it on. At last satisfied, she situated it near the top.

She turned to him, resting a hand atop her slightly rounded belly. Her face was radiant. "It's time we started a new tradition. After all, you helped me decorate the tree last year and you didn't do such a bad job."

"Hey! I did a really good job. You said it was the prettiest tree you'd ever seen."

She arched a brow. "I think they call that revising the past."

He approached her, finding himself unable to keep his hands to himself whenever she was in the room with him. "Maybe you should come down here so we can discuss these new traditions."

She smiled and stepped down the little ladder until she was standing on the lowest rung. Her eyes twinkled with merriment. "Why, Prince Demetrius, if I didn't know better, I'd think that you have a lot more on your mind than talking."

He wrapped his hands around her expanding waistline and lifted her to him. Her body slid down over his. His pulse raced. It didn't matter how long they were together, he couldn't imagine ever being immune to her charms.

Her arms looped around his neck as she gazed deep into his eyes. "You do know that we're expected at Residenza del Rosa soon, don't you? I want to take my mum her presents. I called and this is one of her better days."

He had to hand it to his wife. She was the strongest person he'd ever known. Though her mother's condition was deteriorating, Zoe did her best to stay positive even though her mother recognized her less and less. On the days when Zoe needed a hug, a shoulder to lean on or an ear to listen, he made sure to be there for her. She was his priority. It wasn't all sunshine and roses, but together they were getting through the challenges life threw at them.

"Don't worry. We won't be late. In fact, I think we have just enough time to squeeze in a little of this." His lips pressed to hers. He knew from plenty of experience that it wouldn't take much to sway her into delaying their outing.

"Hey, isn't that how you two got in trouble already?"

With great reluctance, Demetrius released his princess and turned to face his brother. "I don't think you have any room to talk."

"Is my husband causing problems already?" Reese entered the room wearing a blue cotton top with the words Precious Cargo Aboard emblazoned across her rounded midsection.

Demetrius smiled. "He's always causing trouble."

"Don't I know it." Reese pressed a hand to her back. "Did he tell you yet?"

"Tell us what?" Zoe spoke up.

"That he's been up to his antics." Reese frowned at her prince, but her eyes said that she was only playing with him. "It appears that we're not having a baby boy, we're having two—boys that is."

"That's wonderful." Zoe rushed over to hug her.

Demetrius gave Zoe a look. "You aren't carrying twins, too, are you?"

She started to laugh. "Not me. But I do have a surprise."

"I love surprises." The king entered the room. A smile lit up his face. He looked so much more at ease now that both of his sons were taking on a lot of the workload that the king had shouldered for so long on his own. "Well, don't keep us in suspense."

Zoe smiled at her father-in-law. Over this past year they'd grown quite close as they took daily strolls through the flower gardens. Demetrius always wondered what they found to talk about, but he didn't want to pry. Some things were best left alone.

Zoe moved to Demetrius's side. "I was planning to save this announcement for Christmas day, but now seems rather fitting."

Demetrius's chest tightened. "You're starting to worry me. Nothing is wrong, is it?"

She smiled and shook her head. "Everything is fine. Do you think Mirraccino is ready for a queen that looks like me and acts like you?"

He breathed easier. "It's a girl?"

She nodded. Demetrius picked her up and swung her around. He didn't care whether it was a little boy or girl just so long as baby and mom were both healthy. "Hey, you cheated. You weren't supposed to consult the doctor while I was off on that business trip to Milan."

Zoe glanced away. "I… I had some pains—"

"What? Why is this the first I'm hearing of it?"

She pressed a hand to his chest where his heart was pounding as adrenaline raced through his veins. Nothing could be wrong with them. He didn't know what he'd do if he lost Zoe after everything they'd gone through.

"Relax." Her voice was soft and comforting. "The doctor told me that it was normal. They were growing pains. Completely natural."

"You're sure?"

She nodded. "He even did a sonogram to assure me everything was fine." She moved to her purse that was on the couch and pulled something out. "Meet your daughter."

Demetrius stared at the photo and then at his wife. His vision blurred a bit, but he didn't care in the least. He couldn't believe that he'd been so blessed.

"This is going to be the best Christmas ever."

With that he pulled his wife into his arms and kissed her, leaving no doubt about how much he loved her. Now and forever.

* * * * *

COMING SOON!

We really hope you enjoyed reading this book. If you're looking for more romance, be sure to head to the shops when new books are available on

Thursday 15th November

To see which titles are coming soon, please visit **millsandboon.co.uk**

LET'S TALK

Romance

For exclusive extracts, competitions and special offers, find us online:

- facebook.com/millsandboon
- @MillsandBoon
- @MillsandBoonUK

Get in touch on 01413 063232

For all the latest titles coming soon, visit millsandboon.co.uk/nextmonth